ELLERY QUEEN'S
PRIME CRIMES 2

Volume 51

ELLERY QUEEN'S
PRIME CRIMES 2

Edited by Eleanor Sullivan
and Karen A. Prince

THE DIAL PRESS
Davis Publications, Inc.
380 Lexington Avenue
New York, New York 10017

COPYRIGHT NOTICES AND ACKNOWLEDGMENTS

Grateful acknowledgment is hereby made for permission to include the following:

Ashes for an Urn by Frank Sisk; © 1984 by Frank Sisk; used by permission of Scott
    Meredith Literary Agency, Inc.
The Case of the Frozen Diplomat by Tim Heald; © 1984 by Tim Heald; used by
    permission of Richard Simon, Agent.
On Her Feet Again by Anthea Cohen; © 1984 by Anthea Cohen; used by permission
    of John Farquharson, Ltd.
The Canoe by Don Gilbert; © 1984 by Don Gilbert; used by permission of the author.
Born Victims by Edward Wellen; © 1984 by Edward Wellen; used by permission of
    the author.
The Tree in the Forest by Melville Davisson Post and John F. Suter; © 1984 by
    Melville Davisson Post and John F. Suter; used by permission of Robert P. Mills,
    Ltd.
Another Me by Donald Olson; © 1984 by Donald Olson; used by permission of Blanche
    C. Gregory, Inc.
The Girl and the Ghost by Ernest Savage; © 1984 by Ernest Savage; used by per-
    mission of Scott Meredith Literary Agency, Inc.
Things Will Look Brighter in the Morning by Dorothy Benjamin; © 1984 by Dorothy
    Benjamin; used by permission of the author.
The Murder of the Governor by Theodore de la Torre Bueno; © 1984 by Theodore de
    la Torre Bueno; used by permission of the author.
The Beneficiaries by Hillary Waugh; © 1984 by Hillary Waugh; used by permission
    of Ann Elmo Agency, Inc.
Exit, Stage Right by Fred Burgess; © 1984 by Fred Burgess; used by permission of
    the author.
All Business by John Lutz; © 1984 by John Lutz; used by permission of Larry Sternig
    Literary Agency.
The Miracle by Jane Paynter; © 1984 by Jane Paynter; used by permission of the
    author.

"Q"

CONTENTS

INTRODUCTION

A field of opium poppies in the countryside outside Mexico City. The teeming streets of Jakarta, Indonesia. The Governor's palace in the Lima, Peru, of Conquistador days. The ancient temples of Karnak and Luxor beside the Egyptian Nile.

These are the settings for just a few of the stories in this collection, the second in a new series of Ellery Queen anthologies consisting of stories never before published in the United States, most of them never before published anywhere.

Featured are stories by such internationally known mystery writers as Clark Howard, Antonia Fraser, Hillary Waugh, Frank Sisk, Tim Heald, and Edward D. Hoch, and an unfinished Melville Davisson Post story, finished by John F. Suter. There is also a stunning short novel by William Bankier, "Beliveau Pays."

The collection represents an extremely diverse mix—foreign and familiar, past and present, light and dark—all of it prime reading.

Karen A. Prince

Frank Sisk

Ashes for an Urn

That morning the phone rang a few minutes before seven.
Thomas Smith's gruff "Hello" was greeted by a thin high-pitched oriental voice which could have been either male or female:
"Mister Thomas Smith, yes?"
"Yes, this is Tom Smith."
"Speaking on line now?"
"In person."
"A moment, pleece."
Swinging bare feet to the floor, Smith listened to the hollow hum of the international telephone connection. He assumed this was a call from his son Robert. Once a month, from wherever in the world that joyful vagabond happened to be, he phoned the old man. Smith sat there remembering the last call less than three weeks ago. The exchange had gone like this:
"Sawadee, papa-san."
"Sawadee, luk chai. Where you calling from?"
"Jakarta. What's cooking in Connecticut?"
"I cooked a goose last week. How's Pranee?"
"She's one reason I'm calling. Her next birthday's coming up. In June. Remember last year?"
"The seventh. Sure, I remember. Last year she did all the preparation, we did all the celebration."
"That's how Thai women like it, papa-san. Well, she wants me to get you back to Thailand again. Next month I'll be there myself on a three-week furlough. May twenty-eighth to be exact. So perhaps we can synchronize our calendars for arrival that day at Don Muang Airport. I could have Chen standing by with his air-conditioned Humber and the makings of some tall cool ones. How about it?"
"Sounds irresistible, son, but I've got to resist for the time being."
"If it's money, Dad, no problem. My new contract with Hyperion is a real gusher."
"It's not money, Robert. The fact is, I've just signed a contract myself."
"Still teaching the rough stuff? You told me six months ago you were ready to retire from all that."

8

"Well, let's say I—"

The masculine/feminine voice interrupted his reverie. "Mister Thomas Smith, here is your call."

"Hello there, Tom." It wasn't Robert. "Can you hear me all right, Tom?"

He recognized the Nova Scotian accent. It belonged to Harry Oliver. Harry had retired from married life and the Royal Canadian Air Force simultaneously after long and heroic service in each. He now lived with a native girl at Pattaya Beach in Thailand, where Thomas had met him through Robert a year ago. That Harry was phoning him from 12,000 miles away was a source of surprise as well as acute apprehension.

"I hear you loud and clear, Harry," he said. "What's on your mind that won't keep for a letter?"

"A letter, yeah. I'm going to write you one, Tom. Tomorrow. Pranee's here beside me. I'm really calling at her request. She's not too good on phones."

Smith could spot equivocation when he heard it and this of Harry's sent a ball of ice to the pit of his stomach. "What's the matter, Harry?"

Harry cleared his throat. "Damn it, Tom, I'd rather be flying through heavy flak over Berlin again than telling you this. Bob's dead."

Dead.

This dark syllable, falling from Telstar, hit Smith with crushing weight. He felt it was heavy enough to rupture the earth's crust and find the molten center of things.

"Dead." To mask the hard knot of grief, he compressed the word to tidy quiescence: "How did he die, Harry?"

"Pranee's got this cablegram here. It doesn't say much. Let me read it to you, Tom."

"I'm listening."

"Well, here it is. 'Dear Mrs. Pranee Smith: Your husband Robert was killed here this morning while resisting a robbery. Accept our profound condolences. We are prepared to assist you in any way through this difficult time. We await your instructions and arrival.' That's it. A gent named Lem Williamson signed it. Director of Personnel, he calls himself."

"I'm writing that down," Smith said.

"Have you got the company address and phone number?"

"Robert sent it when he signed the contract. Let me talk to Pranee, Harry."

Sorrow muted his daughter-in-law's normally cheerful voice. With her native inability to pronounce "r," she said, "Fatha, I cannot believe yet what happen to Lobbut. It make sun black."

"I know, luk sao. Be a brave lady. I'll see you soon."

"Tomorrow I fly Jakarta. Take care Lobbut's body. You come too, fatha?"

"I can't come that soon, daughter. I must clear deck here first. I'll be in Thailand in four or five days."

"Tell me time, I tell Chen meet you Bangkok Airport."

"Don't bother, Pranee. When I know the exact time and flight number, I'll phone Chen. I have his business card. I'll see you soon."

"Prot reep nawy, fatha."

He thought it meant "Please hurry."

During a few of the ensuing days, while retracting his commitment to the state police academy, he tried to reach Lem Williamson at Hyperion Petroleum in Jakarta, but the man was on ˅ field trip in a impenetrable part of Indonesia.

Five days after learning of his son's death Thomas departed from Bradley International en route to Seattle, where he stayed overnight in a motel near the airport. At 7:45 A.M., he boarded a wide-bodied plane flown by Thai International. On the foredeck, his glum mood brightened briefly when he was greeted by a brown-eyed hostess in a silken green gown, palms joined just beneath her chin in the traditional *wai*.

His seat in the non-smoking section, first class, was beside a porthole. An excellent breakfast was served at 35,000 feet: papaya juice, ham grilled with pineapple, shirred eggs, warm rice cakes, good strong coffee.

He peered out the porthole when the tray was removed. Patches of the Pacific, inky blue, were visible below scattered bundles of scalloped fleece. Once, more than a generation ago, he'd known some of that ocean all too well. Tarawa drifted up from it in memory. Again he could see one of its hellish atolls—Betio—where he'd suffered his one and only battle wound.

Again he could see the Higgins boats, undimmed by time, bobbing sickeningly in the water not far from the battleship *Maryland*. Their cargo was the Sixth Marines, eight hundred strong. And he was one of those sweat-soaked jarheads, crouching red-eyed and dry-mouthed behind a Higgins bulkhead, waiting for some naval wizard to delineate safe fathomage across the coral reefs that had already snagged a dozen amphtracs. The riflemen aboard these helpless vehicles were either dead or dying, but Jap machine guns entrenched on the beach two hundred yards away were still stitching men and metal.

Betio—a spit of burning sand, cruel cutting coral, scrub brush, shell-shattered palm trees. A place that made the final claim on 3,381 Marines.

He wondered who remembered it now. For that matter, who knew much about it even then?

As a boy, Robert loved to trace the campaign in the Pacific on maps. A few weeks after his mother died (he was fourteen), he told his father, "When I finish high school I want to join the Marines."

"No you don't. Marines are obsolete."

"I want to be what you were."

And he finally made it to Vietnam and *two* purple hearts. Yes, two. One up on the old man.

With lunch, Thomas Smith drank a split of Beaujolais. Afterward he watched a movie, *Deathtrap,* without fully comprehending its ricocheting plot. Then he tilted back his seat and dozed.

A voice crackling on the intercom wakened him.

"The sun is shining in Tokyo this morning. We'll be arriving in approximately fifteen minutes. Tokyo time is ten-fifty—ten five oh. And since we have crossed the International Date Line it is now Thursday, not Wednesday."

It was 4:10 P.M. by Smith's watch. He reset it.

The paradox of global travel at high speed, he reflected. You leave Seattle in time for breakfast aboard a 747. You're in the air for nearly nine hours. You skim through a few magazines. You eat lunch. You watch a movie. You take a nap. And you find yourself arriving in Japan before noon of the following day.

The silver bird was banking. Through the porthole he discerned the Kanto plain bathed in golden sunlight. Its patterns were agriculturally asymmetrical—oblongs of yellow, triangles of green, rhomboids of brown. The Sumida River, a livid serpent, squirmed over the cultivated geometry, its wake creating filamentary offshoots to nourish the crops.

The intercom spoke again. "We shall be on the ground for about an hour. Transit passengers may leave the plane if they wish, but they will be limited to a small part of the terminal."

Three thousand more miles to Bangkok, Smith calculated. Five more flying hours. He'd arrive with nightfall.

The plane taxied to a stop. Unbuckling his seat belt, he became really aware for the first time that the chair beside him was unoccupied. All day he'd spoken to nobody but the flight attendants. All day alone but not lonely.

The Thai Customs inspection was generally cursory for Americans. Smith was no exception. His passport was stamped with a smile, his single piece of luggage cordially ignored.

Entering the Arrivals area, he spotted Chen almost immediately in the forefront of the crowd behind the ropes. Short and swart, he radiated an ageless durability. With a wave and a grin, Chen moved toward the opening in the rope barricade. His right hand seized Smith's while his left grabbed the heavy bag.

"Sawadee, papa-san," Chen said. "Gan tawn to Bangkok again."

"Khawp khoon, Chen. This is great service."

"Have to be. When you phone from Amelica for taxi. Yes, yes."

Chen led the way to an elevator which carried them to the ground level. The evening air was hot and clammy. The dignified old Humber was parked advantageously close. Smith got in the front seat with Chen, who started the motor and turned on the climate control.

"In two minutes we be nice and cool," Chen said.

In two minutes they were also out of the lot and on the feeder road to the main highway into Bangkok.

Chen produced a thermos bottle. "I tell hotel bartender make velly cold vodka martini faw papa-san."

Smith poured a few ounces into the thermos cap. "Here's to you, Chen, and the bartender."

"Yes, yes. All peoples in Khatmong Hotel have long face like old horse when they heah what happen to Bob."

"He was always a big tipper."

"Not only reason they sad, papa-san. No, no. Bob good man and they all know."

"Didn't mean to sound cynical, Chen. I understand what you're saying. And thanks." He swallowed what he'd poured and poured more. "Did you put Pranee on the plane to Jakarta?"

"Oh, yes. She come back tomollow noon. I go get her."

"We'll go together."

There was a conversational lull as Chen concentrated on coping with the awesome night traffic on the Bangkok highway. Then, after he'd barely avoided colliding with a mixed trio astride a snorting motorcycle, he said, "We know Bob dead, papa-san, but we don't know how he die. You know how?"

"No more than you do, Chen. I've tried to reach a certain man in Jakarta. No luck. I'll try again in the morning."

"Look in glove compartment, papa-san."

Thomas snapped it open. The interior light glinted on a revolver barrel on a strip of chamois. "A Colt thirty-eight."

"Bob always safe in this car, papa-san. Much money in pocket many time. Nobody ever try to lob him."

"I can believe it, Chen."

"He tell me you teach police how to kill without gun."

"A trade I learned back in the early forties. A war trade."

"He always say you the best in the business."

"There's always somebody better, Chen. And I'm not getting any younger."

Chen grinned broadly. "You stlong old man, papa-san. So say phooying at Khatmong Hotel."

"Thai girls are prone to exaggerate." Smith grinned himself, knowing his use of the word "prone" was beyond Chen's reach.

Smith had breakfast next morning in the hotel coffee shop. He was halfway finished when a tall gaunt man with three phooying in tow entered from the lobby.

Bangkok Bill, by God, Smith thought with an amused smile.

The man's legal name was Henry Williams. He was a CPA who rambled around Southeast Asia auditing the books of an oil conglomerate's subsidiary companies. At quarterly intervals, his rambles brought him to Bangkok in quest of rest and rehabilitation, which took the form of an eclectic preference for more than one woman at a time.

Bangkok Bill's bloodshot eyes roved through the nearly empty room and rested on Smith, then widened with recognition. Trailed by his mini-harem, he sauntered toward the table with outstretched hand.

"Buddha be praised, if it isn't Bob's terrific old man. Tom, man, I'm mighty pleased to see you."

The two men shook hands. The three phooying exchanged glances and giggled.

"Take a seat, Bill," Smith said. "Never realized you were such an early riser."

"Early and late, man." Bangkok Bill, winking a bloodshot eye, sat opposite Smith. "C'est rire. But strictly speaking, Tom, I'm on the way to bed."

"With heavy traffic."

Bangkok Bill smiled benignly upon his entourage and motioned them to a nearby table. "I heard about Bob when I came through Singapore two days ago. Tough, man, tough and sad. Le grand homme, Bob. I owe him untold favors. So what can I do, Tom?"

"Not much, Bill. Thanks anyway. What's your pleasure?"

"I'm here for a beer."

"And the girls?"

"Lips that touch liquor will never touch mine. They drink juice of any kind. It's on me though, Tom. I'm fresh from the fields and loaded for bear." He signaled the waiter and ordered. "A bottle of Singha and three nam som."

"Tell me what you heard about Robert in Singapore, Bill."

"Just that he was dead. Been killed."

"No other details?"

"Fighting off muggers, I heard. But you must know that much, man."

"That's about all I know, Bill. I don't know how he went down. Shot or clubbed or what."

"I heard he was knifed, Tom. Un coup de poignard."

"Oh, Christ."

"A bad way for a good man to go." Bangkok Bill's oldish young face was a weary tragicomic mask. "If you can think of anything I might do to help, give me a jingle. I'll be here at the Khatmong for a couple of days. Then I'm off to Jakarta for a week or so. Staying at the Mandarin. Let me jot that down, Tom."

"Merci, Bill."

"Il n'y a pas de quoi."

Whoreson cutthroats.

With these words resonant in his head he went to his room and placed a phone call to Hyperion Petroleum in Jakarta. This time the previously elusive Lem Williamson was available.

Smith identified himself.

"Well, sir, I can hardly begin to tell you how sad we feel about this tragic event." Williamson's accent was Texan panhandle. "Your son Bob was with us a comparatively short spell but long enough for us to appreciate his value as a technician and a human being. Now if there's anything we can do for you—"

"There is. Tell me in detail the circumstances of his death."

"Well, sir, yes, I, uh."

"Let's start with the time of day."

"Why, sure. According to my notes, he was attacked a few minutes after nine in the morning."

Smith breathed an inward sigh of relief. At least Robert hadn't fallen outside a sordid saloon in the dead of night. "He was on the job then?"

"Right, sir. Matter of fact, he'd just left a brief meeting here at our headquarters and was en route to our construction site at Adhi Guna shipyard."

"Was he driving a car?"

"He was a passenger in a taxi, a Blue Bird, driven by one—I'm trying to make out the name—by one Taryono. Do you want me to spell it, sir?"

"No. Go on."

"The taxi was going east on Martadinata—that's a main thoroughfare here, sir—when it had to stop at a railroad crossing for a passing freight train. The driver says Bob was in the back seat reading a newspaper when two men, apparently Javanese, came up beside the taxi on motorcycles, opened doors on either side, and attempted to rob Bob at knife point. He resisted right strenuously, I gather from the report. Fact is, he managed to eject both assailants from the cab. Unfortunately, he'd already been stabbed a couple of times and one of the wounds proved fatal. Anyhow, the driver got him to a nearby hospital, where he died in the emergency room while being administered treatment."

"What happened to the two bastards on the motorcycles?"

"They drove off."

"And this all happened in broad daylight in heavy morning traffic?"

"Right, sir."

"No witnesses? No arrests?"

"Dozens of witnesses, Mister Smith. So the driver told the police. But who knows their names? They just simply melted away. And no arrests so far."

"What did the cutthroats manage to take?"

"Nothing, it seems. Bob's wife, Pranee, she's been here in consultation with our people. As far as she can ascertain, nothing is missing."

"Damned inept thieves, wouldn't you say?"

"Well, sir, I, uh."

"Robert always wore a gold Rolex wristwatch worth ten grand. Wore a couple of rings worth another five. Wore a gold chain with a gold medallion. And customarily he carried around too much cash. Hell, Williamson, he could be stripped like a Christmas tree by a fast-moving unarmed boy. And you mean to tell me the bloody wogs who knifed him failed to lift a thing?"

"A fact, sir. The watch, the rings, the chain and medallion and the cash—six hundred and fifty-nine dollars, most of it in rupiahs—were all intact and are now in the hands of his wife."

"Does that sound like a robbery, Williamson?"

"An unsuccessful one, maybe."

"I don't think so."

"What else could it be?"

"I'm coming to Jakarta to find out."

"I see. And when may we expect you, Mister Smith?"

"In a few days."

"Where are you now, sir?"

"In Bangkok to see my daughter-in-law."

By prearrangement, Smith met Chen in the hotel lobby at 10:45 A.M., and they drove to the airport to await Pranee's arrival. Her flight was on time.

Encumbered by a variety of luggage only a Thai woman could manage, Pranee led the flux of passengers into the packed reception area. She was thinner than she'd been a year ago, Smith thought.

Brown eyes bright with recognition, she detached herself from the milling throng, set her luggage on the floor, and encompassed Smith's waist with tight brown arms. He buried his nose in her glossy black hair and thought she was smaller than he remembered.

"Been a long time, my daughter," he said.

"Oh, fatha, I so glad to see you heah with Chen."

Chen himself was gathering up the luggage except for Pranee's handbag and a lidless cardboard box containing a dun-white urn of Satsuma ware. Smith soon learned that this urn held Robert's ashes.

Exchanging warm amenities, they followed Chen to the car, and there it developed that Pranee didn't wish to tarry in Bangkok. She preferred to go home to Pattaya City that afternoon on the three-beer bus, so called because that's how long it took a drinking passenger to be transported from the beginning to the end of the line.

The bus was air-conditioned. The happy Thai driver loved the horn; he honked it merrily as a warning and a greeting. The highway south of Bangkok was in good condition, fairly straight and comparatively free of bumps. The only times the bus swerved from its swift, horn-honking course was to avoid the occasional water buffalo which had wandered up on the road from the steamy fields on either side.

Pranee and Smith sat side by side on narrow cane-matted seats designed for oriental physiques. Comfortable, Pranee was holding the boxed urn in her lap and talking in her soft, sometimes barely audible voice. Concentrating as much on the discomfort of his buttocks as on what was being said, Smith sipped at his second bottle of Singha beer.

Pranee told him how she'd viewed Robert's body in the hospital morgue. She described the fatal wound in his left side below the heart.

She said there were other cuts, too—three on the left forearm, another on the left side of his face under the chin.

"My husband fight good," she murmured proudly, eyes tearful. "He not easy to kill, fatha."

"I'm sure of that, daughter."

Then she spoke of the Buddhist ceremony after the cremation. Six monks were in attendance. Also present were men and women from Hyperion Petroleum. Robert, she said in effect, followed no religion (something Smith already knew) but had lately mentioned he objected less to the flexible tenets of Buddhism than to the rigid orthodoxies that claimed to be infallible.

At the ceremony in a joss house, the monks made much merit for Robert with the Buddha. Thirty days hence, other monks in Pattaya City would make more merit for him. Then again, there would be another merit-making ceremony ninety days after his death.

Robert's spirit would be reborn, she said with shy conviction. He would return not in the guise of a diseased tree or a poisonous snake or a crippled child, but as a beautiful bird or a fine man risen from the sea.

She fell asleep before Smith ordered a third beer, the slender fingers of her right hand resting caressively over the top of the urn that held what was mortal . . .

From the bus terminal they took a taxi to the house that Robert had called his home for the last five years. It was an attractive but modest structure of white brick with a roof of yellow tile. Green grass grew around it. Three tall coconut palms leaned over a side-yard patio fringed with tropical ferns and overlooking the Gulf of Siam.

A man got up from a patio lounge chair and greeted them with a hand holding a bottle of beer. Of medium height and balding, with dark glasses and a Captain Ahab muff of whiskers, the man was at first unrecognizable to Smith and then he spotted the outline of the Canadian flag on the faded green T-shirt.

"Harry Oliver!" he called out. "That you, Harry?"

The man advanced, removing the dark glasses. "Noboby else, Tom. I was hoping you'd show up with Pranee."

"I didn't recognize you with the facial fur," Smith said, shaking the other's hand.

"That's right—I was clean shaven last year." Harry reached out for Pranee and squeezed her shoulder. "I made myself at home while I was waiting. With the help of your little housegirl."

"Fine, Hally. You like family. Let me talk to gal, then we all sit down and have to eat little bit."

The equatorial night descended: first as a damp and dusky gauze, then as a light azure veil, finally as a lavender curtain spangled with stellar minutiae. In the gulf's murky stillness, the imponderably slow progress of distant craft was marked by flickering intervals of orange light.

On the patio table Pranee and the housegirl had set out cheese, crackers, sliced melon. Pranee had also served the men gin and tonic. Now she joined them with a glass of iced tea.

The table's centerpiece was the sole illumination, a squat green candle that doubled as a mosquito repellent. Its fluttering virescence imbued the faces around it with a spectral quality, and in this aura of séance Pranee related what she'd learned in Jakarta about Robert's death. Her version was not only more detailed than that which Williamson had given Smith, but it differed critically in several aspects.

Taryono, the taxi driver, for instance, had a standing arrangement to meet Robert each morning at his hotel and take him to the jobsite. He was not, in short, a driver summoned at random.

Pranee had obviously questioned Taryono more closely than anyone from Hyperion Petroleum.

He told her he drove Robert to the Panin Bank building where Hyperion had executive offices. En route he observed (an exercise in hindsight) two men on a motorcycle who seemed to be tailing the cab. At the time he lent no importance to this because persons on motorcycles, singly or paired, were commonplace in Jakarta. But these two wore goggles—*not* commonplace—and that's why he later remembered them.

Robert entered the Panin Bank building, where he remained for twenty minutes. Waiting in the cab, Taryono thought he saw the same two men near a vendor's pushcart half a block away.

Robert returned to the cab and directed Taryono to proceed to the Adhi Guna shipyard, where he was supervising the construction of seagoing oil rigs. Then he became absorbed in *The Jakarta Times*.

As usual at nine in the morning, the traffic on Gunung Sahari Antjol was heavy and noisy. Taryono's concentration was so intense that he failed to notice the goggled men on the motorcycle until he'd turned onto Martadinata alongside the Antjol Canal. Even then he was not sure these were the *same* two men.

Until the slow-moving traffic jammed to a halt at a railroad crossing through which a freight train was rattling. Even then Taryono was not especially aware of the men until the motorcycle came to a stop at the left-hand side of the cab and the man in the passenger seat, dismounting, opened the rear door and lunged at Robert with a wickedly long knife. Robert's reaction was surprisingly quick. Using an attaché case on the seat as a shield, he warded off the first blow. The goggled man slashed out again, this time drawing blood.

At first Taryono was as immobilized as his taxi. He couldn't believe what was happening to his passenger. At last he did all he was capable of—he yelled for help. Of the dozen or so nearby witnesses, nobody heeded his cries. Pranee described Taryono as "small man, eyes ashame of himself, no help to Lobbut."

The attack ceased as abruptly as it had begun. The man with the knife resumed his seat on the motorcycle and the driver maneuvered the vehicle across the stalled traffic and into the comparatively empty lanes going back toward Gunung Sahari Antjol.

Robert instructed Taryono to get him to a hospital, quick. But quickness was impossible in that clutter of motionless metal. Even when the railroad crossing was clear, Taryono required time, too much time, in getting the cab out of the congested traffic. Then he took still more time by stopping at a police station and excitedly and repetitiously reporting the incident to several officers. And only then, with a police escort, did he proceed to a hospital.

Too much time, much too late.

Five minutes after being helped into the emergency room, Robert expired. Nobody remembered what his last words were.

Smith listened to this account with a phlegmatic expression which concealed an inner fury.

"What a damn senseless thing," he said in a flat voice, staring at Harry Oliver's mournful face across the table but seeming to address some other, less visible audience.

"I think same thing, fatha," Pranee said. "I think make no sense. Then a Philippine man, name of Tomas, he come see me day I fly home. He tell me things I nevva know yet. Then it make some sense, yes."

Smith leaned forward. "What sense, daughter?"

Tomas told her he'd been recruited in Manila by Hyperion Petroleum with two other qualified riggers named Luis and Vicente. The trio arrived at the Jakarta jobsite a month before Robert came to replace the resident engineer, a Chinese who was succumbing to drugs and alcohol.

From the beginning, the Indonesian workers were hostile to the Filipinos. They treated them as pariahs not only because they were foreigners but also because, as unionized riggers, they were better paid than most of the natives, who were classified as day laborers.

Tomas said the enmity, expressed in many ways, kept growing. Tea was spilled on blueprints being examined by him or one of his compatriots. Pipe of the wrong diameter was deposited at the wrong location. Concrete was improperly mixed. Cranes broke down because water was in the oil. Whatever operation came under the jurisdiction of the Filipino riggers was in constant jeopardy.

Finally this enmity trespassed on the sacrosanct, the personal, Tomas said. It took the form of jostling, of treading on toes, of elbowing, of deliberately misdirected spitting. Which led to the last unendurable provocation. This occurred when a rowdy named Siswono, usually in the forefront of these torments, dropped a burning cigarette down Vicente's shirt front. Enraged at last, Vicente kicked Siswono in the genitals, delivered a knockout punch as he doubled up, and urinated on him as he lay twitching in the dirt.

Vicente's body was found in a latrine the next morning. He'd been stabbed in the back and emasculated.

Police appeared, asked perfunctory questions, made sparse note of evasive answers, listened with courteous incomprehension to Filipino Spanish while caressing their sidearms, and disappeared. Siswono was still among the work force four days later, glowering balefully at the Filipino riggers.

Tomas and Luis took their case to the Chinese manager, who was too fogged in to give a damn. Besides, as it turned out, he'd just been divested of all authority and given his walking papers. Robert arrived within the week. Tomas and Luis approached him on his rounds and told him what had been happening on the job and about Vicente's death. They pointed out Siswono as the culprit. Robert listened attentively and said he would address all the workers the following day about amity on the job, and he did so.

Siswono leered at the English and laughed at the translation. The following afternoon Luis was found beside a demobilized crane, his skull fractured. He died an hour later in an ambulance.

Tomas sought out Robert—or Roberto, as he called him—and Robert promised to keep an eye on Siswono. He obviously did just that, for he saved Tomas' life within the week.

The little Filipino was drinking from an ice-water fountain near a rig foundation. It was dusk. The spot was isolated. Siswono was apparently poised to deliver a stab in his back when he was pounded into the ground by Roberto—a very good man, su marido, señora—who then literally dragged him to the gate and heaved him off the premises with the injunction that he never come near the jobsite again.

That was two weeks before Roberto's death.

"Siswono is the hediondo bastardo who killed him," Tomas said. "Siswono and his amigote, a man named Mulja."

Pranee said then, "We go to police, Tomas."

"Waste of time, señora," Tomas replied. "Not safe for me, either. Tonight I fly back to Manila. I burn many candles for Roberto with Santa Teresa and pray that his killers soon sizzle en el quinto infierno. Adiós."

"Now I know what I have to do," Smith said.

"Tom, don't do anything rash," Harry Oliver said.

Smith said, "I'll do what has to be done, Harry."

"Will you take some advice?"

"Test me."

"Well, don't try transporting a weapon. Drives them nuts in Indonesia. They find a weapon, Tom, they lock you in the monkey house and feed the key to a crocodile."

"I don't require a weapon. Not in the conventional sense."

"I heard about you, Tom," Harry Oliver said.

"Get me a dowel, Harry. Hard wood. Teak's fine, and it's local."

"What size dowel?"

"I'd like it eight inches long and an inch and a half in diameter."

"When do you need it?"

"I'm going to Jakarta the day after tomorrow. I'd like to take it with me."

Thomas got off the plane at Kemajoran Airport and took a taxi to the Mandarin Hotel. As he registered, he asked if Henry Williams was in the house. The clerk gave him an obliquely knowledgeable eye.

"Not yet, sir. But we do expect him later today."

Bangkok Bill was running on schedule.

Once settled in his room, Smith phoned Hyperion Petroleum and got through to Lem Williamson. "This is Tom Smith," he said. "I plan to be at your office in twenty minutes."

"Well, I, uh—"

Smith cut the connection.

Williamson was a man in his mid-thirties with limp sandy hair parted in the middle and a sandy mustache that drooped over full lips. Smith found his manner smilingly obsequious but not just for present company; he judged it to be a habit cultivated for a long climb up the corporate ladder.

"Pleasure to meet you, sir," Williamson said, offering a thin dry hand. "Take this chair here if you will. Fine. And now that we're face to face, sir, I can't help but remark how much Bob favored you, especially around the eyes. I'm just about ready to have tea. I trust you'll join me. Unless you prefer something stronger."

"Tea will do. I didn't know Texans were addicted to tea."

Williamson chuckled almost penitently. "I spent time in England as a Rhodes scholar and drank it socially. I learned to like it. But judging from your astute observation, I reckon it didn't dilute my Texan accent." He offered a cigarette, which was refused, and then lit one himself. "I know you're here for a good reason, sir, but damned if I can figure it out."

"I'm here to nail the curs who killed my son."

Smoke filtered lazily through the fringes of the man's sad mustache. "Just yesterday, knowing you were en route, I discussed the case with the police again. I regret to say they haven't got a clue."

"Well, I've got a couple."

"You have?"

"Yes."

"Something the police can go on?"

"Not the hard evidence they'd require. Not yet. But I've got a strong lead. To follow it, I'll need information from your personnel records."

"I'm at your service, Mister Smith."

"Two weeks prior to my son's death, you had a couple of laborers on your payroll. Their names are Siswono and Mulja. I want the addresses that go with those names."

Williamson was penciling the names on a notepad as the office door opened and an attractive young woman entered bearing a silver tea service. Smith had noticed her among the several other women in the outer office upon his arrival. Her frosty blonde hair and china-blue eyes had immediately conveyed to him her Dutch origins, the hereditary Dutchness which had ruled this tropical archipelago long before the emergence of Sukarno.

"Punctual as always," Williamson said graciously. "And oh, by the way, Miss Boonstra, this gentleman is Bob Smith's father."

"I guessed it." Miss Boonstra set the gleaming tray on the polished desk. "Though we didn't know him long, your son was much liked here, sir. We understand how great your loss."

"Thank you." Smith was on his feet, the old cavalier. "I appreciate the sentiment."

"I'll do the honors, Miss Boonstra," Williamson said, reaching for the teapot. "Meanwhile, you may do Mister Smith a favor." He tore a page from the notepad and slid it across the desk. "Find out whatever we have in our records on either of these two men. The quicker the better."

Five minutes later the results of Miss Boonstra's efficiency were on Williamson's desk. The name Mulja wasn't a matter of company record, but Siswono's name was there as well as his address.

"It's an area of sorry kampongs," Williamson explained. "Shacks of wood and bamboo. Six people to a room. I wouldn't go down there looking for him if I were you."

"I don't plan to. He'll come looking for me . . ."

Smith stopped at a drug store near the hotel and bought two items—a large can of lighter fluid and a roll of adhesive tape. Back in his room, using a formidable jackknife, he went to work on the teak dowel that Harry had obtained for him.

A little after six, he descended to the bar for a preprandial cocktail. He wasn't surprised to find Bangkok Bill already there. But he was sitting alone and that was a bit of a surprise.

"Where are your ladies tonight, Bill?"

He turned to look at Smith over his right shoulder. Once his weary eyes focused, his gaunt face filled perceptibly with a smile. "Hélas and bonsoir, Tom. What a rencontre! What's your pleasure?"

"A bone-dry martini."

"Tout de suite." He gave the bartender the order. "You inquire after my ladies, mes dames de charité. They don't know I'm here yet. But le bon mot is even now going abroad and soon, voilà, the warm bodies will begin to arrive from all quarters."

"Perhaps you can arrange for one of them to do me a favor."

"One? Why one, mon ami? Try two or three. I have always more than enough for my simple needs."

"You misunderstand. Let me explain."

Smith then outlined what he had in mind.

Bangkok Bill should ascertain which of his ladies was comfortably familiar with a certain district of the city where a man called Siswono lived. This lady should discreetly spread the word around that district that the late Robert Smith's father had just arrived in Jakarta. He should be described as an angry old man dedicated to exposing the men who murdered his son. It should be told that this fierce father had the names of two Indonesians given him by a Filipino pipefitter and not much else to go on. Yet this avenging old devil was so convinced that these names identified the guilty parties that he was already manufacturing evidence against them by suborning witnesses. He had the money to make greedy folks say what he wanted them to say and swear thereto. Give this ugly American a week, let it be rumored, and he will have amassed enough false testimony to indict the men whose names are always on his lips—Siswono and Mulja. And count on his money to arrange a speedy trial and the maximum penalty—a life of daily horror in the monkey house.

"So you set yourself up as a target," Bangkok Bill commented.

"La cible-silhouette. It's a dangerous game, Tom, but it just might work."

"Do you think one of your ladies can help set me up?"

"I'd bet on it. Are you registered here at the hotel?"

Smith nodded.

"Then let me sleep on it. I'll get back to you in the morning."

Bangkok Bill rang at ten. "The game's afoot, Tom."

"You've found the right gal?"

"I've found her, yes. Now she'll find the listeners. When that's done, I'll be in touch."

"Any idea how soon, Bill?"

"Le temps approche, mon ami. Give me a couple of days."

Three days later the phone rang as Smith was leaving the room for breakfast.

"Tom Smith?"

"Yes?"

"Bangkok Bill here."

"I recognize your voice. Any progress?"

"Definite feedback. Somebody wants to know where you might be found alone, outside the hotel."

"Pass the word that I often stroll at dusk around the Istiqial Mosque. Say I'm crazy about its architecture, its well kept grounds and bushes and trees. Add that I'm easy to identify because I wear a yellow straw hat with a wide brim, something like the cowboys wear in American movies."

"Do you stroll alone, mon vieux?"

"Always alone, Bill."

"And how far do you expect to carry this plan, Tom?"

"All the way."

"Well, Tom, bonne chance and au revoir. I'm leaving for Singapore in the morning. Perhaps I'll read of the outcome in the newspapers."

"I doubt it. Robert's murder rated a single paragraph in the local press. So much for the importance of death here. But thanks, Bill, for your aid and comfort."

In latterday mosques the muezzin's call to prayer is often a stereophonic reproduction, and thus it was at the imposing Istiqial. From the balconied minaret atop the eleven story building, the resonant chant, issuing forth five times a day, reached much farther than any unassisted human voice.

"La ilaha ill'Allah." The electronic plangency seemed to make the humid dusk quiver. *"Allah akbar . . ."*

This was Smith's fourth evening of listening to the intoned recording, and as on all previous occasions a deep cognitive sense informed him he was being reconnoitered by one of the pedestrians on the public sidewalk across the avenue from the mosque's well kept grounds.

Again came the ubiquitous chant from the minaret. What was it Robert once said about the Moslems? "Anyone who has to pray five times a day can't feel much at home on this old globe." A dozen of them, facing in the general direction of Mecca, were pressing their foreheads on the mosque's parched grass a hundred yards away. He had yielded that area to the faithful a few minutes earlier and taken a more secluded stand under the drooping branches of a Java willow. As prayerful heads rose and once again bent to the ground, the sun was extinguishing itself in Jakarta Bay.

If nothing happens soon, Smith mused, I may grab one of those terrible tricycle taxis—betjaks, yes—and go over to Raja Kramat where Pesar Senen is—the Monday Market. Today was Monday. Maybe he could find a—

His musing ended with the sound, somehow distinct from the other sounds of traffic, of a motorcycle suddenly accelerating. Stepping from the willow's shadow, he faced south and saw what he'd been waiting for.

The motorcycle bearing down on him was less than fifty yards distant. It carried two brown men, their lank black hair restrained by sweat bands. And they both wore goggles.

Yes, he decided, these are my whoreson cutthroats.

He reached his right hand into the side pocket of his safari jacket and took out the dowel, a much different-looking dowel from the one Harry Oliver had given him. Both ends were honed to a blunt point and the center was irregularly taped for a firm grip. He gripped it firmly now.

Ten feet away the driver skidded the bike to a stop. The passenger, sliding neatly from his seat, reached behind himself and produced a long-bladed knife. Holding it low, he took the few running steps that brought him within striking distance of Smith, and struck.

But Smith did what he'd often trained others to do. Pivoting deftly, much like a matador executing a veronica, he whipped off the big hat and absorbed the knife-thrust in the crown. At the same time, with a swift backhanded motion, he drove a blunt point of the dowel hard into the man's trachea and heard the crunch of cartilage. The man dropped to his knees and rolled over on his back, his mouth distortedly open to scream a scream that wouldn't come.

The driver waited too long. It took him that belated extra second to realize what had happened. Then he gunned the machine to make his escape. But Smith had already retrieved the knife and was ready to throw it. It caught the driver deep in the right lumbar region, knocking him off the bike, which fell on its side several feet farther on, the motor almost immediately stalling.

The entire episode had taken less than ten seconds and the Moslems were still aiming themelves toward Mecca. Nobody else had observed anything, either.

Removing the large can of lighter fluid from a pocket, he twisted off the cap and emptied the contents in equal measure over the fallen figures. Both were still alive and would remain alive a little while longer.

Long enough to get a foretaste of hell, Smith reflected as he struck a match and set each man afire.

Tim Heald

The Case of the Frozen
Diplomat

Simon Bognor, Britain's special Board of Trade representative in
Canada, buttered another slice of toast and spread a thick layer
of Gentleman's Relish on top. The combination of spiced anchovy
paste and butter-saturated crust was immensely appealing and he
allowed himself an indulgent moment of gratitude to Macpherson.
Without Macpherson there would have been no Gentleman's Relish.
Toronto had run out of the stuff. The manufacturers were refusing
to stick on bilingual labels, so Trudeau's excise men were banning
it. Bognor smirked. Macpherson must have bought up every one of
the little black-and-white jars in the entire province, perhaps even
beyond. When Bognor had opened Macpherson's safe three weeks
ago, 79 of them had come tumbling out—Macpherson's last will and
testament.

Bognor remembered his predecessor well, for they had shared a
taste for food, drink, and thin cigars, and occasionally indulged it
in a small Italian restaurant near the office. Bognor did not like to
think of Macpherson lying under the snow all winter. He had gone
missing during the first blizzard of December. Three weeks ago at
the beginning of the thaw, a cross-country skier had fallen over his
boot in a conservation area thirty miles north of Toronto. The consul
general said he was perfectly preserved, though he had been drinking. In one pocket was a frozen ham sandwich, half eaten; in the
other was an unopened jar of Gentleman's Relish. He was, of course,
extremely dead.

Bognor sighed, picked up *The Globe and Mail*, and turned to the
"daily mistake." The persistent apology was, he had decided, a Canadian characteristic. Ever since his arrival, Canadians had been
apologizing: for the unusual weather, for the poor quality of the
television, for the Toronto Maple Leafs. But not so often for Macpherson's death. The man from the RCMP had said, in so many
words, that Macpherson had asked for it; he had become involved
in what should have been left to the RCMP. Bognor had been expecting a man in a red tunic with a cowboy hat. Instead the Mountie

had worn a neat Tip Top Tailors three-piece suit. He was called Jay Walewska and he chewed gum.

"Brits here keep a low profile, sir," he said, pseudo-friendly. "Like you shouldn't bust your ass. Have a good trip. Watch the Blue Jays. Find yourself a cottage. Get yourself a girl. No reason to mess around." Bognor, not wishing to give offense, had nodded agreeably and for the past three weeks had sifted through Macpherson's papers and personal effects.

He sighed again, put down the paper, and dug his knife into the Gentleman's Relish, scooping out another gob of the dark-brown paste. The jar was a masterpiece of packaging: heavy white stone with utterly discreet black lettering and the Latin subtitle *patum peperium*. It was the peanut butter of the English upper class. It belonged on the same shelf as the Oxford Marmalade and the Bollinger Champagne. He spread it absentmindedly and realized with a sudden start of irritation that the relish contained a foreign object.

He paused, then scraped with his knife and revealed a paper sachet that looked like a very small teabag. Odd. He set the packet down on top of his desk and contemplated it. He'd never come across such a thing before. A two-inch nail in a take-out chop suey once and a wedding ring in a bowl of cold soup at a private dinner party. Never this.

He picked it up and tore it open, then frowned as a thin stream of white powder poured out into a neat pyramid. He rolled a little between finger and thumb. Finer than salt, rougher than icing sugar. He licked a finger. It tasted of nothing. In London, he would have taken it downstairs for analysis, but the consulate boasted no such facility. He would send it to Ottawa and on to London in the diplomatic bag.

He sighed again. This Canadian assignment was another piece of miscasting in a life that, in its middle years, was turning from light comedy to farce and might yet end in tragedy. He had meant, on leaving Oxford, to enter the civil service. When the interviewer, oily and ingratiating, had leaned forward and said, *sotto voce*, that there was "*another* branch of the civil service," he had nodded eagerly, wishing to appear keen, not knowing what he meant, and had allowed himself to be swept along by the ensuing charade of clandestine meetings and country-house weekends. Now he was stuck: an undercover agent in the Special Operations Department of the Board of Trade, a secret agent of sorts, ill-suited by temperament, inclination, breeding, and education for the world of codes and ciphers and industrial secrets.

He swept the little pile of powder into an envelope and sealed it with a lick. LSD, cocaine, heroin—he tried to remember the details of the dangerous-drugs course he had been sent on four years ago on the Scottish island of Benbecula and failed. No matter. Analysis would tell him soon enough.

It was 12:30. Time for a cheeseburger. He picked up his notebook, the jar of Gentleman's Relish and Macpherson's diary, then crossed the road to the Crazy Cow Dining Lounge for a light lunch and further research. He had been through that diary every lunch since he had arrived, so that it was filthy with fingermarks, cheese stains, and spilled Molson's. Still it had not yet yielded a plausible secret. Indeed, the only clue worthy of the name was that brand-new jar of Gentleman's Relish in Macpherson's left pocket. It was obviously a new purchase.

Bognor had taken a photograph of Macpherson to every high-class grocer and delicatessen in town. Finally, in a suburban cheese "shoppe" he had found what he feared. Yes, the diminutive gourmet behind the counter recognized the photograph. A Saturday morning last December, the day of the storm. The man had had an English accent and had just bought the last jar of Gentleman's Relish when he was confronted by a ferret-faced person with a ginger moustache and a limp. Ferret-face had two friends, and between them they'd bundled the Englishman outside and into a car. There had been a lot of shouting.

Since then, Bognor had kept his eyes peeled for a ferret-faced man with a limp and a ginger moustache. To no avail. He wiped a streak of warm rubbery cheese from his chin and picked up the half empty jar of Gentleman's Relish. It reminded him of home as he turned it slowly in his fingers, savoring its feel and appearance, remembering nursery teas with Nanny: the smell of charred bread against the gas fire; of the carbolic soap that Nanny used. In a changed world, at least Gentleman's Relish was what it had always been. At least—he frowned. Why in God's name had he not noticed it before?

He stared hard at the label, blinked, turned away, stared again, had another swig of beer, took a final peer, and decided that the undersized teabag was not the only peculiarity of this particular jar. There, tiny but distinct, proudly prancing below the middle letters of the label, was a small rampant beaver with a spoon thrust in its mouth. Bognor's eyes glazed. "Interesting," he said, as he got up to pay the bill.

The beaver and the spoon was the personal emblem of Sir Roderick Farquhar, the world-famous millionaire financier who headed "Mammon-Corp," the Mammon Corporation. Farquhar was so smart that he had kept his name out of Peter Newman's book on the Canadian business elite, allowing such lesser rivals as E.P. Taylor of Argus Corporation and Paul Desmarais of Power Corporation to take the limelight. To those in the know, however, Farquhar of Mammon was the man who controlled Canada; who had half the cabinet in his pocket; who was on Christian-name terms with the Queen; who kept a cruiser-sized yacht in the Mediterranean and apartments in a half dozen countries, as well as a Scottish grouse moor and a private pack of hounds in Dorset.

All this was known to Bognor, who had gone through the Canada files before leaving London. Now a sachet of drugs had turned up in a jar of Gentleman's Relish marked with Farquhar's personal insignia. Bognor's mind struggled inexorably to the obvious conclusion. Farquhar was importing drugs and Macpherson had found out. He had been murdered on Sir Roderick Farquhar's say-so. Bognor's mind boggled.

Bognor was not methodical by nature but he often attempted to remedy the deficiency by drawing up lists on pieces of paper, which he subsequently lost. Now he set about cataloguing the remaining jars of relish. Twelve had already been consumed and discarded, leaving 67. First he examined each one for the distinctive sign of the beaver and was disappointed to find no more. Then he procured a large black garbage bag from Miss Sims and scooped out the contents of each jar in the search for more sachets. Nothing. He could scarcely believe his bad luck. All he had to show for his labors was a garbage bag full of anchovy paste.

"Bloody silly!" he exclaimed, running his fingers through his thinning hair. He decided to telephone and sort the whole affair out personally, man to man. He thumbed through the phonebook clumsily, then dialed and listened to the ringing tone, heard the answering secretary.

"Sir Roderick Farquhar," he said.

"Sir Roderick is in conference. Would you like to speak to Mr. Lewandowski?"

Lewandowski, it transpired, was Farquhar's personal assistant.

He sounded antiseptic, capable of unending evasion, a specialist in a politeness so polite it was ruder than insults. Bognor had dealt with his sort before. There was nothing as insufferable as a great man's flunky.

"I wish to speak with Sir Roderick. It's important. It's about the death of a colleague of mine, a Mr. Macpherson from the Board of Trade."

"I am truly sorry, Mr. Bognor, Sir Roderick does not give interviews. He is extremely busy. Perhaps I can help?"

"I want to see him."

"I am afraid that is not possible."

"What if I were to tell you that it was about Gentleman's Relish?" A pause. A long one. Then a click. Lewandowski had hung up. Bognor stared at the receiver blankly, then hung up himself. Something had happened, though he wasn't quite sure what.

Late in the afternoon, just as he was about to go home frustrated and dispirited, the consul general summoned him.

"Sherry?"

"Thank you."

"I gather you're trying to see Farquhar of Mammon over this damned Macpherson business?" A censorious exhalation of blue tobacco smoke.

"Yes."

"May I ask why?" The consul general wrinkled his nose and squinted down it, then, as Bognor hesitated, examined his fingernails, individually, not much liking what he saw.

"I think he may have killed Macpherson," said Bognor. "I found drugs in a pot of his personal Gentleman's Relish."

The consul general gave him a very old-fashioned look. "Come on, old boy." He smiled like a benevolent uncle. "Between you and me, we're involved in some rather tricky negotiations with Farquhar over the new fighter aircraft. Not to mention the James Bay project. Fact of the matter is, I don't want anything screwed up by your banging around annoying the fellow."

Bognor pinked, his throat dry. "Sir, with respect, a man's dead."

"Precisely, Bognor." The consul general screwed the remains of his cigarette viciously into the ashtray. "And nothing you can do will bring him back. We need these contracts, Bognor. Farquhar's an important chap. Personal friend of the Queen, got most of the cabinet in his pocket. I don't want him offended."

"Oh, for God's sake." Bognor had left then, half his sherry undrunk. He had liked Macpherson and was appalled as always by the private cynicism that governed public life. Well, if no one else was going to do his late lamented colleague justice, he at least would. He returned to his office and pushed the buttons that would connect him to Mammon-Corp. The number rang for a full minute, then a male voice answered.

"This is a personal call for Mr. Lewandowski."

"Are you a friend of his?"

"In a manner of speaking. We have—or had—a mutual acquaintance." Bognor relished the bitter accuracy of the words.

"I'll see if he's still here."

Bognor waited minutes, then there was a sequence of whirring and clicking and a new voice, silky smooth, immediately recognizable as Lewandowski's, came on the line.

"Lewandowski?"

"This is he."

"Bognor here, Board of Trade. Now just you listen to me. If you think I'm going to be fobbed off because your precious boss wants to invoke the Old Pals' Act you've got another think coming. Just you tell Sir Roderick bloody Farquhar that I have his number. Got it?" Bognor slammed the phone down and found that he was shaking. In London he would have found a search warrant, perhaps even indulged in a burglary, gone round to Mammon Corporation and impounded all the Gentleman's Relish he could find. Here in Toronto he found himself surrounded by strangeness and hostility and he was afraid. He needed a drink.

That night, in his apartment in a building on Bloor Street, he got drunk on rye. The apartment was owned by the office. It had been Macpherson's before him and he felt his predecessor's presence more keenly the drunker he became. Macpherson, he was certain as he staggered into alcohol-induced slumber, had penetrated the secret of the Gentleman's Relish and had been about to confront Farquhar. Farquhar had got him first. The ferret-faced man with the limp and the whiskers was obviously a Mammon hit man.

In his dreams that night, Bognor imagined what his own fate might be. He visualized the karate chop from behind; the weights tied to his feet; the early-morning drop into Lake Ontario.

He woke at five, sweating, made coffee, and read two chapters of Hardy's *Jude the Obscure*. It did not improve his temper. On the bus, his umbrella struck a fellow passenger. She glared at him so unforgivingly that he glared back. At the office, his coffee was even weaker than at home so that he complained to Miss Sims—nice, helpful Miss Sims, whose parents had come from Glasgow in the Depression. She sulked, not understanding his ill temper, but still gave him the message: "Sir Roderick Farquhar will see you Monday at four. Mammon Centre, one hundred and first floor."

"He what?"

Mouselike, Miss Sims flinched from such unexpected aggression, and Bognor softened. "I'm sorry," he said, "old war wound. Or an ulcer. I don't know. What did you say?"

"Sir Roderick Farquhar will see you on Monday at four," she repeated, wide-eyed and nervous.

"The devil he will," said Bognor, narrowing his eyes and thinking hard. "Did he phone?"

"A man called personally to deliver the message."

"Really?"

"Yes."

"Ginger-haired? Moustache? Walked with a limp? Ferrety sort of face?"

Miss Sims' eyes widened. Sometimes Bognor's powers of intuition amazed even himself. "Say no more, Miss Sims," he said, smiling for the first time in days. "All is forgiven." He gave her a light peck on the cheek and went to his desk humming the Grand March from *Aida*.

Not that he was under any illusions. He realized that Mammon meant danger and that once inside its portals he might never come out alive. Therefore he took precautions. He sent a coded cable over the CN-CP wires to Parkinson, his immediate superior for many years and now director general of the SOD(BOT). It set out all that had happened and was about to happen. He could rely on Parkinson. Then he sent a similar wire to London Analysis, telling them to expect a sample soonest, to give it their immediate attention and liaise with Parkinson. Then, to make absolutely certain, he telephoned Monica, the loyal, boring girl friend who had been one of the few fixed points in his life for almost as long as Parkinson.

"Monica, it's me."

"Darling, how nice."

"Yes. I'm in Toronto."

"I know. How is it?"

"Cold. Windy."

"How interesting. But I don't suppose you phoned to talk weather."

"No. This is important. I'm seeing someone called Sir Roderick Farquhar at four o'clock on Monday. He's world famous and madly respectable and rich, but in fact he's a drug pusher and a murderer. He killed Macpherson."

"Goodness. Are you sure?"

"Pretty positive. I'll know for certain by four-thirty. The point is, he's dangerous. There's not much he won't stop at."

"Oh, yes." Monica sounded bored. She had been here before.

"Darling, this is important. I may not get out alive."

"Quite."

"So I want you to phone the office at five. If I'm not back, get hold of Parkinson, tell him to send in the troops. The Mounties, that is."

"Right you are," said Monica. "Darling, are you getting enough sleep? You sound peculiar."

"Yes, I'm fine. Just nervous."

"Of course."

They had exchanged pleasantries and Monica had promised, twice, to do as she was told. His life depended on it. He hoped she realized. He hoped she cared.

It was late now, and Friday night. Somehow he did not like the idea of being alone in his apartment. Instead he drove to a country inn at Niagara-on-the-Lake, where he spent as comfortable a weekend as possible with his old service revolver strapped to his shirt and a sick apprehension inside him. On Sunday he came back, ready to face his epic confrontation.

This time he drank only one stiff whiskey before bed. Sleep did not come until after midnight and was shallow and fitful when it did. Nor was it long-lived. His bedside travelling clock showed 2:15 when he heard the crisp click of his lock, expertly picked—probably with nothing more sophisticated than a credit card. Seconds later, they were in the room. He had a fleeting impression of stocking masks, a man with a limp, then the hospital smell of ether clamped hard to his mouth and nose. A perfunctory struggle, a moment of numb despair and panic, then a slipping away of consciousness into a world of darkness and wild, disturbing dreams.

He came round in a room with the feel and smell of basement. The mean cream paint was peeling off the brick walls. There were pipes everywhere. Two heavy men with prize-fighter faces and black-leather jackets lounged by the door, drinking from plastic cups. On the other side of the bare table sat, as he had rather expected, a man with a ginger moustache.

The man smiled and offered a cigarette. Bognor seldom smoked but he had a sense of occasion so took it in his lips and allowed his captor to light it from a gold Dunhill. His own hands were tied to the back of his chair.

"Who are you?" Bognor's voice sounded frightened. He wished he could control himself better.

The man stood and limped toward him. "How rude of me," he said. "Lewandowski. Jim Lewandowski. Executive assistant to Sir Roderick. We have spoken."

From some untapped source, Bognor dredged up defiance. "Executive assistant," he laughed. "Big name for a crummy little job. Yes sir, no sir, three bags full. All you do is answer the phone and arrange your master's life. Buy him his booze, and—" he paused dramatically "—his Gentleman's Relish."

Lewandowski's ferret face froze. "Fritzy," he said, "give our friend a drink." One of the henchmen went to a cupboard and took out a quart of Wiser's Special Blend. The other heavy pulled Bognor's head back, Lewandowski pried his mouth open, and the third man forced a pint of Wiser's down the protesting gullet.

"We have plans for you," said Lewandowski. "As you may realize, your inquiries have become—" he flicked ash onto the floor "—as tiresome as your predecessor's! Like you, he was fond of his whiskey, so that, most unfortunately, he was too drunk to find his way home from Bruce's Mill. In your case, the coroner will be shocked but unsurprised to discover that you attempted to drive at one hundred miles an hour along Lakeshore Boulevard after drinking almost two bottles of rye." He shook his head and smiled thinly.

Bognor began to feel drunk. "We'll keep you here for the day, and then some time after midnight we'll let you drive home on your own. What could be more civilized?" Again that laugh and its echo from the doorway.

"I don't understand," said Bognor, understanding, he feared, all too well.

"Then let me explain." Lewandowski folded his arms and grinned. "Your friend Mr. Macpherson shared our beloved master's love for this absurd British teatime savory paste called Gentleman's Relish. As you now presumably realize, we have a particular interest in ensuring that our own, rather special not to say individual pots of relish do not find their way onto the public market. Alas—" he spread his hands in a gesture of muted despair "—whether it was a computer fault or human error I can't tell. One of our jars went missing. We found it was on the market. When we checked the local outlets, we discovered that for the previous week a strange fat Englishman had been buying the whole Toronto stock. Finally, we trapped him, but by then it was too late. For all of us. Fritzy here became a little, how shall we say—overenthusiastic."

"And you never found your jar?"

"No. We were unable to penetrate the security of your British consulate. Macpherson would not give up the combination of the safe. He was a brave man." Lewandowski lowered his eyes. "But we have all day. Another drink?"

The procedure was repeated, and Bognor felt himself losing all control. He wondered what time it was. He just hoped the basement was in the Mammon Building. That the Mounties would get to him before dark.

"Why the message?" he asked. "Why did you pretend Sir Roderick would see me at four?"

"No pretense," said Lewandowski. "The message was genuine."

He was drunk, blind drunk, when they found him. His early warning distress signals to London had done the trick. The analysis of the tea bag, confirming Swindow LSD, had helped. A Scotland Yard dawn raid had uncovered a London drug factory plus a hoard of Gentleman's Relish jars and an accomplished art student who had been making money on the side painting tiny beavers with silver spoons in their mouths. Parkinson had flown over at once. He was concerned, as he put it, to "give those damned Mounties a kick up the bum. They're too busy doing a Watergate on Quebec's froggoes to worry about crime." But he had other worries, too.

"May I go home now?" Bognor asked, eventually, still drunk.

Parkinson stared at him with the expression that had withered countless colleagues in every reach of the British civil service.

"May?" he repeated finally, with a devastatingly ironic softness. "May, Bognor?"

Bognor swallowed hard. He was not sober but he was not so far off sobriety that he didn't recognize Parkinson's anger.

"I just thought—" His voice trailed away.

"I know what you thought, Bognor." Parkinson was still talking very softly but he was having trouble keeping his voice down. "You thought you were some sort of a hero. Thought you'd broken a great international drug-smuggling racket, involving the most powerful man in Canada."

"Well, yes, actually."

"You're an imbecile, Bognor. It's true there has been a rather amateur little drug-smuggling operation going on. And it's true that one end of it was organized from within the Mammon organization. But instead of seeing it for the small-time nonsense it is, you have to go right to the top, don't you? You can't accept that it's the embittered male secretary on an inadequate salary who's trying to make a fast buck. Oh, no. For you, only the best. 'Multi-millionaire in drug scandal.' You want your name in lights along with Inspector Maigret and Sherlock Holmes."

Bognor bit his lip. The worst was to come, he knew. This was not the first time.

"Farquhar had nothing to do with it. Nothing whatever. Lewandowski was working a little fiddle all on his own. The RCMP were already onto him. But Farquhar's angry now. Not just with you but with us. You've botched the fighter deal; you've screwed up any chance of collaborating in James Bay. The foreign office is livid with rage. The prime minister wants your head on a plate. The external-affairs chappies in Ottawa say if you're not out in twenty-four hours they'll expel you like they did the Soviets. And yet you still manage to ask, all nice and smug and pleased with yourself: 'May I go home?' God help us."

Bognor flew home that night, badly hungover, vaguely regretting that he had never got to see the Blue Jays play, nor found a cottage, nor a girl. It was the only time he had crossed the Atlantic sober.

"Have a good day!" smiled the pretty Air Canada blonde as he slouched out of the 747 into a thin London drizzle.

"Sure," he said.

Anthea Cohen

On Her Feet Again

May was glad when her mother fell downstairs. She hadn't pushed her, though God knows she'd thought of doing so hundreds of times.

Mother was ninety-nine and a half and completely gaga. Apt to get out of bed at night and wander, sometimes naked, bent double, grotesque. She didn't recognize May, and constantly talked about her husband, May's father, who'd been dead for forty years. She often hallucinated he was in her room, standing at the end of the bed.

May slept in a small uncomfortable room opposite her mother's with one ear cocked. But she was getting a bit deaf so that she didn't hear her mother get out of bed that night. What could you expect at May's age?

And it had been an unusually tiring day, which was probably why she was so deeply asleep when her mother progressed to the head of the stairs and fell.

Mother had pushed away the spoon when May was feeding her minced beef and it had splattered over the clean sheet. May's fault, she should have put a towel there. She knew well enough that the unwilling, toothless mouth would often refuse, clamp shut, sometimes spit out the food she shoveled in every day.

May had had to change the top sheet, turn it from top to bottom, so that the soiled part didn't show. She couldn't run to a clean sheet every time something like this happened—there was enough washing as it was. It was the doctor's day, but he hadn't turned up. Not that Mother knew. She didn't know anything, although May chatted away to her.

"The doctor's coming today, we must look our best, mustn't we?" She had tried to comb the frizzled, thistlelike hair as her mother's eyes strayed round the room vacantly and her hands, clawlike, smoothed the clean sheet and plucked nervously at the bedjacket—the blue, best bedjacket reserved for doctor's day.

May had waited in all day, not daring to go out to do the shopping that took her a long time these days. The hill to the town was steep. Mother, even in her good days, would never sell their house on the outskirts and buy something in the town. No, it was either the bus or walk. Few shops delivered these days.

May had come out of her bedroom, switched on the light, and looked, dispassionately, down the stairs. At the foot lay her mother, silent. May hoped and prayed she was dead, but as she stood looking her mother moved. One leg was bent under her. As the light was switched on, she started to moan feebly. Disappointment swept over May as she realized her mother was still alive. She wasn't callous—she'd just had enough. Enough of wet beds, of forcing food into that unwilling mouth, of talking to someone who took nothing in, of spending her life round this old, old woman. Did her mother want to live or die? May couldn't tell. It was because of the good care given her by her devoted daughter that she lived on. In six months' time she would be a hundred.

May had gone cautiously and rheumatically down the stairs to her mother. When she got there, she was tender enough. She had taken her coat from the hallstand, rolled it, and put it under her mother's head, then attempted to straighten the bent leg. But her mother gave a yelp of pain, a noise louder than she had made for months—years?

The old lady was thin and very light, like a dried-up stick. May, long ago—twenty years ago, when her mother had first been stricken and couldn't move—had been able to lift her onto the commode, but now she couldn't.

Having made her mother as comfortable as possible, May had shuffled over to the phone and dialed the doctor's number. At the other end of the line the phone buzzed persistently, then a sleepy voice said, "Yes, Doctor Black here, what is it?" He sounded cross, or maybe just sleepy. Who likes to be wakened at six o'clock in the morning on a dark winter's day?

"It's Mother, Doctor Black. She's fallen down the stairs, she's groaning. I think her leg—"

"Whose mother?"

"Oh, I'm sorry, Doctor, it's Miss Stevens speaking. It's Mother, Mrs. Stevens—she's fallen down the stairs."

"How did that happen, for God sake? I didn't know she could get out of bed."

"Oh, she can. She wanders a bit, particularly at night. I didn't hear her, I was sound asleep. I usually hear her, but I didn't this time."

"Okay. I'll be along." The phone went click and May put the receiver down and went back to her mother. She pulled the nightdress down over the skinny legs, then started upstairs, hanging onto the bannisters, to fetch a blanket. She came cautiously down with it, laid it over her mother, and tucked it round her legs.

"There you are, dear, now you'll be warmer. Does it hurt?" The old woman looked at her apathetically and turned away her head.

It was after seven when the doctor arrived. The dawn was lighting up the hall—a grey, dreary light. It was cold. During the hour May had filled a hot-water bottle and put it outside the blanket at her mother's side.

Doctor Black came in briskly, shaved and dressed, ready for the day's work.

"Well, well, what have we been doing to ourselves?" he said, kneeling down beside the old woman, feeling her pulse. He looked at the now straightened leg, noted that one foot was rolled outward.

"It looks like her femur, her thighbone." He looked up at May. "It looks as if she's broken it." He rose, went to the phone, and dialed.

"I'm dialing the ambulance. She must go to the hospital."

During the hour she had waited for the doctor, May had scrambled into her clothes. Now, wondering how long the ambulance would take, she went toward the hallstand for her coat, then remembered it was under her mother's head.

Doctor Black gave her mother an injection for the pain. "Don't give her anything to eat or drink," he said as he left, and because of this May took nothing to eat or drink herself. What was the point? She couldn't be bothered making tea for herself.

She sat again, waiting. Her mother had stopped moaning, the injection seeming to have taken effect. It was twenty past eight when the ambulance arrived.

"Well, Granny, what have you done then? Been larking about, eh? Fallen down the stairs. Been at the bottle, that it?" The big fat ambulance man turned to May and winked broadly. May did not wink back. She was not offended by his remarks, but during the hour or more she had been waiting, thoughts had been coming into her head—thoughts of freedom at last from this twenty-year-old chain. Her mother would never survive, surely. She was frail, terribly frail, in spite of May's endless, careful nursing. Never a bed sore, hardly a missed meal, never constipated.

May had got used to it. She hated it, but she did it. At the idea of freedom from the endless bedpans, her heart lightened. She felt no guilt. Why should she? She had done her best for so long.

By the time they arrived at the hospital it was nearly nine o'clock. May had given the particulars to the admitting nurse.

Mrs. Mary Stevens, 99½ years old
26, Esther Terrace, Merchester
Doctor: Andrew Black

The nurse had replied kindly, "You can come in and be with her now."

May didn't say, "I don't want to come in, I never want to see her again," but followed the nurse meekly into the Casualty area and went into the corner behind the curtains where Mum was lying on a couch, her frizzy white head on the pillow, her face white, with a yellowy tinge. A red blanket was drawn up to her chin, covering her from head to foot. May turned her head away and said to the nurse standing beside her mother, "She doesn't speak much. She doesn't know what goes on."

As if to prove her words, the old woman suddenly raised her head on her wizened, knotty neck and said loudly, "Where's Dad, where's your dad?" She looked at May, but May didn't bother to look back. She knew the look—confused, the rheumy eyes going to and fro, looking for Dad.

"She wanders in her mind," May said to the nurse.

The nurse nodded. She was all of twenty, bright and pretty. May noticed a wedding ring on her left hand.

They waited for what seemed to be an interminable time. The nurse gave May a cup of tea with sugar in it. May didn't take sugar, but she drank it. She had heard sugar was good for shock. But they wouldn't know she wasn't shocked—only hopeful.

Suddenly the curtains were pulled back and a white-coated doctor came in, followed by another, slightly older. May half rose as if to go, but they waved her back to her seat, threw back the red blanket, and examined the sticklike leg.

"Had some morphia, has she?"

During the examination May's thoughts were still anticipating freedom. She might live to be a hundred, too. She might make a better job of it—might not be helpless like her mother. She might be sprightly. She was pretty sprightly now, at seventy-six. Breathless when she went upstairs, but that was to be expected the number of times she had to do it. Now she could have lunch in a café every day. She could sleep unworried, even take a sleeping pill if she wanted to—one of Mother's. She would make herself very comfortable, sell the house, get a tiny flat . . .

The doctor was speaking. She hastily gave him her attention. "Well, well. Ninety-nine and a half, eh? That's one of our oldest." He pulled the stethoscope plugs from his ears and looked at the nurse, smiling cheerfully. "Heart sounds aren't too bad. We'll be able to pin that hip. Has she eaten this morning?"

May shook her head.

"Good." He turned to the younger doctor. "If we can get the theater before the afternoon list begins, we could push it in, couldn't we?"

The younger doctor nodded. "I'll ring the theater, see what the list's like." He left the cubicle.

The older doctor turned to May. "We'll soon have her back to you as good as new. We pinned an old lady of a hundred and she did marvelously, didn't she, nurse?"

The nurse had looked blank, obviously not remembering.

"Yes, as good as new. Don't you worry, she'll be back with you in a couple of months. What relation are you?"

"I'm her daughter," May said.

The doctor nodded, looked at the nurse, then back again at May. "Well, you'll have some help. She'll have to have physiotherapy and the District Nurse will help you. They'll call for her in the ambulance a couple of times a week, and get her on her feet again."

"She's been bedridden for nearly twenty years, Doctor," May said mildly, but the doctor went on,

"On her feet again, that's right."

He raised a hand to May and left the cubicle, saying to the nurse as he did so, "Get her up to the ward after she's been X-rayed. I'll sign the forms on my way out."

May's face suddenly crumpled, and her old eyes filled with tears and spilled over onto her cheeks. The nurse came over to her, completely misunderstanding, and put her arms round May's shoulders. "Don't worry, she'll be all right. They do marvelously now, they really do. You'll have her home, you'll see—like the doctor said, good as new. How are you going to get home?"

"On the bus," May said.

"You can wait and go up to the ward with her, see her into bed." May shook her head . . .

Every day May went to a café for lunch. She did no housework. Her mother's bed remained exactly as it had been, rather smelly and unmade. For over six weeks, May enjoyed every day. She went to the pictures and went to Bingo (though she didn't enjoy that much because she couldn't keep up, she didn't understand it very well). She went on short walks to get out of the house and breathe the cold air. When she locked the door at night and went puffing up the stairs, she knew she'd go to sleep quite happily. It lasted nearly two months. Then the day came when the phone rang.

"Is that Miss Stevens? It's the hospital. Mrs. Stevens can come home. We can send her home by ambulance this afternoon."

"This afternoon! That's rather quick, isn't it?" May had said, her voice shaking, thinking of the bed upstairs, the preparations.

"Yes, well, I'm afraid we've had a couple of emergencies, and we need the bed." The voice was brusque, businesslike. May put the phone down and looked at the clock. Nine-thirty. She hadn't asked exactly what time her mother would be home. Afternoon, they had said. Still, it didn't matter.

She crossed the hall and locked the front door, went into the kitchen and closed the back door. She took down an old raincoat that hung there, threw it across the bottom of the door, and pushed it close with her foot. She went into the sitting room and fetched a cushion, then returned to the kitchen and closed the door into the hall. She checked that the window was tight shut, still clutching the cushion to her.

Then she opened the oven, put the cushion on the lower edge, and creakingly got down on the floor. It wasn't comfortable, but it would do. She sat there thinking for a full ten minutes, then put her hand up and turned the oven full on. She heard, even through her deafness, the hissing of the gas. She lay her head on the cushion and straightened out her body. The floor was hard, but the cushion was soft. She turned her head on one side and lay there, waiting.

But the North Sea Gas failed her. After lying there for half an hour, she got up, turned off the gas, and went up the stairs to strip and make up her mother's bed.

"Q"

Don Gilbert

The Canoe

A series of unusual events took place in our neighborhood the spring and summer I was twelve.

My cousin Joel came to stay with us for a time. Jenny Price's body was found drowned in The Pond. And her next youngest sister came forward with the news that Jenny had been over three months pregnant. No one was surprised about that and, of course, everyone thought she had committed suicide. Two weeks after that, my cousin Joel had his eighteenth birthday and he went back to Canada to join his country's armed forces. He left me his hunting clasp knife and our birchbark canoe. I never saw him again because he was killed in France in June 1917. The Canadian government sent his family a medal for his bravery.

I loved my cousin Joel.

Mom's and Dad's names are Elizabeth and Henry Grey, but everyone calls them Liz and Hank. Dad claims he's the only stationary Grey in existence, the rest of the family being scattered all over the United States and Canada.

My name is Maurice. It's a name I always disliked, but now it looks pretty good on my office door. *Maurice M. Grey—Attorney at Law.* Mom happened to be reading a romantic novel about the time I was born and the hero's name was Maurice Mannerly.

Maurice Mannerly Grey. That's a mouthful, but Dad always said, "What the heck, a rose by any name would smell mighty fine!" Later Dad started calling me Ticky. Then even Mom did, and the nickname stuck.

"Ticky," Dad said, "you stick as close as a—"

We lived on a farm in central Wisconsin and that was the only world I knew until I was out of high school and into college.

It was in March that my folks had a letter from Canada, from Dad's older brother Timothy. I had never seen Uncle Tim because he lived way up in Manitoba. Dad said he'd wandered up there, married a part Indian girl, and had a raft of kids—well, at least four. Now it seemed the oldest boy, Joel, seventeen, was in a peck of trouble. There had been a wedding dance, a real wingding according to Uncle Tim, with lots of whiskey, food, and dancing. Uncle Tim didn't believe Joel had been drinking, because whiskey made the kid sick, but the dance ended in a free-for-all. Cornered, Joel had got out his hunting clasp knife and cut up one of the braves. We gathered that incidences of this nature were not unusual, but now there was a vendetta out on Joel. The Indians considered Joel more white than red, therefore not really of their people. Joel was already on his way to Wisconsin because Uncle Tim feared for his safety. He might arrive as quickly as the letter.

"Good heavens," Mom said, "we can't take in a savage like that!"

"Liz," Dad said, "the boy's on his way and he's my brother's son! Likely he's a forlorn young one."

"Forlorn, my foot," Mom said. "He's part Indian and he used a knife in a brawl—likely over some girl!"

"Likely so," Dad said.

It was late the next afternoon—a March day of scudding clouds, sunshine, and sleet flurries—that my cousin Joel arrived. I was home from school and Dad and I were down at the barn doing early chores when old Shep started barking. There was a slim stranger in a red-and-black-plaid mackinaw coming up our rutted drive. Shep stood back, hackles bristling, nose testing the air, then suddenly he dashed forward in an extravagance of welcome, just as he did with me.

"Well, I'll be darned," Dad said, "a man has to smell just right to get that kind of a welcome from ol' Shep. Ticky, you go and bring your cousin to me."

I did, feeling this was a very grown-up thing to do.

"I'll bet you're Joel," I said, holding out my hand.

"Yep," the stranger said, looking me square in the eye, "and you're Ticky."

Our hands met in an adult manner and I still remember the odd thought that flashed in my mind. *He's beautiful.* And he was, in a strong, woodsy way. Even in heavy winter clothing, he moved lithe as a cat. His skin was smooth and dark and his features were so sharply defined they seemed almost fleshless. And his eyes were the deepest blue I had ever seen.

He was shouldering a heavy blanket-roll and I said, "Let me take that. Did you have to walk all the way from town?"

"It's okay," he said, not giving it over, "I'm used to walking with a load of traps."

He followed me to where Dad was waiting. "How was your trip?" Dad asked as if such a visit were a common thing.

"Okay," Joel said. "I've never ridden a train that far before."

"Well, you got here safe and that's what counts. Come along to the house and meet your Aunt Liz. I never did get to see any of Tim's young ones before now. Families sure drift apart." We went toward the house and now Joel let me carry his pack. I didn't notice the weight much because I was worried about how Mom would receive our guest.

I should have known better. Joel was a stranger, but he was young and already Mom had placed him in a frame of danger. Besides, she was still close enough to a pioneer woman to meet most situations head-on. She wasn't the kind to kiss every relative who came down the road, but she gave Joel a motherly hug.

When we finished eating supper, Dad pushed his chair back from the table in a way that I knew meant he intended to say something important. It had been a pleasant meal, topped off with one of Mom's special lemon pies, and now the lamplight and the rough wind outside bound us together. I felt very happy.

"Joel," Dad said, "I'm glad to give you a home with us as long as you need it and I'll treat you like a son, just as I'd expect your pa to treat Ticky if the need arose. In return I expect you to pitch in exactly as if this was your own home. I need an extra hand part-time, and I usually hire some neighbor lad, but you can fill that place as long as you're here. I pay a dollar a day and keep. Ticky and you can share his room off the kitchen. It's warm in the winter and cool in the summer. We'll put another single bed in there so you fellows can sleep private. I can tell by Ticky's face he's all for it, how about you?"

Joel looked at me and grinned. "Sounds good to me. There were three of us boys sleeping in one bunk at home!"

And Joel really meant what he said. He seemed to adjust easily. But I learned you never could tell exactly what Joel was thinking by how he reacted on the surface. He was always quiet on the outside no matter how unrestful his mind was. Mom said that was the Indian in him, but that wasn't exactly true. Some people are naturally reserved no matter what their breeding and that was the way Joel was. I knew he appreciated what the folks were doing for him without expressing it in extravagant words. He was neither a true Indian nor a true white man. In a way, his mother's people had turned

against him while his father's gave him shelter (although in ret-
rospect I realize he must have felt there were strings attached). He
was caught between two sets of rules. So, when it was necessary, he
made his own rules. Which I have found, in my law practice, people
do all the time.

The morning after he arrived, a Saturday, Dad, Joel, and I went
down to the wood lot, a heavy growth of poplar, birch, oak, and
maple we kept thinned for firewood. We soon found out that Joel
was handy with an ax and could hold up his end of a crosscut saw
with Dad.

I heard Dad tell Mom, "That boy is muscled like a man. He's had
to work right along with his daddy."

Mom hesitated, then said, "I'm glad to hear that. I must say he's
clean as a cat. I looked through his belongings this morning and
everything is folded just so. And no sign of a knife."

"Liz," Dad said, and I could imagine him shaking his head, "you're
the limit. Don't you know a desperado always carries his weapon on
his person?"

After dinner Dad asked, "You boys want to go to town with Liz
and me or roam the farm?"

I was torn between two desires: wanting to show Joel off in town
and wanting to show him all my secret places on the farm.

"I think I'd like to look the farm over," Joel said, "if Ticky would
just as soon."

I took him down to The Pond first because I liked it best. It wasn't
a big pond, a little over a hundred yards across at the widest and
not more than ten feet deep in the middle. Dad said the beavers had
dammed the creek before the first settlers came and there had still
been plenty of poplar for food. Now the trees were mostly gone except
for scattered stands, and the land was broken into farms. The beaver
had vanished with the trees but their dam had become part of the
terrain, The Pond a jewel of water in the rolling hills. It was really
the center of the neighborhood. We skated and cut ice on it in the
winter, swam in it in the summer, and picnicked on its shores.

I wanted Joel to like The Pond, although in my heart I knew it
wasn't much compared to thousands of lakes in the north country.

"Is there fish in there?" Joel asked skeptically as we stood on the
still-ice-locked edge.

"Bullheads and perch," I told him, wanting to say "musky and bass" but not being that much of a liar.

"We have big lakes and big fish in Manitoba."

"Well, we have them in Wisconsin, too. But this is *our* pond."

"I bet it's nice when it's thawed out," he said quickly. "I bet you and your friends have a lot of fun here."

"Yeah, we do." I guess I sulked. "I know it isn't very big."

"It's just fine, Ticky. Doesn't it get green in the summer?" he asked with interest.

"Along in August," I admitted. "Then we go to a sandy place in the creek to cool off."

"The water shouldn't get too bad out in the middle, away from the cattails and lily pads. I'll tell you what, Ticky. If Uncle Henry has some metal barrels and a few boards, we can make us a float. We'll anchor it out where the water is cleanest."

"We'd still have to swim through the scum to get to the float."

"We could go in where the creek current keeps the water fresh, and from there to the float. You can swim, can't you?"

"Of course!" Dad said I was good as a mud puppy in the water.

Joel beamed suddenly. "You know, I saw a couple of big ol' paper down where we were cutting wood this morning. If Uncle Henry says it's okay, we can cut those down, skin 'em, and make ourselves a birchbark canoe! My mother's father, Grandfather Walks on Water, let me help him make one before he died. He told me that every man who had a drop of Indian blood should make at least one birchbark canoe in his life. Maybe Uncle Henry will have some boards to make the ribs and frame of. Ash is the best. We can cut the boards into narrow strips, then soak and shape them in water. Then we sew the birchbark on the frame with tamarack root fibers and cement the seams with boiled pitch. We'll balance the canoe just so. It may not turn out to be a thing of beauty, although it's hardly possible to make a canoe that is not beautiful. We will then whittle out a paddle for each of us—"

Mom was dubious. "It seems to me you'll be spending most of your time in this foolishness."

But Dad backed us up. "I'll see to that end of it, Liz. It's funny, but when I was a kid I always wanted to make a bark canoe. I just never had anyone to show me how."

"You should have gone to Canada with your brother," Mom said.

And so we began our work on the canoe with every free hour we

could find. We set up shop in the feed room in the barn. It was warm
in there and out of the way. In May, Dad helped us haul the oil
drums and old lumber for the float to The Pond. By that time, I had
to tell my friends at school about the canoe and the float or burst.
The Sunday after I spilled the beans, most of the boys in the neighborhood congregated at The Pond. The big boys stripped down, towed
the float out, and anchored it. There was a lot of shouting and
horseplay but by the time the float was secured, the sun was going
down and we were all glad to get our clothes back on.

As we were, someone saw a couple of girls coming down through
the hill woods. We all knew right off who it was likely to be. Most
girls, under their mothers' guidance, didn't come around where there
was a bunch of boys unless it was a picnic or a ballgame. Jenny
Price and her sister had no such motherly stricture.

Jenny was nearly eighteen and she had finally quit school because
she never got out of the sixth grade. She was really quite pretty in
a big, dusty sort of way. Where other girls were sort of starched, she
never even looked ironed. She had a pretty honey-tan summer and
winter and her blonde hair was like a sheaf of ripe oats. She used
a lot of perfume that she bought at the dime store in town.

I guess we all felt Jenny and her sister had been watching us boys
put out the float. They stopped at the wood's edge and Jenny hollered,
"If you ain't decent, put your pants on! We're comin' down there!"

Everyone except Joel sniggered at that, but I guess we all felt
kind of foolish. Jenny came flouncing across the field, her younger
sister in tow. Jenny's sister wasn't too bright and never talked much,
which was a good thing because Jenny made up for it. I looked at
Joel to see how he was taking Jenny. He didn't seem embarrassed
that the two girls had seen him naked.

Indifference was one thing Jenny couldn't stand. She walked up
to Joel and said, "I hear you and Ticky are building a canoe. You
going to take me for a ride when it's done?"

"I might," Joel said. "But a canoe isn't a rowboat. You have to
know how to act in a canoe. A canoe can tip over easy."

"Well, if it's that kind of a thing," Jenny said, "it ain't much good!"

Joel shrugged his shoulders, but before Jenny could say anything
more one of the bigger boys blurted, "Hey, Jenny, I heard your pa
lost his hired man. How come?"

Jenny tossed her head. "Heck, how would I know? He just took
off one night. Didn't even ask for his wages. Ma says there are things
missin' and she may call the sheriff."

"Heard in town someone saw him catch a westbound freight."

"Good riddance," Jenny said, and, her sister tagging, she started back toward the woods as if she was weary of rude boys.

"Maybe Joel will teach you to paddle his canoe," someone shouted, not wanting to let the moment go.

"Thanks," Jenny yelled back sarcastically. "Likely the old canoe won't float. And I can't swim!"

We all laughed at that because the idea of a girl swimming was funny. When there was a picnic at The Pond, they just waded around the edges.

After that it seemed as if every time Joel and I went to The Pond Jenny would soon appear. She must have had her sister scouting us most of the time.

"I wish she'd stay home," I told Joel.

"Maybe she's lonely," Joel said.

I said a dirty word under my breath. By that time I was sure Jenny had a crush on Joel and I wondered what he'd do if she kept on chasing him.

One evening, with Dad and Mom trailing us, Joel and I carried our canoe to The Pond and launched it. It worked fine and Mom said, "I really don't know why, but I'm proud of you boys! That canoe is a real pretty thing!" However, though Dad was game, she refused to ride in it.

After a time, they left us alone at The Pond. Then, just before deep dark, Joel said, "A lot of people never learn how to handle a canoe, but you catch on fast. In secret I will call you my Brother of the Birch."

If King Arthur had touched my shoulder with his sword, I couldn't have felt more glorified.

It must have been at least two weeks after that evening that I awoke from a deep sleep to lie tense and listening. The night was silent, drugged, somehow ominous. Outside, the moon was shining, filling the room with a filtered radiance. Then I knew what had awakened me. Joel was gone. I couldn't hear his breathing.

Terror seized me. I was suddenly afraid that Joel, like the Prices' hired man, had vanished in the night. The feeling ebbed away as I told myself Joel had just stepped outside and in a moment I was asleep again. I didn't mention this to Joel the next day because he'd think me silly. But a few nights later it happened again and this time I couldn't go back to sleep.

With the first paling of dawn, Joel slipped into the room.

I whispered, "Joel—"

He crouched beside my bed. "I was down at The Pond with Jenny. I'm teaching her how to use the canoe. She's very persistent." After a silence he said, "That isn't quite true, it's only an excuse. We want each other. And after we've used each other, she goes home and I swim down to the creek and scrub my body with sand. Her perfume sticks to my skin."

"Why do you go, then?"

"That is a question you'll be able to answer soon enough."

"I'm not so dumb! I'm twelve! How did it start with you and Jenny?"

He chuckled as he patted my face. "Wise one, how does something like that start? She sent for me to meet her at The Pond. She wanted to go out in the canoe. She wanted to learn to paddle it. I felt sorry for her at first. Then things got complicated. But she did learn quick about the canoe."

"As quick as me?"

He rumpled my hair. "Never, Brother of the Birch."

"What then?"

"We went out to the float—and there is where it happened for the first time. And there is where we meet now. I swim out from our end of The Pond and she comes from her end with the canoe. Later I take her back to the creek and hide the canoe. She wants it that way."

"Joel, you'd better not let Mom and Dad find out about this."

"Do you think I'm crazy?"

"Well—does she make you happy?"

He groaned. "I never knew about being happy until I came down here. Jenny has nothing to do with it. I guess my folks are happy, but not like your folks—"

Knowing about Joel and Jenny gave me a worry for the first time in my life. Mom worried me the most. Dad was easy-going but Mom had pretty set ideas.

A few nights later, Joel was beside my bed again.

"Ticky, Jenny wants us to run away and get married. We don't love each other—we just like what we do together—but she's got this idea in her head. An Indian girl would never ask a man to marry her, but Jenny! She told me she slept with the hired man who ran away in the night. If she really wants to marry, why didn't she marry him?"

Remembering all the farm animals I helped care for, I said, "Maybe Jenny's going to have his baby."

Joel jerked backward as if I had hit him in the face. "I'm a double damned fool! The hired man ran away when she told him, so now she wants me to play the goat. —Well, I won't run away, but what she wants will never happen."

"We better go to Mom and Dad," I said.

"We?" he repeated. "Ticky, you're a true friend. But I won't drag your folks into this mess. They've been too good to me. Jenny can't make me marry her, because the baby will come too soon to be mine, but if I run back to Canada it will look like I was a coward and people would blame Uncle Henry and Aunt Liz for sheltering me. I'll meet Jenny one more time and make her see she's met her match."

That day I saw Jenny's sister slip across the field to where Joel was working.

She was there only a moment before Joel walked away.

"What did she want?" I asked him later.

"Jenny wants me to come to the float tonight—one last time."

"Are you going?"

"I told her sister no. I told her Jenny was not to use the canoe again."

I'll never forget that night. After chores, Joel told me he was going for a walk. I called Shep and we went down back of the barn to chase young rabbits along the cornfield. I didn't want the folks to ask me any questions about Joel's whereabouts. When I went to bed, Joel was ahead of me, already asleep. Troubled as I was, sleep came swiftly to me, too.

But I awoke in the dead of night, struggling in the twisted sheets, shivering and sweating at the same time, a terrible dream sound echoing in my ears.

"What's the trouble?" Joel said from his bed.

"I thought I heard someone calling—"

"You were dreaming."

"No, it woke me!"

It came again—eerie, ululating, suddenly choked off.

"That?" Joel asked. "Ticky, you know there's a pair of loons nesting in the cattails on the far side of The Pond. That's just them talking to each other in the night."

"But this sounds different."

"Brother of the Birch, go back to sleep."

They found Jenny's body just below where the creek entered The Pond. It was enmeshed in water-lily pads. The canoe had drifted away on the lazy current to the farther end of The Pond, where Joel and I found it and lifted it ashore, the sodden canvas still folded in the bottom where Jenny had knelt on it to paddle. We found the paddle caught on a sandbar down the creek.

The sheriff asked us about the canoe, so we told him we always kept it on our land and no one else was supposed to touch it. Of course, everyone knew how headstrong Jenny had been and her sister finally admitted that Joel had ordered her to leave the canoe alone unless someone else was with her. It was then she told that Jenny had been pregnant and it came out that the departed hired man had been sleeping with Jenny.

The week later was Joel's eighteenth birthday and on that day he told us he had decided to go back to Canada and enlist in the Army. By that time the United States was on the brink of war with Germany, too, so it seemed the right and patriotic thing to do.

The day he left, we walked down to The Pond together.

The canoe was still there, hidden in the bushes. "Brother of the Birch," Joel said, "it was good being with you for even a little time. When I get back from France, I will come here even before I go home."

I dared not speak because of the lump in my throat.

"I want you to have my hunting knife," he said.

I took the knife, clutching it tight in my hand as we walked back to the house where Dad and Mom were waiting for us in the Model T.

The day after we took Joel to the train, I went back to where the canoe was hidden. Lifting the folded canvas from between its ribs, I opened the hunting knife Joel had given me and slipped the blade into an exposed slash in the birchbark. It slid easily along the wound, so I knew it had been there before. The proof made no difference to me. I put the knife back in my pocket and sewed the rent shut with tamarack fibers just as Joel had taught me. Then I covered the seam with pitch, rubbed it with sand, and left it to dry.

In the night I wakened to a voice whispering: "Brother of the Birch—"

I still have the birchbark canoe in my garage loft. My wife says it's taking up room we could put to better use and she's right, but I'm keeping the canoe for our son. When he's old enough, we'll use it as a model and make one of our own.

Edward Wellen

Born Victims

Detective Third Grade Andrew Flint took the topmost complaint card from the waiting stack of fresh forms and made ready to fill in the blanks.

Complaints. He had his own complaints, but could do nothing about them. An already overwhelming case load, and here came one more. A sweltering day, the air-conditioning still on the blink, yet because the precinct commander had a thing about his people's appearance—anyone who met the public had to look buttoned-down neat—no shirtsleeves.

He looked at the young woman in the chair beside his desk and lost some of his resentment. Someone that pretty shouldn't look that worried. The chair she sat in, the desk she rested her hand on, the air about her, all vibrated to her nervousness. But he had to remain the cool professional.

Complainant. "Your name?"

"Analisa Sanders. One 'n' in Analisa. My problem is—"

Marital status. "Miss or Mrs.?" Hardly any insisted on Ms.

"Miss. I—"

Address. "Where do you live?"

"Four twenty-three Montvale Avenue. Apartment 5 C. What I—"

Crime. "All right, Miss Sanders, what's the complaint?"

"A man is following me around and threatening me."

He eyed her sharply. She looked much too young and pretty and undried-up to be one of those wackos. "Do you know the man? Can you describe him?"

She gave a small ironic laugh. "I know the man. I can see him with my eyes closed."

"Do you know his name?"

"Sam Locke."

"Description?"

She ran a vaguely measuring gaze over Flint. "He's a bit taller and heavier than you, with dirty-blond hair and hazel eyes. He has a pleasant face that can turn mean in an instant." Though it was hot, she shivered.

Flint put down "6'1″, 190 lbs., medium-blond hair, brown eyes."

Distinguishing characteristics. "Any scars? A limp? Anything like that?"

She shook her head. "Nothing to make him stand out in a crowd." But her haunted eyes said they could always pick him out.

Flint nodded. "How long has he been following you?"

It was as though his question had pricked a balloon. She let out air and sagged. "One year."

He stared. "And you're only now reporting it?"

She shook her head wearily and managed a tired smile. "I reported it back home a year ago."

Flint tried not to show his relief. He had it figured now, saw how to get out of this one. If in one full year they had been unable to resolve the case back home—wherever back home was—then the job was clearly one for Detective Cann: the wastebasket. This was simply a lovers' quarrel and she and Locke would have to work it out themselves. Still, he had to hear her out.

"How did it start?"

She looked back through him. "This was up in Ridgeway, where we both come from. I met Sam at a party. We got to talking and he seemed nice so I dated him a few times. But he soon showed his other side—his mean, jealous, egotistical nature, his explosive temper."

Miss Sanders kept watching Flint to see how he reacted to what she said. He kept nodding but maintained a noncommittal expression.

"Once he knocked out a waiter who spilled a drink on him. Another time he slugged a man he said was staring at me. These things frightened me and I decided to have nothing more to do with him. But it proved impossible to let him down gently. He seemed to think the few times I went out with him made him my steady.

"I told him I wasn't ready to go steady with anyone just yet, but he said I was his and he wasn't about to share me with anyone else. He hung around and scared off any other men that showed interest. That's when I went to the Ridgeway police. But they said Sam hadn't actually done anything they could book him for and they suggested I see the district attorney about a restraining order.

"I went to the district attorney, but he said I hadn't told him anything he could get a restraining order on and he suggested I see the police."

She looked at Flint, but he was busy doodling on a sheet of scrap paper.

"I couldn't take it any more. I packed up one night and left town without telling anyone. I didn't know myself where I was going. I just took the first bus out. It brought me here." She smiled. "I really thought I lost him." Then the smile faded and she spoke dully. "But somehow he tracked me down and followed me here. I had a few good months here before he showed up. I not only found a good job but got to know and like a man at the office, George—a kind, compassionate widower who says he loves me. He asked me to go out with him, and I agreed."

Her eyes pooled. "But that very day, I spotted him—Sam. And I had to tell George I was sorry but I wasn't in love with him and it wouldn't be fair to lead him on. I couldn't bring myself to tell him the real reason."

Flint looked up. "The real reason being that you believe Sam would threaten this George?"

She leaned forward. "Not just threaten, kill. He'd kill another man rather than let him have me."

Flint shifted uncomfortably. "Look, Miss Sanders, this is all conjecture. We can't proceed against Sam until he actually does something."

She herself seemed ready to explode. "All I want is to live a normal life! Is that too much to ask?"

Flint thought it was, but didn't say so. Normal life, as he saw it, was full of harassment and fear. "Why not take a positive attitude? Confront Sam. Reason with him."

"That's what all you law-enforcement people seem to think: that it's always the victim's fault, that in some perverse way victims like myself goad the victimizers on. Well, I never led Sam on. I told him when I tried to break up with him that time wouldn't change my mind. I've kept away from him, but he won't keep away from me. He has this sick idea that because he loves me—whether or not I love him back—he owns me. That if he can't have me, nobody will. Try and reason with that."

Flint sat mute.

She sighed. "I see it's no use. I could plead myself hoarse and you'll say the same thing: there's nothing you can do."

"That's right. Because it's the truth. You don't know how sorry I am, but that's the way it is." He put his hand on top of the pile of file folders on his desk. "Lady, look at my case load. We don't have enough personnel. We can't spare the people to guard you and this man around the clock against somebody who may or may not be a nut."

She eyed the folders. "I get the message. If Sam kills George, *then* you can take action against Sam."

Flint flushed. He drew a long sigh.

She spoke more to herself than to him. "I slipped out the back way to come here. Sam will be waiting in front of my office building, watching for me to leave for lunch so he can follow and see who I have lunch with." She stood and gathered herself to go.

Flint watched her. He had told her the truth, but he felt uneasy. And in some measure, as part of a society that lets bad things happen, guilty. But what could he do? This Analisa Sanders had to live out her fate. Some people were born victims. He stood as they said goodbye and watched her go, no starch in her back, no lift in her shoulders, no snap in her walk.

Then, as she reached the doorway, she straightened and though he could no longer see her face he felt it had lost its beaten look. He stared after her for a wondering moment, then picked up the complaint card, tore it in four, and fed it to Detective Cann. He looked at the clock and a wry smile surfaced. It was about time to eat.

He nearly choked on a sparerib. Somehow Analisa Sanders had found out where he ate lunch and was sashaying straight to where he sat alone at a table for two.

Her eyes seemed unnaturally bright, fueled by some fever of excitement. She kissed him on the cheek before taking the seat opposite his and picking up the menu.

"Hey, what—"

"I'm glad you went ahead without me. I'm sorry to be late, but you must be getting used to it by now," she chattered gaily as her eyes roved the menu.

She made up her mind, looked around, and a waiter appeared. She smiled up at him. "A tunafish sandwich and a cup of coffee, please."

The waiter nodded and left.

Flint was in a daze. What the hell was this? *Was* she wacko, after all? The best thing for him to do was hurry through his meal and get out of here.

He tried to do just that, but she kept putting her hand on his arm and chattering as though the two of them were intimate friends. He wanted to tell her to shut up and leave him alone, but he was too polite and finally he saw it wasn't going to go on forever. She glanced at her wristwatch, took a last bite of her sandwich and a quick sip of coffee, wiped her mouth with her napkin, and said with a laugh that she had better get back to the office before they realized they didn't really need her.

And at least she wasn't going to stick him with her lunch. She placed a five-dollar bill under her plate, then she was on her feet, her hand on his shoulder as she leaned toward him and whispered in his ear. "I know one thing: the police go all out to catch a cop killer."

"What are you talking about?"

She gave him a dazzling smile. "You don't know how sorry I am, but it's my only chance." Her hand pressed on his shoulder as she bent to kiss him soundly.

As he sat in frozen disbelief, she slipped gracefully between the tables and left the restaurant. Outside, through the window, she stopped briefly and blew him a kiss.

With a thrill of fear, he grew aware of a nondescript man who had been watching her from the sidewalk register his presence, take a long look after her as she disappeared from sight, and then reach for the door and enter the restaurant.

Melville Davisson Post and John F. Suter

The Tree in the Forest

The case for the plaintiff was apparently unshakeable, and although the defendants were of the highest integrity they seemed destined to lose.

The defendants' lawyer, Henry Preston, was examining the plaintiff's doctor. Preston was a thin, sober man, and his questioning matched his appearance.

"Doctor Parker, you have testified that Mr. Dickerman has lost fifty percent of his hearing. Are you certain of that?"

The doctor smoothed his grey moustache. His reply was as calm as the surface of a millpond in summer. "I am very certain. In fact, his hearing might even be less than fifty percent of what it should be. He has lost hearing completely in one ear. What the deterioration of age has done to the other ear, I could not say."

At the prospect of dealing with an opponent who was even more handicapped than was claimed, Preston seemed to withdraw. He failed to follow the opening the doctor had made. He asked no question which would relate the effect of age on the plaintiff's bad ear. "The alleged hearing loss is in the left ear, I believe you testified," he said instead.

The doctor smiled. He would not be drawn into a contradiction. "It was the right ear."

In the rear of the courtroom, one of the spectators shook his head. He appreciated Preston's dilemma. Doctor Parker was well known, not only in the community, but in the county. His integrity was unquestionable. Parker could not attack it.

The spectator was another lawyer, a huge man. He was nearly sixty, but there was no grey in his thick, black hair. That glossy hair was as carefully brushed as his immaculate clothing was carefully arranged. His thick features gave some key to his age. They were greyish-white, with no tone to the skin. The pores of his nose were enlarged. His thick lips loosely held an unlit cigar.

The lawyer, Preston, had begun to ask the doctor to describe again the tests he had made to determine the plaintiff's loss of hearing.

He was barely into it when his critic's attention was distracted by the person who sat down beside him.

"Colonel Armant?"

The big lawyer looked around. His narrowed eyes widened.

The principal defendant was seated on his right, looking at him with large brown eyes. Her dark hair was artfully done, but the air of confidence her proud face usually wore was replaced by worry and distress.

"Yes?" the lawyer answered.

"It's not going well, is it?"

Colonel Armant made no immediate reply. He seemed to be listening to the questioning. Finally he said, "No, it is not goin' well."

"Do I have a chance?" She motioned toward the front of the room. "Or is it Preston?"

The big lawyer blinked. "There's always a chance. But I do have to agree, a lot of your trouble is Preston."

The conversation was producing a distraction, and the judge looked in their direction. Before any remark was made from the bench, Colonel Armant held up a big hand.

"Let's discuss this in the hall," he whispered, gently urging the girl to her feet.

Outside, in the marble corridor, the inquisition in the courtroom was shut out. A measure of the girl's confidence seemed to have returned.

"Do you know me, Colonel Armant?" she asked.

The old lawyer grinned faintly. "We don't travel in the same circles, but I know who you are. You're Florence Ross. You're tryin' to run the Vandalia Traction Company while your father's sick."

The girl inclined her head. "I've noticed you in court. Are you familiar with this case?"

"I'll give you what I've heard," Colonel Armant replied. "Your father is ill—seriously ill. He's at Terra Alta, with consumption, they tell me. It's takin' nearly every penny his streetcar company makes to pay his medical bills and to give you a bare livin'.

"Now, at the end of last winter, your streetcar to Mill Creek was out near city limits when a wagonload of flour from McAllister's Mill broke down across the tracks. It was an icy day. The motorman tried to stop the car, but he misjudged conditions. The streetcar hit the wagon—hard."

The lawyer shifted his cigar and paused. The girl did not contradict him.

"Nobody was on the car but one passenger," Colonel Armant went on. "That was this Raymond Dickerman. At first it seemed that nobody was hurt. Not the teamster, not the motorman, not the conductor, not Dickerman—until Dickerman found out that he wasn't hearin' sounds with both ears. He could only hear with his left one. When he realized that, Dickerman brought suit against your company. What he wants would force you into bankruptcy. *Then* what would keep your father alive?"

The girl's classic mouth set in a bitter line. "I had been hoping that the normalcy which President Harding has been promising would mean an improvement in business. Then this creature, this leech, Dickerman had to appear!"

"You tried to settle with him. And he wouldn't."

The girl looked at him closely.

"You know him, then?"

"I know him. Not to speak to, but I know him. All about him."

The girl gestured toward the courtroom. "You don't think Preston can beat him, do you? Dickerman and his lawyer?"

The big man shook his head. "Preston's a company lawyer. Maybe even a textbook lawyer. He won't even make Doc Parker look human. Doc might admit that Dickerman's age could have caused some loss of hearin'. Besides, how do we know he's qualified to test a man's ears? Preston ought to cast some doubt, but he respects Doc too much."

He removed his cigar for a moment.

"Dickerman already has money, but he's just a guttersnipe. To beat a guttersnipe, it helps to know how he thinks. That's not in Preston's textbooks."

The girl gripped his arm. "Colonel Armant, would you take over this case for us?"

The big man looked at her steadily. "Well, you can't fire Preston."

"There must be some way to have him step aside."

"He's a proud man, Miss Ross. You might need him. There are some things he's good at."

"It doesn't matter. For my father's sake, will you do it?"

Colonel Armant looked at the courtroom door.

"I will. There's a way. However, I couldn't take a part in the examination of Doc Parker. The judge wouldn't allow it. For the kind of case they have, all they need do is put Dickerman himself on the stand. The circumstances have been established. All that's left to be done is to show Dickerman's side, then your side. Do you have anything strong enough to offset a man who can hear only half what he used to?"

"If we have, Preston has not mentioned it."

Colonel Armant looked down at her. "Then it would have to depend on cross-examination of Dickerman."

"Would that be enough for you?"

"I don't know. It would be a chance."

"I'm willing to take it. Are you?"

The old lawyer drew out his watch and consulted it.

"Chance gave Dickerman the hold he's trying to use on you. Maybe chance will break it." He snapped the watchcase closed. "Miss Ross, you must let Preston finish with Doc Parker. Then have him get permission to consult with you. If he will have me, get him to request my appearance as co-counsel. Since Dickerman has not yet begun testimony, I will be permitted to cross-examine when he does.

"It's now close to lunchtime. By the time the judge agrees to my entrance into the case, he will want to recess. I'll join Preston when court reconvenes."

Hope now made the girl's face glow. She started for the courtroom, then turned. "Will you have lunch with us, Colonel Armant? You might want to get some background from Preston."

The big man shook his head.

"I'm afraid I can't. I have some business to transact, and I have to get my thoughts together. I'll see you after lunch."

Colonel Armant's appearance at the counsel table caused a stir in the courtroom. In that small city, he was a familiar figure. Although his office was in the courthouse basement, he was more often seen on a bench on the courthouse lawn.

An acquaintance had once come up to him when he was sitting in the shade and asked: "Colonel, why aren't you studying your law books?"

The big lawyer did not look at him, but kept gazing at the passersby. "I am, Tom, I am," he replied.

When the plaintiff's lawyer put his client, Dickerman, on the stand, Preston was taken aback by his co-counsel's behavior. Throughout the direct testimony, the old man had sat motionless, his eyes almost closed. A pencil lay by his right hand, but he made no move to use it to make notes on the pad of foolscap before him.

Finally Dickerman's direct testimony was finished and it was time to cross-examine.

When Colonel Armant got to his feet, the plaintiff eyed him with the same calm which had been evident throughout the case. He was a small, dark, lean man with a bald area which went halfway back on his head. His small, muddy eyes were close-set.

Colonel Armant stood in front of him for a moment, then moved to his right side. "Mr. Raymond Dickerman," he said. It was a statement.

The witness shook his head and smiled. It was a smug smile. He was not one to be caught.

"I don't know what you said, sir. I don't hear in my right ear anymore."

The lawyer inclined his head and walked slowly to the other side of the witness.

"Can you hear me now, Mr. Dickerman?" he asked.

"Not as good as I used to, but I can."

"Suppose I stood directly in front of you?"

Dickerman glanced at the judge. He seemed anxious to conduct himself correctly. "I could still hear you, but it would be better the way it is now."

"Then I'll try to stay here," the old lawyer said. "I'm not much of a one for repeatin' myself when I don't have to. Besides, it's easier on you."

"Thank you for that," Dickerman said.

"Let's get back," the big lawyer rumbled. "Raymond Dickerman. I seem to remember that you've often had business in this building."

The lean man considered the remark. It did not seem to call for an answer. He made none. The judge, who was used to Colonel Armant's ways, did not request interrogation.

"I remember a case a few years back," Colonel Armant drawled. "Involved an old fellow name of Wyatt—Jerry Wyatt. Had a little twenty-five-acre piece over in the east end of the county. He'd bought it so he and the old lady could have a nice little place to live out their days on. Trouble was, the fellow who sold it to him kept the mineral rights. Assured Jerry that there'd never be any worry. He wanted to keep the rights because his own land joined Jerry's and he didn't want some coal company movin' in next door early some mornin'. That's assumin' Jerry might sell to the company.

"Trouble was, this fellow sold his own land and the mineral rights to both pieces to a coal company. Jerry had to sell out cheap because the company wanted to mine under that land."

The big lawyer stopped and stared at the plaintiff.

"Ever hear that story, Mr. Dickerman?"

Dickerman sat in the witness chair, imperturbable. "I am familiar with it. I sold Wyatt that land. Sold it in good faith."

Colonel Armant removed his cigar and looked at it. "What would you consider bad faith, then?"

Dickerman's lawyer stood up. "Your Honor, I fail to see what bearing this has on the present case."

The old lawyer replaced his cold cigar. "Your Honor, I have another matter I want to call to the witness's attention. Then I intend to show how both of these tie in with what we have here."

The judge addressed the plaintiff's lawyer. "Colonel Armant's methods may be somewhat relaxed, but I have found that he knows where he is going. I'll allow it."

The huge man thanked the judge and turned again to the witness. "Something else I listened in on, Mr. Dickerman. About ten months ago, a man named Nathan Lewis bought a farm pony for his kids. It seemed to be healthy, with plenty of spirit. Less than two weeks later, it died. Neighbors of the man who sold that pony told Lewis that it had been sickly not long before he bought it. Its owner fed it some jimson seed a few times and it perked up. Perked up long enough for him to get rid of it.

"Lewis was boilin' mad about that, and he tried to get his money back. Even took it to the JP. He didn't get anywhere."

Again Colonel Armant looked challengingly at the plaintiff. "Ever hear of that case?"

Dickerman leaned forward. "You want me to say that I sold that pony. Well, I did. And it was a healthy beast when I sold it."

His own lawyer interrupted again. "Your Honor, it would seem that counsel is attempting to besmirch my client's character."

"I am only casting light on his character," Colonel Armant said calmly. "He has admitted his part in both of these incidents. I haven't besmirched his character. He did."

Dickerman's lawyer snorted. "He still has his rights!"

The judge looked at Colonel Armant. "I must remind you of the truth of counsel's statement. You can scarcely expect him to denounce his client's character in court or to agree with any black picture you paint, no matter how accurate it is. If Judas Iscariot came into this court with a legitimate claim, he would be entitled to a fair judgment."

The old lawyer nodded both to the judge and to his opponent.

"Your Honor is quite correct. And I might represent that miserable creature."

When he said this, Preston's lips pressed into a thin line. The girl, whose hopes had been building, sat stunned.

"However, Your Honor," said Colonel Armant, "I hope there is no need to strike the testimony which has been given on cross-examination."

"I'm sorry, Colonel, but there is," the judge replied. "The witness's testimony will be stricken, and the jury will disregard it."

"Then I'll go on," said the old lawyer.

The plaintiff had settled once more into his old calm. If anything, his features had taken on a faint contempt for his adversary.

"Mr. Dickerman," said Colonel Armant, speaking in his deep drawl, "you and I see each other around the courthouse quite often, don't we?"

"I guess so."

"A lot of these fellows who hang around here are always tryin' to get me into arguments. Do they ever do you that way?"

Dickerman looked puzzled. "Sometimes. But I don't have time for that."

The big attorney made a gesture. "There's one hypothesis some of 'em have tried on me, and I'd like to get your opinion."

The plaintiff's lawyer spoke up. "Your Honor, my client and I didn't come here to be involved in some back-corridor argument."

Colonel Armant turned to the judge. "This man's predicament reminded me of something, Your Honor, and I think his observations could help us all. You might say he almost illustrates this hypothesis."

"Very well," replied the judge, "you may proceed."

The big attorney addressed the plaintiff. "Mr. Dickerman, do you have any idea what sound is?"

Wrinkles in Dickerman's forehead seemed to go up into the bald area. "Sound? Why, I guess something makes what you'd call a noise, then—there's waves in it somewhere, I understand."

The big man nodded. "About the way I've been told. Then at the end you and I and maybe Jake Casto's dog hear it."

Dickerman withdrew a little. "I'm not doing so well in that part of it, nowadays."

"So we've been told," Colonel Armant said. He moved closer to the witness chair. "Now here's the question they like to spring on me:

if a tree falls in the forest, and there's nobody around, is there any sound?"

"That's just one of those Natural Science riddles!" the plaintiff's attorney interrupted.

The judge smiled. He was long used to the old lawyer's eccentricities. "There may be some bearing," he said. "Do you mean to ask, Colonel, if there would be a sound for Mr. Dickerman?"

The big lawyer shrugged. "In this case, I'd have to ask: would there be half a sound? No, I only want to know the other answer."

The judge looked at the plaintiff. "All right. Mr. Dickerman?"

Dickerman's long face was still a study in puzzlement. "If a tree falls, and nobody's there, is there any sound? Why, I don't know. I'd have to leave that to the scientists."

"Maybe," said Colonel Armant, "we can fool these arguers, you and I. I think it's a matter of defining it. We were on the track of a definition a bit ago. You said that something makes a noise and some waves come into it. That would be sound waves from the noise source, I think. Then I said somebody received these waves in his ears, and the sound is heard. You agreed. Am I right?"

"Yes."

The big man held up one of his hands and began telling points on his putty-colored fingers.

Nearly everyone in the courtroom was smiling at the picture of the Colonel confounding these back-corridor savants. Even Preston, the company's lawyer, had a lift at the corners of his mouth.

"So maybe we could define sound as a process involving three things: the origin, a carrier—that's the waves—and a receiver—that's the ears. Does that seem likely to you?"

"Yes."

Colonel Armant leaned toward the plaintiff. He seemed to be conspiring. "That ought to give us an answer if these fellows bring the question up again. It would seem as though there wouldn't be sound if you took away the receiver—the ears. Would you agree with that? Our definition covers it."

Dickerman relaxed. "I would."

The big attorney reached into his vest pocket. "We could demonstrate that now."

He took out his large, gold stem-winding watch. The cover was closed over the face.

"My watch," he said, holding it up. "I'll leave the case closed so that it can be heard, but not seen. If a man can see as well as hear, he sometimes gets ideas."

The big fingers held the watch near Dickerman's right ear. "Is there a sound—as we defined it?"

The lean man shook his head.

"That is my injured ear. I hear nothing. I guess you'd say there's no sound."

"You're sure? Listen closely."

Dickerman smiled.

"There is no sound, to me."

Colonel Armant dropped his head and pursed his lips. "You say there is no sound."

He switched the watch to his other hand and held it near Dickerman's left ear. "What do you say now?"

The plaintiff's smile was even broader. "I can hear it ticking. There is sound—by our definition."

The lawyer looked at him. "Do you want to test this ear again?"

"If you like." Dickerman inclined his head toward the watch for a moment. "I can still hear it."

His lawyer was smiling, too, now. And faces at the defense table were long. Colonel Armant's first testing of his opponent had failed. What else could he do to save the case?

The old lawyer's eyes fixed on the lean man's face. He raised his free hand and ticked off items with his fingers once more.

"Our definition of sound, and you agreed to it, covers three parts: the origin, the waves, and the receiver—the ears. In one case, the receiver was bad. In the other, it was good. In the one, there was no sound. In the other, there was. This is what you say?"

Dickerman leaned forward, grinning. "That is what I say."

Colonel Armant held his hand high for all to see. He folded his third finger.

"No receiver, no sound." He opened the finger again. "Of course, our definition has three parts."

"What of that?" Dickerman demanded.

Colonel Armant folded his first finger. "Take away any of the three parts, and there is no sound. What if there is no origin?"

He walked ponderously to the judge's bench and placed the watch on it. He turned to the witness chair.

"Dickerman," he said, and his rumbling voice seemed to fill the room, "you should consider the consequences of perjury. You have said that you could not hear my watch with your right ear. That is true. You also said you could hear it with your left ear. That is impossible."

He turned to the judge.

"Open the back cover of the watch, Your Honor."

And simultaneous with the judge's exclamation, Colonel Armant said to Dickerman, "It is impossible to hear an empty watch tick. I had the works removed at the jewelers' at noon."

Donald Olson

Another Me

To enter the shop dressed as she was on so dry and mild a spring day might have seemed injudicious to anyone but Rose Mabee. It didn't occur to her that with her coat buttoned to the neck, floppy rain hat pulled low over her forehead, an umbrella in her hand, and dark glasses covering her fine dark eyes certain people engaged in Mr. Blodgett's trade might regard these Garboesque touches with cynical mistrust, detect furtiveness where there was only timidity and intentional disguise where there was only fear of exposure.

The bell over the door brought Mr. Blodgett himself shuffling into view, strings of grey hair smeared across his bony skull, eyes distorted by thick glasses, teeth so yellow they ruined the effect of his too-quick smile.

"Why, it's Miss Smith, isn't it?"

As if in fact concealment had been her purpose, she felt obliged now to remove the dark glasses. "I—I've brought some spoons. Commemorative spoons. They're sterling. I wondered—" She dug them out of her shoulder bag and set them on the counter. Mr. Blodgett examined each spoon, rubbing them with chalky white fingers as Rose gazed about. The shop was a jumble of antiquities: lamps, clocks, pictures, trays of flatware, jewelry, and coins. On a shelf behind the counter she spotted the bisque figurine she had sold on her last visit—the delicate, painted figures of the embracing children seemed to regard her with reproachful perplexity as if wondering why they had been dispossessed from Aunt Ethel's bow-front china cabinet where they had been so tenderly cherished over the years.

"Very nice, Miss Smith. Yes, there's always a market for such pieces. May I inquire what you're asking for them?"

Timidly she ventured a figure. "Would fifty dollars be unfair?"

Neither now nor on earlier visits had Mr. Blodgett haggled. She could not have borne that. Picked at random, Mr. Blodgett's shop had proved a lucky choice. He was such an obliging old gentleman.

As she turned to leave, a young man sailed into the shop. At the sight of his weasel-eyed, slickly handsome face, Rose hastily recovered her eyes with the dark glasses, recalling with displeasure his jauntily flirtatious manner on a previous visit.

"Ah, there you are, Augie," purred Mr. Blodgett. "You remember Miss Smith."

The young man winked at her. "Miss *Smith*, of course. And how *is* Miss Rose *Smith* today? More goodies, have we? Spoons?" He held one up. "Heirlooms, are they?"

Rose nodded, backing toward the door. The young man's boldly insinuating manner produced a disagreeable sense of panic in her. "What about jewelry, Miss Smith? Old pieces are all the rage. Do you have any old gold or ivory?"

Rose dropped her umbrella and nervously snatched it up.

"Where do you live, Miss Smith? I'll be glad to drop by and look over all your stuff. Save you these trips."

Stammering a rejection of his offer, Rose escaped from the shop. It was as if he could see right through her. And the way he spoke her name, as if he knew it was phony. "We mustn't tell them our real names or where we live," Aunt Ethel had cautioned her on that single long-ago visit to another dealer, when a temporary financial crisis had obliged her to sell one of her treasures. "In times like these, child, if people know you've got good things . . ."

The discomfort of her encounter with the appalling Augie was forgotten by the time Rose arrived home. Her mind for the past week had been occupied with a mystery almost anyone else would have found scarcely worth pondering. Had Rose herself not been still a child in many ways—a child of twenty-eight—the discovery of a name identical to hers, another Rose Mabee, in the new phonebook might have inspired no more than passing curiosity. In so large a city, the coincidence was hardly extraordinary. Rose, however, had reacted with a startled thrill of astonishment. Possibly the conviction of having nothing in common with another human being, of being set apart by her own grave difficulties of temperament, of being one of nature's solitary creatures, inspired this singular delight in learning that she shared her name with another woman somewhere else in the sprawling city—that somewhere being Chelsea Terrace, a street Rose had never heard of.

So immediate and pressing had been her curiosity about this woman that Rose had promptly dialed the number in the book, wanting only to hear the woman's voice. In a sense, the telephone was Rose's only link to the world outside her apartment. She ventured out only on the most necessary errands. The noises of the street, the crowds and the traffic aggravated that chronic disorder of the nerves which had afflicted her since childhood, leaving her unfit for what few occupations her education might have made possible.

Before the onset of those multiple infirmities which had left Aunt Ethel gratefully dependent upon Rose's constant presence, the older woman had often fretted about her niece's future. "I won't be around forever, child," she had said. "I really don't know what's to become of you when I'm gone."

The *practical* consequences of her aunt's death had created no problems until some months following the event. During that period, Rose's life remained unchanged, aside from no longer having to wait upon an invalid. Nor did the removal of her sole companion leave Rose as shattered as she might have been had not the old lady's condition already reduced her, quite deaf and nearly blind, to little more than a breathing presence requiring to be bathed and fed and nursed. It was as if Aunt Ethel had deliberately withdrawn herself from life by gradual stages in order to spare her niece the possibly traumatic effect of being too suddenly left alone in the world.

A vast effort of will had been required for Rose to resort to the only means at hand to pay the bills once Aunt Ethel's meager savings had been exhausted—to sell, piece by piece, Aunt Ethel's treasures: silver, china, crystal, porcelain, antique jewelry. What would happen when there was nothing left to sell, Rose couldn't bring herself to contemplate. There would be no one to turn to. She was quite alone in the world.

Alone in the world, but not alone in the house—a modest duplex owned by a dentist who lived in one of the distant boroughs. His aged uncle, Ira MacBride, occupied the adjoining apartment and for years he had been delegated to collect Aunt Ethel's rent. A recluse whose sole interest in life was the breeding of parrots which he sold to pet shops in the city, old Ira had only once, years ago, invited Rose to see the vivid, exotic specimens in cages lining the walls of two upstairs rooms. Yet she was constantly aware of their presence. Her own bedroom lying contiguous to the aviary, the screeching of the parrots was distressingly audible. At times Rose felt she was awakening in some tropical forest, so ferocious was the clamor beyond the wall.

Even more eerily nerve-wracking was the plaintive monotony of that "*Hello—hello—hello—hello*" filtering through the wall during those periods of the day when Ira MacBride played a recording designed to teach the parrots to talk. Aunt Ethel's deafness had left her immune to these distractions, but there were times when Rose's more acute spells of neurasthenia were so exacerbated by the endless, savage squawking that she was obliged to sleep on the sofa downstairs.

Obsessions, healthy or unhealthy, wise or foolish, become not infrequently the refuge of those whose temperaments leave them unfit for normal social intercourse—those all-absorbing, excessive preoccupations (in Ira MacBride's case, parrot life) that serve to fill the emptiness of the solitary life. Thus it happened that Rose Mabee, bereft of her aunt's companionship, fell victim to an obsession inspired by the discovery of another Rose Mabee living in the city. It might have been the timing of the discovery, occurring as it did so shortly after her aunt's death, that accounted in part for the mystical significance it acquired in Rose's mind. And there was also Rose's ignorance of her own family history. As if wishing to protect her niece's precarious mental equilibrium, Aunt Ethel had always been reticent about Rose's parents, both of whom had died when Rose was an infant, so that now, so utterly alone, it wasn't surprising that Rose began to fantasize about her namesake, to imagine that there might exist some link between them beyond the mere coincidence of their shared name.

At first she was content to call the number in the book, hopeful of hearing the woman's voice, as if some quality in her voice might yield a clue, suggest some kinship, bring the woman closer, make her more real. Yet each time Rose dialed the number, the phone rang and rang without being answered. Not only during the day but late at night, when, sleepless, Rose would reach for the phone and dial the number. Then the sing-song drone of Ira MacBride's bird recording, drifting through the wall to where Rose lay staring at the ceiling, acquired a mocking urgency. "Hello—hello—hello—hello." A shadowy face would swim into view behind Rose's wide-awake eyes—a woman's face—and Rose would rise up, listening, and again reach for the phone to dial the other Rose Mabee's number. And to the measured ring of the distant phone she would move her lips in reply, beseeching the response that never came: "Hello—hello—hello—hello!"

The appalling Augie didn't immediately look up as Rose entered the shop, intent as he was on examining some article lying on the counter between himself and a seedy-looking youth wearing faded jeans and a denim vest with some sort of motorcycle emblem on the back. Mr. Blodgett was nowhere in sight. As Rose, her hand still on the door, hovered indecisively, Augie lifted his dark head. "Miss Smith! Come in! Nice to see you." He whispered something to the youth, who glanced around at Rose with dull-eyed curiosity. Augie came around the counter.

"So how are you doing, Miss *Smith?* More goodies? I'm in a buying mood."

Rose remained by the door. "Is Mr. Blodgett here, please?"

"Sorry, love. He's sick today. Bum ticker, you know. Don't worry, I'll give you as square a deal as the old man." He winked at the youth, who now lounged against the counter eyeing Rose with an impish grin. Her get-up, especially the umbrella on this clear sunny day, seemed to amuse him. But then he slapped an impatient hand on the counter and said, "So how about it, Augie? It ain't never been out of the box. If you don't want it, I'll take it to—"

"Who said I didn't want it? Like I said to Miss Rose here, I'm in a buying mood." Turning his back on Rose, Augie conferred in whispers with the youth for a few moments. Money passed between them. Then Augie leaned closer, put a hand on the youth's shoulder, and murmured something in his ear. The youth nodded, pocketed the money, and shambled out of the shop, not glancing at Rose.

Hastily now, eager to escape, Rose opened her bag and placed a pair of ivory beads, a garnet brooch, and a set of gold earrings on the counter. Augie, humming under his breath, examined them closely, and when Rose named a price he agreed to it quite as readily as Mr. Blodgett would have done. But then as she took the bills from his hand, his fingers closed over hers.

He laughed as she snatched her hand away. "Hey, you're as nervous as a little bird, Miss Smith. A pretty little bird. Pretty hair, pretty eyes. What are you so jumpy about, love?" He glanced down at the jewelry. "You can trust me, you know. I'm not the nosy type."

His tone implied some offensive innuendo. Rose grew flustered and stuffed the bills clumsily into her bag.

"Do you live around here, Rose? You don't mind if I call you Rose, do you? Like I said before, tell me where you live and I'll stop by." He picked up the garnet brooch. "You got any more stuff like this?"

"Not like that, no. Thank you. I—I'm late. I've got to go now."

"Hurry back, love. Any time."

She was several blocks from the shop when she chanced to look around and spotted the seedy youth not far behind her. That he might be following her did not enter her mind until she had crossed the street into the park, intending to take a short cut to the bus stop. She had advanced halfway through the block-long park when she glanced over her shoulder and saw him still behind her. Instantly he flopped down on a bench and flung his arms out along the top rail. Rose quickened her steps and at the edge of the park, disregarding the traffic, plunged recklessly across the street against the light. At the opposite curb, she looked back and saw the youth waiting for the light to change.

Aunt Ethel's constant warnings about muggers came back to her and she thought of the money in her bag. Quite a lot of money. The youth knew she had entered the shop for the purpose of selling something. Truly alarmed now, she proceeded along the street as rapidly as she could without actually running. At the next corner, she waited anxiously for a break in the traffic, jay-walked across the street, then ran up the broad steps of the cathedral halfway down the block. She paused in the shadowy vestibule to catch her breath before hurrying down the long left-hand aisle and slipping out the side entrance. An old woman with a cane was just stepping out of a taxi parked at the curb. Seconds later Rose was seated in the cab, breathlessly giving the driver her address.

With that innocence of vision her lack of worldly experience had left as uncorrupted as a child's, she regarded the frightening incident in only the simplest terms: the youth, surmising she would leave Mr. Blodgett's shop with money in her bag, had followed her with larcenous intent. Any suspicion of complicity between the youth and the appalling Augie did not enter her mind.

As the months progressed, Rose's loneliness grew increasingly painful, as did her preoccupation with thoughts of the other Rose Mabee. At the root of this obsession may possibly have burned some dim hope of an actual kinship of the flesh, no matter how remote. Would it be so exceptional a coincidence? Once, years ago, Aunt Ethel had received a letter from a cousin she had never known existed, a college professor in Alabama who had sought her out while doing research for a genealogy of the family to which Aunt Ethel belonged. So such things *did* happen.

The mystery of why the other Rose Mabee never answered her phone grew so compelling and frustrating that eventually Rose took it into her head to leave the sanctuary of her apartment and seek out the Chelsea Terrace address. Garbed in her protective armor of raincoat, hat, and dark glasses, she set off one afternoon when an overcast sky and steady drizzle produced the sort of mildly tranquilizing effect upon her nerves which Rose had always been conscious of without being able to explain.

She strolled past the narrow brownstone several times before venturing to climb the steps of Number 28. The front door, surprisingly, was open. In the hall, traces of bygone splendor survived in the golden oak wainscoting and faded elegance of an antique chandelier with flower-etched globes of frosted glass. Rose Mabee's name on one of the mailboxes in the vestibule kindled a peculiar warmth of proprietorship, encouraging Rose to mount the stairs to the second floor, where she stood outside the door of Apartment 2C before timorously pressing the bell. It soon become evident that as she had half feared but half expected, Rose Mabee was not at home.

As Rose retreated toward the stairs, the door of an adjoining apartment opened and a woman's head appeared. "Lookin' for Rosie, are you, dear?"

Rosie. Rose frowned. The appellation struck her as vaguely offensive, even vulgar, recalling to mind the obnoxious boy in high school who had insisted on calling *her* Rosie.

"Rose Mabee?"

"She's been away weeks, dear. Due back today, though. Any time, in fact. Want to leave your name?"

If I did, thought Rose, secretly amused, wouldn't you be surprised? "No," she said. "No, thank you. I'll come back some other time."

As she started down the stairs, the woman uttered a coyly inquisitive chuckle. "Not one of Rosie's girls, are you, dear?" As Rose turned to stare at her, she laughed. "No, I didn't think so. Not quite the type."

Rose had no sooner reached the sidewalk when a taxi pulled up. Some instinct of recognition identified the woman to Rose even before she stepped from the cab and the driver handed out a smart alligator overnight bag, accepted payment from the woman, and said, "Thanks, Miss Mabee. Welcome back."

Rose's preconceived image of her namesake was more than flattered by this vision of elegance. The woman was about Rose's height and as slim, and though her hair was arranged in a casual, short-cropped, expensive cut, it was nearly the same dark-auburn shade as Rose's. She wore a pale-blue-suede suit, a string of pearls, and a fur jacket. Perhaps if Rose had not been so in awe of her namesake's air of formidable chic, she might have ventured some shy self-introduction then and there. However, she was too acutely conscious of her own graceless attire. So fashionable a creature as Rose Mabee of Chelsea Terrace would surely be strongly influenced by first impressions.

Still, it took the cab driver to resolve her indecision, so compelling was her desire to follow the other woman up the steps of the brownstone. "Cab, lady?" he said.

Rose gave a little start, glanced once more at the retreating figure in blue suede, then moved toward the taxi.

To have seen the other Rose Mabee, almost close enough to touch her, added substance to the fantasy Rose had invented and nurtured in the privacy of her own dream world. She pictured herself being invited to Rose Mabee's apartment, long cozy chats over cups of tea, the exchange of confidences—the forging of a bond.

"How amazing," she could imagine Rose Mabee saying. "Imagine living here in the same town and never even knowing . . ."

She delayed phoning Rose Mabee until after nightfall, when darkness, dulling the razor-sharp edges of reality, eased the tension of her embattled nerves.

"Is this Rose Mabee?" she said when the other woman answered. "It is."

The beguiling tone of Rose Mabee's voice might to others have betrayed a spurious warmth, a practiced intimacy, but to Rose, savoring its richness, it conveyed an immediate promise of sympathy.

"Miss Mabee, I've been trying to reach you for weeks. I wanted—I—this may sound strange—"

"Who is this, please?"

"My name is Rose Mabee."

There was a pause and then, with a faintly arctic overtone, Rose Mabee said, "No jokes, please. I'm not in the mood."

"Oh, please listen. I'm not joking. My name *is* Rose Mabee. Just like yours. It sounds funny, I know, my calling like this, not knowing you—"

"Did one of my girls tell you to call?"

"Girls? No, I—"

"Are you in the business, honey? Because if you are—"

"Please! Please listen to me! It's like this, see—I saw your name in the phonebook—"

The line went dead.

At first Rose thought they might have been cut off, but then with a sense of wounded astonishment she realized that Rose Mabee had hung up on her. She felt as if an unseen hand had slapped her smartly across the face. Still clutching the phone, she shut her eyes and lowered her head to the pillow. But then the longer she thought about it, the easier it became to blame herself for the rebuff. Blurting out her name as she had done, stammering like an idiot, what could she expect? Rose Mabee must have assumed it was a crank call. Wouldn't she, herself?

Phoning her like that, after dark, out of the blue, had been a mistake. She must call her back, of course, but not before morning and not without forethought as to what she would say. She mustn't stammer and babble like a child.

If Rose Mabee should form the opinion that she *was* talking to a crank, everything would be ruined. There would be no invitation to meet, no tea by the fireplace. The warm, wonderful friendship would remain nothing but a dream, and that's all there would be for the rest of her life. Dreams. Nothing.

She must choose the right words, write them all down beforehand, organize her thoughts just as she would do if she were writing a letter. But, of course! Why hadn't she thought of it before? A *letter*. People were always suspicious of phone calls from strangers, whereas a letter would be certain to make a better first impression on a woman like Rose Mabee. She would write first and *then* call her again.

At first, Rose tossed and turned in bed, trying to compose the letter in her mind. But this proved as impossible as sleep. Finally she sprang out of bed and ran downstairs to the desk in the living room, where she seized paper and pen and began the struggle of composition.

Words flowed onto the paper—all about her situation, her fears and uncertainties, and her agony of loneliness. She wrote about her aunt's death and her own nervous disorder and her excitement at discovering another Rose Mabee in the phonebook. "It was like discovering there was another me," she wrote, revealing in that one sentence far more about the nature of her obsession than she could herself have understood.

Rereading what she had written in her sprawling, childlike hand, it did not occur to her that such an effusion of bewildering sentiments might produce as unrewarding an effect as her muddled attempt at explanation over the phone . . .

Rose opened her bag, her fingers nervously plucking out the cameo brooch so hastily that her letter to Rose Mabee was swept out with it. Before she could pick it up from the counter, the awful Augie's hand closed over it. Playfully, he snatched it up and handed it back to her, but not before glancing boldly at the name and address: Rose Mabee, 28 Chelsea Terrace. His face betrayed no furtive glee at having penetrated, as he must have supposed, the true identity of Miss Smith. Instead he examined the brooch in silence and paid the price she asked. But then, the transaction concluded, his tone once more acquired a provocative slyness.

"Like I said before, Miss—er—" his glance slid briefly across the letter in her hand "—*Smith,* why sell your valuables piece by piece? It's not safe, you know, keeping stuff like that around the house. Don't you read the papers? I could pay you a little visit. It wouldn't take long to look over what you have. Will you be home tonight?"

"No! No, not tonight." Where was Mr. Blodgett, for heaven's sake? She made up her mind then and there she would never return to the shop. There were other dealers. She might even ask Rose Mabee's advice. Yes, perhaps Rose Mabee would know someone. Oh, there was so much to talk about, she and Rose.

"Well, you just give me a call any time you want me to come over. Remember, it's not safe, and you living alone like you do. You do live alone, don't you?"

A tiny sliver of a smile touched Rose's lips. "For now, yes."

The confidence she had felt ever since writing the letter, a sense of purpose and direction such as she had never before known, returned once she was away from the shop. No, never again would she pass through that door. But she had had no choice this morning. Without money she wouldn't be able to make the purchases she planned. And now, with money in her bag, she decided to take a taxi instead of walking all the way to Chelsea Terrace.

Once there, she told the driver to wait. In less than a minute, the letter was slipped into Rose Mabee's mailbox and Rose was glad she had decided to deliver the letter in person. Sending it in the usual way would have meant waiting another whole day before calling her new friend. Back in the cab, the little sliver of a smile again settled on her lips as she thought about her next stop, the department store, and the things she would buy: the dress, the shoes, the gloves.

During the drive downtown she made another decision. There was a hair salon in the department store. If she was lucky, she might get in without an appointment. She didn't care what it might cost—she would have her hair done exactly like Rose Mabee's.

That evening she went up to her room early, lay on her bed, and prayed for the phone to ring. She had written her number very clearly in the letter and had twice underscored the words *I must talk to you before it's too late.* As twilight deepened, she didn't turn on the light. It was more comfortable in the dark. She felt safer, calmer. The flush of the evening sky faded beyond the window; the silver glimmer of the mirror on the wall evaporated. Still the phone did not ring. The only sound was the squalling chatter of the parrots behind the wall. A gathering of lunatics might have been holding a party in the other apartment.

By midnight Rose was forced to concede the possibility that Rose Mabee might not be going to call. If she didn't . . . The endless hours of the night loomed threateningly. She knew she would never be able to sleep, and when tomorrow came, and the next day and the day after that . . . At last, unable to suppress her rising agitation, she sat up, switched on the light, and with damp trembling fingers dialed the familiar number.

It rang at least six times and at the lifting of the receiver, Rose uttered a gasping cry of relief. She began to babble. "I'm sorry to call so late. But I thought *you* would call *me*. It's me, Rose. Did you get my letter?"

"Oh, yes. Don't apologize, honey, I just got in. I'm dead on my feet. Deliver me from conventioneers. But I read your letter, honey, and I'm sorry I hung up on you when you called yesterday. It just seemed so—well, far out, you know? But, listen, I've got to be honest. What exactly *is* the problem? What is it you want from me? It's not that I'm not sympathetic, you know, but—oh, hold on a minute, will you? Someone's at the door. God, what a night. I'm a little tipsy. I don't think I remembered to slide the bolt— Hold on."

Rose heard the sound of the phone being put down and then, barely audible, Rose Mabee's voice, an inquiring unalarmed murmur, and then a man's voice, followed by a startled exclamation of protest from Rose Mabee. Perched tensely on the side of her bed, Rose hugged the phone to her ear. Suddenly a scream tore along the wire, a wild, piercing scream of utter terror. Then total silence on the other end of the line. Presently, as Rose listened, unable to breathe or move, there could be heard the gentle, almost noiseless click of the other phone being replaced on its cradle.

Rose pressed the mouthpiece closer to her lips. "Hello? Hello? Hello?" She kept saying it even though she knew the line was disconnected. "Hello? *Hello?*"

Profound silence seemed to settle upon the house. At first even the birds behind the wall were silent. No sound penetrated that infinitely small corner of the world in which Rose sat alone, endlessly and forever alone. Until abruptly, into that silence, floated not the sing-song human syllables of the recording she had heard so often but the guttural raspy utterance of a single parrot, as if it had finally learned its lesson and now could not stop repeating the word, over and over and over again: "*Hello—hello—hello—hello—*"

Ernest Savage

The Girl and the Ghost

I had just begun to eat lunch at Sheldon's on Van Ness, a few blocks north of my apartment. It was a little before twelve and the noon crowd hadn't gathered yet. I concentrate when I eat, the way I do when I put fuel in the Dart, eyes on the job.

I saw her middle portion first—hips, waist, upper thighs. She was standing still, facing me, waiting. My eyes reluctantly crept upward to her arms, Xed across her breasts, cuddling a book. She was wearing a sober-grey pantsuit, a leather purse hung from her right shoulder. My eyes rose to a slender, soldier-straight neck, chin, then the full face, and my mouth fell agape.

She closed her eyes briefly in a moment of bored disgust. She resented the involuntary primal, slavering reaction of men—which must be her hourly lot.

I snapped my mouth shut, greatly miffed with myself. "What you should do," I said, "is wear army boots, an ankle-length muumuu, and your grandmother's straw summer boater with a ten-inch fine-mesh veil. Then you wouldn't have to put up with this sort of thing."

"I have no grandmother."

"Any Salvation Army store will do. You're Miss McClure, aren't you?"

"Miss McLain. May I sit down?"

"If you must. I told you an hour ago on the phone that I was leaving town this afternoon and won't be back until Monday. What you said—about some book, was it?—didn't strike me as urgent. Is that the book?"

"Yes."

Her face was now opposite me at eye level. The Devil had framed it in long, lustrous black hair. Her eyes were cut and polished jewels—amethysts, I think. I put down the fork, stomach full of small UFOs, and said, "How did you know I was here?"

"I know where your apartment is, Mr. Train. I followed you. The problem may not be urgent to you, but it's much on my mind. If you'd just give me—"

"In one hour I leave here for a place in the mountains called Inskip. There's a dinky hotel there that's a hundred and thirty years old, formerly used by gold miners. I'll sleep there tonight. Tomorrow, early, I'll walk about four miles deeper into the mountains and fish a stream that no more than six people know about. Tomorrow night I'll sleep on its banks, and maybe Sunday, too, depending. Monday afternoon I'll be back here and—"

"Gosh," she said, "that sounds wonderful!" Her eyes had gathered new lights—but her spell was suddenly broken. I could quit being tough. "Trout," she went on wistfully. "Fried crisp over an open fire and under an open sky—"

You mean *you* camp out? I nearly blurted. *You* fish? Does Queen Elizabeth vacuum the palace halls? But I said cautiously, "Brook trout, Miss McLain, and rainbows. German browns up to ten pounds. Do you fish?"

We stared at each other, letting the moment pass in peace. My appetite was returning, my belly settling down. The hard-won equilibrium of my years resumed its function. But she was not that much younger than I—about twelve years maybe, her beauty gaining vintage. I was *seeing* her now, with eyes unblurred by awe.

"Yes," she said. "But it's been years, Mr. Train. Years ago my father and I—"

"I've got plenty of equipment," I said. "We could pick up a sleeping bag for you on the way if you haven't got one. But I'm no father, lady."

She must have gone through this a million times, the pitch—old hotspur on the make. "I don't know, " she said, "what you mean by that."

"Hell," I said, "I don't either. Forget it and tell me about your book—my rush is not all that great."

"I could tell you about it," she said, "on the way."

One thin wall separated my room from hers. Not enough. Through my open window, the cleanest air left in this world abundantly flowed. We were 5,000 feet high in the Sierra, the place I admire the most—more than the sea, the city, or the plains. The night was a symphony of silence, if you'll accept the paradox.

I had heard her stir in her room and get up, and my eyes snapped open as though a shot had gone off. It was well after midnight. I'd been fed a bounteous supper by Kathy Duffey, who with her husband Bob owns and runs the Inskip Inn. I should have slept like a baby. I'd left all my cares in San Francisco, save the one I'd brought with me, now walking around on the wide pine floorboards of her room, clomp, clomp. Now getting back in her bed, creak, creak.

Sleep ruined, I wrenched my mind off her recumbent form, nestled down so near to mine, and put it on her problem, which she'd said was urgent. The book.

It was a hefty tome, over four hundred pages, a current bestseller. It was written by a man named Winston X. Rhodes, whose picture was on the back of the dust-jacket—a nondescript face, shaded by a hat. But it was not written by him, Miss McLain proclaimed vehemently. In fact, part of it, the last chapter, was written by Miss McLain herself. The rest of it had been written by a woman named Sarah Loring, now dead.

"Who was what to you?" I had asked as we tooled north on I-5.

"A friend—a casual friend. We shopped at the same Mom and Pop grocery store. I first met her there nearly two years ago. She was in her seventies. She had badly crippled fingers—from arthritis. She'd dropped some packages and I picked them up for her."

"You're a nice girl, Miss McLain. She was a neighbor?"

"Three blocks distant. We kept bumping into each other at the store. She was a pleasant woman, friendly but reserved, gentry fallen on hard times. She had lovely luminous eyes. Many old people in pain do."

I said, "I bet you get along well with old people, don't you?"

"They're very nearly the only people," she snapped, "that I do get along with."

"What was she to this Rhodes fellow?"

"Nothing I've been able to discover. But one day after shopping we had coffee together and she asked me if I could type. I said I could and she said she'd like to hire me to do some work for her. We went to her apartment—a tiny place over somebody's garage—and she told me about her book, showed me the whole manuscript—"

"Typed?"

"Yes. All except that last chapter, which was written in a barely legible scrawl because of her hands. She insisted that I take the whole thing home with me and read it. That was important to her, Mr. Train, that I *read* it. I think she knew she was running out of time—"

"So you read it."

"Yes, and it was wonderful, a truly heart-gripping story. But I changed the last chapter when I typed it—had a character live that she'd had die."

"Did she approve?"

"Yes. She agreed it was a change for the better."

"Do you still have the typewriter?"

"Yes."

"Good. Then what happened?"

"I don't know. I never saw her again. I got this job I've held until today—and I had to move."

"What do you mean you've 'held until today?' You mean you quit?"

"Yes. After you dropped me off at my apartment, I phoned and told them I quit."

This disquieted me. "Why?"

"Because I've come to despise them. It's a partnership of three lawyers. Two days ago they settled a personal-claim case for an outrageous amount of money. They're still gloating over the arithmetic of the thing—they made $9,800 an hour for twenty hours of work, most of which I actually did. I simply couldn't stand it any longer."

"You mean no bonus for you—"

"Of course no bonus for me—there *never* was. But that's not the point. Never once was justice mentioned in that office—just fees."

I grinned, sharing her sentiments about lawyers. She said, "That's where I heard about you, Mr. Train. You were mentioned several times in that office—always opprobriously, which is what caught my favorable attention. You are not well liked by lawyers."

"My single claim to fame. So," I said, "what about the book? You read it, recognized it—"

"Yes—by the sheerest fluke. I almost never buy a book—and the title had been changed—but something drew me to it, I don't know what."

"Yeah, sure. And?"

She was a moment before saying, "At first I actually thought about discussing it with my bosses, of taking some legal action against this Rhodes—if that's his name. But the idea of working *with* them as well as for them was simply too repugnant. Besides, I'd have to find him first. And that's what you do, isn't it?"

"Sometimes. So you want to hire me. Do you know my fees?"

"What are they?"

"Two hundred dollars a day plus expenses."

"Oh." She was shocked. She made a sweepingly sardonic gesture at the beautiful countryside. "Is *this* an expense, Mr. Train?"

"This is a vacation, Miss McLain. I hope . . ."

She walked the way Indians walk—softly, sure-footed, with no wasted motion. I'd made her precede me, in case she fell, calling directions to her as she went. She set a brisk pace, carrying exactly one half our gear on her back and in her hands. She'd insisted on that. She fended off men by not needing them.

She'd been silent all morning. Not uncivil, just withdrawn. But I'd regained my poise. It would be a fine two days.

There's a stretch of clear swift water about fifty yards long on the north bank of which we made our camp. She changed from hiking boots to fishing shoes and was rigged up before I was.

From under a rock at the stream's edge she nabbed a helgamite, fat and ugly as sin, and strung him on her hook. On her third cast, placed precisely right, she caught a rainbow and began to play him. I watched admiringly. Her father had taught her well, and she'd remembered. She brought the colorful fish deftly out of the water, a big one, wriggling, mad at himself, glistening in the rays of the early-morning sun. She unhooked him and put him in her creel. Then she turned and we traded vivacious grins. She was standing thigh-deep in the water, legs braced against its rush, jeans soaked to the waist. It was a fine moment. Now she was just a fellow fisherman, a worthy competitor. Now all I had to do was catch more fish than she did.

I had brought a hip-flask of cognac. After supper we shared it, drinking out of cups. We were seated on the cushiony upper surface of a long-fallen pine. In front of us, the fire was dying slowly. In front of it the stream hissed and burbled along. She had fallen silent again, reflective. I was planning sleep—it had been a long and tiring day and the silence would be hers to break.

Then she did, barely audibly. "Last night," she said, "a man came to my room."

I was startled and instantly defensive. There was only Bob Duffey and myself within ten miles of the Inskip Inn. I asked her how that could be.

"A ghost," she said, straight-faced. And I thought at once, my God, Charley Stokes! Who else? Charley Stokes had come to see Miss McLain, gone through all that hell just to see Miss McLain! I took a deep breath, wide awake and suddenly pleased as punch. I knew about Charley Stokes.

But I was cautious, skeptical.

I said, "What kind of a ghost?"

She was impatient. "A *ghost* ghost. Transparent. Translucent?" Her face swiveled my way. "I could see *through* him."

"As apparently you can most men. Describe him."

"Why? Do you know who this person is? Was? Is?"

"I think I do. Describe him for me."

"He was tall and slender. He had what you'd call a saturnine face. He had dark eyes."

"What was he wearing?"

"Old-fashioned clothes. A long black waistcoat, a brocaded vest, a white shirt, a string tie, a wide-brimmed flat-top hat. A watchchain was strung across his vest." She was getting huffy. "Mr. Train, I wasn't asleep. It wasn't a dream."

"I know. Were you frightened?"

"No. I was more cold than frightened. Cold is what wakened me. I was startled, of course, but he wasn't threatening. When I got up, he stepped aside politely, giving me room."

"And then?"

"I went to the window and looked out, and then looked back at him. I could see him perfectly plainly. He seemed to be—inner lit. I could see his lips move."

"Could you hear him?"

"No. But he was trying to tell me something—I think. Why else would his lips move?"

"I don't know. Mrs. Duffey never mentioned him trying to speak."

"Mrs. Duffey?"

"Yes. You met the resident ghost of the Inn, Miss McLain. His name is Charley Stokes. A hundred and some odd years ago he owned the place. He's been seen a number of times—once by Mrs. Duffey herself a few years ago. But mostly he's just heard, walking around, up and down the stairs, down the halls, clomp, clomp."

"It doesn't please me that I'm one of the few he chose to present himself to."

"Then you *were* frightened."

"No," she said firmly. "But I found it disturbing. Most particularly when I became sure it was real."

"And Mrs. Duffey didn't tell you about him last night? Just a word, a hint?"

"What? No. How could she have? You were with me every minute. Besides, if I'd known there was a ghost in her hotel, I'd've slept in the car. I found it *very* disturbing, Mr. Train."

I got up, legs stiff, and fed the fire, hunkered down for its warmth.

We were face to face, her eyes sparkling from the flames. But I was used to her beauty now, if not inured to it. "Miss McLain," I said, "you attract men and you attract the ghosts of men. You're no longer a dewy-eyed girl. How come you're still on the loose? Surely you've had dozens of proposals."

"Yes—I suppose."

"From every kind of man there is. From every type."

"Yes. Probably."

"But none have met your bill of specifications. What is it—do you have a dream man or something? You'll know him when you see him?"

"No. That's been my fear—that I'll walk right by him, that I already have. Mr. Train," she said, roused now. "I want to be *useful* to a man, not an adornment. Men are either afraid of me or they want to possess me, as they possess, say, an expensive car—something to show off."

"That's one of the classic motives for marriage, Miss McLain. Both for him and for her."

"But not for me, Mr. Train."

"Miss McLain," I said, "how old are you, and for Christ's sake, what's your first name?"

She laughed. "I'm thirty-two," she said, "and my name is Jean. And yours is Sam. And now we're friends, aren't we?"

"You bet."

A little later we crawled into our sleeping bags, she on one side of the fire, I on the other. She went to sleep first.

She exercised a gentle, ladylike snore. She was at peace now under the open sky, but last night in Charley Stokes' hotel her magnetism or something had compelled him into that agonizing journey from there to here. That is why it's always cold around a ghost. To make the trip consumes all the energy they can get their bony hands on, all the heat. Or so it's said, and why not? Surely something had troubled Jean's night last night—and mine, too. That clomp, clomp I'd heard had been somebody's boot, not milady's bare and delicate foot.

When Charley Stokes owned the Inn, Inskip was booming. A thousand men gathered there to pick the gold from the hills and streams. Charley had a sister. She lived in the Inn under his wing. One of the miners wanted to marry her, but Charley said no, and according to the legend the enraged suitor burned the Inn to the ground. It's possible that Charley killed him, but that isn't known for sure. What is known is that Charley rebuilt the Inn and sent the sister somewhere north out of danger's way. After that, peace apparently reigned—except in Charley's heart, else why would he haunt the nights?

The stream's answer to that question—and all others—was a lullaby.

"The thing is," Jean said, "you're sullen and angry because I caught the biggest fish."

"I'm not sullen and angry, this is the natural set of my face. And silence means I'm thinking."

"About what?"

"If I answer that, the two hundred bucks a day starts now."

"You were thinking about me."

"I'll be thinking about you off and on for the rest of my life. I was thinking about another woman—dead a hundred years."

"You should be thinking about Rhodes and how to find him."

"That will be done."

"How?"

"Professional secret."

We were on our way home, having picked up I-80 off I-5, the late-afternoon sun now slanting into my eyes. She had her left leg up and folded on the seat, left arm hooked over the back the way my teen-years girl friends used to sit when they weren't pressed against my side. We were pals now, easy with one another.

In the trunk of the Dart an ice chest contained eighteen trout, ten of which were hers, including the largest. She was good; not necessarily better than I, but good. She'd been born in Yreka, which is near the Oregon border. Her father had taught her the fishing art in the streams of the Trinity Mountains. He was dead. She was alone in the world. Alone with her beauty, as you are alone at the top.

"Just what," I asked, jockeying through the thick going-home Sunday traffic, "do you want from this guy Rhodes?"

"The truth," she said crisply. "I want the credit given where the credit is due." Justice. The old elusive goal.

"No money, Jean?"

She was silent for an eighth of a mile, then said, "Should I want money?"

"Well, it seems almost unAmerican not to, doesn't it? Besides, shouldn't he be punished? Damaged? Hurt? Your ex-bosses would skin him alive and sell his bones to the zoo."

She straightened on the seat and stared straight ahead. She was frowning as she said, "I don't know what I want from him, Sam. I don't know, really, what I *should* want from him. I don't know why I bought the damn book in the first place."

"Serendipity," I said. "It brought you to me."

"Yeah, sure," she said. The copy-cat.

I was up at eight-thirty Monday morning, an hour later than usual, but it had been another restless night. I plugged in the coffee, drank a glass of orange juice, and then looked up Winston X. Rhodes in the phonebook. He was there—sometimes this business is simple—but when I dialed his number I got told it was no longer in service. Sometimes this business is tough.

I'd spread the morning *Chronicle* on the table and had steeled myself to read it when she came. She said, still standing in the hall, her amethyst eyes aglow, "I know where he is."

"Where?"

"Or will be," she said, striding past me, "at two o'clock this afternoon."

"Where?"

"At Walton's Book Store on Grant Street. From two to five. To sign his books."

"Good work, my dear."

"It's in the *Chronicle,* page forty-eight. See?" She thrust the paper before my eyes. I probably would have missed it. I don't read the ads. She was roaming around my living room, full of energy. She would make a judgment on the room, women can't help it. She rendered hers, smiling at me. "I like your place," she said—and, God help me, I was in love again.

We were at Walton's a little before two, part of a growing crowd, mostly female. It was a woman's book, Jean had told me, a love story, true to the heart, with discreet, gentle sex and only Nature's violence.

Rhodes hadn't yet appeared, but his place had been arranged, a table stacked high with the book. Jean was wearing a bulky camelhair coat, cinched in at the waist, a scarf at the throat. A beret capped her lustrous hair and dark glasses screened the troublesome eyes.

We separated as the milling crowd grew. I heard one woman ask another, "Did you see him on Johnny Carson last night? Two million for the paperback rights and God knows how much for the movie!"

Rhodes appeared at precisely two and the crowd fell silent as he was introduced and ushered to his table. He was a surprise. I had one of his books in hand and he looked little like the fuzzy, behatted figure on the dust-jacket. His hair was an unkempt reddish-brown mass streaked with grey and his moustache and Van Dyke beard were of a noticeably different hue. A craggy, bony face, flushed and freckled. Small round glasses, dark as an Arab chief's, over his eyes. He was broad-shouldered and five foot six or seven. He looked tense and tired, almost frazzled. I placed him at thirty-five, but aging fast. Jean appeared at my side. She was staring at him, frowning. I said, "Have you ever seen him before?" and she shook her head.

I got in the line that was forming in front of the table and she asked what I was going to do. "Get him to sign this book," I said.

She gripped my arm as the line began to move. "Be kind to him, Sam."

"Why, for God's sake? He's—"

"Just be kind to him, please. He looks so tired."

"As well he should."

When my turn came, I opened the front cover of the book and laid it before him. He raised his eyes high enough to discover I was a man and said, "Thank you, sir. How would you like it inscribed?"

"To Sarah Loring," I said, and he began, reflexively, to write. "In memoriam," I added, "with three million dollars' worth of thanks. Roughly. Up until now."

His pen had stopped. From my vantage point I could see his eyes behind the dark glasses close, then open and blink. I had scored. His pen moved again and he said into his beard, "As you wish."

"What I wish," I said, "is a nice long talk with you, Mr. Rhodes. To discuss literary matters."

He muttered, "Impossible."

"Either here, before all these wonderful people, or tonight at your hotel. Where are you staying since you gave up your apartment?" The tension between us had stretched taut. The people behind me began to stir. Jean had turned and gone away. "Name of the hotel," I said, "and number of the room."

He growled an answer and I told him I'd be there at eight o'clock sharp . . .

Outside, Jean said she wouldn't come with me and I asked her sharply why not.

"Because I think it's going to be bloody," she said, "and I don't want to watch."

"But you're my chief witness, Jean, as well as my employer. I need your testimony."

"You know everything I know, Sam—and you do very nicely on your own."

"Yeah, sure," I said.

He was wearing a robe when I got there. He'd removed the false moustache and beard, which had been awkward fakes. I pointed at his empty chin and said, "How come?"

He shrugged, more or less at his ease. He'd bathed and eaten and had a few drinks. "My agent," he said, "didn't think I looked writerish enough. What's your name?"

I told him, but we didn't shake hands. "I'm a private investigator," I said. "I represent the estate of Mrs. Sarah Loring. From which you've swiped a fortune."

"You're not the first, Train."

"Meaning what? There's only one Sarah Loring."

"Maybe—whoever she is. But there's a world full of highbinders. Every time a new writer hits the bestseller list, dozens of people claim they had a hand in the thing. It's one of the oldest established cons. The only reason you're here is that I wanted to avoid a public fracas this afternoon. Now you can go."

"Your agent's right, Rhodes. You don't look writerish. But I know why, if he doesn't. You're not a writer. You're a fake, and you're losing your nerve. You don't have the guts to bluff this thing through. I've got the woman in hand who wrote the last chapter for Mrs. Loring, who—as you know—couldn't type." Now he sat gracelessly on a couch and reached for the drink he'd left to answer the door. His face, ruddy this afternoon, had gone pale, his freckles looking more like liver spots. He lit a cigarette and pressed heavily into the cushions of the couch.

"The dust-jacket," I said, "says you're working on your second novel. That's a lie. If you're working on a novel, it's your first, and you know it. Your heart stopped when I mentioned Mrs. Loring's name this afternoon. Your heart probably stops ten times a day, you can't handle much more."

"Train," he said wearily, blowing smoke, "you can't prove a thing."

"I haven't tried yet. Give me two days and I'll have you and Mrs. Loring stitched together like a quilt."

He got up and went over and looked out his ninth-floor window at the lights of Union Square. His suite was spacious, high-ceilinged, and furnished for a king. The carpet under his bare feet was plush and service was at his fingertips—the trappings of success. He turned and blinked his moist, unprotected eyes. His hair, damped down, was springing loose again.

"She's dead," he said, "she has no heirs. I checked. I spent two months and quite a lot of money checking."

I watched him stiffen up his drink back at the table. "How did you get the manuscript? You swiped it."

"No. She gave it to me."

"Why? Who were you to her?"

He sighed, visibly relieved by a lightened load. "This friend of mine," he said, "was teaching a night-school course in creative writing. She got sick and asked me to fill in for her. I used to teach composition at a private boys' school and was halfway qualified."

"And Loring was one of the students?"

"No. The course was half over by then. She came in the first night I was there, a Tuesday, and asked if she could monitor the class. Hell, I didn't know the rules or the rates or anything and I said sure. Then after class she handed me this pacakge—said it was a novel she'd written and wanted a professional opinion."

"Professional, huh?"

"Yeah, Train, professional. But I'm as good as anybody at reading a book. You don't have to be a pro to tell good from bad. Sure, I thought it would be a clunker, a piece of junk, but I took it home, anyway. She was a sick little old lady and I didn't want to hurt her."

"Good of you."

He shrugged. "My friend," he said, "was still too ill to work, so I began to read it. The next class night, Thursday, Mrs. Loring was there and I told her I'd finish it over the weekend and give her a judgment on Tuesday."

"But she didn't show up."

"Believe it or not, Train, it's true. She couldn't. She died on Saturday."

"How did you know?"

"The cover sheet of the manuscript had her address on it. Hell, it had a half dozen addresses on it, all but the last scratched out. She'd been working on it for years—that was obvious—and she'd moved a lot. She was on welfare. Welfare buried her a month later. I was the only one there. They'd tried to find an heir, even just a friend, but they couldn't. Then I tried—" He shook his head, recalling it, the forgotten drink swirling in his hand. He stared at me. "What was I supposed to do? It was a hell of a book—as subsequent events proved. What was I supposed to do?"

"You had options, Rhodes. You could have told her story. You could have published it under her name. Books get published posthumously all the time."

"Yes, but by somebody's estate. Somebody's heirs, somebody's agents, someone connected. If I'd done what you suggest, Train, everybody in the country named Loring would have claimed to be a cousin."

"And this way all the money's yours."

"Right," he asserted. "And all the credit. I'm a writer now, and there's nothing you or anybody else can do about it."

He was facing me, massive shoulders squared. He'd released the fester of all this ill-stored hugger-mugger and was feeling a lot better. But there *was* something I could do about it. I said, "Where's the manuscript?"

"In the publisher's files. But that won't help, Train—I retyped the whole thing."

"All," I said, "but the last chapter, which didn't need it, which was nice and fresh." His face fell a notch. "And I've got the typewriter that wrote it."

He waffled. "So? I hired this girl to type it for me."

"No good. You don't even know who she is. And believe me, she's unforgettable."

It occurred to him that he held a drink in his hand and he downed half of it. "Train," he said, "this is common stuff, trying to horn in on the action. Look, right after you leave here, I'll call my publisher and tell him to destroy the manuscript. Or lose it."

"I can still hook you into Loring, Rhodes. No problem. And the big thing, pal, is this. Let's see this so-called second novel you're working on. One glance at that, if it exists at all, and any grade-school scholar can—"

He stepped toward me, lowering. "It *does* exist," he said hotly. "And it's—it's—"

"Awful?"

"It's—"

"Juvenile?"

"It's a damn good novel. It may—it may—"

"Need work? Need help? Need Mrs. Loring's hand?"

His hair had sprung all the way loose. He ran his free hand through it and bolted the rest of his drink. "Okay," he said grimly, "do your best—or your worst. I'll simply deny it all. And I've got three million dollars to buy lawyers with, if it comes to that."

"Your money is tainted, Rhodes. Money from the grave. Haunted."

"So what? Lawyers don't give a damn where their fees come from. You or your client couldn't begin to match it."

"We won't have to. You're about ready to spill the beans yourself. I mean publicly, not just to me. You're on the ropes, Rhodes. The only thing that could save your hide and your ego would be if you came up with a book of your own as good as Loring's. But you can't. Even at your best you couldn't, and you're at your worst."

To my surprise, he bolted into the bathroom, robe flying in the wind. I thought to be sick. But when he came back in fifteen seconds, he had a gun in his hand, a snub-nosed revolver. The great arbiter. "Get out!" he roared. "Leave me alone!"

I took a deep breath. I hate guns, especially in nervous, angry hands. But I'm living proof that if they don't go off at once, they don't go off at all. Generally speaking.

"Just don't," I said, "put that thing in your mouth and pull the trigger. It makes a nasty meal and you're hungry for it. But you've got a good clean way out, Rhodes—just tell the truth. Give the dead old lady her due. Hell, it'll probably increase sales! You know how the American public loves its crooks."

The gun had calmed him, as it had uncalmed me. "What I'm going to do," he said, "is get on with my work. I've got a bookstore date in Oakland tomorrow. I've got a talk-show date in San José the next day. Thursday I fly to Salt Lake City for more of the same." His smile was cold. "Get out, Train."

"The trouble," I told Jean, after I'd told her everything, "is that I don't know what the hell I'm working for. Or even who. You? Sarah's shade? What could I tell Rhodes? That we'll expose him for the fraud he is?"

"I don't want you to do that, Sam."

"See? So what the hell's the point?"

She'd been waiting for me in the downstairs bar. She'd nursed a single Coca-Cola and Seagram's 7 the hour I'd been gone. It wasn't enough tariff for the expensive table at which she sat alone, the cynosure, needless to say, of all eyes. I had ordered a double Boodles martini on the rocks to help pay the rent, but I needed it more than they did.

"The point is—" she said.

"What?"

"He's got a conscience, Sam."

"Yeah, sure, but if he gets through the next few days it'll curl up and die. Most consciences have a short half life. And he doesn't have to prove he can write at all, Jean. He's got all the money right now that he'll ever need."

"But that's not what counts with him, don't you see? He didn't know the book would be a terrific success. He saw in it what I saw—truth, beauty. Not mere money. And most first novels don't make a nickel, everybody knows that."

"Yeah, sure."

"Read it!"

"All right, I will, since I bought the damn thing. And that's an expense, incidentally."

"Fine," she said. "Now I want you to see him tomorrow."

"Why, for God's sake?"

"I want you to leave a note at the desk telling him you'll see him tomorrow at the same time."

"And you, I suppose, will sit down here nursing another teenage drink."

"I'll wait for you," she said, "right where I am now." Then she paid me, two full days plus $15.85 for the book, tax included. I told her she didn't have to do that as she wrote out the check, but she pretended not to hear.

When I called him on the house phone Tuesday night, he said he'd gotten my note but he wouldn't see me, then or ever. I went into the bar and told her that, but she said to go up anyway, to knock on his door.

And I did—for two minutes, during which he told me to go away. Then finally the door gave way under my hand and I walked in. He was backing away from me, the gun in his hand. I followed him all the way across the room to the Powell Street window and took it away. It was plastic, as I'd known it would be. He had flown in yesterday morning from L.A. and you can't buy a gun in this town that quickly. I should have known that last night, but I wasn't myself last night. He stumbled over to the couch, sagged onto it, and held his head.

"How'd it go in Oakland?" I said conversationally.

"I wanted to change my room," he mumbled, staring down at the floor. "But they said they were full. Tourists." He looked up at me. "How did you do it?"

"Do what?"

"It wasn't Sarah Loring," he said abstractedly, "because I know her. It was a man. How did you do it?"

Oh, Christ! I thought, but said, "I didn't do anything, Rhodes. I got moderately tanked last night and slept in this morning. What man are you talking about?" As if I didn't know—I and the hair on the back of my neck. Charley Stokes travels. The ghost had come west.

I grinned like a fool and went over to the phone and asked the man at the desk to page Miss Jean McLain in the bar and send her up to Room 907.

"What was that for?" Rhodes asked.

"You'll see. Tell me about this man. What did he look like?"

"Like John Carradine in some old western—as if you don't know. He was standing by the side of my bed. His lips were moving. I got up and swung at him and fell down. I hit my elbow on the bedside table." He raised his robed arm to show me the bruise. "I didn't go to Oakland today," he went on. "I called it off. I want them to change my room. For one thing, it gets too damn cold in here. How did you do it, Train?"

"Winston, I didn't do a thing. This is somebody else's work. Change your room and Carradine goes with you. But his name isn't John Carradine, it's Charley Stokes. A nice guy who loved his sister. A girl," I added musingly, "who went north a hundred years ago—and maybe just recently came back."

"I don't care," he said. "I want my room changed."

"That won't do it, Winston. You've got to change your life."

"It's not fair," he said, staring back at the floor. "I can't write, I don't have the knack."

"What you need," I said, "is help. Which is just now at the door."

I went there and opened it and let Jean McLain in. She looked bewildered but lovely. "There he is," I said, "on the couch. He's not a writer, but maybe he was a miner once—God knows. Work it out for yourselves."

Then I went downstairs and spent the entire price of the book on Boodles gin poured over rocks with just a smell of vermouth. It went down my throat like a cold silken rope.

AUTHOR'S NOTE: The Inskip Inn is real.
Bob and Kathy Duffey are real.
Charley Stokes is real; I've heard him walk.
Jean McLain is real; but she doesn't know that.

Dorothy Benjamin

Things Will Look Brighter in the Morning

When I graduated Lemister High School, I wasn't so much pushed from the nest as mercilessly ejected by my mother, who declared her intention to relocate in a more equable climate. We lived forty miles from Valley Mountain, from which direction unfailingly blew icy blasts in winter and, paradoxically, a minimum of cooling breezes in summer. Painfully shy, I quailed at the prospect of being on my own and begged my mother to reconsider.

"We've taken care of you for eighteen years, Carol Ann," she said. "It's high time you began taking responsibility for yourself. Your father and I deserve time to ourselves now." Actually, my gently retiring father had little say in the matter.

With my parents gone, I settled in a boarding house, permanently I thought. But it was only the first in a series of eventful changes I'd experience in less than a year and a half. My life was by turns exciting and frightening—and overshadowed by violence.

I spent just the summer at the boarding house. Lacking a steady job, I soon fell behind in my rent. The landlady, a waspish replica of my mother, informed me I could remain provided I helped, meaning full-time work without pay. When a boarder confided that Matilda Krim, owner of a drugstore in the distant town of Tonville, was looking for a girl, I fairly flew to the bus depot.

The drugstore was similar in layout to the one in my hometown—magazine section to the side of the entrance door, soda fountain opposite, and prescription area in the rear. Tilda, as Mrs. Krim asked me to call her, was a cheery plumpish widow in her fifties. She'd run the store since her husband's death, and declared that if she could learn at her age, it ought to be a cinch for me. Mainly, I'd work at the fountain and fill in wherever there was a need.

On my very first day I faced a dilemma. In the morning, the bus brought me to work late. Then, when I informed Tilda that I'd have to leave before closing time to catch the last bus to Lemister, she told me bluntly, "This won't do, Carol Ann. If you want the job, you'll have to move to Tonville. Make up your mind now."

"I haven't the money," I said tearfully. Anyplace that I rented would require payment in advance and I had barely enough money for a few days' bus fares.

Tilda's solution was to offer me a room in her home, rent to be deducted from my salary.

"I'll be glad for your company," she said warmly. "I'm tired of rattling around alone in a big house." There was nothing to keep me in Lemister and I accepted her offer gratefully, imbued with a feeling of expectancy that life in a larger town would be more exciting than the drab restrictive existence I'd led before.

With his muscular build and rugged good looks, Sheriff Hale Esker was an impressive figure. The first time I saw him, he was accompanied by his deputy, Dewey Trant. Even without Hale's identifying badge there would have been no mistaking who had the authority.

"Sheriff, meet my new girl, Carol Ann Stow," Tilda introduced me. "From up Lemister way. Pretty little thing, isn't she?"

I was wiping the counter and flushed self-consciously under Hale's scrutiny. He affected tinted glasses which, shaded by the brim of his Stetson, imparted a subtly menacing air that I, in my naiveté, found romantic, and was smoking a stogie. "You like our town?" he asked me.

Awed by him, I mumbled, "Yes, I do," though I'd hardly seen anything of Tonville yet.

He nodded approvingly. "It's a good clean town—and I aim to keep it that way."

If Hale was an impressive figure, his deputy was the reverse. Younger than Hale, Dewey was a big, sloppy man with hooded eyes and a furtive air.

After Hale left, Dewey sidled up to the fountain and drawled, "How 'bout you and me takin' in a movie tonight?"

"I'm sorry," I stammered, disconcerted when he stalked out before I had the chance to explain I wasn't dating yet. But I wouldn't have cared to date him, in any case.

"Small potatoes. Take no mind of him," Tilda sniffed. "Thinks *he* ought to be sheriff. Hah!"

To Tilda, absolutely no one measured up to Hale. Not only had Hale received a commendation from the governor for keeping Tonville's crime rate the lowest in the entire state, but at thirty-two he was the youngest man ever to head the Association of Regional Sheriffs. Tilda admired Hale's courteous manner, totally unsuspecting that it was a deliberate pose to cloak his penchant for brutality.

I enjoyed living and working with Tilda. I was the daughter she'd never had and she clucked over me like a mother hen. And like a fond mother, she set about playing matchmaker.

While I was out on an errand, she made arrangements with Hale to take me to Tonville's annual Halloween Dance on Saturday, crowing, when I returned, that she'd snagged the town's most desirable bachelor for me.

Not only was it my first date, it was the first dance I'd ever attended, and I felt like Cinderella. With Hale my Prince Charming.

Arriving at the town hall, where the affair was held, Hale went off to confer with an official and nineteen-year-old Jimmy Fulton, who worked in his mother's bakeshop next to the drugstore, asked me to dance. It didn't enter my mind that Hale might object to my dancing with anyone else and I accepted.

Chatting while we danced, Jimmy confided his intention to drive up to Valley Mountain the next day. The mountain was considered the most scenic area in our state, and all my life I'd longed to go there.

"I've never been to Valley Mountain," I said wistfully.

"Would you like to come with me tomorrow?"

"*Would I!*" I exclaimed, with such exuberance that we laughed in unison.

I became aware that Hale was watching us. He stood glowering, with one hand balled in a fist and caressing the knuckles with the palm of his other hand—a gesture I would learn to dread. As Hale started toward us, Jimmy excused himself and left the floor.

Hale paused to say coldly, "I'll get you a cup of punch," and disappeared.

Dewey brought the punch, muttering that there was a ruckus outdoors and Hale had gone to have a "look see." His eyes raked me with hostility as he left.

As I stood sipping the punch, a friend of Jimmy's stopped to relay the rumor that the sheriff had beat up on Jimmy. "Sheriff Esker would never do anything like that," I declared loftily. Since when did Prince Charming indulge in brutality?

But when Hale appeared, his look of smug satisfaction set my nerves to jumping. I went home with a splitting headache.

On Sunday morning, Tilda, still matchmaking, invited Hale to dinner. The drugstore was open until noon and we had to hurry home to prepare the meal. I hadn't seen or heard from Jimmy since he'd left the dance floor the night before. After dinner, Hale and I went for a walk. He was so attentive and charming that I fell for him all over again, and chided myself for my nervousness the previous evening.

Several weeks passed before I saw Jimmy. Usually when he came into the store he'd order a cola, but this time he just looked at some magazines.

Noting faded marks of discoloration around his eyes, I asked, "Were you in a fight the night of the dance?"

"The sheriff pushed it on me," he said defensively.

"Why, Jimmy? What reason did he have?"

"I was horsing around outside with a couple of my friends—the sheriff knew that's all it was, but it gave him the excuse he wanted. The real reason was because you danced with me."

"Maybe he thought there really was a fight and was trying to stop it."

"You believe what you like, Carol Ann," Jimmy said bitterly. "You'll find out the truth someday."

I'd hoped Jimmy had come by to renew our Valley Mountain date, but he left without saying another word.

During a midwinter stroll, with a light snow falling, Hale proposed marriage. I'd spent every Sunday since the Halloween Dance with him and had become known as the sheriff's girl. Flattered, I fantasized that I was in love. At his urging, we set the date for early spring, after my nineteenth birthday.

Though Hale made much of my looks, what really must have appealed to him was my docility. He liked having his own way. It never occurred to him—or to me either, then—that the time might come when I'd stand up to him.

Following the wedding ceremony, I moved into Hale's house. It consisted of dark, cramped rooms cluttered with oversize furniture that I couldn't dispose of because it had belonged to Hale's mother. She had lived with him until her death.

But what I disliked most about the house was its proximity to the jail. With our back door only a few steps away, Dewey was a constant visitor.

The only consideration Hale showed for my joining his household was a new refrigerator in the kitchen. In the corner opposite the refrigerator stood a small utility table. Here, Hale would deposit his holster and revolver when he arrived home at the end of the day. I was terrified of guns and begged him to keep the revolver somewhere else, out of sight.

"I've always kept it on that table, Carol Ann, and that's where it stays," he told me.

Within a short time, life assumed a humdrum routine. Somehow, I'd expected more from marriage than just working and keeping house. Hale's idea of spending his off-duty hours was to loll about, drinking beer with Dewey and discussing the merits of various types of firearms, a topic of which they never wearied.

Our life might have continued on its dull course if I hadn't managed to persuade Hale to take me to the movies one evening. As it was, we hadn't gone anywhere since our marriage and I left the house feeling excited. The weather was balmy, a perfect June evening. While Hale drove, I mused happily that we'd stop someplace for ice cream after the movie.

As we turned into a road adjoining the highway that traversed the outer perimeter of Tonville, a car came hurtling off the highway, music blaring from a radio. Hale sped alongside, imperiously waved the teenaged boy who was driving to pull over, slammed on his brakes, and strode purposefully to the other car.

"You from Tonville?" he demanded.

"No, sir!" the boy answered fliply.

He gave the girl seated beside him an arch look, eliciting a fit of giggles from her.

"Where are you from?"

The teenager mentioned a town near Lemister.

"Then what are you doing here?" Hale snapped. "And where do you think you're going?"

"Just taking a ride, Sheriff. It's a free country, ain't it?"

The boy was asking for trouble, I thought, and then I saw Hale's balled fist, the menacing intent in the way he caressed his knuckles. I leaned out the car window. "Hale!" I called. "We'll be late!"

Hale swung around, flashed me an angry look, and swung back. But I had the teenager's attention, which was what I'd wanted. Praying that he'd understand its import, I signaled him to go back the way he'd come, breathing a sigh of relief when he said, "Okay, Sheriff, I get your message," and quickly backed up and drove off.

Hale stood staring in frustration after the car, then walked back slowly and opened the door. Glancing at me, his expression turned baleful. I felt a chill of foreboding.

"You," he snarled. "You warned him off."

Berating me for my lack of wifely loyalty, he turned the car around and sped home. Inside the house, ignoring my screams and pleas for him to stop, he beat me until, his rage expended, he dumped me on the bed and slammed out of the room.

When I hadn't shown up for work in two days, Tilda came by to check on me.

"Carol Ann, honey!" she cried. "What *happened?*"

I mumbled that I'd tripped and fallen down the stairs. Somehow, I couldn't bring myself to tell her the truth.

I returned to work on the Saturday before the Fourth of July. My body was healing, but I didn't know what to do. I was married so short a time it didn't enter my mind to leave Hale. Even if I'd thought of it, I'd have been too afraid of him to make the move. There had been no apology or word of regret from him. He acted as if the beating hadn't occurred. But it had, and the memory of it shadowed my days like a dark cloud.

On my first day back, Mark Prest walked into the store. Despite the heat, he looked fresh and cool in a crisp summer suit, his handsome face a golden tan. I guessed him to be about twenty-five. Mark introduced himself as an aide to the governor. He explained that on their way to the governor's mountain lodge to spend the holiday weekend, the governor had come down with a severe headache. He needed some aspirin.

"No need to buy any," Tilda said graciously. She shook a few aspirin tablets into a paper cup and gave it to him. "Carol Ann, dear," she said, "take a glass of water out to the governor, please."

The governor, seated in the rear of a sleek black limousine, was fatherly-looking, with a shock of silvery hair and tired eyes. "Thank you," he said, handing me the empty glass with a smile. To Mark, he said, "Shall we get going, Mark?"

Rounding the car to the driver's side, Mark whispered to me, "I'm coming by to see you again next Saturday, Carol Ann. Watch for me."

I figured he was just flirting, but true to his word he appeared on Saturday, good-humoredly bewailing the uncomfortably hot drive from the capital in his own modest car. Then, drinking a lime cooler, he exclaimed, "You're *married*, Carol Ann. I didn't notice your ring last week." He smiled ruefully. "And I drove all this way to ask you to have dinner with me. How long are you married?"

"Four months," I said. "To Hale Esker—he's sheriff here."

"I know." Mark was impressed. "You must be proud of him. He's done a great job for this town."

I nodded, wishing I had the nerve to tell him the truth about Tonville's noted sheriff.

All summer, right up to the Labor Day weekend, Mark drove up every Saturday to see me. Sipping a cold drink, he'd discuss the governor's upcoming re-election campaign. Once he confessed he'd tried to stay away and changed his mind at the last minute. I was glad. His visit was the high point of my week.

Dewey chanced into the drugstore twice while Mark was there, eyeing him with the suspicion both he and Hale reserved for strangers, but Mark's behavior was always circumspect. And I'm sure Dewey had learned that he was the governor's aide.

During the month of August, we suffered a prolonged drouth. Tilda turned on the store radio repeatedly during the day for the latest weather report. She complained that I looked peaked. I wasn't feeling well and blamed it on the heat, certain I'd recover as soon as the weather broke.

I welcomed the holiday weekend. With Hale out of town for the Regional Sheriffs' Association meeting, I counted on spending my two free afternoons, Sunday and Monday, resting.

When Mark came by the store on Saturday afternoon, he said he was staying overnight at the mountain lodge. He'd been assigned the task of drafting a speech for the governor to deliver before a labor group on Monday and planned to work on the speech in the quiet of the lodge. He was explaining that Labor Day was the traditional kickoff for a political campaign, when Tilda broke in. "Mark, would you do something for me? I'm worried about Carol Ann. She's too pale. I think she needs fresh air and the only place there is any right now is Valley Mountain. Can you spare the time to take her there for a few hours?"

"Sure," Mark said. "I'd be glad to." He turned to me. "What do you say, Carol Ann?"

As I hesitated, Tilda said, "Go, for heaven's sake. I can manage."

I could hardly believe my luck. If Hale hadn't been away at the meeting, I'd never have dared go.

When we reached Valley Mountain, I walked about in the cool, refreshing air, hugging myself with delight. In every direction there was a breathtaking view. At sunset, we sat on the terrace of the lodge watching descending peaks become bathed in a rosy hue. When the sky faded, we went inside and Mark made sandwiches and coffee. Stepping outdoors later to leave, we were held spellbound by the splendor of the night. In the mountain dark, the sky glittered with stars. Linking hands, we ran like carefree children to Mark's car.

Sunday morning, Tilda grumped about her decision to keep the store open both Sunday and Labor Day mornings. What with the heat and it being the last weekend of the summer, she was sure there would be no business. Mark stopped in for a quick goodbye. He'd worked on the speech late into the night and had overslept, so he had to drive back to the capital immediately to give the governor time to check over the speech.

"Thank you for the lovely day yesterday, Mark," I said.

He gripped my hand. "It was nice for me, too, Carol Ann. We'll go again, I promise. Listen—things will become hectic now. I won't be able to drive up here until after the election. But I'll be thinking of you."

I nodded. "I hope the governor wins."

He grinned, "I'm counting on it." He shook hands with Tilda and was heading toward the door when it opened abruptly and Hale stomped in, grim-faced, Dewey behind him.

"Hale," Tilda greeted him. "How was the meeting?" She introduced Mark. "Mr. Prest is the governor's aide."

Disregarding the introduction, Hale said, "You the guy who took my wife up to Valley Mountain yesterday?"

"Hale, you've got it all wrong." Tilda was studying his menacing face. "*I* asked Mr. Prest to take Carol Ann up there for some fresh air. Haven't you noticed how pale she is lately? Look at her. Carol Ann—*Carol Ann!*"

I had caught sight of Hale's balled fist and felt the blood drain from my face. I made a desperate grab for the edge of the counter for support, but my nerveless fingers gave way and I slumped to the floor. Mark was the first one to reach me.

"Darling, are you all right?" His anxious voice came to me as though from a distance.

Then Hale roared, *"Get away from my wife!"* and I blacked out . . .

When I came to, Mark had gone. I was seated on a chair. Tilda was hovering over me solicitously and Hale was standing near the door.

"I have some business to attend to," he told me curtly. "I'll take you home now."

"Carol Ann is in no state to be left alone, Hale," Tilda protested. "Let her come home with me and stay the night so I can keep an eye on her. You go take care of whatever it is you have to do."

Shrugging, Hale gave me an enigmatic glance, nodded to Dewey, and the two left the store.

All that day, a presentiment of impending doom hung over me. Tilda prepared light meals for lunch and supper, but I only picked at the food. Lying in bed, my spirits lifted, thinking of Mark, then succumbed to brooding despair when my mind settled on Hale. Would I suffer again at his hands?

In the middle of the night I woke up screaming. Tilda rushed to my bedside and tried to comfort me. "It's just a bad dream, dear," she said. "You're worrying too much. Things will look brighter in the morning."

But the morning was a carbon copy of every recent day—cloudless sky, burning sun, and a record high temperature. Listlessly, I followed Tilda into the store.

"Will this heat never end?" she grumbled, switching on the radio. Seconds later, we stood, stricken, listening to an announcer report that during the night governor's aide Mark Prest had been found brutally beaten. He'd undergone surgery, but had yet to regain consciousness. As the announcer noted the cancellation of the governor's scheduled Labor Day speech, I keeled over again.

Reviving me, Tilda insisted on phoning her doctor. "You've fainted twice in two days, Carol Ann. It's unnatural, even in this heat."

Despite the holiday, out of courtesy to Tilda the doctor agreed to see me in the afternoon. Before I left the store, I telephoned the hospital. Mark's condition remained unchanged.

"Please call me when you get home," Tilda said. "I want to know what the doctor says."

"I will, Tilda," I promised.

But I didn't call her. Heartsick over Mark, and tense and jumpy waiting for Hale to come home, it slipped my mind. I was seated at the kitchen table when Hale came in. Skirting my chair, he divested himself of his holster and revolver, deposited them as usual on the utility table, and went to the refrigerator for a beer.

"Hale," I said. "I have some news."

His hand on the refrigerator door, he turned and gave me a searching look.

"Yeah? What is it?"

Nervously, I stood. "I went to the doctor today. He told me I'm going to have a baby."

Hale smiled unpleasantly. "Am I supposed to believe the baby is mine?"

"Of course it's yours!" I cried.

Hale scowled. "I've heard that a guy's been driving a good distance every week just to see you."

"You're responsible for Mark's beating, aren't you?" I said. "That was your 'business' yesterday."

He made no attempt to deny it. "Some people have to be taught not to play around with another man's wife."

"Nothing happened between us, absolutely nothing."

But he wasn't listening. He was caressing his fist.

"You need a lesson, too, Carol Ann. You're gonna learn you can't make a fool of me."

Cringing in terror, I backed away from him and bumped up against the utility table. Idea and action were simultaneous. Before Hale realized it, I had his revolver in my hand. I pointed it at him, warning, "Don't come any closer!"

"You haven't the guts," he sneered. He stepped forward.

In a panic, I fired—and watched hypnotically as he staggered, then crashed to the floor. After a few minutes I came out of my daze and fell to my knees beside him. I checked his body for signs of life. There were none. Numbly, I rocked on my heels, unable to think what to do next.

The ringing of the telephone brought me to my feet.

It was Tilda. "Carol Ann, I'm sorry to be the bearer of bad news but it just came over the radio—" her voice shook "—Mark died."

I stood, immobilized, trying to absorb this latest shock. It was only two days since Mark had driven me up to Valley Mountain.

Tilda sighed. "Did you see the doctor?" she asked.

I answered dully, "I'm going to have a baby."

Tilda's voice regained vigor. "That's wonderful, dear. Now listen. Don't bother to come to the store tomorrow. I want you to stay home and rest."

I didn't have the heart to tell her that I'd probably never enter the store again . . .

For a while I paced the room, coming to a halt from time to time beside Hale's body. In a way, this was retribution, I told myself—a life for a life. Hale had caused Mark's death. Wasn't it fitting he pay with his own?

But what about Dewey? His was the initial responsibility for what had befallen Mark. The forces he'd set into motion had culminated in two deaths. And he now stood to profit from his actions.

Not if *I* have my way, I decided.

With a revived sense of purpose, I went to the telephone and dialed the jail. Dewey answered.

"Hale has been shot," I told him. "He's lying here on the kitchen floor."

"Is he—dead?"

"Yes."

Dewey hung up quickly, but not before I had caught the rising tone of exultance in his voice. He was already anticipating himself as the new sheriff.

Grimly, I began preparing for Dewey's visit. Opening the kitchen door wide, I unlatched the screen door. There was a rumble of thunder and I glanced at the twilight sky. Ominous dark clouds were rolling in. The weather was going to break at last. Retrieving the revolver from where I'd dropped it, I sat down at the kitchen table and waited for Dewey.

Theodore de la Torre Bueno
The Murder of the Governor

The assassins were on their way to murder the Governor. The news swept through the city like leaves driven before the wind. It flew through the streets and to the four corners of the plaza, and at last it reached the doors of the high house of the Governor.

The Governor rose to his full height. Grim, grey, and old, he was still a powerful figure. The Governor crossed himself, called for his body armor and sword, and sent for his brother.

Nothing was heard in the streets but the heavy tramp of twenty pairs of conquistador boots as the Almagrists marched shoulder to shoulder, their hands on their sword-hilts. The news flying on the wind had emptied the streets and filled the courtyards. In the shadows, hundreds of eyes watched as the assassins marched by with their cockades in their caps. Even the dogs were silent.

The Governor stood erect, waiting for his armor and for his brother. So death was coming for him after all these years. Death which a thousand times had taken his comrades at his right and left hands, death which a thousand times had cut down Spain's enemies before his eyes, death which he himself had inflicted a hundred times. Death did not daunt him. He would meet death like a Castilian and hidalgo. (Of course, like all of us in those days he was an Extremaduran, but of course all of us in those days referred to ourselves as Castilians.)

The page boy came running with the sword, as was his duty. The Governor bethought what he faced and said to the boy: "Thanks."

The pretty page blushed. He had never before heard that word from the Governor.

The ugly page came running with the body armor. Solid and stolid, he said nothing. The two page boys fell to arming the Governor, buckling on the pair of breast plates. It was the pretty little page, Tordoya, who had brought the news of the Almagrists' coming. The

ugly big page, Vargas, looked as he always did, like one in dire
straits—as indeed he was.

The assassins were marching down the main street that led from
their lodging into the principal plaza. There were Pérez, Bilbao,
Narváez, Barragán, and the other Knights of the Cape, and behind
them marched the followers of the Almagrists.

Juan de Rada was the leader of the assassins. You could tell he
was the leader by his look of command, by his position in the center,
and by the fact that he wore the cape. The faction of Almagro, under
house arrest in Lima, were so poor that they could afford but one
cape among them, wearing it out to the paseo or to market. So it
came about that the wits of the Spanish capital on the coast had
dubbed them the Knights of the Cape. Today Juan de Rada wore
the cape and it was their day to avenge the executed Almagro.

Juan de Rada, older than the others, looked like one bent and
broken on the wheel of life. Bent over with arthritis, gnomelike,
with a face darkened and lined like that of some wise monkey of
the rainforest, Juan de Rada was accounted one of the best brains
in all of Peru. So he marched at the head of his faction, and they
walked down the main street toward the principal plaza, where the
Governor's palace stood across from the cathedral.

The Governor's brother hurried into the room in his body armor
and carrying his sword. Shorter and much younger than the Governor, the young brother was of humble birth, while the elder was
the son of an hidalgo. The two brothers embraced briefly, then the
younger guarded the door while the elder went on arming. The
Governor was in his small-clothes, having taken off the scarlet robe
in which he had been playing the host at luncheon, and it lay on
the floor like a harbinger of things to come. He had kicked off his
alpargatas and put on his white boots. The Governor had not grown
stout, but he was stouter than when he had last worn his body armor
and the two page boys struggled with the straps and buckles.

In this moment, both men knowing what was to come, it is likely
that each of the two brothers would have thought about their
mother . . .

The pretty Francisca stood by the well and raised her head to
listen. She knew the voice and recognized the sound of the lute: it
was the young hidalgo whose attentions had caused her, an honest

girl, to be sent here to the convent by her respectable working-class parents. Not indeed as a postulant (for all the nuns were from families of the better classes) but as servant girl to the good holy sisters. She heard a scrambling on the outside of the convent wall, and there he stood silhouetted against the sun: her Gonzalo. With a graceful leap, he landed lightly on his feet and took her in his arms—her hidalgo who could not be avoided or denied.

In due time then, Francisca was brought to bed and delivered of a man child, not within the sacred precinct but in the home of her humble parents. The boy was named Francisco after his mother. Francisco (now the Governor) retained a memory picture of Francisca as his beautiful girl-mother, like the Blessed Virgin in the paintings in the church. The picture stood apart from his dim memories of the humble home of her parents—his grandparents, the old-clothes merchants. This was before he was sent away, first to herd the pigs and then to follow the soldiers. The picture of his mother was the only tender memory the Governor conserved out of a long and a hard life.

The handsome Francisca later stood before the altar in her parents' parish church and was honorably married to a man of the commons, one Tal de Alcántara. Her beloved bastard was gone for a soldier, her hidalgo lover was long since married in his own class and off to the wars, and Francisca was starting over. San Martín was a favorite saint of the working people because he divided his cloak with a beggar, and his name she gave to her son born in wedlock.

The boy, Martín, was to remember his mother as strong and still beautiful, her face lined and her hair already grey by the hard life and hard work of the working people. Martín was a good boy and worked alongside his parents, but in Extremadura in those years what could a young man do, whether he was of the commons or of the classes? So Martín, too, had gone for a soldier. And he had stayed in the ranks until, like a folk tale come true, his hidalgo brother had appeared from the other world as the conqueror and Governor of golden Peru . . .

The Governor, body armor half on and hanging down, turned to the page boys and said, "Hurry." The page boys hurried. Nobody said "wait" to the Governor.

The assassins had come to where the street led into the plaza.

Here the ground settled and a standing pool of water was enriched with horse piss and dung. Juan de Rada and most of the men walked straight through the puddle, but the man on the outside skirted around the edge. Juan de Rada stopped.

"Go back," he said. Juan de Rada, bent on the wheel of life, his cape dripping, stared down Pérez, the miscreant. "Go back. We are about to wade in human blood, and you cannot wade in water and piss. Go back." Head down, Pérez turned and walked back to the lodging of the Knights of the Cape.

It was high noon on the Sunday after San Juan's Day. South of the equator this meant that it was midwinter. Under a leaden sky, the people of Lima were coming out of the cathedral after High Mass. As the Almagrists walked shoulder to shoulder across the plaza, hands on sword-hilts, the masses of the faithful parted to left and to right and the wits of the paseo said, "At last they are going to murder the Governor."

The Governor stood in the room at the head of the stairs with his brother at his right hand and a guest at his left hand. The other luncheon guests had left, some by the doors and some by the windows, and the host had put down the Guadalajara pitcher in which he was serving Peruvian wine from his own vines.

Who was he, this guest who had stayed while the others had gone? What was his name? His name was Don Gómez de Luna. What kind of man was he? He was an hidalgo.

The Governor had held the faction of Almagro in such contempt that he had not mounted any guard in spite of their threats. So this was his guard in the final moment: one luncheon guest, two page boys, and his brother. It was in God's hands. He had stood with six, he had stood with twelve, and he would stand with three. (For in the field arithmetic of the illiterate captain-general, two boys or Indians stood for one man.)

Where were they now, those six brave men who had gone with him to the conquest of an Indian kingdom in Panama when he was a captain under Balboa, and they had come back seven men gravely wounded?

Where were they now, those twelve brave men who had stood with him on the Isle of Gallo when all the others had turned back from the conquest of Peru? Where was Sancho de Cuellar, scribe of the twelve, who had acted as court reporter at the trial of the Emperor of the Incas? Captured and garroted by the Indians in revenge.

Where was Don Juan de la Torre, last and longest lived of those twelve heroes of Gallo? Keeping law and order and teaching the Indians their doctrine in the white city of Arequipa, which he, de la Torre, had founded under the volcano, El Misti.

Where were they now, those four faithful brothers Pizarro who had come with him and his partner Almagro to the final conquest of the golden realm of Peru?

Hernando Pizarro, the hidalgo—the legitimate son of old Don Gonzalo—he who had ordered the execution of Almagro in the civil war, where was he? Back in Spain to plead the cause of the brothers, and imprisoned without charges or trial. Well did Francisco Pizarro remember how he himself had ridden out of Lima to stop the execution of his old comrade-in-arms, and how after an all-night ride he had met in the vale of Abancay, between the Andes and the Andes, the messenger from Cuzco with news of the execution. But the execution of Almagro was his own responsibility in the end, and Francisco Pizarro accepted the consequences of it.

Juan Pizarro, the warrior—old Don Gonzalo's son by his servant girl, María Alonso—he who had led the troops in the battle for Cuzco, the Inca capital in the mountains, where was he? Killed under the massive stone fortress, Sacsahuaman, by a great rock hurled down—beside him the body of Cahuide, the Incan chieftain who had thrown himself down off the fortress.

Gonzalo Pizarro, the princely—old Don Gonzalo's son by his servant girl, María Biedma—he who was the hope of all to carry on the government of Peru for the conquistadors, where was he? Far beyond the Andes Mountains in the headwaters of the Amazon River, seeking the Land of Cinnamon to add to the conquests of Pizarro for the crown of Castilla and of León.

Martín de Alcántara, the laborer and new hidalgo—not the son of old Don Gonzalo but son-of-a-mother with Francisco—where was he? Here by Francisco's side.

The assassins reached the great double door of the high house of the Governor of Peru.

Juan de Rada drew his sword and gave the order to rush the doors before they could be closed. He and his men crowded through the great iron-bound double doors into the entrance portico and slew one of the few servants who tried to fill the place of the absent guards.

De Rada took off the black cape and wrapped it around his left arm for a shield. He was wearing shiny new body armor. He gave the order and the assassins rushed up the stairs. At the top of the stair one of the guests who had left and then returned, Chávez, tried to parley with the Almagrists. He was stabbed and thrown down the steps, dying.

Governor Pizarro heard the clatter of boots on the stairs. His brother Martín stood at his right hand and his luncheon guest Don Gómez stood at his left hand. "Stand behind me, boys," said the Governor to the pages. His unbuckled armor hung down like the wing cases of a beetle in flight. He picked up his scarlet robe and wrapped it around his left arm for a shield. Then the three men drew their swords and crossed themselves with the hilts.

As Francisco drew his sword from its scabbard, he muttered a pagan invocation which had stood him in good stead in a thousand scrimmages: "Come to me, companioness of my labors."

As Martín de Alcántara drew, he said within himself: My brother, son of my mother.

As Don Gómez de Luna drew, he said nothing. Of him it had been said one thousand five hundred and forty-one years before: "Greater love than this hath no man, that he lay down his life for his friend."

The pretty boy drew his short-sword and made the sign of the cross, his mouth a tight line and his eyes brimming with tears. The ugly boy did the same, stolid as ever. As he drew, the pretty little page said: "Our father, who art in heaven . . . " As he drew, the ugly big page said: "Hail Mary, full of grace . . . "

Here stood the Governor, Francisco Pizarro, Marquis of Spain, in a room with one door, a room of the same size and shape as the one in which he had imprisoned the Emperor of the Incas and which the Inca had half filled with gold before Pizarro ordered his execution. Here in this room Pizarro stood with three, as he had stood with six and with twelve.

The door was flung open and the Almagrists crowded between the jambs. Juan de Rada's gnomelike face thrust into the room down low. The ten Knights of the Cape formed a corolla around and above him and eleven bloody swords projected through the doorway. The second rank of Almagrists, back in the shadows, filled the short corridor to the stair landing and waved their bright swords. Standing on the threshold, Rada looked like an angry bee in a flower whose petals were spokes of steel.

The Governor spoke, looking down the shining blade over the scarlet robe: "Be gone, traitors."

Juan de Rada spoke, looking down the bloody blade over the black cape: "Almagro shall be avenged."

The men at left and right jamb leaped into the room. Gómez de Luna and Martín de Alcántara stepped forward and parried. A clash of steel and a thrust, then Gómez de Luna fell dead without a word, but one assassin went down with him, skewered on his sword. Martín staggered back, wounded and bleeding. The Governor thrust, parried, and feinted, making the rest of the attackers stand back on the sill.

Two more Knights leaped over the doorsill into the room. Martín staggered forward, and with his workingman's arm he smashed one man's sword aside and ran the other man through. Then he slumped from loss of blood and the first man stabbed him in the throat. Martín fell dead on top of the man he had killed. Once more the Governor's swordplay held the rest of the pack at bay.

Without turning his head or taking his eyes off the corolla of sword points, Francisco Pizarro said: "Adios, hermanito," which means: To God, little brother.

Martín, the former workingman, had said "Thanks" to the little page several times in his life. The pretty page boy leaped in front of the Governor and with his little sword held straight out he ran at Juan de Rada, the shortest of the assassins. A tall Almagrist leaned down and ran his sword into the boy's chest. The Governor's sword flashed silver and came back scarlet.

The boy fell dead, eyes half closed, mouth half open. He had not cried. Now the blood and tears poured out together. His killer fell beside him, tall head to little feet.

The big page leaped around the Governor and ran at Juan de Rada and almost got to him. Another Almagrist stepped forward and caught the boy on his sword point. With a slashing stroke, the Governor cut the man's throat. Blood spattered up the wall as high as the Inca gold had reached. Two more bodies slumped onto the floor.

Juan de Rada pulled his men back into the doorway. Four of the attackers lay dead at his feet and the Governor had not been touched.

Breathing heavily, covered with sweat, Francisco Pizarro stood firmly in his white boots while his slate-grey eyes blazed at them over the scarlet robe and his bloody sword-point went back and forth in front of them like a snake. His breast plates hung down in front and he said without knowing what he said: "Die, villains!"

Juan de Rada grabbed the man at his right, who was Narváez, by the scruff of the neck. "Die for Almagro!" said Juan de Rada, and so saying he threw Narváez onto the point of Pizarro's sword.

Narváez went down, dying, and Pizarro put his foot on the man's chest, but before he could pull out the sword Juan de Rada had run him through. The Governor slumped to his knees. The Knights of the Cape crowded into the room and ran their swords into his body. As each of the assassins struck, like one of Brutus's conspirators, he shouted a slogan such as "Death to the tyrant!" The Governor slumped to the floor. The murderers pulled out their swords and, in the rough chivalric code of their race, stood back to let their man die his own death.

In a later age, another great Spaniard, whose conquests in art equalled the Governor's conquests in arms, would say that if imprisoned by fascism he would open his veins and draw one last painting with his own blood. Picasso, Pizarro. The Marquis Governor was illiterate and could not write or sign his own name.

Slowly, painfully, Pizarro raised his head. His blood was pumping out. He had seen so many men, boys, and animals die that there was no doubt of this moment. Very slowly, very painfully, Francisco Pizarro raised his right hand and dipped it into his blood. Then this illiterate Marquis reached out and on the floor he drew a cross with his own blood. The Governor Marquis Francisco Pizarro spoke one word: "Jesús."

He leaned down his head and kissed the cross drawn on the floor. Then he collapsed. His head rolled over onto one side. His slate-grey eyes, half closed, stared into eternity. And on his grim mouth, half open in a tender smile, was imprinted the cross of blood.

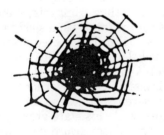

Hillary   Waugh

The   Beneficiaries

"The evidence might be circumstantial, Captain," the young
detective said, "but the gardener did it and no question. Come
around to the broken window and I'll show you." Pointing his flashlight, the young detective led the Captain to the rear of the large
mansion. A light gleamed through the narrow, shattered casement
window of the upstairs bedroom, faintly lighting the soft earth of
the garden underneath.

"Go careful, sir," the young detective warned. "I fenced off the
clues with sticks and string to keep them untouched." He played the
beam of his flash on the soft trammeled dirt enclosed by twine and
stakes. "The story tells itself," he explained proudly. "Let me show
you." He pointed his flash. "There are the marks where he set the
ladder. Here, where the broken glass is lying on top of the footprints,
is where he stood before he climbed up to rob the safe and stab the
old man to death to keep from being recognized. Here, where the
glass has been pressed into the dirt, is where he came down with
the old man's money." The young detective grinned. "And that's not
all. If you'll follow me over to the shed, sir, I'll show you the rest."

The weathered shed was fifty feet behind the mansion, halfway
to the cottage the gardener shared with his deaf wife. "Look," said
the young detective, taking the Captain inside, "here's the very
ladder, put back where he took it. He thought no one would ever
know, but see there, on the bottom of the side rails? See the earth?
It's from the garden, you can tell, and not even dry yet. And here!"
He moved on with excitement. "The overalls hanging on the hook
here. The gardener's overalls. You might want to feel into the left-
hand pocket, Captain. You'll be interested in what you find."

The Captain explored the pocket and came out with a small folded
paper on which was written: L30-R4-L10.

"You want to guess what that is?" The young detective beamed.

"I'd rather you tell me," the Captain answered.

"It's the combination to the old man's safe. You want to know
what was in the safe—what *used* to be in the safe? Fifty thousand
dollars—what old Mr. Brewster kept on hand for pin-money, you
might say. And do you know where *that* is?" The young detective

119

couldn't wait for an answer. He leaped to a toolbox sitting on the dirt floor against the wall nearby. The tools under the upper tray had been dumped into a handy cardboard carton and in their stead lay a small ivory chest with the name *Brewster* embossed on it in silver. It bore no lock and when the young detective lifted its lid, neatly bound stacks of hundred-dollar bills were revealed, filling it to its brim.

"Open-and-shut case," the young detective announced. "I only left the money here for you to see it the way I found it. Shall we take it with us now?"

"It would be a good idea," the Captain said drily. "I wouldn't want to see it stolen a second time."

"Don't worry, sir. I've had an eye on this shed every second."

"Besides the gardener and his deaf wife, who else lives on the estate?" the Captain asked, leading the way back to the mansion.

"Well, Mr. Brewster had a butler and a part-time cook and a cleaning woman who came in once a week—"

The Captain stopped. "I asked you who *lives* on the estate, not who works here."

"Oh, yes." The young detective's grin was now definitely uneasy. "There's the gardener. And Wallace, of course. He's been Mr. Brewster's faithful manservant for nearly twenty years. And there's Miss Young, the nurse Brewster hired when he took sick last year. She's a pretty thing. I don't know how competent she is."

The scene of the crime was Mr. Brewster's bedroom and it was not a pretty sight. The wizened old man lay half on and half off the bed. There were deep stab wounds in his chest and blood everywhere. The casement window had been pulled wide, the glass shattered all round the inside handle. The wall safe lay exposed and open, its contents, except presumably for the ivory box, scattered on the desk beneath, the wall plaque which had hidden its location face-down on the foor.

The Captain assessed the scene and called in the members of the household. First was Wallace, the butler, who was six feet two and a man of tremendous girth and thinning grey hair. It was he, Wallace said, who had discovered the body. He had awakened without knowing why, but with a sense of unease. At first he tried to go back to sleep, then decided to have a look around. The first thing he saw was light shining under the master's bedroom door at the end of the hall, past the nurse's room. He had knocked and entered to see if all was well, only to find the master dead and bloody on his bed, the narrow casement window broken and open, and the contents of the safe scattered on his desk, except for his ivory money box. As soon as he determined that the master was beyond help, he hurried to the phone to call the police.

Amy Young was next. She was young and blonde, probably not yet thirty, and she broke down at the sight of the old man's body. "I loved him," she cried. "We were to be married next month." The Captain noted a generous diamond ring on the third finger of her left hand. She wiped mascara-stained teardrops from her face. "Who could have wanted to harm such a dear old man?"

"How long have you worked for him?" the Captain asked.

"Six months," she wept. "Since just before Thanksgiving. He was ailing badly. Wallace could no longer take care of him."

The gardener was last. He was a slight man, rail-thin and angry. "You aren't going to blame this on me," he said, gesturing at the open window and the safe's contents scattered on the desk. "I was home asleep when this young detective came knocking on the door. Somebody else broke in and killed the old gentleman, not I."

"Can you support your alibi?" asked the Captain. "Your wife will so testify?"

"My wife, who's been stone deaf for five years? Not likely. When she sleeps, she can't hear nothing, she can't see nothing. She's as good as dead. And she wouldn't if she could. She'd like to see me hang."

When the Captain dismissed the gardener, the young detective said, "Aren't you going to arrest him?"

"Not yet," the Captain answered, going to sort through the strewn papers that had been tumbled from the safe. After a while he said to the young detective, "Call Wallace back in here, if you please."

The massive butler reentered the bedroom, puzzled. "You asked for me, Captain?"

"I did. Would you know what this paper is?" He held it up.

"It looks like Mr. Brewster's will, sir."

"Do you know what's in it?"

"Yes, sir. He made no secret of it, sir. Upon his death, the gardener and I would split the property, one third for him, two thirds for me."

"And you knew that once Mr. Brewster married Nurse Young, all that would change. So you decided to kill him before he could rewrite his will. And you thought if in the doing you could frame the gardener to take the blame, you just might end up with the whole estate. Isn't that right?"

"Sir, my apologies, but you must be crazy. Even if I wanted to do such a deed, there's no way I could have got through that narrow window."

"Nobody came through that window, Wallace. All you did was prop a ladder against the house, kill Mr. Brewster, open the safe, break the window, then replace the ladder, putting Mr. Brewster's money box in the gardener's toolbox and the combination to the safe in his overalls pocket."

It took three patrolmen to overcome the ox-strong Wallace and take him downtown to be booked. The Captain then turned to the young detective. "Let that be a lesson to you," he said. "You must analyze all the evidence you find carefully. It's too easy to leap to wrong conclusions."

"But how did you know it was a frame?" the young detective said, the easy confidence gone from his face.

"The broken glass," the Captain explained. "If the window had been broken from the outside, the glass would have been all over the carpet. But it was out in the garden, which indicated the window had been broken from the bedroom. That made it more than likely to be an inside job, with Wallace and the nurse the most likely suspects.

"Miss Young's engagement ring pretty well told the story and pointed the finger at Wallace. But it was the will that solidified my suspicions about him. It will take a judge and jury to justify them now."

Fred Burgess

Exit, Stage Right

The idea in a battle is that nobody gets hurt. While I'm not the ranking expert, I've staged fights in shows from *Macbeth* to *West Side Story,* and the worst injury for one of my warring actors was a twisted ankle from an overly enthusiastic leap. Then I took on *The Brave Banners.*

That's one of these quasi-historical dramas performed outdoors, usually hailing the region's Most Famous Historic Figure, usually ten percent history and the rest the playwright's imagination. But *The Brave Banners* did have a full-scale battle scene in Act One and a free-for-all fistfight in Act Two, and when director Tony Parent insisted I coordinate these scenes I figured I'd enjoy it more than spending the summer with those regular-semester Fs who go to summer school trying to pull their grades up to C level.

In the final week of rehearsals, Tony Parent finally quit equivocating and begged me to play the role I'd been taking on more and more in the practices because the actors who tried the character couldn't do the fighting. And so suddenly I was going to spend the rest of the summer commanding a battalion of His Majesty's loyal Highlanders in the famous Battle of Wherethehell, leading my band of kilted performers to nightly disaster at the hands of the gallant American rebels, commanded of course by the Most Famous Historic Figure. Six nights each week (no show on Mondays), I would wrap on my kilt, carefully drape my Clan Ross plaid on the left shoulder, tuck my *sgian dubh* into the right stocking top, strap on my claymore, and, after a pleasantly competent but increasingly sisterly kiss from the third girl and an increasingly heated argument with the assistant stage manager, march bravely forth to my certain but spectacular fate. Afterwards, I would go up to the air-conditioned control booth and watch the rest of the show with refrigerated refreshments. Not much pay, true, but not a lot of work, either. In fact, quite enjoyable—until during the third performance of the second week, the assistant stage manager was shot to death.

The victim was Rodney Barlow, rising senior drama major at State. Low B student, Low C assistant stage manager. F as an actor, which was why he had been tagged as assistant to stage manager Charles Tunnell. Barlow was one of the worst of the mistakes Tony Parent made when he selected his cast and crew. But we had him and we had to live with him—until he wasn't living any more.

Barlow was a tall, thin kid who talked incessantly about himself. No matter what anybody had done or was doing, Barlow had done it, too, and better. And he had the impression that part of the assistant stage manager's duty was "improving" the scenes. I came down on him when I heard him instructing one of my Scots to run a route different from the way I'd designed it. I came down on him harder the next night when he improved the battle by firing off the pyrotechnic special effects in an unfamiliar sequence, leaving us on stage wondering when the next charge was going off—and where.

The next night he left the battle alone but improved the placing of furniture for a touching scene between the Most Famous Historic Figure and the girl he loved but couldn't marry, a shift that meant Dewayne May, as the M.F.H.F., would have been totally upstaged if he'd stuck to Barlow's blocking. I don't know if Barlow's oft-voiced opinion that he should have been cast in the lead role had anything to do with that, but Dewayne offered to give him broadsword lessons and Cynthia, who played his loved one and broke character because she couldn't improvise very well, swore she would poison whatever Barlow drank if she could figure out what it was.

His rearranging the furniture didn't bother me so much—a competent performer can see where a physical object is located and act around it—but rearranging the pyrotechnics did bother me because one doesn't see them until they ignite and that's a very good way to get somebody hurt.

On the night Barlow was killed, I began to get concerned when the fourth cannon salvo wasn't fired.

The plot for the Battle of Whocareswhere called for a first blast in darkness, to begin the scene. Area lights rose and the Americans, led by Dewayne as the M.F.H.F., took positions along the downstage apron. Second cannon salvo: the Highlanders appeared atop the upstage parapet, Rebel rifles fired. I leaped off the parapet and took position center stage. Dewayne ran forward, waving his cutlass and yelling. I waved my claymore and yelled back. As the third cannon salvo was fired, our blades met.

The blast came, I started a slash, and jumped aside as something stung me on the outside of my left knee.

"Sorry," I told Dewayne and repeated the basic movement. He

blocked my cut, but the impact knocked the sword from his hand, right on cue. He whirled, dived for it, as I lifted my single-shot pistol and fired it, aiming at the stage right palisades to keep him out of line in case the wadding didn't burn off cleanly. He retrieved his sword, charged back, and that was where the fourth cannon salvo was supposed to fire the cue for the rest of the Highlanders to engage the rebels in individual combat.

No fourth cannon salvo. No Highlanders attacking on cue.

Dewayne and I locked swords, hilt to hilt, hands grasping wrists, and with his face inches from mine Dewayne asked, "What's happening?"

"Nothing, damn it!" I whispered. "Come on, let's make it happen!"

I broke the lock, took two quick steps back, turned upstage, and yelled as loudly as I could, "Charge!" Dewayne, catching on quickly, faced his troops and cried, "At 'em, men!"

Happy to have something to do, the two armies came together, and Dewayne and I renewed our duel. He swung. I ducked and thrust. He blocked and thrust. I parried and made a terrific low swing, clanging my blade on the concrete as he jumped over it. I blocked his cut, slashed again, lifted my claymore high, and he thrust expertly, his cold steel piercing that inevitably fatal spot between body and upstage arm. I sank down, mortally wounded.

Taking their cue from their brave leader, the other Highlanders began to die. As the area lights faded, leaving Dewayne and his comic-relief sergeant in a spotlight, only the Americans were left alive. In the darkness, we dead men picked ourselves up and joined the survivors filtering silently offstage.

I went directly to the first-aid station. The sting, bite, or whatever on my knee had puffed up to about the size of a dime. There was a spot of almost-dry blood. I squeezed it, and along with fluid there was a speck of grey. An insect's stinger? I cleaned the area with antiseptic, covered it with a plastic strip, and moved around to the property shed. There I gave my pistol to Charles and my sword to the prop mistress, Lillie. "What happened to the fourth salvo?" I asked Charles.

"Who knows!" he snarled. "I'm sure Barlow doesn't. Maybe a wire broke. Or a fuse blew. Or Barlow went to sleep. Or Barlow went home."

He finished clearing the pistol and handed it over to Lillie to be cleaned and stored. His attention shifted and he barked, "All right, third scene finale! Flute and drums! Dancers! Where's that damned second girl?"

He hurried off and I watched a while as he tried to separate cast from chorus in the near-dark offstage, then I went on to the robing shed. The Scots and the rebels had already made their costume changes and were gone, but Dewayne was still there, and so was the damned second girl (Jerri? Terri?), who was chirping through a one-sided conversation that seemed intended to arouse his amorous interest. She didn't know.

"Pardon," I told her, "but I think Charles is wanting you." She listened to the stage sounds coming through the robing-shed loudspeaker, then squeaked and fled.

I began to divest myself of the Highlander outfit while Dewayne was getting into his suit for the next scene.

"What do you think happened to our cannons?" he said, pulling on a pair of knee britches.

"Charles said it might have been a blown fuse or maybe a broken wire. Or Barlow might just have gone home."

"Wonderful thought," Dewayne said. He studied himself in the mirror. The former rebel, now very nearly a prosperous farmer and merchant just elected to the young state's legislature, carefully adjusted his stock and placed a tricorn precisely atop his powdered wig.

"By the way, Trooper, a group of us are having an after-the-show party Saturday night. I confess I don't know which way you swing—I don't even know if you *do* swing—but we'd be happy to have you come by for a drink, at least."

"Thank you, Dewayne. I'll see."

"Which probably means no. You ought to come by, Trooper. You don't know what you'll be missing."

As an exit line, it rated about a one on the proverbial scale of ten, but it got him into a graceful bow and out.

I hung my Highlander costume on the rack, got into my real-world uniform of corduroy jeans, knit shirt and moccasins, said good night to the wardrobe mistress, and exited. I went through the side-stage gate, up the hill, through the parking lot, in the main entrance, and up to the control booth.

In the booth, Larry, the technical director, handed me a can of beer without looking away from the stage. Tony Parent, headset hanging around his neck and only slightly more distraught than usual, was at it before I could get the top popped.

"What happened in Scene Two?"

"Everybody's asking the same question, Tony."

"Well," he said, "it was nice, the way you and Dewayne covered. I've been trying to get Barlow on the phones, but either he's refusing to answer or he's not wearing his headset."

Tony is a decent enough chap, but he's the kind of director who takes a play from line to line and never quite sees the entire work as a single statement. In real life, he's much the same. He runs from crisis to crisis.

But while he was concerned about Barlow not answering the phone, I was beginning to be more concerned about the unfired effects. The fourth cannon salvo had six charges, all at ground level, and there were some people in the cast who didn't know where they were. I could just imagine Barlow deciding to plug the cannon into, say, the ballroom scene.

"Look," Tony said, "everybody else on the hookup is too busy to check and see what's going on with Barlow. Could you—I mean—"

I looked at my can of beer. It was the first of what had become a customary three during the rest of the play.

"You don't have anything else to do right now," he persisted. "How about going down there and finding out what Barlow thinks he's doing."

"Sure," I said, draining the beer.

Backstage, I cut through the darkness in the right wings to the assistant stage manager's station.

Barlow was there, wearing his headset. But he hadn't answered his phone because he was unconscious and bleeding.

I worked the assistant stage manager's station for the remainder of the performance, after the company paramedic summoned a silent ambulance and Barlow was removed to the county hospital a mile away.

The cast knew something had gone wrong, but nobody knew exactly what. It pains me to recall what was on my mind. I wasn't thinking about the kid on the operating table. I was thinking that I was two beers behind schedule and probably not going to catch up. I was thinking how much fun it was to be doing tech after so many years. I was thinking of the increasingly sisterly third girl.

When the county sheriff's chief investigator arrived after the performance, it took me a moment to figure out why he seemed familiar. Then I made the connection.

We'd already met, at three one morning during the first week of rehearsals, one of those nights when I wasn't sleeping. I had discovered the 420 Truck Stop, only 24-hour place within fifty miles. I had eaten an omelette, drunk coffee, smoked a cigarette, read the first edition of the morning paper from the city, and listened to crossover country from the radio behind the counter. Gradually, I realized I had company.

He was about my age, a little better than average size. In khaki windbreaker and cap, he looked like a trucker or somebody getting an early start to the coast for a little surfcasting. He struck up a conversation but I never got his name and occupation. In fact, when I thought about it later I realized there was a lot I didn't get while he had been learning a lot about me. It was a very efficient grilling.

Now I learned his name was Autry. He was wearing a neutral grey suit, well pressed despite the heat and humidity. He was hatless, revealing the most impressive pompadour I've seen north of the 1950s. His maroon tie was knotted just below the collar button and his shoes had the immaculate gloss impossible for anybody who isn't retired military. At our first meeting, I'd have described his eyes as sleepy. Now I recognized them as sniper's eyes, inured to patient waiting for that single instant when the target presents itself in the sights.

Those eyes were fixed on the stage, where the cast and crew were gathered, talking among themselves in little clusters. A squad of deputies was circulating.

"I load every one of the firearms," Charles was answering his question. "It's a fundamental safety rule, to make certain each gun contains nothing but blanks. I check every weapon when it's issued to the performer and when it comes back, to make sure there aren't any unfired charges."

"Uh-huh," Autry said encouragingly.

"You have to be very careful with firearms onstage," Charles went on. "Even blanks can do a lot of damage."

"Uh-huh," said Autry. "Look, Charles, blanks aren't supposed to leave holes in people. This guy was shot with a bullet."

"But we don't use real bullets," Charles protested.

"Somebody did," Autry observed. "Somebody sure as hell did."

I made a contribution. "We do try to follow some basic safety procedures, Chief, and we drill the actors who are going to use weapons just as if they were out on the firing range. The first rule is never to point any shot in the direction of the audience. The second is never to aim directly at another member of the cast."

"I assume," Autry remarked drily, "it's acceptable to aim directly at the crew members." He turned to Charles again. "How many pieces are onstage in that battle scene?"

Charles said, "Trooper has the only handgun, a single-shot muzzle-loader."

Autry's eyelids lifted. "An antique?"

"No, it's designed for stage use. And we have a dozen rifles. The patriots carry them. They ought to be muzzle-loaders, too, but we use repeaters so we can have what looks like more firepower in the scene."

"I don't think a shot could have come from the rebels," I said. "They're spread out along the front of the stage—most of them can't even see Barlow's station from there. Anyway, they're supposed to shoot upstage. I can't swear to it, but all the muzzle flashes seemed to be in that direction tonight."

"Who in the cast shoots in another direction?"

"I do," I replied. "I fire one shot at—oh."

"It had to come from somewhere out here," Autry said. "I don't think it could have come from behind him. Let's say somebody's shot. Chances are they're going to fall in the direction the gun is aimed. Bullet hits them from the front, they'll probably fall backward. You say you found Barlow lying on his back, head that way, feet here. For now, let's assume the bullet came from the stage area."

"Maybe one of the actors smuggled in a, say, a .38 and while he was shooting off blanks in one direction, he was taking a real crack at Barlow."

"That's possible," I said. "It's also possible somebody was in the opposite wings with a gun."

Autry nodded. He called to a deputy. "Everybody here? I mean, *everybody?*"

Assured they were, he climbed onstage. I followed and so did Tony Parent.

Autry took a couple of steps toward the apprehensive assembly, looking down with curiosity at the white marks on the boards.

"What are these?" he asked, stopping.

"Markers," I explained. "This one is where Dewayne and Cynthia play their second-act romantic scene. This one here is where the preacher stands for the funeral. This one over here is where Dewayne and I meet for our swordfight—where we're supposed to meet, I mean. The idea is, if you're on your marker the lighting is correctly focused on you."

"Doesn't the audience see them?"

Tony Parent finally found his voice. "Oh, yes," he said, "but they're not that obtrusive. The audience forgets about them."

I added, "They don't mean much to the average person seeing the show. Sometimes even the actors don't see them."

Autry gave me a cool look, then addressed the cast and crew. "Well, now, ladies and gentlemen, as I'm sure you all know by now, there's been a serious accident here, and this department is responsible for investigating it. It's getting late and if you're like me you don't want to stay here any longer than you have to. If everybody will cooperate, we'll all get home earlier."

He paused. "Now, here's what I'm going to ask from everyone here. I want each of you to give one of these officers your very best recollection of exactly where you were and, if possible, exactly what you were doing from the end of the first scene to the end of the battle scene. I am for the moment presuming the accident occurred within that time because Mr. Barlow didn't answer his phone after the battle scene."

He took a couple of slow, deliberate steps. "Just two more things. Don't leave tonight without making sure we have your name and address—where you live here, not your home address. And I'm afraid we're going to have to search you."

"That's unconstitutional!" somebody exclaimed.

"So is shooting folks," Autry agreed pleasantly. "Don't misunderstand. I don't mean a pat-and-poke. We've got one of those metal-detector gadgets like you see in airports. We won't touch anyone unless that thing thinks it smells metal and beeps. If it does, we'll want to know what made it beep. What we're looking for is a weapon. I don't give a damn about anything else you might happen to be carrying. Got it?"

It looked like everybody, actors and crew—and deputies—got it.

"Fine," said Autry. "You first, little lady."

He pointed to the ranking feminist in the company and she exploded to her feet, primed to react to Autry's term of address, but when she saw the sniper gaze in those eyes, she bit back whatever she might have had in mind to say and crossed to the down right corner of the stage, where the deputies had set up a briefing table. There was grumbling, but in a few minutes the procedure was moving smoothly. Two officers operated the detector and two others interrogated.

In little over an hour the job was done.

Tony, Charles, and I were in the business office with Chief Autry, who was talking to the telephone. The telephone was doing most of the talking.

When he hung up, Autry said, "The boy's still in surgery. Did somebody say you've got some beer around here?"

"You mean, you drink on duty?" Charles asked.

"Not if I have to pay for it."

"Maybe Larry's up there closing down the control room," Tony said. He reached over to the intercom and pressed the talk-bar. "Larry?" Squawk. "Larry, how about bringing some of that beer in the refrigerator down to the office."

Squawk.

Autry leaned over and pushed the talk-bar down. "Larry, while you're at it, just bring the refrigerator, I'm thirsty."

Squawk?

"Do as the man says, Larry," Tony said.

Squawk.

I waited for somebody to say something, but nobody did. So I said to Autry, "I suppose now you'll want to get down to the one thing you'd really like to know."

Autry's eyes opened briefly. "That's right, Mr. Burgess."

"What's that?" Tony asked.

"Mr. Parent, I'm surprised at you," said Autry. "I mean, *you're* the director. *You're* the one who examines the plot and discerns each character's motivation. When we figure out who didn't like the guy this much, we could be halfway to court."

"I don't have any idea who that might be," said Tony primly.

"I do," I said. "Me, for starters."

"You?"

"Sure. He was screwing up the play left and right, trying to 'improve' it."

"I really had to ride him to keep him on his job," said Charles. "But shooting him? I don't think so. However, Tony, I have thought about shooting you."

Tony paled.

"Me? *Why?*"

"Because you hired Barlow."

Larry arrived with an armful of beer and passed it around. "Thanks," Autry said. "Keep talking," he told us.

Charles said, "He messed up one of the most important scenes in Act Two by shifting the furniture around. Larry had to improvise fast to keep it properly lighted. Cynthia was just about hysterical when she came off, but Dewayne, I think, got a kick out of it. It gave him a chance to show what a great actor he was—you know, meeting the challenge, rising above the adversity."

Autry's eyes veiled again.

Charles continued. "If anything, it was Barlow who was uptight about Dewayne, not the other way around. He spent a lot of time telling anybody who would listen he should be playing that role."

"Well, now—" Tony started to say.

"Not to worry, Tony," said Charles. "Nobody in the cast could hear that without laughing. And, another thing. He got really wound up at the opening-night party. The way I heard it, he thought he had something going with one of the girls and that Dewayne was moving in on him."

"He didn't know," I murmured and got a sideways glance from Autry.

"I remember," said Tony. "You're talking about Sheila. She and Dewayne were together almost the whole time. Dancing. They're both very good dancers."

"It strikes me," said Tony, "that when you get a group of performers together, there's something larger than sexual relationships that causes controversy."

"And that would be?" prompted Autry.

"Billing," Tony said. "All performers want top billing. Dewayne May's name is first on the billboards and the posters and the ads. Barlow's name is on the last page in the souvenir booklet."

"So," said Autry, "you have a would-be actor working in the wings watching a headline performer on stage, and you've got yourself a case of jealousy."

"Of the most extreme sort," Tony said. "Add the matter of Sheila and it increases its intensity."

Autry opened his second can of beer and said, "But what if Dewayne wasn't very much interested in females except as dancing partners? This Barlow, could he have been upset because Dewayne came between him and this girl, or was he upset because this girl came between him and Dewayne?"

I looked at Charles. Charles looked at Tony. Tony looked at me.

"I take it," Autry said, "you don't know."

I tried to explain. "It's a lot like the military, Chief Autry. We've got officers and personnel. We—the director, the stage manager, the technical director, me—we're the officers, and the cast and the crew are the enlisted personnel. There's always a gap between the 'creative' people who put a show together and the 'performing' people who actually do the show. We're not part of their group. Unless there's an affair for the entire company, or unless we're specifically invited, we don't take part in their social activities."

"All right," Autry said. "Who do I ask to find out?"

Charles thought of a couple of names, Tony of another, and I observed that Dewayne might be a good source for the latest backstage gossip.

"Well, we can talk to them in the morning," Autry said. "Is there any more of that beer?"

Of course there was.

Shortly after, both Tony and Charles made their excuses and left. Autry's sleepy eyelids were at half mast as he gazed at me. "You got anyplace you're in a hurry to get to?"

"Outside of a bed and a book, not while there's any beer left. Throw me one, will you?"

We sat and drank silently. Then he asked, "What are they all doing here?"

"Some of them, it's just a way to have some fun during the summer and get a little pay for doing it. Some are hoping to be the next Katharine Hepburn or Marlon Brando and this is another credit on their résumés. It's a better credit than anything they might have done in school, no matter how good that might have been, because this is classed as professional theater and college isn't. And a few of them are here because they really care about outdoor drama and this is an opportunity to experience it. I guess I'm in that last category."

"You know," Autry mused, "you folks have had a fairly wild reputation, but until tonight there's never been any real trouble." He squeezed the can and I could see he was thinking of reaching for another—I was hoping he would, so I could, but instead he asked me if he could see how the special effects were operated.

We navigated from the office down to the stage, where I displayed the fire-control console.

"This panel does all the firing for the pyrotechnics," I explained.

"Each of these switches—forty-eight of them—will be wired up to one effect, the wires connecting to these screwposts back here."

He walked around, aimed the flashlight at the back of the box, and peered closely at the incoming lines. He felt the ten empty terminals where no wires were attached.

"When we want to fire one of the effects, all we have to do is flip a switch. Like so." I flipped a switch.

"Nothing happened," Autry said.

"Of course not." I smiled at him. "The set pieces are empty. We don't put charges in until just before showtime. And the power's off. The main switch is here."

I clicked that, and the "live" glow lamps under each toggle switch lit up across the board, forty-eight little green dots of light.

"Who rigged this up?"

"I did. Part of my job as fight coordinator. I designed the special effects and oversee their loading each night. I earn an extra six hundred that way."

"Each week?"

"Each summer. Four weeks of rehearsal, seven weeks of the show."

Autry flipped one of the toggles up and down. Then, "Didn't you say a couple of these things didn't go off?"

"Yeah. One cannon salvo and the impact bursts."

"Hell, let's shoot one off."

"We've had too much beer, Chief. It's 2 A.M. They'll call the law."

"I'm the law," he said. "Shoot it!"

I shrugged and triggered No. 9. Nothing. Again. Again nothing. Same with No. 10.

"Why didn't it go off?"

I checked the terminals, and they were tight. Then I remembered.

"Charles! He would have unloaded any unfired charges after the show. Barlow wouldn't, but Charles never forgets."

"Too bad," Autry said. "I like fireworks."

We walked up the amphitheater steps, back up to the office.

"How much do you spend for these special effects?" he asked.

I calculated. "The budget's eight thousand for forty-two performances, plus a few rehearsals. A little under two hundred dollars a night. That doesn't include ammunition. We have a budget of about a thousand for that."

"How many of these effects do you shoot off each show?"

"When everything works, thirty-seven."

"After Barlow got shot, who handled the controls?"

"I did. As I said, I designed the effects and I know where every-thing's supposed to fit in the show."

We were in the office now and he glanced at his wrist. "Want me to read you the full drill?"

"What drill?"

"About staying available for further questioning if necessary. I'd hate to lose my Number One Suspect, even if I don't think he did it." The phone rang and he scooped up the receiver before the ring finished.

"Autry. Yeah . . ." He listened and his expression changed dras-tically before he replaced the receiver on the cradle. The sniper eyes were cold and bleak.

"The kid's dead," he said. "Died on the table."

Because of a compulsion etched on my brain years ago by a psy-chiatrist friend very adept with hypnosis, I couldn't drive after drink-ing, so I left the Mustang in the parking lot and hiked the half mile to where I slept. It was a fine night for walking, with a couple of curious dogs to keep me company and the summer constellations falling westerly. But I would have enjoyed it a lot more if I could have kept from thinking about Barlow.

He hadn't been a pleasure to work with or to be around, but now he wasn't anymore, and somewhere there were probably a few people who would miss him.

At the cabin, I brushed most of my teeth, got most of my clothes off, and in that last twitch of consciousness before sleep a thought began to tickle the edge of my mind, something about numbers that didn't add up. But I was too far gone to make sense of it.

Autry and a platoon of deputies were at the amphitheater when I arrived a little after noon. The chief investigator was sitting front row center, looking exactly as he had at 3 A.M., suit just as neat, shoes just as glossy.

"Find anything yet?" I asked.

He rose, brushed off his trouser legs, and we walked across the grassy verge between audience and stage.

"You know," he said, gesturing toward the deputies, "this is work. In the stories, the detective thinks a little and pinpoints every clue. He thinks a little more and comes up with a brilliant solution. Me, I think a little and come up with a headache. What we do mostly is look for the things that are right there—if we can find them."

He led me up the stairs and across the stage, then stopped and squatted down, staring at a scar on the stage floor—a few streaks across the grey concrete near the marker where Dewayne and I do our swords routine.

"One of the moves in the fight has me slashing low at Dewayne so he can jump over the blade. I try to hit the concrete. Sometimes it brings sparks," I told him, "and that adds to the excitement of the routine."

"This one isn't a sword cut," Autry said, fingering a different, ragged scar about an inch long and half as wide, a half inch deep, the raw concrete showing white through the surface of the marker. "Any idea what might have caused this one?"

I shook my head.

"It's fresh," Autry said. Then he looked up toward the audience area as Larry came loping down the steps toward us. "Who's this?"

"Our technical director. Larry. He's the guy who brought us the beer last night."

"Oh, right. Good fellow."

Larry leaped onto the stage.

"Bloody hell!" he complained. "Barlow was scheduled to check all the lighting instruments this morning, and now I've got to do them. All sixty of them!"

Numbers. What was it I had been trying to put together when I passed out this morning?

Ten something . . .

Ten? What was ten?

I excused myself and went to the assistant stage manager's station stage right.

There I studied the effects control box. The forty-eight toggle switches were all in the off position. I flipped the power switch and watched the ready lights blink on.

I looked behind the box at the terminal posts and counted the empties.

"Chief," I called, "you might take a look at this."

"What?" Autry asked as he came over.

"We've got an extra circuit here that I didn't install. There aren't supposed to be but thirty-seven lines going out, and there are thirty-eight."

"Can you trace it?"

I didn't have to. Before I could reply, we heard Larry yell, "What in hell!"

A deputy came to the foot of the tower and called up to him, "Is something the matter, sir?"

"There's a gun up here!"

When I had it worked out later and realized what might have happened if I'd been placed a little farther forward and to the left of where I had been, the shakes came.

Very carefully, the deputies removed the rifle from the brackets that clamped it between a pair of the big 16-inch Leko spotlights. Very carefully, they took down the little solenoid unit hooked to the trigger and followed the wire from the solenoid back to the effects console.

The fingerprints on the rifle were Barlow's, of course.

"Go on," Autry said. "Tell me."

"Okay," I said. "Let's assume the jealousy factor. Would anybody do something like this without being a little off?" I tapped my head.

"I don't know," said Autry. "Can you give me a good definition of sanity?"

"No way," I said. "But anyway we have Barlow mad enough at Dewayne to rig up the rifle so it's aimed where he's supposed to be standing. He expects he'll be able to come up here this morning and remove it and he can also take up the extra wire at his convenience, lose the weapon somewhere, and everything's cool. Right?"

"Sounds right so far."

"I don't know where the gun came from, but rifles aren't hard to get, not like handguns. No license necessary—just walk into a sporting-goods store with cash, check, or credit card.

"As for the triggering gadget, Barlow was a competent technician, regardless of what else. He wouldn't have much difficulty rigging that."

"Simple," agreed Charles.

"So when it comes time for Dewayne and I to play swords, Barlow waits until he thinks Dewayne is on the aim point and when the next charge goes off, he also triggers the rifle. And misses, because Dewayne is a step off the mark. That had to be what stung me on the knee—a speck of concrete or a flake of lead from the bullet. In the noise and activity, nobody would notice the sound a rifle would make, just as we didn't notice the impact. The bullet struck the floor between us, ricocheted, and got Barlow."

"Ten-four," Autry said. "Or as you creative people might say, poetic justice."

John Lutz

All Business

Erica was worried. The people bustling past her in the Tampa International Airport terminal building seemed totally caught up in their own affairs. She stooped slightly and her long fingers, sun-bronzed from her two weeks in Mexico, absently caressed the brown-vinyl suitcase at her feet. It was a large suitcase that sported a Plaza Mexico bullfight decal. Though Erica, as instructed, carried the ceramic pot and wore the distinctive two-piece white casual outfit that so complimented her deceptively frail figure, she knew it was the suitcase that would single her out for her contact.

Davidson nonchalantly walked over and, without looking at her, slumped in a plastic chair near where she stood. He pretended to offer her the newspaper he was finished reading, then engaged her in seemingly casual conversation. Like Erica, Davidson was with the international police force, Interpol.

He said, "You've been standing in that spot for over an hour. He's not going to show."

"Maybe he's spotted one of us," Erica said, referring to the half dozen Interpol agents stationed in the terminal building and disguised as travelers or airport employees.

"Possible," Davidson agreed, "but there's no way to be sure. Leave here and take a cab to your apartment. We'll follow, just in case your contact decided to wait until you're alone somewhere to approach you. If anybody's tailing your cab, we'll know it."

Erica glanced at her watch and then turned and began pulling the wheeled suitcase behind her by its vinyl strap as she walked toward the nearest exit.

Fifteen minutes after she had entered the furnished apartment she'd rented under the name Maureen Marshall, there was a knock on the door. Her throat dry, her blood racing, Erica peered cautiously through the peephole into the hall.

She saw only Davidson, distorted by the concave glass. She let him in.

"Nobody followed you," he told her. He settled his lanky six-foot-three into the sagging sofa and propped his size thirteen shoes on the coffee table. "Whoever was supposed to pick up the shipment must have been tipped."

"Nobody knew my true identity," Erica assured him. "Everything in Mexico went smoothly."

Davidson eyed her. "But you can't pinpoint the location of the opium and marijuana crops. And something must have tipped Dumond that you weren't genuine."

"If that were true," Erica said, "he never would have given me the five thousand dollars and the ceramic pot and suitcase full of narcotics."

"You're probably right," Davidson said. "If your cover was blown down there, you likely would have been shot."

"I don't think so," Erica said. "Not by Robert."

Davidson glanced sharply at her. "So he's Robert to you, the most notorious dope smuggler in this part of the world. I suppose you two became quite intimate."

"Not in the way you suggest. Robert fell for the information we planted about my flight from an attempted embezzlement charge in Detroit. To him I was Maureen Marshall, girl on the run who needed the five thousand dollars he'd offer to bring a pot lined with narcotics into the United States." She stared at Davidson until he looked away. "You and I have had a few dates together," she told him. "That's all. I made that clear from the beginning. If you've got a male ego hangup over this operation because I had to spend some time with Robert Dumond, that's your problem. Don't make it mine. Anyway, my relationship with Robert was all business, though my business wasn't what he thought."

And suddenly Davidson was all business. He stood up and shoved his big fists into his pants pockets. "How come you have no idea where the crops are grown?"

"It's in the report I mailed," Erica said. "We left the Mexico City airport at night in a small private plane. We were airborne for several hours and made numerous course changes. The return flight a week later was at night, too. I didn't even get to look out a window when taking off or landing. That's how Robert works. He's cautious."

"And as debonair as rumored, no doubt."

Erica didn't answer. She'd had enough of Davidson and she was tired from her long flight and from the fruitless wait for her contact to approach her. Davidson took the hint and left, taking with him her suitcase and telling her almost with malice that her apartment would be kept under guard . . .

Erica undressed and lay in bed, unable to sleep, thinking about the past several weeks. Everything had seemed to go perfectly. As instructed, she had traveled to Mexico City and appeared to be exactly the sort of woman Robert Dumond invariably employed to run his narcotics through Customs. Tall, sharp-featured, and with a dazzling smile, every bit as charming as rumored, Dumond had approached and befriended her, made the expected pass and been rebuked, and then, as a friend who understood her difficulty with the law and her finances, offered her $5,000 to pass through Customs with several pounds of heroin concealed in a souvenir piece of pottery with double walls. Her problems were in Detroit, he'd assured her, and she'd be supplied with excellent forged identity and travel papers so no one would bother her at the Tampa airport. She would simply be another American tourist returning from Mexico with the usual duty-free souvenirs. His face, however, was sometimes recognized by alert Customs inspectors, so he would take a flight the next day and join her in Tampa.

Erica had pretended to think about the proposition, then with seeming reluctance had agreed. That same night she and Robert boarded the private plane at the airport and flew in a generally southeastern direction. Their pilot put them down in remote jungle territory, on a grass landing-strip illuminated only by kerosene blazing in five-gallon buckets.

In the morning, after a sleepless night on a cot in a crude metal hut, Erica had gone outside and seen the acres of cultivated cannabis plants that were lush and shoulder-high, the fields of opium-rich poppies beneath camouflage netting. The surrounding country was beautiful and vast. And cannabis plants themselves were unidentifiable from the air. Erica understood how difficult it would be to spot the huge drug operation using aerial reconnaissance.

The many peasants who toiled the fields seemed to think little of the fact that they were growing and harvesting what with simple processing was sold in parts of the world for amounts that made fortunes for drug-runners and pushers. Manolo, the wizened old foreman, proudly showed Erica around the illicit farm and even introduced her to his wife Aleta and their teenage daughter at one of the series of dilapidated huts where the workers and their families lived. The workers had barely adequate food and housing and did a great deal of weaving, sewing, and grinding of meal. Whoever owned the cannabis and poppy farm obviously didn't believe in profit-sharing.

Erica and Robert spent an entire week at the farm. He never repeated his amorous suggestions. Most of their conversation centered around how she would conduct herself passing through Customs and how she was to wait at a certain place in the Tampa airport to be contacted by the man who would take the ceramic pot. It was as if Robert had tested her that night at the hotel and decided that since she wouldn't become a conquest of passion she qualified as a business associate.

Before Robert had gone with her back to Mexico City, Erica had noticed immediately the change in her suitcase. Someone had slit the lining and inserted dozens of packets of whitish powder, then skillfully repaired the lining so that only the most conscientious Customs inspector would notice anything had been altered. The piece of pottery she was carrying, Erica was sure, would be filled only with powdered sugar or some similar perfectly legal substance with which she could be trusted. It was the suitcase that contained the real bounty.

Robert hadn't seen through her cover, she was positive, yet somehow someone had gotten wise, something had gone wrong. Erica was still trying to figure out what that something was as she fell asleep.

Davidson was back early the next morning. "It's get-up time, sleepyhead," he told her. "You'll be interested to know that the ceramic pot *and* your suitcase were packed with refined sugar."

Wearing slippers and robe, still groggy from being awakened by the doorbell, Erica backed a step. "Then everything I brought back from Mexico was legal substance. But why?"

"You were used as a diversion," Davidson said, almost as if he were angry with her. "We were concentrating all our efforts on some nonexistent courier who was to contact you, and we let the real smuggler slip through without a hassle. A diversion like you was easily worth five thousand dollars if it made it easier to pass several million dollars' worth of drugs into the country."

Erica walked to a chair and sat down. Her pulse was hammering in her temples. "Now what?"

"Now I go to the airport to meet Robert Dumond when he gets in on the noon flight from Mexico City. Nobody will look more like a tourist than Dumond, and probably nobody will be cleaner and more legal. But there's no point in passing up a chance to search him."

"I'm going with you," Erica said. "It won't matter now if he knows who I really am."

"Are you sure you want to go?"

"You'll be glad I came," she assured him, and stood up to put some coffee to perk while she showered and dressed.

The flight from Mexico City arrived at the Tampa airport on time. Robert Dumond really did look as much like an innocent tourist as anyone else in the Customs line. There was a camera slung about his neck and he was lugging the usual souvenirs that wouldn't fit into his suitcases—a bullfight poster, pottery, and a large woven sombrero.

Erica stood out of sight and watched him feign bewilderment, then shrug casually and leave the line with a Customs inspector while another inspector confiscated his luggage. The inspectors stood aside to let Robert struggle through the door of a private room with his bulky souvenirs. Davidson glanced at Erica, asked her to wait outside, then also entered the room.

Half an hour later Davidson emerged, his face red with frustration. "They're still questioning him," he said, "but he's as clean as I thought he'd be and twice as cunning, chock full of continental charm and confidence." He slapped a palm against the wall. "The devil was too smart for us again."

"Not necessarily," Erica told him.

Davidson squinted at her in puzzlement.

"That hand-woven sombrero he was carrying," Erica said. "I gave it to him. Robert told me he always passes through Customs with a souvenir sombrero—nothing makes him look more like an ordinary tourist."

Davidson shrugged in irritation. "So what? Nothing was concealed in the hat."

"I told you the peasants toiling in the illicit crops are used to what they're doing and work at it as if it were any other low-paying field job, hardly noticing what crop they're farming." Erica smiled. "I gave Aleta, the foreman's wife, the stalks to use in the making of the sombrero Robert just brought in. It's woven out of dried cannabis."

It took Davidson a few seconds to get the point. "Which means—"

"The sombrero itself is an illegal substance."

Davidson gaped at her, grinned, and spun on his heel to hurry back into the interrogation room . . .

Minutes later Erica watched as Robert was led handcuffed from the room. Davidson was walking directly behind him, carrying the huge sombrero and looking blissfully smug.

Robert would talk plenty now. The authorities would strike a deal with him. That was how the game was played. A reduced sentence was important to Robert, and the location of millions of dollars' worth of narcotics still in the ground was important to the authorities. So there would be a trade negotiated by clever lawyers. The vital consequence was that a major source of narcotics could be destroyed.

Just as Robert was being ushered through the terminal door, he turned and saw Erica. He looked surprised, then angry. Then he shrugged and smiled. With a slight bow, he made a motion toward her as if tipping his hat. Then the door swung shut behind him and he was gone.

Jane Paynter

The Miracle

"What stupid nonsense!" Roberta said. "Why did you bring me this?" She threw down the newspaper and glared at Meg.

Meg, who was unpacking Roberta's suitcase, glanced in dismay from her cousin's tight-lipped face to the paper on the floor. Meg had bought the *Pine Grove News* half an hour before in the town drugstore. She crossed to the bed where Roberta lay propped up on pillows, picked up the newspaper, and straightened it. There, on the front page, topping a two-column picture of a woman's brilliant-eyed, large-boned face under coiflike white hair, was the headline FAMOUS HEALER VISITS PINE GROVE. The story ran down from the picture: "Mother Nadina Rancke, who is said to have healed hundreds of crippled and ill persons medical experts considered hopeless, will share what she calls her God-bestowed gift with residents of Pine Grove tomorrow when she—"

Meg thrust the paper aside. "I'm sorry," she whispered. "I didn't notice that story. I know you want a newspaper every day and this was the only one—"

Roberta turned over, away from Meg. "Don't make excuses, just get rid of it," she said. "I'm going to take a nap."

"I'll go out for a while." Meg grabbed up her purse, raincoat, and the paper. Feeling Roberta's displeasure like a prod, setting off the fearful inner spasm as it invariably did, she hurried out of the room.

By the time she reached the downstairs hall, the wild urge to scream, to strike out, made her clutch the newel post for support. She'd had these spells since childhood—"temper fits," Roberta had called them then. She had castigated Meg until she had learned to internalize them. The spells had become severe again last spring when Roberta was especially irascible. But Meg knew now that Roberta couldn't help her crankiness, and it was wrong of her to feel resentment and rebellion when Roberta was so ill . . .

There, the inner frenzy was easing. Think about something else. Meg drew a shuddery breath as she directed her attention out the window at the rain streaming off the porch roof. Storms such as this came yearly to these North Carolina mountains in October, the weatherman had said on the car radio this morning. If the deluge hadn't hampered their progress, she and Roberta would be in a Raleigh hotel instead of in the Shady Rest Tourist Home in Pine Grove, where they'd stopped because Roberta had suddenly announced that she was too exhausted to go farther.

Meg's tension subsided. With the newspaper under her coat, she went out to the porch. Remembering that there was a coffee shop at the corner, she pulled up the hood of her raincoat and ran along the puddly sidewalk.

Inside the restaurant, she made her way between the crowded tables to an unoccupied one at the front window.

She'd read the story about the healer and was trying to figure out why her face looked so familiar when the waitress came and took her order for coffee.

"Sorry to keep you waitin'," said the woman, whose hair and perspiring face were the same tallowy shade. "We're terrible busy and she's why." She pointed her pen at the healer's picture. "She brought mosta these people here. They're sleepin' in cars, tents, wherever, waitin' to see her."

"The story says she performs miracles."

"I never seen none with my own eyes but they do say she can do everythin' but raise the dead. Some say even that." The woman went for the coffee. Returning, she set it in front of Meg, looked her over, and asked, "You ain't here for healin'?"

"No," Meg said. "Just passing through."

"Even so, if you have a problem or anythin', you might's well give Mother a try."

After the waitress went to answer a call from the kitchen, Meg reread the story about Mother Nadina. Phrases stood out. Medical authorities couldn't explain. Parents marvelled. The doomed were restored to health. The account ended with the announcement that Mother Nadina would be available to all at the Pine Grove High School Auditorium from 10:00 A.M. to 3:00 P.M. tomorrow.

The story probably *was* all stupid nonsense, as Roberta had said. On the other hand, the woman was credited with many miraculous cures. Suppose, Meg mused, just suppose she *could* heal the sick, could even save someone as doomed as Roberta? She felt an exultant thrill as she imagined returning her cousin to their home in Lenham, Massachusetts, and hearing their family physician, old Dr. Risteen, in amazement, pronounce her perfectly well.

Meg gazed at the rain-streaked window and recalled Dr. Risteen's advice that she and Roberta should start this trip, which they'd been planning since last winter, as quickly as possible. That had been in mid-August, the day he told Roberta that the spells of weakness she'd been experiencing were forerunners of the incurable wasting disease that would ultimately render her a helpless invalid.

When Roberta relayed the diagnosis to Meg, Meg had sat sick and shivering although Roberta spoke as matter-of-factly as though she were reporting a pedestrian chat with a friend. It seemed impossible that strong, hearty Roberta, at fifty-two the only mother Meg could remember, would someday be helpless and bedridden.

Meg, who was now thirty-five, had been two months old when her parents were killed in a boating accident. With the help of sitters for Meg, Roberta, an orphaned cousin who had then been living with them for fifteen years, managed to get through college and became a professor of English. She and Meg lived then, as they did now, like mother and daughter in the antique family house in Lenham. Meg's parents, who had never really expected to have a child of their own, had bequeathed the house along with a moderate amount of investments to Roberta long before Meg was born. They had meant to change their will after Meg's birth but, having no sense of urgency, never got around to it.

"You're not listening, Meg," Roberta had said after reporting Dr. Risteen's diagnosis. "I still want to take that trip through the North Carolina mountains. Dr. Risteen would rather I didn't go, but I told him no six-syllable disease is going to stop me."

Roberta had forced Meg to make all the travel arrangements because it would be good practice for the future when she, Roberta, wouldn't be able to manage everything for them as she did now. And so Meg had planned the trip, with much prompting and correction from Roberta. So far, the reservations and sightseeing had been mostly satisfactory except for a motel Roberta had called "lower class" and a digression to explore a cave that turned out to be closed when they reached it after a twenty-mile detour. It seemed to Meg that such mishaps could befall anyone but Roberta was angry and reprimanding.

Making decisions and taking responsibility had been exhilarating, though—it made Meg speculate hesitantly and guiltily on the shape her life would take when Roberta had to go to a hospital and she was on her own. She'd first contemplated being independent last spring when Roberta had grudgingly listened to her tentative suggestion that she get her own apartment someday. Roberta's half acquiescence that she might think about it had opened a peephole into a frightening but fascinating scene. Meg began to envision herself in a sunny apartment with fluffy white curtains and yellow walls instead of in the somber old family house. In these imaginings, she saw a pretty, happy woman, like the After picture in a magazine makeover instead of the harried one she saw in her mirror.

Often this other Meg chatted, easily and charmingly, with an attentive man who sometimes looked like Richard Chamberlain and sometimes like Burt Reynolds. But the depressing aftermath of these reveries was the realization that they hinged on being parted from Roberta. So after such fantasizing Meg was extra solicitous to her cousin—to the point yesterday where Roberta had exclaimed, "Stop *hovering!* I'm not an invalid yet!"

Perhaps that attitude helped Roberta ignore the signs of her illness. Certainly the medications Dr. Risteen had prescribed didn't help. Roberta would have none of them. She'd handed them over to Meg. "I won't take them—I hate the damned things." When Meg reported this to Dr. Risteen, he said to accede to Roberta's wishes and that she mightn't need them before she got home. He advised seeing that she got plenty of rest and not prolonging the tour, adding that her disease could progress so swiftly that she might need nursing care early in the new year. They'd left Lenham on September 28th, planning to be home by October 21st.

But this was only October 10th and Roberta had suddenly become exhausted today. Suppose she suffered a collapse and had to be hospitalized somewhere around here, far from Dr. Risteen? Meg dreaded the idea of overseeing such an arrangement. Dr. Risteen would think her stupid for not discerning earlier signs of Roberta's decline and getting her home, and Roberta would scold if her arrangements were less than perfect.

With a start, Meg saw by the wall clock that an hour had passed. She quickly paid her bill, left the restaurant, and hurried through the downpour to Shady Rest, still clutching the newspaper and wondering where she had seen that strong face and those fixating eyes before. Then suddenly she remembered the occasion, and the enthrallment of that night three years ago. Roberta had gone to bed and Meg had turned on the television, keeping the sound low. Roberta scorned most of what was offered on TV, claiming it dulled the intellect. Although Meg contributed a portion of her salary as bookkeeper at Lenham's one small department store toward household expenses, which presumably entitled her to use anything in the house, she knew that watching any television program not sanctioned by Roberta annoyed Roberta.

The picture had come into focus on an imposing woman in nunlike garb gazing directly out at Meg. "I make no claims," she was saying. "The healed make claims in my name." With that, the picture had shifted to the interviewer, who said, "Thank you for being with us, ladies and gentlemen. And now, this message." The woman had been Mother Nadina, Meg realized now, recalling the instant rapport she had felt in that one glance from those compelling eyes.

Approaching the room where Roberta waited, Meg was seized by the conviction that Roberta's salvation lay in Mother Nadina, that Roberta must be persuaded to consult her.

Roberta was sitting in the room's only armchair, studying a road map. She wore a fresh dress and her grey-streaked dark hair was drawn tautly back into a knot. Meg smiled carefully at her and said, "You're feeling better?"

Roberta removed her reading glasses and watched Meg cross the room.

"You still have that damned paper," she said.

"Yes. I—I didn't see a wastebasket."

"There's one, in the corner."

"But—Roberta, won't you please read the story about this Mother Nadina?"

"I read as much as I could stomach," Roberta said testily. "Don't you *dare* suggest I go to that faker. It's an insult to think I'd consider it."

"I don't mean to be insulting. But shouldn't you try anything that might help? She's healed a great many people." As always, when she dared to argue with Roberta, Meg's heart began to pound and the inner trembling started.

"Who says so?"

"A—a waitress in the lunchroom down the street said she's heard—"

"You believe hearsay from a waitress? You've got to stop being so silly and gullible, Meg. No more about this charlatan, hear me?" Roberta put on her glasses and consulted the map across her knees. "If we leave early tomorrow and take the shortcut I've marked, we can make up for lost time."

"Please, won't you think about going to Mother Nadina?"

Roberta's brows drew together. "This *healer* is bilking the igno-rant, Meg! I'm *not interested!*"

Meg didn't answer. She collected a change of clothes, went into the bathroom, and undressed. While the tub filled, she pushed her short brown hair into her shower cap, noting in the mirror the lines between her hazel eyes, the faint wrinkles around her mouth. She was thinking that she looked as tired as she felt when the inner frenzy which had started during her conversation with Roberta surged into full force. She clenched her teeth against the scream in her throat and grabbed a towel, twisting it hard until the compulsion to strike out, to fight off invisible constraints, dwindled and passed. Then she shakily got into the tub and lay in the warm water with her eyes closed. Roberta hadn't actually said no to her last plea. How wonderful if she could be cured. Then she'd be the old Roberta, strict but not so angry. And maybe if she were cured she'd let Meg go, the way they'd talked about last spring.

That evening, in an Italian restaurant downtown, Meg and Ro-berta ordered manicotti and salad. After Meg filled their glasses from a small carafe of chianti, Roberta raised hers somewhat un-steadily and said, "I wonder how much longer I'll be able to hold a glass—or anything."

"Didn't Dr. Risteen say?"

"He was vague about it. He said the deterioration could go fast but I could live on for years." She picked up her fork with the slight-est fumbling. "Well, eat, drink, and so on. Tomorrow—who knows?"

That night in her bed, Meg listened for Roberta's regular breath-ing to indicate she'd fallen asleep. So much time passed that she was dozing when Roberta said, "Meg?"

"Yes?"

"I've decided something. I was going to tell you when we got home but you may as well know now. You must do me a favor when the time is right."

"Of course. What?"

"You must help me die quickly—not out of my mind on drugs, stuck full of tubes and needles. It may not be for years, but when the time comes you're to do as I say."

"Oh, Roberta—"

"Don't moan! You'll have to be strong, to help me."

"I couldn't do *that*, Roberta. We'll be home before long. Dr. Risteen will—"

"What he can do won't be much."

Meg gripped the blankets. "Roberta," she ventured, "why not give Mother Nadina a chance?"

"And humiliate myself by accepting the placebo of the hoi polloi? Never! But I refuse to hang around like a living corpse. You're to see that I don't."

In a tiny voice, Meg said, "But if you're in the hospital, how—"

"I'm not going to a hospital. I have it all planned. You'll quit your job and we'll manage very well on my retirement pay and the investment income. But I'm not going to have nurses—you're to take care of me. It's no more than you owe me for raising you. Besides, you know how I like things. I couldn't stand months and months of bossy nurses."

Meg wanted to ask what had happened to the idea of her, Meg, living independently, but of course she knew—the issue was dead.

"Reaching this decision has brought me some peace of mind," Roberta went on. "I'm going to sleep." Presently the rhythmic sighings of her sleeping breaths was the only sound in the room.

Meg lay stiffly for a time, staring into the darkness. At last she stole out of bed, slipped on her robe, and huddled in the armchair. Her inner chill seemed to be intensified by the keening of the wind outside. She tried futilely to concentrate on the beauties of the scenery in the mountains while Roberta's directive resounded through her mind. Then the prospect of living alone called up the sweet, illicit excitement it always did. Quickly Meg squelched it and focused on how much she owed her cousin, on her fearful loneliness when Roberta was occasionally out of town. She crept back into bed and finally fell asleep.

Rain was drenching down harder than ever the next morning. Branches and blowing leaves littered the lawn and a sizable limb lay on the hood of their car. Meg pressed close to the window, perceiving the storm as her co-conspirator, detaining her and Roberta here within reach of Mother Nadina.

When Roberta woke half an hour later, Meg told her hesitantly that it was still too stormy to travel. Roberta listened with half closed eyes, then said, "I don't feel like going anywhere, anyway."

Meg leaned over her. "I have Dr. Risteen's pills. Or shall I find a doctor here?"

"Neither. Just let me rest."

"I'll find us some breakfast and bring it here."

Downstairs, Meg met their landlady, Mrs. Kreble, in the hall. When she saw that Meg was going out, Mrs. Kreble said, "There's coffee, juice, and rolls in the kitchen. Come and help yourself." She led Meg to the kitchen where a steaming urn, a basket of buns, and a pitcher of orange juice waited.

When she'd fixed a tray, Meg said, "We'll probably need to stay another night. My cousin's not feeling well."

"I thought one of you was sick. I'm filled up because of Mother Nadina. She can cure anything, I've heard. Oh, sometimes the ailments don't go away right off and it don't work for everybody. You have to believe a hundred percent and do exactly what she says. By the way, I've heard she has only so much power a day and when she's healing it kinda runs down. Get your cousin there first thing while Mother's charged up is what I'm saying."

"I'm going to try to." Meg thanked her for the breakfast and carried the tray to the bedroom. The curtains were still drawn. When Meg hesitated in the doorway, Roberta stirred and said, "I'm awake."

Meg set the tray down. "Do you feel better?"

"No, I don't."

"Are you in pain?"

"No. I'm just—weak. I want to lie still."

Meg placed coffee, juice, and a roll on Roberta's bedside table, noting with a pang of dread her cousin's sunken eyes and greyish pallor.

Roberta grimaced and averted her face. "I'm not hungry. I want to sleep."

"Please listen, Roberta, Mrs. Kreble says Mother Nadina—"

"Spare me her superstitious prattle! Leave me alone."

"All right."

Carrying her purse and raincoat, Meg tiptoed out of the room. Outdoors, she breathed the cool, fresh air gratefully and went to the car. The rain had slackened. There were breaks in the fast-moving clouds and the wind was stronger. After tugging the limb off the hood, she started the car and headed downtown. She had no specific goal except to occupy herself so that Roberta could rest.

When she came to the shopping district, she parked, got out, and wandered down the street but she soon realized it was too windy and cold for strolling. Besides, after half a block, rain pelted down again. She ran for the nearest store. Inside, she wiped her wet face with a handkerchief and looked around. Signs over the aisles listed diapers, vitamins, toys, cosmetics. She started vaguely up an aisle.

She'd collected a tube of toothpaste and several postcards when she came to a display of scarves. She examined them, struck by their good quality and pretty colors. There was a long red one she thought would look nice on Roberta and might please her. She lifted it from the rack and went to the checkout counter.

Back in the car, she turned off Main Street onto a one-way street and saw too late that it was clogged with cars. She rolled down the window and peered ahead.

A policeman four cars up was making urgent forward motions to speed traffic. She heard him shout to one of the drivers, "Yessir, straight on for the healin'."

Eventually, her car crept the long block. While she meant to swing the wheel at the intersection she'd been inching toward for what seemed an hour, instead she steered straight ahead as though guided by a dominant will. Wasn't it her destiny to see Mother Nadina in person? Wasn't that why she had been caught in this throng of believers?

Half an hour later, she was standing in line at the door of the high school auditorium where a young woman was passing out cards. The one she gave Meg said #5.

"What does this number mean?" Meg asked.

"You'll be fifth to consult Mother Nadina."

"I'm not here to consult her. And there are lots of people ahead of me."

"No one's ahead of anyone else," the girl said. "Some who are most afflicted have the greatest difficulty gettin' here. The cards aren't distributed in order. Mother Nadina wants everyone to have the same chance of consultin' her first. Move along to the seat with your number, please, ma'am."

Before Meg could explain she was here only as an onlooker, she was pushed forward by the crowd. An usher checked her card, led her to the front-row seat labeled 5, and hurried off.

The high-ceilinged auditorium seated perhaps four hundred. But soon all the metal chairs were taken and standees were crowding into the space along the sides and rear of the room.

Faded green curtains framed the front of the stage, which was bare except for a wooden chair and table at its center. A sign reading VOLUNTEER GRATETUDE OFFERINGS leaned against a large gilt bowl.

Presently the young woman who had distributed cards went up the ramp to the stage, raised her hands, palms outward, and stared the crowd into silence.

"I know you're right anxious to see Mother Nadina," she said in a high, carrying voice. "She's backstage prayin' for the strength to grant your requests. You may receive her priceless gift for nothin' if that's what the Spirit within you wills. But as she remembers you generously in her prayers, so *you* be generous. Praise be!" There was a stirring behind the tan curtains at the rear of the stage. The young woman stepped back and swept aside the folds, revealing Mother Nadina.

She was older than her picture showed, much older and more powerful-looking than she'd appeared on TV. Her wide face was almost as colorless as her white robe and her cap of white hair. She advanced on the arm of the young woman with the plodding steps of an automaton, her thick hand heavy on the young woman's arm. As she approached the chair, her large, ice-grey eyes swept across the audience as though perceiving the need of each person separately.

For the space of a breath, the audience sat hushed. Then, with a clashing of chairs, many of them sprang up, cheering and calling, "Help us, Mother! Help us!" One of the ushers began to sing "My Faith Looks Up to Thee" and immediately the crowd joined in.

When the hymn ended, the young woman seated Mother Nadina in the chair and again held up her hands for quiet. The audience gradually settled back into their seats. "Please line up five at a time in the order of your numbers," the young woman called. "No shovin'. There's ushers to help those that need it."

The first of the supplicants took her place at the foot of the ramp and waited, leaning forward slightly—she had a grotesquely swollen foot. A boy on crutches hobbled up to stand behind her. Then a starved-looking baby unfretting in its mother's arms and a man who shook with palsy. Two young male ushers escorted them singly to Mother Nadina.

Eyes closed, lips moving as though in silent prayer, the healer passed her hands over each one as though searching out the root of their affliction. The young woman stood behind the table and lifted the bowl toward them as they turned from Mother Nadina. In no case was she disappointed—they all dropped bills into the bowl.

The audience murmured "Praise be" as the woman with the swollen foot came down the ramp unaided and the boy followed, using only one crutch. The baby emitted a couple of weak yelps and kicked off its blanket, which its mother acknowledged by crying, "Praise Mother Nadina, he's healed!" She kissed Mother Nadina's sleeve and the crowd cheered. But when the palsied man straightened and began to jig awkwardly, the audience let out shrieks and whistles that hurt Meg's ears. She was absorbed in the man's progress up the aisle when one of the ushers hurried to her.

"You're next," he said, pulling her to her feet. She shook her head and tried to make him hear over the shouting of the crowd that she was merely an onlooker. With the patiently harassed look that said there was a way to handle the mentally ailing, he signaled the other usher. Meg barely managed to snatch up her purse before they had her up the ramp and facing Mother Nadina.

Mother Nadina looked at her deeply, then motioned the ushers away. "Why are you afraid?"

"Because—I only came to watch."

"No. You have a request."

Meg took an unsteady breath. "Well—yes, I have. For my cousin. She didn't come. She's too ill."

"And I see that you are very disturbed."

"Yes."

"Tell me about it."

"She—Roberta—says I'm to take care of her until she decides to die and then I'm—to help her do it."

"You have agreed to this?"

"I do what she says. You see, she raised me—she's been a mother to me all my life."

"Ah. She will not let you go."

"I think she was going to—but then she got sick, so she can't."

Mother Nadina looked knowingly at Meg. "When she dies, you will be free. You are afraid and yet not afraid."

"Yes . . . no . . . " Again the mirage of the apartment, a party in progress. Music . . . laughter. A handsome man clasped Meg warmly to him as they danced, guiding her masterfully through intricate steps she followed perfectly.

Smiling slightly, Mother Nadina asked, "What is your wish?"

"Why, that Roberta be cured."

"I must touch her or something of hers. What have you brought me?"

"I don't— Wait, I have a scarf I just bought her."

"Give it to me."

Clumsy in her eagerness, Meg took the scarf from the paper bag in her purse.

Mother Nadina bent intently over the scarf and drew it slowly through her hands. Fluttering and clinging to her strong fingers, the red silkiness crackled like rubbed cat fur. When Mother Nadina replaced it in Meg's hands, Meg felt a tiny tingle.

"Your dearest wish will be granted when you put this scarf on your cousin."

"I hope she'll let me. Sometimes she's very stubborn."

"It's *essential* that she wear it. Don't let her refuse! My strength will be with you." Mother Nadina's brilliant eyes held Meg's.

"How can I thank you?" Meg whispered. Mother Nadina inclined her head toward the gilt bowl. Meg fished several bills from her wallet and placed them in the bowl, then hastened back to her seat, snatched up her raincoat, and hurried outside.

In the car, she gazed at the scarf as reverently as though it were a sacred relic. It shimmered with an iridescence she hadn't noticed in the store. The scarf would free Roberta from her illness, and free Meg, too! But of course the visit to Mother Nadina and the scarf's miraculous quality must never be mentioned.

She found Roberta sitting on the side of the bed as if willing herself the strength to get up. "Where have you been all this time?" She eyed Meg suspiciously. "You look different, like a star-struck kid. What have you been doing?"

"Getting you a present!" Meg took out the scarf and held it up. "Isn't it pretty? Let me put it on you."

"I've never worn that stringy kind." Roberta studied the scarf for a moment. "No, I don't like it, Meg. You'll have to return it."

Shaken by a sickening rush of disappointment, Meg went to her with the scarf. "Oh, please, Roberta, it's important to me—do put it on!"

Roberta cast an incredulous glance at Meg. "Don't be ridiculous." She turned away from her.

As Meg approached Roberta's rejecting back, her inner frenzy began, mounted, and swelled to a black storm that obscured her surroundings. She saw only the taut red line of the scarf and heard Mother Nadina's command: *"Don't let her refuse! My strength will be with you."* Suddenly, as though with Mother Nadina's powerful hands, she flung the scarf around Roberta's throat, twisted it twice, and strained it tight against her frantic struggling.

"Must—keep—it—on," Meg heard a harsh voice say. It was not her voice, although it came through her gritted teeth. With fierce strength, she hung onto the scarf until Roberta went limp, toppled sideways on the bed, and lay still. The scarf, like a bandage of blood around her throat, was the last thing Meg saw before blackness overwhelmed her.

When the dark fog gradually cleared, Meg was standing over Roberta in dazed puzzlement. She remembered advancing with the scarf and then—nothing.

Why was Roberta lying so still? Was she sicker? Had she collapsed? But no, she was wearing the miraculous scarf, she was cured! Soon she would sit up and say she was well again. Meg rejoiced. Praise Mother Nadina! She sat down to wait.

Isak Romun

Christmas Is Over

I waved aside the other barbers' invitations and waited until the second chair from the window was free. I'd been coming to Tony's Barber Shoppe for over twenty years and only once in those years was my hair cut by someone other than Mr. Fisher, who officiated at the second chair from the window.

It wasn't that Mr. Fisher was one of the great barbers of all time. It was just that he cut my hair the way I wanted it cut: short on top, whitewalled on the sides. He never tried to talk me into a trim.

We had a ritual. He would brush off the chair and beckon me into it. I'd make some comment about the weather as I sat down. Then he'd say, "Same as usual, sir?" and snap a sheet over me. I'd answer, "Same as usual, Mr. Fisher." After that, I'd settle in for the duration and would often be dozing or even sound asleep when he'd ask, "How's it look?" I'd gaze into the mirror he held, check my front and back, sometimes the sides, mumbling appreciative sounds and nodding my head. Then I'd pay and tip him.

Impersonal, maybe, but satisfying. I don't believe he even knew my name. I only knew his because his last name was on a plate above his station and I'd hear Tony call him "Julie" from time to time.

As Tony did that day. The proprietor came over to Mr. Fisher's chair, nodded perfunctorily at me, and handed the barber an envelope. "For you, Julie."

The envelope passed more or less under my nose and I had a chance to see the barber's name on it care of Tony's. Mr. Fisher ripped the envelope open, took out some advertising flyers on slick paper, then crumpled the lot and threw it in a nearby trash basket.

"Hair-tonic companies," he said disgustedly. "They send their stuff in a plain envelope, knowing you'll open it."

"If they want to sell you something," I said, "they should at least get your name right."

He fished the envelope out of the basket and showed it to me. "No, the name's okay."

I looked at the envelope and read "Julian Fisher. Isn't your name *Julius* Fisher?" I asked.

"Nope. Been Julian ever since I can remember." He threw the envelope back in the trash basket.

Then, of course, I asked the dumb question, "You sure?"

"Just to check, I'll call up my mama tonight when I get home."

We both laughed and he got on with the haircut. But I didn't doze off as usual. At one point, I said, I hoped casually, "I was down around Independence the other day. Nice part of town."

"I don't know. I think it's kind of tacky."

"Where do *you* live—if you don't mind my asking?"

"Montrose," he answered, and I could hear the puzzlement in his voice. "The Montrose section."

"You just move there?"

"I've been there since I come to Paulsburg twenty-five years ago."

"How's the phone service in that part of town?"

"Not bad, not good. Why?"

"Well, I get a lot of wrong numbers. At first I thought they had me listed wrong."

"I'm unlisted."

"Oh."

He must have thought I was crazy, all those questions, all those departures from ritual. But it was like I was seeing him that day with a piece missing.

And that piece was the annual Christmas check.

About ten years before, in appreciation of getting my hair cut exactly the way I wanted it, I had started sending him a check at Christmas time. I'd consulted the phonebook to get his address and came up with Julius Fisher, 907 Independence. I often wondered why in all those years he didn't mention the checks, but reasoned he felt it less than tactful to talk about money—or that among the other tips he might receive, my contribution was less than spectacular. Besides, as I said, he probably didn't know my name, didn't connect me with the checks.

But apparently *my* Mr. Fisher, *Julian* Fisher, wasn't getting and cashing my checks at all. Some unknown individual who never cut a hair of my head, never stimulated my scalp with trained and sensitive fingers, was unconscionably enjoying an annual windfall he didn't deserve.

I didn't think any more about the matter beyond making a mental note to send the next check to the right Fisher. I didn't think about it, that is, until a month or so later when I found myself early one evening driving along Independence Street. On an impulse, I slowed down at the 900 block and found the house numbered 907. It was an ordinary house in a row of ordinary houses, all hemmed in by ugly bushes—and probably by ugly mortgages, as well.

I got out of the car, went up a small path of cracked bricks to the door, and rang. A dog barked and I heard someone coming toward the door. The someone said, "Rex, stop!" and the barking stopped. I heard the click of an electric switch, but no light came on.

The door opened and a short, gone-to-weight, guppy-eyed man with a pale, almost transparent face said, "Yes?"

I asked, "Mr. Fisher? Mr. *Julius* Fisher?"

"Yes."

I said, "Christmas is over."

His face fell, a worried look flickering briefly on his lined, drooping features. I expected him to say something like, "What is that supposed to mean, mister?" Instead, he said, "I understand." Then he shut the door in my face.

I should have pushed the bell again and asked *him,* "What is *that* supposed to mean, mister?" But I was too nonplussed by his response, by the door shutting on me. So I went back to my car and drove out of Independence, thinking, What happened back there?

And that, I thought, was the last I'd ever see of Julius Fisher. But in less than a week I saw him again.

He came into my office at the newspaper late one night. He stood at the desk and looked down at me. He said, "Please don't move." And in my face, he waved a large, ugly automatic pistol.

March had come in roaring and then blustered around for thirty-one days. It was more than just a bad month of cold and windy weather, it was a bad month at the typewriter. My column had taken on a bland and sterile tone and my editor, with menacing jocularity, had let me know he knew. Toward the end of the month, I began to get myself in hand, going back to the office at night in hope that a staring contest with the typewriter would induce something. It didn't.

But that's why I was in my office at *The Paulsburg Advance-Indicator* that last night of the month when Julius Fisher barged in on me.

"Monahan, is it?" He glanced at my desk sign.

"Right."

"Now then, Mr. Monahan, don't try anything and you'll be fine.

I'm just going to take you where the rest of your people are being kept." He looked again at the sign. "What's the O stand for?"

"Oscar," I answered unwillingly.

"And the X?"

"Xavier."

"Curious. The name is familiar."

It occurred to me then that he was as nervous as I was and he was trying to cover it up with meaningless small talk. Another thing occurred to me. He didn't recognize me, probably because the porch light was out the night I called.

He gestured me out of my office and marched me to the city room, and on through it to the windowless morgue, which the modern-day purists who work there insist on calling a library. Inside was the whole nightside crew, guarded by an above-middle-aged individual with a submachinegun. Wan and unhappy-appearing, he looked as if he'd rather be home watching TV.

That's what a third one *was* doing. Outside, in the city room, a superannuated gunman was at a TV set he must have lugged in because there hadn't been one there before. Another had his ear pinned to a radio. Both instruments were tuned to Paulsburg stations.

A fifth man, a really old lad, came up to Julius and in a strained voice said, "They're not where they're supposed to be, any of them. Where in God's name are they?"

Julius said, "Quiet!" and the other shut up. That was my first indication that Julius was the leader of this hangdog group.

A moment later he addressed us, his captives.

"We're going to keep you good people in there under guard. Not that you could get out—but if you should, we have all the exits blocked. It's futile to try anything. You might get hurt." His voice rose, fighting a quaver. "You might get killed."

He waved the pistol around some more and indicated the submachinegun in the hands of the guard. "We're all armed and we know how to use our weapons. If you make us have to use them we'll use them to greatest effect."

"Mister, maybe you can tell us what this is all about." That was Abe Slaughter, the paper's top lensman and resident bigmouth. He liked to hang around the paper at night answering police calls, trying for the shot that would win him another press-association award.

"I can't. Won't. And neither can he." Julius stared meaningfully at the guard and strode from the room.

Abe Slaughter edged back, found a chair next to mine, and sat down.

"What *is* it all about, Monahan?" he asked, *sotto voce.*

"I wish I knew. It's a sweetheart of a story, though. 'Over-the-Hill Gang Takes Over City Paper.' " I felt the professional lassitude of the last thirty-one days slipping away. "Any chance of sneaking a few shots when they're not looking? Available light okay?"

"The light's okay, but what am I supposed to take photos with? My hands? They took my camera. They're pros."

"They don't look like it. They're past the age for this kind of thing, whatever it is."

"Maybe, but they're organized. You didn't see them come in. They were on us all at once. And they knew what to do. My camera wasn't out, but they went looking for it. They're even fielding calls coming into the night desk."

I sneaked a look at the phone on the librarian's desk. "Has anyone tried that?"

"They cut the wires."

I looked out at the city room where the old boy who had talked to Julius was dialing a phone. He had dialed it several times, for that matter, each time listening for what must have been a ring or two, then putting down the instrument and shaking his head. Julius said, "Keep trying," then went over and talked to the man at the TV set, who also shook his head. Julius then consulted the radio addict and got the same results. They were all pretty grim.

I checked my watch. It was getting late, minutes to midnight. I decided if there was a story here I'd better start getting it.

I got up and went to the door. The guard port-armed his submachinegun, blocking my exit. I shouted over his head, "Mr. Fisher!"

It was as if I'd pulled the pin on a grenade and rolled it out into the city room. They were transfixed, all of them, staring unbelievingly at me.

Julius called across the city room, "Who are you talking to?" I thought I saw, flickering again on his features, that same worried look I had seen some nights ago.

"I'll answer your question if you answer some of mine."

He took out his gun and pointed it at me. "Come out of there, Mr. Monahan."

I did as I was told.

"Your office, Mr. Monahan," Julius said. "We'll see who answers whose questions."

In the office, he sat behind my desk and I sat on a straight chair placed by him in the middle of the floor, out of reach of anything I could pick up and use as a weapon.

"Now, Mr. Monahan. How did you know my name?"

"What about my questions?"

He raised the pistol and rested his arm on the desk so that the line of sight was directly on my heart. I noticed his hand was steady, his manner businesslike, as if he had grown into his role and, maybe, might be enjoying it.

"You don't remember me," I said, "but I visited you recently. About five nights ago."

The gun snout went down, and so did my level of panic.

"What did you say that night, Mr. Monahan?"

"I asked if you were Julius Fisher. There's a funny story behind my asking."

"Never mind the funny story, what else did you say?"

"I don't recall I said very much. You closed the door in my face."

"Something about Christmas?"

"Oh, yes, I said—" I looked steadily at him and I think I smiled "—I said, 'Christmas is over.' "

"You're Cassius!" he whispered in a thick, urgent voice.

"I'm Monahan." I nodded at the nameplate on my desk. "I work on this paper."

"And I'm Mary Poppins. I'm not interested in any part of your other cover names. I just want to know where everyone is."

"Everyone?"

"Listen, I worked my tail off getting these guys out. After thirty years! They've settled in. So have I. Do you know I'm a deacon in the Independence Street Methodist Church?"

"No, I can't say I knew that."

"Well, where did you go after you gave me the code? You were supposed to alert the other cells. How come the TV and radio stations aren't taken? The police department? Where are the *troops?*"

I almost laughed, because in a way it was funny. Funny even though a man sitting just feet from me was threatening to tear a chunk out of my body. I *didn't* laugh, but maybe a certain amusement showed on my face because the gun was up again and pointing at me.

"Don't futz around with me, Cassius. How come we're out here on a limb waiting to be sawed off? Chrissakes!"

I looked at him and saw desperation.

And so I told the whole story.

Afterward, he sat for a long while, unbelieving. He didn't lower the gun, though.

"That's why your name was familiar. It was on the checks."

"Where did you think they came from?"

"From them. They told us we'd get them periodically to help us get set up, take care of later expenses. They often came with different names. Back in the Forties and Fifties they came regularly, and for pretty good amounts. Then they stopped. When yours came, I thought they were starting up again but that the Bureau's budget was tight." He paused. "And then you show up and give me what sounded like a code phrase."

"Sounded like?"

"Yes, sounded like. I couldn't remember the one in the plan, which was never written down. I thought the plan was dead. I thought they had forgotten us. I thought we'd live out our lives here, part of good old middle America. Then you came and you sounded so—so authoritative. I thought the plan was on again after all this time. Listen, I worked like a Trojan to get these old guys out of their houses. I'm supposed to head a cell of ten specialists charged with commandeering this newspaper. Do you know how many I got left? Seven, including me. Two flat out refused to take part, wouldn't even open their doors. The other three are long dead."

His eyes seemed to go in on him. He fell back in the chair. The hand holding the gun relaxed. He said in a strained, hollow voice, "When a man's old it isn't what he believes in that shapes his life, it's what he lives in. Do you know what I want most? To be back in my place on Independence. All of them want the same thing. They never wanted to come out in the first place, but I pushed them and got them moving."

"A man must not swallow more beliefs that he can digest."

"I've read Havelock Ellis, Monahan."

"Why don't you all just get the hell out of here?"

"But those newshounds will come looking for us. The police—"

"They may have a hard time finding you. Maybe you can get away. Leave town tonight."

"Get away. Yes, get away." He stood up and pushed the gun into his belt. "What time is it?" he asked.

I looked at my watch. "About twenty after twelve."

He smiled a tight, small smile. "You know, there's one part of the plan I haven't carried out."

"What's that?"

"We were supposed to liquidate the lot of you." He pulled the gun out of his belt.

"That would—solve problems."

"Come on. I think you should join the others."

We were free and in a frenzy.

Julius had taken me back to the morgue, closed the door, and locked us in. Apparently, he and the others had no taste for killing. About ten minutes after we heard their departing footsteps, we broke through the door. Everyone went for a phone, some to call the police, others to call home. The night editor, who had been uncharacteristically silent during the takeover, called the publisher for approval to put out a special edition. Abe Slaughter rattled drawers and slammed closet doors until he found his camera, no harm done to it. Reporters started interviewing each other to get personal reactions down on paper.

I went to my typewriter to write my own account of my feelings.

As I was about to pull the final sheet from the typewriter, Abe Slaughter came and picked up my copy from the desk. There was no use telling Abe to keep his hands where they belonged. Besides, I wanted his reaction. As he finished the last sheet in his hands, I gave him the one from the machine.

When he finished reading, he said, "Nice, Monahan. You got the monkey off your back. Good. But there's nothing in here about that guy. You know, the one you called by name. What about him?"

"I didn't know him. He resembled my barber, so I just tried out the name."

"And you have no idea what it was all about?"

"No idea at all."

"Funny the way they took off after their boss had his little chat with you." Abe looked at me skeptically and walked out of the office.

What I was doing, of course, was just putting down observed facts, colored by the experience of a participant, a little comedy of sorts. But nothing about where the gunmen came from, who financed them, what their grand plan was, or who their leader was. Nothing Julius had told me, and no speculation.

I wanted to give all those tired, faded men a chance to fall back into their cover lives, which, as they must have come to realize, were their real lives. I was especially hopeful that Julius Fisher would go unnoticed, could live out his days in that crummy little house he obviously loved.

I could have saved myself the trouble. The next night, in the regular edition of the *Advance-Indicator,* there was a short item about Julius Fisher, 62-year-old widower of 907 Independence Street, who had apparently blown off his head with a nine-millimeter handgun found near the body. A neighbor heard the weapon's report, then Fisher's dog barking, and went over to check.

Christmas really was over for Julius Fisher—and in a way for the others, too. For the rest of their lives they'd never be able to answer the door without wondering who was on the other side.

I made certain of one thing. I would never mis-send another check. A couple of weeks before Christmas I delivered Julian Fisher's check to him in person. He thanked me with a large smile and said, "Haircut, sir? While you're here."

"Why not," I said and got into the chair.

Behind me, I heard the sound of the envelope being opened.

"Mr. Monahan, eh? Many thanks, sir. Are you the one who does that column for the *Advance-Indicator?*"

"Right. I'm the one." I straightened up in the chair, looked around to see if anyone had overheard. No one had.

As he put the sheet over me, the barber continued, "I've always thought writing for a newspaper must be interesting. You must learn something new every day."

"Don't take so much off the top like you always do," I said irritably.

"Q"

LaVonne Sims

Behind My Lace Curtain

Envy. Pity. Scorn.

Most often it is the latter emotion I see mirrored on your pinched, unadorned faces when unwilling to hide myself as you would have me do, I pass you on the street. In the sparkle of day-bright, no less.

Harlot! Silently, your condemnation screams at me. You glare at the pink of my cheeks and then turn away lifting the hems of your skirts, sniffing disdainfully.

How I've wished to laugh aloud upon seeing your drawn-down brows and lip-curls of contempt. Yet, I dared not. I have held my mirth firmly in check, letting it bubble up and out only when I am in my own world, peeking out at yours through the lace curtain of my balcony window. It would not have done to outrage the public decency beyond endurance. To commit such an offense, to laugh outright at the prim wives of our noble townsmen—the judges and councilmen and officers of peace—would have been to break a final barrier and thus ruin business. Then would I have been thrust upon the mercy of some charitable sisterhood.

God forbid!

God. No doubt you assume I give neither thought nor heed to The Deity. But how could you believe it, knowing from whence I came? I thank Him often. Were it not for His bountiful endowments. . .

Ah, well. It will suffice to say I have been most abundantly blessed, be it by Divine Hand or an admirable heredity. My skin is fine and clear—not powdered, as you whisper to one another behind gloved hands. My hair is like ripe burnished corn silk—an invitation in itself. I have only to nibble at my lower lip to turn it cherry red.

As to what I might have been bequeathed by my long-departed mother I cannot say. The few photographs I saw of her were brown and yellow, her features fuzzy and indistinct. The painting Father kept over the mantel was lovely in its way, though perhaps a bit exaggerated. I have learned that painters are not above placating clients with a touch or two of gentle subterfuge.

Father once said my eyes were like hers, an observation which sent shivers up my spine. I remember them and how, sad and stormy grey through the day, they turned stern at eventide. And at night, by firelight, looking down at Father and me, they became glowing, catching the very sparks of hell.

In my father I see myself more clearly. He is tall—strong of bone and proud of bearing. I have his full mouth and the same white, even teeth. My fingers are long and tapered just as his are. When I was a girl, I used to believe that his strong white hands had as much to do with salvation as did his convictions. I sat enthralled upon the foremost pew, watching him seduce his congregation. His deep voice rose and fell like summer thunder, fairly rattling the rafters with its resonance. And all the while he preached, all the while those threats of damnation fell from his lips, he caressed the Good Book with soft strokes, gentle tappings.

My father was glorious at the pulpit. An angel in black. At least once every Sunday morning he raised his Bible high into the air until sunlight streaming through the stained-glass windows caught the tarnished cross engraved on its cover. How different he was before the parsonage hearth. Then he wept and cursed. Through the anger and tears I knelt before him. He laid his hands upon me and ordered the demons away. I prayed, too. An eternity of contrition on raw, bended knee.

Now, sitting upon the edge of my bed, I look away from the window and down at my hands. Beautiful white hands. Strong hands.

You envy me. You envy the glitter on my fingers and wrists. You cast resentful eyes at the velvet and lace of my gowns and the fine tasseled carriage which conveys me through your streets.

When I move, even a little, men pause. They lift their heads to inhale the sweet essence of me, all the while careful to keep their glances discreet lest you notice. Your men. Husbands and brothers, sons and fathers. My men.

I was a child when I first became aware of your small jealousies. They reached out and touched me—tangible, malevolent graspings. First you envied me my goodness and beauty, and now you envy my evil—for so you perceive me to be. You envy me and wonder at what I have become. Soon you will wonder even more.

You more high-hearted souls pity me. You mistake acquiescence for subjugation and pray for my miserable miscreant soul. For you at least I save a small, soft place, because in one sense you are quite correct. I *have* been a slave—though a willing one. A slave to the opulent smoothness of my life. To the sighs, murmurs, pleadings,

and cries of gratification that fill my nights. And a slave most of all
to that one night.

I would die without my special night. Starve. Wilt and be cast out
on the wind.

You scorn me. Or do you really? Is it fear, perhaps?

It can hardly matter. I have most gladly borne your façade of
contempt—smiling behind my lace curtain—in order to practice my
secret pleasures. And I will bear yet more. I will embrace your
judgment wholeheartedly, kiss your most vehement condemnation
full on the mouth to have my ultimate pleasure.

It is Sunday. There is no one beneath my window, none of you in
your drab frocks to cast hostile, sidelong glances of reproach toward
the door of my gracious house. But there are no patrons, either—no
seekers of warmth. It is Sunday, a day of rest as well as worship.

Those who serve with and for me slumber in the rooms surrounding my own. Their breathing seems to catch hold of the very walls.
So many of them came here as I did, coaxed here with loving arms
and forbidden stroking hands. Like me, their bloom of womanhood
was forced to flower early. But no one else here is as fortunate as
I. Each of them fled, carrying with them a secret knowledge and the
burden of their beauty, and the guilt, too, rightfully owned by their
male betrayers.

But then I have always been different, and so I am lucky. A self-
sought, self-brought luck.

I left the big, rambling parsonage with its accusing portrait over
the mantle. I walked out of the church, leaving behind once and for
all the aroma of oaken pews and yellowing hymnals, the bright
patches of multicolored light. However, beyond such feeble deser-
tion, I chose to remain in the town where I was born. How else to
receive my punishment? Or my reward. My window is open. The
lace curtain sways in a faint breeze. I can see myself in the gilded
mirror on the wall beside the window and my breath becomes shallow. Suddenly my eyes are different and yet somehow hauntingly
familiar. My mother's eyes. Glowing. They have captured the bright
beams which seem now to radiate from beneath my pillow.

The gas streetlamps have all been doused. Even from a block away
I can hear his tread on the wooden planks of the sidewalk. It is a
firm, steady tread, one footfall coming in even time upon another.
My heart is pounding, as it always does. I wait and want to weep.

But I will not weep—not yet. Not until I've been held and rocked and stealthily caressed. Not until I've knelt and been chastised in full. Not until my final passion has been gratified.

Reaching beneath the silken pillow sham, my fingertips tremble. The blade I fondle is smooth and cold as ice. The hilt is warm. Comforting.

I will not look away from the window again, for in a moment I will see him. He will step from the shadows and raise his right arm high in the moonlight. And through the lace curtain I'll see the shimmer of a tarnished cross and the glow of strong white hands. And the pale, beautiful, tapering fingers.

James Holding

The Grave Robber

It wasn't until the afternoon of that hot, sticky, airless day that Henry Carmichael met the grave robber.

Not that Henry had been idle in the morning. Far from it. With the group of American tourists, of which he was a member, he had wandered bemused for three hot hours among the mists of history that hung almost palpably over the ruins of the temples of Karnak and Luxor—built millennia ago to the glory of Amen in what had been the ancient Egyptian capital of Thebes.

During those three hours, their Egyptian tourguide, a Miss Abdullah, told Henry and his fellow sightseers more than they really wanted to know about hypostyle halls, avenues of rams, lotus columns, and long-dead pharaohs. But Henry, who was nothing if not polite, bore patiently with it all while he studied at leisure and at close quarters an Egyptian artifact that interested him far more than temple ruins. Miss Abdullah herself.

Obviously one of the new generation, thought Henry. Liberated, ambitious, dedicated to her job, marinated while in school (and college?) in the compelling liquor of Egypt's ancient history, and now dispensing her garnered wisdom enthusiastically to dull American tourists. With a little kohl outlining her eyes, Henry thought, she'd look a good deal like one of those ancient queens she told them about—Nefertiti, perhaps, or Hatshepsut. On the other hand, thought Henry, with a small *frisson* of homesickness, if she were just a trifle taller and broader in the beam, she'd be almost a dead ringer for Lorene, his favorite waitress in Adele's Inn-Between Bar and Grill at home.

At length Miss Abdullah shepherded her twenty tourists back to the Winter Palace Hotel in Luxor for a hurried but excellent luncheon, the central ingredient of which, according to the tour's funny man from Chicago, was a camelburger.

Immediately after luncheon, the tour members set out lightheartedly enough, their strength restored, to visit with Miss Abdullah the Valley of the Kings across the Nile, where many of Egypt's ancient pharaohs had been entombed in underground chambers carved into the red cliffs of the Theban hills.

They crossed the Nile from the hotel wharf in a small felucca. When they stepped ashore in the waste of sand on the farther bank, they found they had several hundred yards of desert sand to negotiate on foot before reaching the cavalcade of dusty automobiles that waited to taxi them to the Valley of the Kings.

"Come along, please," said Miss Abdullah briskly, "it's just a short walk," and she determinedly began to slog through the sand. The disembarking tourists followed after her in a straggling line.

Henry Carmichael, polite as always, and considerably younger and stronger than most of the tour members, volunteered to stand on the tiny jetty to which the felucca had tied up and help his fellow sightseers climb out of the boat onto the desert's edge. As a result, he brought up the tail end of the procession that ploughed after Miss Abdullah toward the waiting cars.

It was tiresome, sweaty work, and after fifty yards Henry stopped momentarily to mop his face with his handkerchief and catch his breath. He wasn't all that anxious to visit a bunch of underground graves, anyway, so why hurry? He knew the party wouldn't go forward without him, since Miss Abdullah carefully counted noses before embarking on any expedition.

It was then, as he stood in the hot sunlight, looking around at the featureless desert landscape and wishing he'd thought to bring his sunglasses, that he saw approaching from a southerly direction, and gamboling over the hot sand as blithely as though it were cool green grass, four scrawny goats, guarded by an even scrawnier-looking shepherd—or goatherd, Henry supposed was the proper word.

Three of the goats were piebald black-and-white creatures. The fourth was pure white—greyed-down a trifle, to be sure, by desert dust, but unmistakably white. The goatherd wore a ragged brown burnoose, a filthy turban, and a pair of scruffy, sand-colored sandals over dirty bare feet.

As he came closer, Henry saw that his oval face was also exceptionally dirty. He had mud-colored eyes and a straggle of wispy, dirt-colored beard on the point of his receding chin. And he carried a long river reed with which he occasionally reached out to touch a recalcitrant goat.

Henry stared for a moment at this raffish genie of the desert, then resumed his journey toward the waiting cars.

But the goats and their guardian were now upon him. Henry was about to nod a friendly greeting to them when the goatherd, to Henry's surprise, suddenly held his reed staff stiffly across Henry's

line of march with a hand from which half the thumb was missing.
The stump, Henry noticed, was ridged and rough and untidy, as
though the man's goats might have nibbled off the end of his thumb
in an absent-minded moment. Maybe they had, Henry thought,
amused. People said that goats would eat anything.

His amusement turned to disquiet, however, when the villainous-
looking Arab reached his free hand inside his dirty robe.

The gesture was somehow so dramatic, so singularly provocative
of curiosity as well as trepidation, that Henry found himself helplessly waiting with inexplicable interest for the goatherd to withdraw his hand from his robe and reveal what he had concealed
beneath it. For his manner left no doubt whatever that something
was concealed there.

Yet when he withdrew his hand and extended it toward Henry,
his words were in the blurred whine of Arab salesmen everywhere.
"Souvenir of Egypt, sir? Memento of ancient Nilotic civilization?
Very rare. From secret tomb." He waved a dirty paw toward the
Valley of the Kings.

Henry looked at what he offered: a carved stone head, perhaps
three inches high, of an Egyptian queen wearing the royal ancient
headdress over slanting aquiline features. The smooth patina of
untold centuries seemed to darken the queenly cheeks.

Despite himself, Henry was impressed. He took the carving from
the goatherd's hand. "Where'd you say it came from?"

"Pharaoh's tomb," the goatherd repeated solemnly. "Over there."
He pointed again with his river reed. One of his goats ducked as
though expecting the raised staff to strike it. "Secret tomb. Nobody
know but me. I steal at night. Break off wall carving. Nice souvenir
of Egypt, sir! You believe?"

Henry, though polite, was not gullible. "Oh, no, pal," he said. "You
probably run these things off by the thousand in some little factory
in Luxor and sell them to unsuspecting tourists like me. Isn't that
right?" He grinned disarmingly, a tall, lanky man with a deceptively
mild expression. "But it's pretty damn good for a fake, I'll hand you
that." He stroked the carved head with admiring fingers.

The Arab said, "No fake, sir. That head of Hatshepsut. Great
queen, Eighteenth Dynasty." He paused, then threw in the clincher.
"She marry her brother, Pharaoh Thotmose the Second."

"How much you want for Queen Hatshepsut?" Henry asked.

"Five pounds," the goatherd said. He looked completely uninter-
ested.

Henry laughed. "Sold!" he said. "Dirt cheap for an antiquity thirty-five hundred years old." He handed over five pounds, grinning, and put the queen's head into his jacket pocket.

"Wait, sir," the Arab said. He brought out a second treasure from beneath his grimy burnoose. He held out his hand, palm up, and passed it slowly under Henry's eyes. "Not fake," he said earnestly. "Real."

Henry stared at the pointed circlet that glinted with a dull gold luster against the dirty palm. The circlet had several rough-shaped studs of what looked like carnelian and turquoise set into it. "Hey!" Henry exclaimed. "What's that?"

The Arab showed a trace of animation now. "Pharaoh's fingertip cover, sir. Worn by kings and queens at banquets. Or when buried in tomb. This one from secret tomb, also. But cost more. One hundred and twenty-five pounds." He shot a sharp glance at Henry. "You like?"

Henry's eyes narrowed. "Prices are certainly going up fast," he said. He took the circlet into his own hand and hefted it thoughtfully. It looked like gold, it felt like gold, it weighed heavily in his hand like gold. Or at least, lead. Maybe it *was* gold. If so, with the price of gold currently over four hundred dollars an ounce, the circlet must be worth considerably more than the goatherd was asking for it. And if it wasn't gold, it would make a nice gift for Lorene, his waitress at the Inn-Between. Lorene, bless her heart, wouldn't know the difference between fake and genuine, anyway.

The goatherd stood stolidly, his dirty face expressionless again, keeping the goats in a tight knot about him by occasional taps with his rod.

Henry made up his mind. "Okay," he said. "I like it. I like it a lot. But a hundred and twenty-five pounds! Let's dicker a little, shall we, pal?"

As he caught up with the other tourists a few minutes later, entered the last taxi in the file, and started off for the Valley of the Kings, Henry looked back from his car at the goatherd. The self-confessed grave robber was now placidly watching his goats drink from the river. Soon he was hidden from Henry's view by the cloud of dust raised by the motor cavalcade.

On the short flight back to Cairo the next morning, Henry maneuvered skillfully and successfully to occupy the seat beside Miss Abdullah, the tourguide. He noted with approval that she looked her usual neat, attractive self this morning, clear-eyed and rested despite yesterday's rigors in old temples, sandy deserts, and underground tombs. Yielding the window seat to her with a gallant bow, Henry thought to himself, not for the first time, this kid is quite a girl.

He decided to begin their conversation by telling her so and she was obviously quite pleased with his praise, but denied, with becoming modesty, having any special talent as a tourguide.

Henry said, "I still maintain you're an outstanding representative of your profession, Miss Abdullah. Why, yesterday on that sandy walk through the desert I thought I'd never catch up with you. There you were, miles ahead, floating along through the sand as though on snowshoes, while I was tagging way behind, sweating and panting for breath!" He grinned at her. "So at least physically, you'll admit, you're something special in the way of girl guides."

"The rest of the party didn't find it so difficult to keep up with me." She gave him a curious side glance. "You kept us all waiting for quite a few minutes at the cars, Mr. Carmichael. What delayed you? Were you ill?"

Henry shook his head. "I was winded and hot, all right, but what kept me from joining you sooner was a traveling souvenir salesman, believe it or not."

"In the desert?" Miss Abdullah gave him another curious look.

"Sure. I guess he was really a goatherder, but he also sold souvenirs. A dirty guy with four goats. But I must say his souvenirs were very genuine-looking. He got them from some pharaoh's tomb, he said. He claimed to be a grave robber."

"He spoke English?"

"Enough to give me quite a sales pitch."

"About robbing a king's tomb for his wares?"

"Or a queen's. I forget which."

Miss Abdullah nodded. "That's a claim many of our souvenir salesmen make when tempting gullible Americans like you, Mr. Carmichael," she said, deadpan.

"Ouch!"

"Because," she went on, "it's just a little white lie that makes you prize your souvenirs so much more highly when you get them home and show them to your friends." She was silent for a moment, looking out the plane window beside her. Then she turned back to Henry. "But a goatherd? In the desert? Speaking English? That really is a new one on me, Mr. Carmichael."

"Want to see what he sold me?" asked Henry, reaching for his flight bag in the rack over Miss Abdullah's head.

"I'd love to," she said with undisguised interest.

Henry took the flight bag into his lap, zipped it open, and brought out the lovely little head of Hatshepsut. He handed it to Miss Abdullah. "So what do you think?" he asked hopefully. "That's Hatshepsut, the man said. Broken off a wall carving in a secret tomb. He also said that Hatshepsut married her brother or something scandalous like that. Now, don't you think it looks at least three thousand years old?"

Miss Abdullah hid a smile. "Oh, at least," she said. "I'm sorry, but you can buy one just like this at any bazaar shop in Cairo or Luxor for a pound or two. They're molded by the gross out of marble dust, then aged by smoking them over a slow fire, the way you smoke fish." She handed it back to him. "It's definitely a fake. I hope you didn't pay too much for it."

Henry said, "I'm a sharp bargainer, Miss Abdullah. I got it for five Egyptian pounds. The sales pitch alone was worth five pounds, even if it is a fake."

For the first time, Miss Abdullah laughed aloud, a very musical cascade of sound that made Henry tingle gently with pleasure. "You didn't *really* think it was a genuine antiquity stolen from a tomb, *did* you, Mr. Carmichael?"

Henry replied honestly, "No, I didn't. But I wasn't so sure about this thing." He brought out the golden fingertip circlet from his flight bag and held it out to her. "Maybe this one *did* come from a pharaoh's tomb. It looks good enough to eat, doesn't it?"

Miss Abdullah froze. She became as motionless as the Great Sphinx Henry expected to see in Gizeh that afternoon. Dead silence seemed to descend on the aircraft in spite of the continuing drone of the engines and the chatter of nineteen American tourists.

At length Miss Abdullah spoke in a hushed, reverent tone. "You bought *that* from your goatherd in the desert?"

Henry nodded and handed the circlet to her. "*You* like it, too, don't you?" he said warmly. "I couldn't resist the darn thing. It's a fingertip cover for some pharaoh, right?"

"That's right," said Miss Abdullah absently. She turned the gold fingertip cover this way and that, held it to the light at the window, then announced, "But *this* souvenir, Mr. Carmichael, is *not* a fake. I think it's the genuine article—a three-thousand-year-old miracle of beauty and craftsmanship." She seemed almost awestruck, Henry thought. Her voice had the rich, deep undertone of respect and nostalgia that had suffused it the last two days whenever she lectured to the tour members about ancient Egypt and its rulers.

He grinned at her solemn expression. "Hold it, Miss Abdullah," he said lightly, "let's not get carried away, okay? Suppose it is genuine? It just means that Arab goatherder *did* stumble on a secret tomb and looted it of everything portable. What's the big deal? I got me a bargain, that's all."

Miss Abdullah said, "Don't you realize, Mr. Carmichael, that there have been more than sixty tombs discovered in the Valley of the Kings, but the tombs of Tut-ankh-amen and Semirameb are the only two that weren't plundered by grave robbers *centuries* ago? I can't believe that when all the archeologists in the world have failed to find another undisturbed tomb, an ignorant goatherd could find one. Even if he *can* speak English!"

"I'm sorry," said Henry. "I didn't mean to upset you, Miss Abdullah. You think that my fingertip cover is genuine, then? A real antiquity?"

"I'm not an expert on Middle Kingdom antiquities," she said, "but I'd be willing to wager my dragoman's license that this fingertip cover is genuine." Miss Abdullah straightened in her seat and looked directly into Henry's eyes. It was a pleasant experience for Henry, because her almond-shaped eyes—as large, brown, and beautiful as two matched topazes—had a strange quickening effect on his breathing. "Mr. Carmichael," she said earnestly, "I must ask you to permit me to show this fingertip cover to the curator of the National Museum in Cairo.

Henry shrugged. "Why not?" he said. Then, after a pause for thought, he said, "On the other hand, *why?*"

"Because he will know instantly whether it is fake or genuine. And if it is genuine, he can perhaps, with good luck, trace the goatherd who sold it to you. And find out how the goatherd came into possession of such an antiquity. And prevent him from selling any more national treasures to tourists. Do you see?"

"Not exactly, no. If my fingertip cover is genuine, the Museum confiscates it, right? And I lose a nifty souvenir." Henry's voice was rueful. "That doesn't seem quite fair, does it?"

She said impatiently, "The Museum would certainly reimburse you for whatever you paid the goatherd." She looked at Henry again, eye to eye. "How much *did* you pay the goatherd for it?"

"A hundred and twenty-five pounds," said Henry. "That's what made me suspect I had a bargain—its steep price compared with the Hatshepsut head."

"Aha!" said Miss Abdullah triumphantly. "You see?"

"All I see is I stand to lose a neat souvenir if it's genuine. A souvenir worth a lot more than what I paid for it."

Miss Abdullah frowned at him. "Don't you understand, Mr. Carmichael, that this little gold fingertip cover is part of Egyptian *history?* A rare and precious relic of the greatest civilization the ancient world ever produced?" She was using her impassioned lecture voice again. "To us, it is a possession beyond value, an artifact to be kept triumphantly in its own land, not carried off to America as a cheap tawdry souvenir of a five-day trip to Egypt."

Henry was enchanted with the way her eyes flashed at him, with her almost religious fervor. "Well—" he murmured weakly.

"Furthermore," said Miss Abdullah, pressing her advantage, "Egypt does not look kindly upon foreigners who try to smuggle national treasures out of our country. You could end up in jail, Mr. Carmichael, do you realize that?"

"I suppose I could," agreed Henry, watching with pleasure the emotional rise and fall of her bosom under the neat uniform blouse. "Where I made my mistake, it's clear to me now, was in showing you the darn thing in the first place." He sighed, then said reluctantly, "Okay. You can show it to your Museum guy if you want to. But only on one condition."

She smiled warm approbation. "What's the condition?"

"You've got to promise me that if the fingertip cover proves genuine, you won't put the cops onto my goatherd until after I've left for Greece tomorrow."

"Oh? Why?"

"Because he's a grave robber, that's why—selling stolen goods to tourists. And the minute you lay him by the heels, I become the star witness against him. And it's well known what happens to witnesses in Egypt. You throw 'em into jail until the trial comes up."

"That is a—a canard!" Miss Abdullah gasped indignantly. "It is simply not true!"

"Just kidding," grinned Henry. "But you've got to admit I might be delayed for a few days if I got involved to that extent. So is it a deal? No putting the cops or the Museum on the goatherd till I'm gone?"

"Of course." Her agreement was prompt. "I'm sure the curator of the Museum will understand your problem. Why don't you come

with me to see him? Then you can tell him personally about everything."

"When?"

"This morning. As soon as we land in Cairo."

Henry shook his head regretfully. "Our party is scheduled to visit
Gizeh this afternoon—the great pyramid, the Sphinx, the House of
the Dead. I thought you were going, too."

"No. I guide only a single Luxor tour once a week. You'll have a
different guide this afternoon for Gizeh. Why don't you skip Gizeh
and come with me to the Museum? You haven't seen it yet, and it's
just as interesting, in its way, as Gizeh."

"There's nothing I'd like better. But I've already paid for the Gizeh
tour—and we're flying out to Athens first thing in the morning." He
paused. "You wouldn't want to see me gypped out of my Gizeh tour
as well as my souvenir, would you?"

"Gypped!" Miss Abdullah's eyes flashed angry lightning. "Do you
realize the origin of that odious word, Mr. Carmichael? It comes
from the word *Egypt!* And you use it as though all Egyptians were
dishonest, deceitful, and larcenous."

She's magnificent, thought Henry. He soothed her. "Now, please,
Miss Abdullah. I used the word innocently. Let's forget it. I apologize,
okay?"

Stiffly she said, "I shall give you a written receipt for your fingertip
cover, Mr. Carmichael. I want that distinctly understood. And I shall
return the cover to you at once if the Museum curator says it is not
genuine."

"Never mind the receipt, for Pete's sake," said Henry, enjoying
the delicate aroma of the spicy perfume she was wearing. Chypre?
Musk? Who cared? He said, "Listen, Miss Abdullah, I trust you, I
trust you. If that is distinctly understood, I'll tell you what we can
do about this conflict of schedules we seem to have. You go to the
Museum with my fingertip cover, I'll go to Gizeh. Then, when you've
done your research and I've finished sightseeing, why don't you join
me for dinner at the Nile Hilton? Say about nine o'clock tonight?
And you can either return my souvenir or reimburse me for it while
we dine. How does that sound to you?"

Miss Abdullah gave Henry a radiant, almost flirtatious smile.
"You are a very kind and understanding man, Mr. Carmichael," she
said quietly. "Thank you. I'll be happy to have dinner with you
tonight."

"I'll be waiting for you. Nine o'clock in the Hilton lobby."

"You must tell me in detail about your goatherd, though. So I can pass it on to the curator if it seems called for. Everything you remember, please—so the police can find him if we discover he is selling genuine artifacts to tourists."

"He's an Arab," Henry said. "Medium height. Herding four goats, three of them black-and-white fellows, one a plain white. He had a dirty turban, dirty face, dirty burnoose or whatever you call those robes, dirty feet, dirty sandals. A wisp of a beard. A four-foot river reed for a staff. Half his right thumb is missing." He grinned at Miss Abdullah. "And you know where I met him in the desert. So he must have come from a village or a goat farm or something not far away."

Miss Abdullah nodded thoughtfully. "There is a village near Deir el-Bahri," she ruminated. "Maybe he came from there."

"Near what?"

"You *saw* it yesterday, Mr. Carmichael. Weren't you listening to my lecture?" Her tone was rallying but forgiving. "The Temple of Queen Hatshepsut."

"Oh," said Henry, "that one. The one that looked like a big wedding cake."

Miss Abdullah gave a ladylike snort of disgust.

Ten hours later, when Miss Abdullah entered the lobby of the Hilton, Henry scarcely recognized her. Her natty uniform was gone, replaced by a jade-green cocktail dress that left her shoulders bare and did sensational things for her figure. Her sensible shoes of yesterday, suitable for trudging through sandy deserts and ruins, had been abandoned in favor of green pumps with four-inch heels that increased her height and lent a regal quality to her carriage. Her hairdo now looked more Parisian soubrette than Egyptian girl-guide. Her makeup had been applied with a light and skillful hand. Henry, smiling his approval of this new Miss Abdullah, went to meet her.

She held out a hand to him and began with a rush, "Oh, Mr. Carmichael, the most wonderful news!"

He took her hand, tucked it under his arm, and turned her toward the hotel dining room. "Hold everything, Miss Abdullah," he said, "you can tell me all about it over dinner."

She drew every male eye in the dining room as they were ushered to a table for two by a window overlooking the Nile. Once seated, she burst out, "Don't you *want* to hear my news, Mr. Carmichael?"

"Sure," said Henry, "although I'd be perfectly happy just sitting here looking at you."

She ignored this puerile sally. "I was right, Mr. Carmichael! Your fingertip cover *is* genuine! The curator identified it instantly." Her eyes were shining. "And wait until you hear the rest of it! The curator told me that some months ago a number of items were stolen from the Museum's Semirameb Collection—artifacts found in the tomb of Pharaoh Semirameb. The stolen artifacts have never been traced, nor has the thief been apprehended. A man named Achmed Fayed, who used to be a night caretaker at the Museum and who suddenly resigned his job and disappeared, was suspected of the theft."

"Oh-oh," said Henry, "I think I can see what's coming next."

"Yes! Your fingertip cover is one of the stolen antiquities from the Semirameb Collection! The Curator identified it at once!"

"Ah-ha. And my English-speaking goatherd, then, is—"

"Achmed Fayed! Without a doubt. Achmed Fayed had half his right thumb missing. As did your goatherd."

"Your Mr. Achmed Fayed is a pretty smooth operator, I'd say," Henry commented. "Hiding in the desert with his loot from the Museum. Masquerading as a dirty old goatherd until the heat dies down."

"Heat?"

"Never mind. I get the impression on second thought that he isn't too bright, after all. He was safe up there in the Valley of the Kings, but the dummy started selling golden souvenirs to tourists. What did he do that for, do you suppose?"

Miss Abdullah's ivory cheeks were suddenly suffused by a maidenly blush. She shrugged her shapely shoulders. "Maybe he has a girl friend up there—working at the Winter Palace Hotel, perhaps—and he needs money for her."

"Ah," said Henry, "love will find a way." He cast a quick glance at Miss Abdullah, hoping at least for a smile of acknowledgment.

"And the curator thinks it quite likely," she continued seriously, "that when the police capture your goatherd, they will recover most of the artifacts he stole from the Museum—all except those he has sold to tourists. So—" she regarded him warmly "—do you understand what you've done for us, Mr. Carmichael? You have helped Egypt recover part of her history! Part of her inheritance! Isn't that wonderful? Doesn't it make you feel good?"

"Yeah," said Henry.

"The curator," said Miss Abdullah, "requests that I tender you his respects and his thanks—and indeed the thanks of our whole nation for your helpful and unselfish behavior in this matter."

"Well, now, I appreciate that," said Henry. "But did your curator agree not to nail the goatherd until I've left Egypt?"

"Of course. And—" she smiled teasingly "—I'm to give you back the money you paid for the fingertip cover." She took a roll of bills—American—out of her purse and handed it across the table. Henry accepted it gravely. "A hundred and twenty-five pounds," Miss Abdullah said, almost to herself, "for a treasure like that! Fayed must be mad!"

"Or in love," said Henry.

They ate their dinner in companionable silence. Then, when it was time for after-dinner coffee, Henry said, "Well, it's nice to have the thanks of your Museum and your nation, Miss Abdullah, but how about you? Are you grateful, too?"

She beamed at him. "I certainly am! Do you realize that this will be the talk of Cairo within forty-eight hours? That I shall become, as a result, one of the most popular and best paid tourguides in Egypt? That you have enabled me to strike a blow for Egyptian women, who have been second-class citizens in our land for centuries? Of *course* I'm grateful to you, Mr. Carmichael! More grateful than I can say!"

"Then why don't we go upstairs to my room to have our coffee?" Henry suggested.

After a moment of electric silence, Miss Abdullah fixed Henry with a level, appraising look that was so cool it could have been termed frosty without exaggeration. "I'm grateful to you, Mr. Carmichael," she said at length, "but not that grateful."

Henry sighed. "Okay. I understand. And I apologize. But look here, Miss Abdullah, you can't blame me for trying, can you? *You're* the prettiest Egyptian artifact I've seen since I left home, even if you're not part of the Semirameb Collection."

That melted the ice in her eyes. "It's almost eleven o'clock," she said, "and you have an early flight tomorrow. You'll want to be packing." She pushed back her chair, gathered up her purse, and smiled at him warmly once more. "So I'll be saying goodbye now, Mr. Carmichael. And thank you again from my heart for everything."

She stood up, turned, and left the dining room while Henry was still fumbling for the dinner check . . .

Folding shirts, pairing socks, he whistled softly to himself, re-
viewing the evening's adventure with Miss Abdullah. He was quite
disappointed, actually, that his pass had failed. Still, he told himself,
there were compensations. Miss Abdullah had been successfully
conned into getting his gold fingertip cover authenticated by no less
an authority than the curator of the National Museum, which ought
to be enough authentication to satisfy anybody. So now he knew,
without the shadow of a doubt, that the fingertip cover was genuine.
It was solid gold, it was from King Semirameb's tomb, it was over
three thousand years old, and it was what Miss Abdullah quite
simply described as "beyond value."

So, he told himself happily, if *that* fingertip cover was all those
wonderful things—genuine, old, solid gold, and priceless—then it
followed that the *other* four fingertip covers he had purchased from
the goatherd yesterday were also probably genuine, old, solid gold,
and priceless.

He dug them out of his flight bag and held them under the bedside
lamp for a moment to admire their silken golden sheen, their carnelian and turquoise studs, their aura of mysterious antiquity. Then
he rolled them up in a pajama top and put them into his suitcase,
contemplating the future with some satisfaction.

Although he considered it the better part of wisdom to remain
abroad until the heat generated by his most recent bank-float scam
at home had cooled off a bit, he would eventually return home. And
when he did, he thought to himself, if he couldn't sell his four gold
fingertip covers for half a million dollars to some American museum
or private collector with no questions asked, he deserved to be buried
alive in some desert, somewhere, or have his thumbs chewed off by
four scrawny black-and-white goats.

Clark Howard

The Dublin Eye

Kilkenny heard the phone ring as he was unlocking his office door. He hurried in to answer it.

"Kilkenny," he said.

"Is this Mr. Royal Kilkenny?" a hesitant female voice asked. The caller sounded very young. "Mr. Royal Kilkenny, the query man?"

"Yes. How can I help you?"

"Mr. Kilkenny, my name is Darlynn Devalain. I'm the daughter of Joe Devalain, of Belfast."

An image mushroomed in Kilkenny's mind. Not of Joe Devalain, but of the woman Joe had married. Of Sharmon. This girl on the phone was probably Sharmon's daughter.

"How is your dad, then?" Kilkenny asked. "And your mother?"

"My dad's not so good, Mr. Kilkenny," the girl replied, and Kilkenny, though he had never laid eyes on her, could almost see her lip quivering as her voice broke. "He's been in a bad accident. An explosion in his shop. They've got him over at St. Bartholomew's Hospital, but it's not known if he'll live or—"

"Did your mother tell you to call me?" Kilkenny asked, frowning. It had been eighteen years since Sharmon Cavan had picked Joe Devalain over him and he had gone off to America to try and forget her.

"No, she doesn't even know I'm after calling you," Darlynn Devalain said. "Me dad told me once that he knew you before you went to America. When he heard you'd come back and set up as a query man down in Dublin, he told me you were a man he could always count on. He said if I should ever find myself in serious trouble of any kind to get hold of you and tell you I'm the daughter of Joe Devalain. You'd help me just as if I were your own. So that's why I'm calling, sor. Not for me, but for me dad. He needs somebody to look out after his interests. The police, they don't seem to care much about who blew up his shop."

"How badly was he hurt in the explosion?" Kilkenny asked.

"As badly as one can be and still be called alive," the girl said. "Oh, Mr. Kilkenny, he's in terrible shape. Can you come, sor? Please."

The girl's voice reminded Kilkenny of Sharmon. Sharmon, with her deep-rust-colored hair and dancing emerald eyes, the smile that showed crooked teeth that somehow made her even prettier, the wide, wide shoulders, and the strong peasant thighs that even at sixteen could lock a man where she wanted him, for as long as she wanted him there.

"Yes, I'll come," Kilkenny said. "I'll take the train up and meet you at the hospital this evening."

Kilkenny bought a first-class seat on the *Enterprise Express,* which made the Dublin-Belfast run in two hours and twenty minutes. Dundalk, an hour north of Dublin, was the last stop in the Irish Free State. After Dundalk, the train crossed into Armagh County, which was part of Northern Ireland.

At Portadown, the first stop in Armagh, British soldiers boarded the coaches and checked all passengers. From Portadown on into Belfast, an armed British soldier rode at each end of every coach. Most passengers didn't leave their seats even to go to the lavatory during that leg of the journey.

At Belfast Central, the passengers stood for a pat-down, baggage search, and questioning at a British Army checkpoint in the middle of the station.

"Identification, please," a pink-cheeked young lieutenant requested. Kilkenny handed over his billfold. "What's your business in Belfast, sir?"

"To see a friend who's in hospital."

"What's the duration of your stay, sir?"

"I don't know. No more than forty-eight hours, I shouldn't expect."

"Your occupation is listed as a 'personal enquiries representative.' What is that, exactly?"

"I'm a private investigator. A detective."

The young officer's expression brightened. "You mean like one of those American private eyes? Like that Magnum bloke?"

"Yes, sort of. Less hectic, though."

The lieutenant frowned. "Not armed, I hope."

"No." Kilkenny wondered why he asked. A sergeant had already patted Kilkenny down and two privates had rummaged through his overnighter.

"Pass through," the officer said, returning Kilkenny's billfold.

Outside the terminal, Kilkenny got into a square black taxi. "St. Bartholomew's Hospital," he said.

The driver glanced at him in the rearview mirror, then looked out the side window at the darkening late-afternoon sky. "That's in the Flats," he said.

"The Flats?"

"Aye. Unity Flats. The Catholic section. I'll take you in, but I can't wait for you or come back to get you. I'm not Catholic, so I can't risk being in the Flats after dark."

"Just drop me at the hospital," Kilkenny said. "That'll be fine."

On the way through the city, it started to rain—one of those sudden, blustery rains that seemed to be forever blowing in off the North Channel and turning the already dreary grey streets a drearier black. Kilkenny hadn't thought to bring a raincoat—it had been so long since he'd been to Belfast he had forgotten how unpredictable the weather could be.

"Bit of a heavy dew out there," he said.

"Aye," the driver replied, turning on the wipers. He made no attempt at further conversation.

Kilkenny wasn't familiar with the section called Unity Flats. He, Joe Devalain, and Sharmon Cavan had grown up in a slum known as Ballymurphy. It was a savagely poor place, worse than anything Kilkenny had seen during his ten years as a New York City policeman. In New York, he had worked both Spanish Harlem and the South Bronx and neither of them was nearly as poor, ugly, or deprived as Ballymurphy. Ballymurphy wasn't the gutter, it was the sewer. Both Kilkenny and Joe Devalain had sworn to Sharmon that they would take her away from the life of poverty in which they had all grown to adolescence.

It had not been Kilkenny Sharmon picked to do it. "I've decided in favor of Joe," she told Kilkenny one night after they had made love under the back stairs of Sharmon's tenement building.

"I thought you loved *me*," Kilkenny had said.

"I love you both," Sharmon had answered. "Do y'think I'd do this with the two of you if I didn't love you both? It's just that I can't *have* you both, so I must choose, mustn't I? And I've chosen Joe."

"But why? Why him and not me?"

"Lots of reasons," she said lightly. "I like the name Sharmon Devalain better than I like Sharmon Kilkenny. And I think Joe will do better in life than you. He's got a good job at the linen plant—someday he'll probably be a foreman. While you've done nothing at all to better yourself."

"I go to school," Kilkenny protested. "I want to be a policeman someday—"

"I don't like policemen," she said loftily. "They're a smug lot. Anyway, Joe'll earn lots more when he works his way up to plant foreman than you'll ever earn being a policeman."

Kilkenny had been sick with disappointment. "If it's just the money, maybe I could be something else—"

"It's not just that," she said.

"What else, then?"

"Well, y'see," she replied with a little reluctance, "Joe is—well, *better* at—well, you know—" She sighed impatiently. "He's a bit more of a man, if y'know what I mean."

Kilkenny had thought he would never get over that remark. It left him impotent for six months. Only after leaving Ireland, going to Southampton, and boarding a ship for America, meeting on board a fleshy Czech girl just beginning to feel her new freedom after escaping from behind the Iron Curtain, was he able to function physically as a man again. He had never had a problem since—but he had never forgotten Sharmon's words.

"Here you are," the driver said. "St. Bartholomew's."

Kilkenny collected his bag and got out. The driver made change for him, glanced up at the waning daylight again, and sped off.

From the front steps of the hospital, Kilkenny looked around at what he could see of Unity Flats. It was a slum, as Ballymurphy had been, though not quite as stark and dirty. But definitely a ghetto. Sharmon hadn't made it very far with Joe, he thought.

In the hospital lobby, a young nun, wearing the habit of the Ulster Sisters of Charity, consulted a name file and directed Kilkenny to a ward on the third floor. He waited for the lift with several women visitors. The women in the north were not as attractive as the women down south, he noticed. Most of them wore white T-necks that clearly outlined their brassieres, wide-legged, baggy slacks or skirts that were too short, no stockings, and shoes with straps that made their ankles look thick. Their hair seemed to be combed and in control only down to their cheeks, then appeared to grow wild on its own, as if it was too much to take care of. They were poor women, clearly. As they grew older, Kilkenny knew, they would all become noble mother figures who would strive to keep their husbands sober, their children God-fearing and Catholic, and their homes decent. They were the silent strength of the poor Northern Irish Catholic household. Kilkenny wondered if Sharmon had become like them.

At the third-floor ward, Kilkenny stepped through double swinging doors and looked around. The instant he saw Darlynn Devalain, he knew who she was. She looked nothing at all like Joe, but though he saw only a trace of Sharmon there was enough so there was no mistaking who she was. Burnt-blonde hair, eyes a little too close together, lips a little crooked, almost mismatched, there was something distinctly urchin about her. That touch of the gutter, Kilkenny thought. It never entirely leaves us.

She was standing just outside a portable screen that kept the last bed on the ward partitioned from the others. She was staring out at nothing as if in a trance. Kilkenny put his bag by the wall and walked down the ward toward her. When he came into her field of vision, it seemed to break her concentration and she watched him as he walked up to her. Their eyes met and held.

"You're Darlynn," he said. "I'm Royal Kilkenny."

She put out her hand. "Thanks for coming." She bobbed her chin at the bed behind the screen. "Me dad's there. What's left of him."

There were a doctor and two nurses on one side of the bed, the nurses just turning away with covered aluminum trays in their hands, walking past Kilkenny on their way out. When they left, Kilkenny had an unobstructed view of the bed. What he saw did not look like a man at all; it looked like a large pillow under a sheet, with a head placed above it and several rubber tubes running down to it from jars of liquid hung on racks next to the bed. There was an oxygen mask over part of the face. Kilkenny saw no arms or legs under the sheet and felt his mouth go dry.

"Who are you, please?" the doctor asked, noticing Kilkenny.

"A friend. Up from Dublin. His daughter called me." Kilkenny tried to swallow but could not. "Is he still alive?" he asked. The form did not appear to be breathing.

"Yes. Why or how, I don't know. The explosion totally devastated him. Apparently he was right on top of whatever detonated. The flash of the explosion blinded him; the noise destroyed his eardrums so that he's now completely deaf; and the hot gases got into his open mouth and burned up his tongue and vocal cords, making him mute. The force of the blast damaged his lungs and shattered his limbs so badly we had to amputate both arms above the elbow and both legs above the knee. So here he lies, unable to see, hear, or speak, unable to breathe without an oxygen mask, and with no arms or legs. But he's alive." He led Kilkenny out to where Darlynn stood. "I've sedated him for the night," he told the girl. "You go home and rest, young lady. That's an order."

Kilkenny took Darlynn by the arm and gently led her out of the ward, picking up his bag on the way. There was a snack shop still open on the ground floor, and Kilkenny took her there, found a remote table, and ordered tea.

"How's your mother taking it?" he asked.

Darlynn shrugged. "It's not the end of the world for her. She and Dad haven't got on that great the past few years."

Kilkenny decided not to pursue that topic. "What kind of explosion was it? How'd it happen?"

"We don't know. It's supposedly being investigated by the RUC. But you know how that is."

The RUC was the Royal Ulster Constabulary, Northern Ireland's civilian police force. Like all other civil service in Ireland's British-aligned six northern counties, it was controlled by London and more than ninety percent Protestant.

"They're trying to put the blame on the IRA," Darlynn added.

"Of course." It would be the natural thing for them to do, Kilkenny thought. But he knew, as most Irishmen did, that for the IRA to be responsible for every crime attributed to it, the outlaw organization would have to be fifty thousand strong instead of the less than a thousand it actually was. "Was your dad still active in the IRA?" he asked.

Darlynn glanced at him and hesitated a beat before answering. Kilkenny expected as much. He was, despite her father's recommendation, still a stranger to her, and to speak of the IRA to strangers could be dangerous. But something about him apparently prompted her trust.

"No, he hadn't been active for about five years. He still supported the organization financially, as much as he could afford, but he no longer took part in raids or anything like that."

"Had he any trouble with the Orangemen?" Kilkenny asked, referring to the pseudo-Masonic order of Protestants that opposed a united Ireland. Their activities were often as violent as the IRA, though never as well publicized.

"Dad had no trouble with them that I know about," Darlynn said. "Except for his IRA donations, he stayed pretty much out of politics. All he cared about these past few years was that shop of his. He was very proud of that shop."

"What sort of shop?" Kilkenny asked. The last he'd heard, Joe Devalain was still trying to work his way up the ladder at the linen factory.

"It was a linen shop. Tablecloths, napkins, handkerchiefs, a few bedcovers, a small line of curtains. If there was one thing Dad knew, it was cloth. He worked in the linen factory for eighteen years and never got a single promotion, but he learned all there was to know about cloth. Finally he decided to pack it in. He drew out all his pension benefits and opened the shop. Mum was furious about it, said those benefits were half hers, for *her* old age as well as his. But Da did it anyway."

"Was that when things started going bad between them?"

"Not really. They'd been at each other off and on for a long time." Darlynn looked down at the tabletop. "Mum's had a boy friend or two."

"Did you tell your mother you were calling me?" Kilkenny asked.

"I told her after."

"What was her reaction?"

"She got a funny kind of look on her face, like I haven't seen in a long time. When I was a little girl, she used to get a look like that whenever Da would bring her a bouquet of posies. When I mentioned your name, it was like I had done something special for her. Were you and my mother close?"

Kilkenny nodded. "Your mum and dad and me were all three close. Your dad and me were best friends, but we were rivals for your mum, too. Your dad won her. He was too much a match for me."

"He wouldn't be much competition now, would he?" she asked. Suddenly tears streaked her cheeks.

Kilkenny calmed her down and got her to finish her tea, then walked the two miles home with her because she didn't feel like riding a bus. It had stopped raining and the bleak, poorly lighted streets smelled wet and the air was heavy. Kilkenny's palm sweated from carrying the suitcase. There was something about the way Darlynn's hair bounced in back that reminded him of Sharmon.

Somewhere along the way, he promised the girl he would look into the matter of the explosion that had destroyed everything about her father except his life.

The Devalains lived as tenants in a little timeworn house that looked like wet newspaper. As Kilkenny and Darlynn got to the door, Sharmon Devalain opened it for them.

"Hello, Roy," she said.

"Hello, Sharmon."

The sight of her reduced him to astonishment. She seemed not to have aged as he had. There were no plump cheeks, no wide hips, nothing even remotely in common with the women he had seen at the lift in the hospital. She didn't look a day over thirty, if that.

"Come in, Roy. I'll make tea."

"We've just had tea, actually. And I've got to go get a room."

"You can stay here. I can sleep with Darlynn. The place isn't much, but it's clean."

"Thanks, anyway, but I'd better stay downtown. I told Darlynn I'd try and find out about the explosion."

Sharmon threw her daughter a quick, irritated glance. "She's quick to ask for anything she wants. Even with strangers."

"I don't really feel like a stranger to her. After all, she *is* yours. And Joe's."

"Yes. Well, I'm sure the RUC will appreciate any help you can give them." Her eyes flicked up and down his tall frame. "You're looking well, Roy. Prosperous."

"Hardly that. I make a comfortable living is all. But it's what I want to do."

"Well, you're one of the lucky ones then. Most people never get what they want out of life. Are you sure about tea? Or staying the night?"

"Yes, thanks. I'll be off. Is there a bus at the corner?"

Sharmon nodded. "Number Five. It'll take you to Great Victoria Street. Will I see you again?"

"Sure," Kilkenny said. "I'll be around."

Only when he was walking down the street did Kilkenny realize that he had not said he was sorry about Joe.

He got a room at the Europa Hotel downtown and spent the night alternating between restless, fitful sleep and sitting on the windowsill, staring out at the night city, remembering.

When the night finally ended and daylight broke over Belfast Lough, when from his hotel window Kilkenny saw smoke rising from the great stacks of Harland and Wolff, the mammoth shipbuilding complex, and when civil servants began hurrying along

Howard Street to their jobs in nearby Donegall Square, he showered and shaved and went down for breakfast.

After he ate, he walked over to Oxford Street where the Royal Courts of Justice were located and found that the Royal Ulster Constabulary Headquarters were still situated nearby. After telling his business to a receptionist in the lobby, he was sent up to the first floor and shown to the desk of Sergeant Bill O'Marn of the Bomb Investigation section.

"Well, well," O'Marn said, looking at Kilkenny's identification. "A real flesh-and-blood private eye, just like on the telly." He was a handsome man of forty, with great bushy black eyebrows. One of the "black Irish" that women seemed to find so attractive. He wore a sprig of light-green heather on the lapel of his Harris tweed jacket. Dapper, Kilkenny thought. "You realize your detective license is no good up here, don't you?" O'Marn asked.

"Certainly," said Kilkenny. "I'm only making enquiry at the request of Mr. Devalain's daughter."

"Who, I believe, is a minor."

"Yes, I believe she is. As I started to say, though, I haven't been retained or anything like that. The girl just wants to know who detonated her father. As I'm sure you do also."

"We already know," O'Marn said. "It was the IRA."

"I see. May I ask *how* you know?"

"The explosion was caused by gelignite. Nobody but the IRA uses gelignite. Every time we raid an IRA headquarters, we confiscate a foot locker full of the stuff."

Kilkenny nodded. "What reason, I wonder, would the IRA have for blowing up Joe Devalain."

"They don't need reasons for what they do," O'Marn scoffed. "They're madmen, the lot of them."

"Are you saying they simply decided to blow up a shop—any shop—and picked Joe Devalain's place randomly?"

"Looks that way to us."

This time Kilkenny shook his head. "I'm sorry, Sergeant O'Marn, but I can't accept that premise. It's always been my understanding that the IRA was much more precise in its operations than that. I thought it only set off bombs in strategic locations where the British Army mustered or patrolled, or where the explosion would produce some subsequent economic impact. I don't see how blowing up a small linen shop is going to do them any good at all."

"Neither do I," O'Marn agreed with an artificial smile. "But then, you and I aren't IRA terrorists, are we?"

"Is the matter still under investigation?" Kilkenny asked, ignoring the sergeant's question.

"Technically, yes."

"But it isn't being worked?"

"I didn't say that, Mr. Kilkenny."

Kilkenny rose. "You didn't have to. I wonder what you'll do about your crime statistics if the IRA ever disbands. Anyway, thanks for your time, Sergeant. Good day."

From RUC headquarters, Kilkenny rode a bus back out to Unity Flats. On the way he became aware of some of the graffiti that scarred the city. NO POPE HERE! read one. NO QUEEN HERE! countered another. PROVISIONALS FOR FREEDOM, GOD SAVE OUR POPE! was offset by NO SURRENDER, GOD SAVE THE QUEEN! Some city blocks warned: ARMY KEEP OUT! SOLDIERS ARE BASTARDS! Others proclaimed: ULSTER WILL FIGHT! The most ominous said simply: INFORMERS BEWARE.

Twice along the way, the bus passed moving Saracens, big, six-wheeled armored vehicles that carried three soldiers and patrolled the Catholic sections. The great tanks lumbered past children playing on the sidewalk. They didn't even glance at it, never having known streets without such patrols.

At St. Bart's hospital, Kilkenny found Darlynn sitting by her father's bed, gently stroking the stump of one arm above the bandage. She looked scrubbed and fresh, like a schoolgirl. Kilkenny drew a chair round and sat by her.

"When your dad was active in the IRA, did you ever know any of his contacts?" he asked very quietly.

Darlynn shook her head. "The only time the organization was ever mentioned was when he and Mum would fight about it. She claimed it was because he was suspected of being IRA that he never got promoted at the linen factory. According to her, it's been the IRA that's kept us in Unity Flats all these years."

"Did you ever know of any meeting places he went to?"

"I'm not sure. There was a pub out on Falls Road—Bushmill's, it was called. I used to find match boxes from the place when I emptied the pockets of Da's trousers for the wash. I know after he left the IRA I never found them again."

While she was talking, Darlynn had unintentionally stopped

stroking her father's mutilated arm. To Kilkenny's surprise, the reduced figure on the bed began emitting from under the oxygen mask a pitiful, begging noise. Darlynn resumed stroking at once, and what was left of Joe Devalain calmed down.

"I don't even know if he's aware it's me," Darlynn said.

"I'm sure he is," Kilkenny told her, though he wasn't sure at all.

"I wish there was some way to communicate with him," the girl said. "Maybe *he'd* know who did this to him."

Yes, Kilkenny thought, he might. But how *did* one communicate with a living soul who could not see, hear, or speak, and had no hands with which to write or feel or make signals?

"Would you like to come for supper tonight?" Darlynn asked. "Mum's going out, but I'm a better cook, anyway—at least, Dad's always said I was. It wouldn't be anything fancy, you understand."

"I'm sorry, I'll be busy tonight, Darlynn. I want to make contact with the IRA if I can."

She put her free hand on his knee. "Stop by later, then. Just so I'll know you're all right?"

He promised he would.

As he left the hospital, Kilkenny imagined that his leg felt warm where she had touched him.

Bushmill's was not unlike a hundred other neighborhood pubs in Belfast. It had a stained-glass window or two, a few secluded nooks, one private booth with frosted glass, and a bar as shiny as a little girl's cheeks on First Holy Communion Day. There was always an accordion player about, and always a stale beer odor in the air. Anyone ordering anything except a pint of stout drawn from the tap got a sidelong glance. All conversation ceased when a stranger entered.

Kilkenny stood in the silence at the end of the bar and ordered his pint. When it came, he paid for it and drank it down in a single long, continuous swallow. Wiping off the foam with the back of his hand, he then spoke to the bartender in a tone that every man on the premises could hear.

"My name is Royal Kilkenny. I'm a detective down in the Free State, but I grew up here in Belfast, over in Ballymurphy. My father was Doyle Kilkenny. My mother was Faye Quinn Kilkenny. My grandfather on my mother's side was Darcy Quinn, who was Padriac Pearse's man in Longford County and served four years in His Majesty's prison at Wormwood Scrubs for the privilege. I'm up here because a friend of mine named Joe Devalain was blown up in his linen shop three days ago. He's still alive, what there is left of him, but that doesn't include eyes, ears, voice, hands, or feet. The RUC tells me the IRA did it. I don't believe that. But I want to hear it from the mouth of a man who knows for sure. I'm at the Europa Hotel, Room seven nineteen. I'll be back there within the hour."

As Kilkenny suspected, it worked. Two men came for him just after dark, escorted him to a panel truck parked near the hotel, put him in the back, and blindfolded him. The truck was driven for about thirty minutes, on rough streets, making many turns. When finally it stopped, Kilkenny was taken out, led into a building and down some stairs, and finally had his blindfold removed in a small, cluttered room in which a white-haired man sat behind a scarred desk.

"My father was in prison with your grandfather," the white-haired man said. "I'm Michael McGuire."

"It's an honor to meet you, sir," Kilkenny said. Iron Mike McGuire was a legend in Northern Ireland. A third-generation Irish freedom fighter, he was the most wanted man in the country. There wasn't a child over six in Belfast who didn't know his name, yet fewer than a dozen people had seen his face in nearly a decade.

"I know about Joe Devalain's misfortune," Iron Mike said. "I was saddened to hear of it. Joe was once a loyal soldier fighting for a united Ireland. He left the cause some years back, for reasons of his own, but I understand he continued to contribute money to us, for which we are grateful. There was no ill will when he left us. There never is. A man does what he can, for as long as he can, and that's all we ask. If Joe had still been one of us, actively, we'd right now be after finding out who bombed him. Since he was not, we choose to stay out of it. I can assure you, however, that the IRA had nothing to do with the incident."

Kilkenny nodded. "I see. Well, I thank you for telling me, sir, and for the trouble of bringing me here."

"It's not been that much trouble. I'd be particular, though, if I were you, where I made that little speech you gave in Bushmill's. There's some pubs you'd not've walked out of. Pubs that are patronized by the other side."

"I understand," Kilkenny said. "I appreciate the advice. May I ask for a bit more?"

"A man can always ask."

"How would I go about contacting the Orangemen?"

McGuire exchanged a fleeting glance with the two men who had brought Kilkenny. "For what purpose?" he asked.

"The same purpose as my coming here. To see if they were responsible. If it was political, what happened to Joe, then I'll let the matter go. But if the Orangemen also disclaim the act, then I've still got work to do."

Pursing his lips, McGuire silently drummed the thick, stubby fingers of one hand on the scarred desktop. "All right," he said after a moment. "I don't believe the Orangemen were involved, but I could be wrong. At any rate, the only Order of Orange faction that is authorized to take lives is the Black Preceptories. It's an internal terrorist group that specializes in kidnaping, torture, and house-burning. It was them that torched the two hundred Catholic homes in Bogside back in '78. The leader of the bunch is Black Jack Longmuir. He works in the shipyards. You can usually find him through the union office." McGuire smiled as cold a smile as Kilkenny had ever seen. "When y'see him, tell him I'm thinking about him. Day and night. Always thinking about him."

With those words, McGuire nodded and Kilkenny was once again blindfolded and led away.

The union office was open around the clock, because Harland and Wolff Shipbuilding was running three shifts. The office was situated in a little corrugated metal building just outside the shipyard entrance. There was no doubt where the union's sympathy and support lay. Immediately inside the door was an Order of Orange flag and a framed rhyme:

Catholics beware! For your time has come!
Listen to the dread sound of our Protestant drum!
In memory of William, we'll hoist up our flag!
We'll raise the bright orange and burn your green rag!

William was William of Orange, who married the daughter of the last Catholic king of England, James II, then betrayed him, drove him from the throne, and turned Britain into a Protestant country. Five years later, the Orange Society was formed in Ireland by the new gentry to whom William had distributed the land. Its purpose, by its own charter, was to maintain the Protestant constitution of the country. Nearly two hundred years later, it was still trying to do that, although it had since met failure in twenty-six of Ireland's thirty-two counties. The organization was strongest in Belfast, where it controlled the trade unions. Nowhere was there a better example of that strength than at Harland and Wolff, Ulster's greatest single industrial complex. Of ten thousand employees, only one hundred were Catholic.

"Might I be of some service, sor?" a bulldog of a man asked Kilkenny when he entered.

"I was told I might find Jack Longmuir here," Kilkenny said. Several men in the little office glanced at him, then looked away quickly.

"May I ask what your business is, sor?"

"I'm a detective from Dublin. An old mate of mine was seriously injured by a bomb in his shop three days ago. I'd like to ask Mr. Longmuir's advice about how best to go about finding out who did it."

The little bulldog cocked his head. "What makes y'think he'd give you advice on a matter like that?"

"What makes *you* think he wouldn't?" Kilkenny countered. "Or are you authorized to speak for him?"

The little man turned red. "I'll see if he's here."

Several minutes later, a young man in coveralls, with metal shavings and dust on his sleeves, came to fetch Kilkenny. Giving him a visitor's pass, he led Kilkenny past a security gate and into the shipyard. They walked in silence for two hundred yards, then the escort guided him into a welding hangar where at least thirty men were working on sections of steel hull. Pointing, he directed Kilkenny up a metal ladder to a catwalk where a tall man stood with a clipboard in his hand.

Kilkenny climbed the ladder and moved around the metal catwalk until he was near enough to speak. But the tall man spoke first.

"I'm Longmuir. What d'you want?"

"Do you know of Joe Devalain?" Kilkenny asked.

Longmuir nodded. He was a cadaverous man with a jaw that was steel-blue from a lifetime of using a straight razor. His eyes looked like two perfect bullet holes.

"I'd like to find out who did it to him," Kilkenny said. "But only if it was nonpolitical. If it was a political act, I'll leave it be."

"Why come to me?" Longmuir asked. "I'm a law-abiding British subject. I work, take care of my family, and support the Presbyterian Church and my trade union. I know nothing of bombings and such. Who sent you to me?"

"Michael McGuire."

For just an instant, Longmuir's face registered surprise, but he quickly contained it. "Iron Mike, eh?" he said, as if the words were a foul taste in his mouth. "You saw him, did you?"

"Yes. He assured me the IRA wasn't involved in what happened to Joe. He said only you could tell me whether the Black Preceptories did it."

"How does Iron Mike look?" Longmuir asked curiously. "I've not seen even a photograph of him in ten years."

Kilkenny thought for a moment, then said: "He looks old. And tired."

Longmuir grunted softly. "Aye. Like me." He squinted at Kilkenny. "Did he say anything about me?"

"Yes. That he thinks about you a lot."

Longmuir smiled a smile as hateful as McGuire's had been. "I hope he's thinking of me when he draws his last breath." The tall man stared out at nothing for a moment, deep in thought. Then he emitted a quiet sigh. "No one associated with the Order of Orange had anything to do with blowing up your friend," he told Kilkenny. "You'll have to look elsewhere for them that's guilty."

Kilkenny thanked him, and Black Jack Longmuir had him escorted out of the shipyard complex.

It wasn't too late, so Kilkenny rode a bus out to the Devalain house to ask how Joe had fared that day and to question Sharmon and Darlynn, now that a political motive had been eliminated, about who else might have had reason to harm Joe. When he got to the house and knocked, no one answered right away. Kilkenny thought they might already have gone to bed. The past few days had to have been very trying for them. Darlynn, especially, looked on the verge of exhaustion. Kilkenny had just turned to leave when Sharmon opened the door, wearing a housecoat.

"Hello, Roy. Darlynn's not here—she's staying at the hospital all night. Joe's mind seems to be going. He's bucking up and down on the bed, making that pathetic sound he makes, raising havoc. The only thing that seems to calm him is to have Darlynn there, patting him. The doctor says her touch is all he relates to now, he's been reduced to the primitive level, whatever that means. I'd offer you tea but I'm just out."

She had not stepped away from the doorway or invited him inside.

"Tea's not necessary," Kilkenny said, "but I would like to ask you a few questions."

"I was just ready for bed, Roy. Can we do it tomorrow?" She must have noticed the curious expression that came over his face, because she amended her reply at once. "I suppose we can do it now. It won't take long, will it?"

"Shouldn't."

She led him to the modest parlor with its threadbare sofa, worn rug, and scratched coffee table. She conducted herself very much like a lady, keeping the housecoat well around her, even holding it closed at the throat. Her reserved demeanor brought back Darlynn's words to him: "Mum's had a boy friend or two." Kilkenny had expected Sharmon to make advances on him first chance she got. Now it appeared she was doing just the opposite.

"I'm sorry Darlynn isn't here," she said. "She'll be sorry she missed you. She fancies you, y'know."

"Nonsense," Kilkenny scoffed. "She's only a girl."

"Look again, Roy. She's older than I was when we first went under the stairs together."

"That was different. I'm sure she only looks on me as an uncle or something." He sat down. "Now, then, to business. I've made contact with the IRA and the Black Preceptories. From both quarters I've been assured that there was no involvement in blowing up Joe's shop."

"And you believe them?" Sharmon asked.

Kilkenny nodded. "No reason not to. If either group had done it, there would have been a purpose—the IRA because Joe had betrayed it in some way, the Black Preceps because he was still providing financial support to the IRA or some other unknown reason. Whatever, the bombing would have been to make an example of him. Not to take credit for it would be defeating the purpose of the act. If either group had done it, they'd have claimed it and said why."

"So who d'you think did it, then?"

"That's where I go from here. Who do *you* think might have done it?"

"I haven't a notion."

"Did he have any enemies?"

"Joe? Not likely. You have to *do* something to make enemies. Joe never *did* anything. Sure, he joined the IRA, but only because a lot of his mates was doing the same. And he ended up quitting that. The only thing he ever done on his own was leaving the linen factory and opening up that silly shop. That was the only independent decision he ever made in his life, and you see how that turned out."

"Was he gambling, d'you know? Could he have been in debt and you not know it?"

Sharmon grunted scornfully. "He didn't have the guts to gamble."

"Do you think there could have been another woman? A jealous husband or a boy friend?"

She shook her head. "Never."

"Well, *somebody* didn't like him," Kilkenny said. "Can't you think of anybody?"

"Just me," Sharmon answered evenly.

"You?" Kilkenny had known it, but had never expected her to be so candid about it.

"Yes, me." With just a hint of defiance. "And why not? Look around you," she challenged, waving an arm. "This here is what my whole *life* is like. Worn, tattered, musty, colorless. This here is what I gave up my *youth* for, Roy. This here is all I *have*. It's all he's ever given me. Oh, yes, I disliked him. And if he'd been poisoned or cut up with a kitchen knife, I'd be your number-one suspect. But I wouldn't know how to make a bomb even if I had the proper stuff."

"No, you wouldn't," Kilkenny said. He thought he heard a noise from the rear of the house—a creaking, as if someone had stepped on an unsteady floorboard. "Could that be Darlynn home?"

"No. She always uses the front. It's probably a loose shutter. Listen, can we finish this another time, Roy? I've a raging headache and really would like to get to bed."

"Sure."

On his way to the front door, Kilkenny noticed an ashtray on one of the tables with something purplish in it. He saw it only for a second, for just as his eyes came to rest on it Sharmon picked it up and emptied it in a wastebasket under the table. "Goodnight then, Roy," she said. "God bless."

"Goodnight, Sharmon."

He did not return her "God bless" because it had just registered in his mind what the purplish thing in the ashtray was.

Irish heather. Green Irish heather. It turned purple when it died.

Kilkenny went to the hospital and found Darlynn asleep on a couch in the waiting room. "She was all wore out," the nun in charge of the ward told him. "When her father finally got calmed, we made her come in here and lie down. She was asleep that quick."

"Is he asleep, too?" Kilkenny asked of Joe.

"We never know, do we?" the nun replied quietly. "He doesn't have to close his eyelids to sleep."

Kilkenny went into the ward and stood by Joe's bed. Devalain's form was still, his eyes wide and fixed. "I might know who did this to you, Joe," Kilkenny whispered. "But I must be sure before I do anything."

Stepping to the window at the end of the long room, Kilkenny stared out at the blackness, seeing only his own dim reflection from the nightlight next to Joe's bed. If only I could ask him simple questions he could answer with a nod or a shake of his head, he thought. But how in bloody hell can you communicate with somebody who can't hear or see? If he had fingers, he could use children's wooden alphabet blocks. Joe could feel the letters.

If, sure, Kilkenny thought with frustration. *If* he had fingers, *if* he had eyes. If I could work goddamned miracles, I could read his bleeding mind! He turned from the window and looked at Joe again. Sighing, he walked into the hall, wondering if he should wake Darlynn and take her home. Across the hall, above the door to one of the other rooms, a red light was blinking on and off. One of the patients had pressed the call-button to summon a nurse. Kilkenny walked away from it. Then he stopped, turned, and stared at it.

Blink-blink. Blink-blink.

Dot-dash.

Hurrying back into the ward, Kilkenny drew a chair up to Joe's bed and sat down. It had been a long time, thirty years, perhaps too long. Yet if there was a chance—

Gently, Kilkenny placed the palm of his hand on Joe's sternum, just below the clavicle. Joe stirred. Kilkenny thought back thirty years. Thought back to the blue neckerchiefs and khaki caps, the gold patches they pinned to their shirts with the letters BSI on them. Boy Scouts International. It was the only youth organization that had ever come into the Ballymurphy slum to help the kids there. The first thing they had learned in the Morse Code class, Kilkenny remembered, was how to do their names.

With his index finger, he began to tap lightly on Joe Devalain's sternum. Dot-dash-dash-dash. That was J. Dash-dash-dash. That was O. Dot. That was E. J-O-E. Joe.

Joe Devalain frowned. Kilkenny began tapping again. He repeated the same letters. J-O-E.

Under the oxygen mask, Joe's lips parted. He began breathing a little faster. He's got it, Kilkenny thought. *He understands it!*

Kilkenny rubbed his hand in a brief circle to indicate he was erasing and starting a new message. He tapped dot-dash-dot for R. Dash-dash-dash for O. Dash-dot-dash-dash for Y. His name. Roy.

Joe's lips parted even more and he forced a guttural sound from his throat. All it sounded like was a long "Aaaggghhh," but it was beautiful to Kilkenny. It meant he had reached Joe Devalain's mind.

Kilkenny began tapping again, slowly, carefully. Making his message as brief and simple as possible. He tapped: Use eyelids. Dot short blink. Dash long blink. Then he waited.

For a brief, terrible instant, he was afraid Joe wasn't going to be able to do it, his lips remained parted, his sightless eyes unblinking. But then the eyelids closed, remained closed, opened, blinked once, closed again and remained closed for a second, and opened. Dash-dot-dash. That was the letter K. He was doing it!

Kilkenny watched the eyelids as they closed, opened, blinked. The letters they were making etched in his mind. K-I-R-R-G. Then the blinking stopped.

K-I-R-R-G? What the hell did that mean?

Kilkenny took out his pen and tore a sheet of paper from the medical chart hanging on the end of the bed. Turning the paper to its blank side, he wrote down the entire International Code that he and Joe had learned as Boy Scouts. Then he went to work breaking down the blinks Joe had used. The K and the I were all right, he decided. But the two R signals had to be wrong. Unable to quickly decide *how* they were wrong, he moved on to the G. That, in all likelihood, was M-E. One of the most common mistakes in Morse was to misread M (dash-dash) and E (dot) as G (dash-dash-dot). Simply a case of too short a pause between letters, causing the receiver to think it was a single signal.

Kilkenny now had K-I-R-R-M-E. Frowning, he scanned the code symbols he had just written. What was similar to R (dot-dash-dot)?

Then it hit him. Dot-dash-dot-*dot*. Two dots at the end instead of one. The letter was L. Joe had signaled K-I-L-L-M-E.

Kill me.

Kilkenny tapped a new message. No.

Devalain blinked back. Please. Pain. Going crazy.

Kilkenny: No.

Why?

Kilkenny tapped: Darlynn.

Joe shook his head furiously and blinked: Burden.

Kilkenny tapped: Sharmon.

The answer came: Finish me. Please.

Who bomb? Kilkenny wanted to know.

Why?

Pay back.

Again the emphatic shake of the head. Hurt Darlynn.

How?

Sharmon.

She bomb?

No.

How hurt Darlynn?

Sharmon.

Involved?

This time Joe nodded as he blinked. Maybe. No matter. Finish me.

No. Who bomb?

Then finish me? Joe asked, blinking a question mark at the end of his signal.

Kilkenny thought about it for several long moments. Then he tapped: Okay.

Joe's next message read: O-M-A-R-N.

Kilkenny nodded to himself. O'Marn. The bomb-investigation sergeant. Neat. He had access to explosives that had been confiscated from the IRA. He knew how to use them. And he was in a position to bury the case without resolving it.

O'Marn. Yes. Kilkenny had suspected as much when he saw the sprig of dying heather in Sharmon's ashtray. The same kind of sprig O'Marn wore on his lapel. He wondered how O'Marn and Sharmon had met. How long they had been lovers. Sharmon, who didn't like policemen, who had picked Joe over him when he told her *he* was going to become a policeman.

He wondered exactly how much Sharmon knew about the bombing. Not that it mattered. If she was still seeing O'Marn after what had happened to Joe, that was enough. And Kilkenny was sure she was still seeing him. That noise he had heard earlier from the back of the Devalain house. Along with Sharmon's eagerness to send him on his way. O'Marn had been there, listening.

Another guttural sound from the bed drew Kilkenny's attention back to Joe. He was blinking rapidly, repeating a message over and over. Do it. You promised. Do it. You prom—

Kilkenny put his hand back on Joe's sternum. He tapped: Later.

Darlynn was still deeply asleep on the couch in the waiting room.

One of the nuns had covered her with a blanket. Kilkenny quietly opened her purse and took her door key.

It was very late now, dark and quiet in Unity Flats. He walked the two miles to the Devalain house, passing no one, seeing no one. When he arrived, he let himself in and stood just inside the door. The house was silent. A night light burned dimly in the hall. Kilkenny moved slowly toward the rear of the house, taking care to stay close to the wall where the floorboards were less likely to creak.

At the door to a bedroom, he saw in the faint glow two naked bodies asleep on the bed. On the doorknob hung a Harris tweed sportcoat. Kilkenny moved into the room and over to the single window. It was shut tight and locked.

Slipping back out of the bedroom, he edged along the hall until he found the kitchen. Its window was also shut. Pulling a handkerchief from his pocket, he turned on all the gas jets on the stove.

Before he left, Kilkenny shut the door to Darlynn's small bedroom and the parlor, closing off all the house except the kitchen and the bedroom in which the two lovers slept. Then he let himself back out.

He waited down at the corner, concealed in the dark doorway of a small store, watching the house. No light came on and there was no sign of movement anywhere. Kilkenny gave it an hour. Then he returned to the hospital.

Darlynn was still asleep when he put her door key back in her purse. But Joe was wide awake and responded instantly when Kilkenny tapped his first message: Paid back.

Who? Joe blinked.

Kilkenny signaled: O'Marn. Sharmon.

A great, weary sigh escaped Joe's chest, the first sound Kilkenny had heard from him that sounded human. Then he blinked: Now me.

And Kilkenny answered: Yes.

Kilkenny reached over and pinched the tube that was feeding oxygen to Joe Devalain's lungs. As his breathing started to become labored, Joe blinked: Darlynn.

With his free hand, Kilkenny responded: Yes.

Joe's throat began to constrict, his face contorting as what was left of his body struggled for oxygen. He had time for only one more message.

God bless, he blinked . . .

Kilkenny sat in the waiting room watching the sleeping Darlynn Devalain until daylight came and the buses began running. Then he woke her and they left the hospital together. On the bus downtown, he told her how her parents had died, but not who killed them. Her mother and O'Marn would be considered suicides. Her father simply had not survived his trauma.

When the bus reached Great Victoria Street, they got off.

"Where are we going?" Darlynn asked.

"First to the hotel to get my things."

"And then?"

"The part of Ireland that's free. Dublin."

Darlynn accompanied him with no further questions.

Edward D. Hoch

Last Year's Murder

D avid knew the man was a reporter as soon as he walked in the
door. There was something about the plaid sportcoat and wrinkled pants and hornrimmed glasses that reminded him of his years
in Greenbrier. He'd never seen the man before, but he knew instinc-
tively what he was after.

The man glanced around, not recognizing him at first, and went
up to Max Renkler, who was working behind the shirt counter. "Do
you have a David Witan working here?"

"Behind the tie counter," Max answered with a smile. He always
smiled at customers even when they asked to see someone else.

David busied himself arranging the tie rack, pretending he hadn't
heard the exchange. When the man came over, he looked up and
asked, "Would you like a tie, sir?"

"You're David Witan?"

"That's correct."

"Mr. Witan, I'm Carroll March from the *Greenbrier Banner-Times.*
I've come a long way and I hope you'll consent to an interview."

"Sorry. No interviews."

"It'll be a year next week since your wife was murdered back in
Greenbrier. We're doing a story on it and we'd like your cooperation."

"My wife's death is too painful to discuss."

"Why won't you even talk to the police?"

"I told them what little I know. I returned home from work to find
her dead on the kitchen floor. I never saw the thief or whoever it
was."

"Some people are calling it a perfect crime, Mr. Witan. Do you
think it was?"

David tried to control his temper. "I said no interviews and I
meant it." Then he added, "Do you think it's right to bother me
where I work?"

"If I came to your apartment—"

"No."

The reporter stood there another moment, then turned and left.

"What was all that about?" Max Renkler asked. "He didn't buy
anything, did he?"

"Not a thing," David said.

He'd arranged to meet Annie Lyme after work. She was a part-time fashion model the store had used a few times and he'd met her at a photo session. They'd been to dinner a half dozen times and she'd come to his apartment twice. He liked her and he imagined she liked him. She was a slim, golden-haired girl in her mid-twenties. When he arrived at the Blue Note, she was already at a table, already the object of a few stares from men at the bar.

"Hi," he said, slipping into the chair next to hers.

"How are you, David?" She smiled warmly. "I ordered a drink for you," she explained as a waitress placed two glasses in front of them. He raised his glass in a toast to Annie and was about to drink when a new arrival at the bar caught his eye. "What's the matter?" she asked.

"I'll be right back."

He went to the bar and tapped Carroll March on the shoulder. "You're following me, aren't you?" he asked.

"Not really. I had nothing to do and I thought you might lead me to a good restaurant."

"This isn't it. Get out."

"Now wait a minute—"

"Get out!"

"Who's the young lady?"

David's vision blurred with anger and he grabbed the reporter's shirt near the shoulder. Hearing it rip, he let go and walked back to the table, where Annie was already on her feet. "Let's go," he muttered, tossing down some bills for the drinks.

Outside, she turned to face him. "I want an explanation, David."

"I owe you one," he agreed. "Let's drive for a bit."

They headed north along the river, and after a time he began to speak. "Something happened a year ago, Annie. It'll be a year next week, and that's why that man is here looking for me. He's a reporter from Greenbrier, where I used to live. I told you I'd been married and you assumed I was divorced, but that's not what happened. My wife Julia was murdered. I came home from work and found her dead on the kitchen floor."

"My God, David! Why didn't you tell me?"

"I don't like to talk about it. After the funeral I left Greenbrier and came here to stay with my brother Sam. I've only been back

once, to get rid of the furniture and put the house up for sale. I quit
my bank job and came here to make a fresh start. Working at Monarch's isn't exactly a lifetime career but it's helped me survive this
past year."

"Why is this reporter bothering you? Certainly he can't believe
you killed her?"

"That's exactly what some of the press—and the police—believe.
They couldn't prove it or they wouldn't have let me leave town, but
I could see it in their faces."

"Tell me about it, David. I need to know all about it."

He pulled up along the river and parked. "Julia and I had only
been married a year when it happened. We'd bought the house and
moved into the neighborhood a few weeks earlier. The neighbors
didn't know us—my roots were back here in Central City—and
maybe that was one reason everyone was so quick to suspect me. It
was a quiet neighborhood where there hadn't been as much as a
house burglary in two years. On the day it happened, I left for the
bank around eight-thirty. Julia got my breakfast and that was the
last time I saw her alive."

He paused and Annie had to say, "Go on."

"Sometimes she'd phone me at the bank after lunch. She didn't
phone this day but I thought nothing of it. She was looking for a job
and I thought she might have been called out for an interview. I
drove home around four-thirty and her car was in the driveway
where it had been that morning. I used my key and went into the
kitchen and then I saw—"

His voice broke. Annie reached out and touched his hand. "I
shouldn't be putting you through this."

"You have a right to know. She—Julia was on the kitchen floor,
dead. She'd been stabbed twice with a long-bladed kitchen knife that
was on the floor beside her. I phoned the police and they came. The
detective in charge of the case was a young lieutenant named Gerber.
He mentioned right away that there'd been no robberies in the neighborhood recently. He asked about enemies Julia or I might have
had, but there were none. It wasn't until the second time he talked
with me, after midnight, that I realized I was a suspect."

"Have you had any contact with this Lieutenant Gerber since you
moved here?"

"He came here once to question me, but I wouldn't talk about it.
I wanted to forget it and start a new life. That's what I'm trying to
do with you, Annie."

"Tell me, David—what do *you* think happened?"

"I don't know. I think of it every day. I just don't know."

"Was anything stolen?"

"No," he admitted. "But a burglar might have been frightened off after he killed her."

"Did she have any old boy friends?"

"No, no one." David started the car and drove back the way they'd come.

"I'm glad you told me," Annie said. "Do you think that reporter will try to cause trouble because you ripped his shirt?"

"No more than he will otherwise." They drove in silence for a time and then he said, "You haven't asked me yet."

"Asked you what?"

"If I killed her."

"Did you, David?" she asked, and then immediately corrected herself. "Please don't answer! Of course, you didn't kill her! You could never kill anyone."

"Thank you," he said.

When he arrived at Monarch's the following morning, Max Renkler was waiting just inside the door. "Your brother was here looking for you," he told David. "He's across the parking lot, having a cup of coffee."

It was only minutes after the nine-thirty opening and the store was empty. "Thanks, Max," David said. "Can you handle things alone here for ten minutes?"

Max looked a bit uncertain. He was a middle-aged man who'd been with the store only a few months and he was reluctant to take the responsibility. "Go ahead," he said finally. "Things look slow this morning."

"Thanks, Max. I'll be back before the boss arrives."

He went across the lot to the fast-food franchise where his brother sat at the counter with a cup of coffee. "Hello, Sam. Were you looking for me?"

Sam Witan turned on his stool, looking very much the successful older brother David had spent his life admiring but not quite liking. "There's a reporter in town asking about you," he said without preamble.

"I know." David slid onto the stool next to his brother's and ordered coffee.

"What's it about? Have they got new evidence?"

David shrugged. "The paper's doing a follow-up. It's a year next week that Julia was killed."

"They still think you did it?"

"Hell, you're my own brother and *you* think I did it!"

"I never said that."

"You didn't have to." He calmed down and asked, "How do you know about the reporter?"

"He came to the house last night and got Francie all upset. You know how she is. He asked me if you have any girl friends and I told him to get lost."

"Thanks, Sam."

"Look, how about coming over to the house for dinner tonight? I know this is a tough time for you. You don't have to work tonight, do you?"

"No, the store's open but I'm off. Is it all right with Francie?"

"Sure. We talked about it this morning. Anytime after six."

"I'll be there." David pushed aside his half finished coffee. "Thanks for the invitation. I'd better get back now."

"David, that reporter said you roughed him up."

"Yeah, I guess I did. I felt like killing him."

Sam patted him on the shoulder. "Take it easy, kid. We'll see you tonight."

Sam's wife Francie had always been more than a sister-in-law to David. They were the same age—thirty-one—while Sam was five years older. They shared many of the same interests, too. Even while Julia was alive, their occasional reunions often found David and Francie together on the tennis court while Sam and Julia talked and drank on the sidelines. After Julia's death, when he'd fled Green-brier without any rational plan, it was Francie who took him into their house and helped nurse him back to something approaching sanity until he was up to finding an apartment of his own.

"How are you, David?" she greeted him at the door, kissing him lightly on the cheek.

"Fine." He handed over a bottle of red wine.

"You know you don't have to bring anything."

"I wanted to."

Sam came in from the kitchen and said, "That reporter's still in town. I saw him outside my office today."

"Just ignore him," David advised.

Francie was a good cook and David always enjoyed the company of their two small children. After dinner, when the kids went off to bed, he decided to phone Annie. "May I make a call?"

Francie waved her arm. "You know where the phone is."

Annie answered on the third ring. "I just called to say hello," he told her.

"Oh, David!" She sounded close to tears.

"What is it? What's the matter?"

"That reporter, the one at the bar last night—he's been here. I think the bartender told him my name."

"What did he want?" David asked, his anger rising.

"He asked all sorts of questions about you. About us. He asked if we were getting married. He even asked how I'd feel being married to a man whose first wife was—" Her voice broke and she couldn't continue.

"I'll be right over," he said grimly.

"No, David—not tonight. I'm going to bed. After that man, I don't want to talk to anyone else right now."

"All right," he said. "I'll see you tomorrow."

He went back to the living room and told them what had happened.

"You'll never have any peace from that guy," Sam said.

David left soon afterward, and drove around town for a while before heading home.

He was awakened in the morning by a ringing doorbell. It was only seven-thirty and he went to the door with a feeling of apprehension.

"Who's there?" he called out.

"Police, Mr. Witan. Open up, please."

David opened the bolt and peered out at a uniformed officer and one in plain clothes. "What do you want?"

"We'd like to speak with you." The detective showed a card identifying himself as John Sebastian. "It's about a reporter named Carroll March. He was found dead shortly after midnight, apparently a murder victim."

"But—"

"We understand from various witnesses at the Blue Note bar that you had a fight with him there the night before last."

Somehow it was Greenbrier all over again, and Lieutenant Gerber had become Detective Sebastian. "I know nothing about his death, if that's what you're implying."

"I'm not implying a thing, Mr. Witan. We just want to know where you were last night."

"I had dinner at my brother's house."

"What time did you leave?"

"Around ten. Maybe a bit earlier. I drove around and then came home."

"Did you go near the Blue Note?"

"I might have driven past it, but I didn't stop."

"See anything of Carroll March?"

"Last night? No. What happened to him, anyway?"

"He was found dead on a side street behind the Blue Note. There were head injuries and the first report listed it as a hit-and-run. But we found traces of blood on a loose brick nearby. We think now that he was struck three or four times with it. A bartender at the Blue Note recognized him. He said you manhandled him. Want to tell me about it?"

David sighed. It would all come out now. "He followed me here from Greenbrier, where I used to live. My wife was murdered there a year ago and March wanted an interview about it. When I declined, he started following me around, bothering my family and friends."

"Did you threaten him?"

"No. I just told him to stay away." He described the events with Annie Lyme, reluctantly giving the detective her name and address. "You're not going to involve her, are you?"

"I'll have to question her. Where are you employed, Mr. Witan?"

"Monarch Men's Shop, in the mall."

"We'll want a statement from you down at Headquarters. Would this afternoon at two be convenient?"

"I work all day."

The detective's face hardened. "We could take you down right now if you'd prefer, Mr. Witan."

"No. I'll be there at two."

After they left, he tried to call Annie but there was no answer. Some mornings she had early modeling assignments. Next he called his brother and Francie answered. "You just missed him, David. He left for the office."

He told her about the murder of the reporter. "It's just like before, Francie. They think I killed him."

"Of course they don't! They'd have taken you with them if they thought that."

"I told the detective I was with you and Sam last night. I wanted to warn you to expect a call."

"We'll back you up, David. What time should we say you left here?"

He felt a passing chill. "Tell them the truth, Francie. Say I left a little before ten. I'm not asking you to lie."

"I know it, David. Calm down."

"I didn't kill that reporter."

"Of course you didn't! It's just that—well, Sam got to worrying about you last night. He phoned your apartment about an hour after you left and no one answered. He even went out looking for you."

"I was driving around. I got home around midnight."

"I'm sorry," she said with a sigh. "I'm not accusing you of anything. I'm just trying to be your friend."

"I know, Francie. Forgive me. Look, tell Sam I called." He hung up and finished getting dressed.

The story about the reporter's murder hadn't made the morning paper, but he knew it would get a big play in the afternoon edition. When he reached the store, Max Renkler was already inside, straightening the shirts on the shelves behind his counter. "Morning, Max," David said. "Is McIntire in yet?"

"I haven't seen him."

"I need some time off this afternoon. Personal business."

"He'll probably let you. It's been slow all week."

"How did last night go?"

"I sold one of those new monogrammed shirts just before closing. That's the first one. If Monarch's is much of a test, the company'd better forget about them."

"Max, remember the man who came in to see me the day before yesterday? In the morning? The one with the plaid sportcoat?"

"I guess so, yeah."

"Did he ever come back and ask about me?"

Max shook his head. "I haven't seen anything more of him. Why?"

"He got himself killed last night. The police came to see me this morning."

"No kidding!"

"That's where I have to go this afternoon."

Just then he saw McIntire, the store manager, park his car and stroll toward the door. David intercepted him as he entered and quickly outlined his problem. "The police want a statement from me," he said. "It shouldn't take long."

"All right. Get back as soon as you can," McIntire said, looking unhappy.

The morning passed slowly. When David saw the newspaper truck delivering the noon edition to the fast-food restaurant, he ran across the parking lot to buy one. Carroll March's killing was on page one, but David's name wasn't mentioned. He wondered how long it would be before some local reporter got wind of what had brought March to Central City.

He arrived at Headquarters promptly at two and asked for Detective Sebastian. The man appeared after a moment and held open the swinging gate for David to enter the squadroom area. "An old friend of yours is here," the detective said. "You'll want to see him."

He led the way to a rear office and opened a door with a frosted-glass window. A man studying some papers looked up and smiled. "Hello, David."

It was Lieutenant Gerber, from Greenbrier.

A police stenographer was brought in while David ran through the events of the past few days. Sebastian handled the questioning, and when he'd finished David asked Gerber, "What brings you here?"

"The dead man was a reporter in Greenbrier, as you know. When we got news of the killing this morning, I decided to hop on a plane. There's always a chance the killing might be linked with that of your wife."

"Meaning you think I killed them both?"

Gerber shrugged, keeping the smile on his face. David remembered that smile. "No, but you admit he made you angry enough to grab his shirt."

"That was the night before he was killed. I only saw him twice."

"He infuriated you."

David's rising anger began to show. "Isn't his murder a bit out of your jurisdiction, Lieutenant?"

"No, I'm still working on your wife's murder, David. I've never stopped working on it."

"My wife was stabbed. March was hit with a brick."

"The killer used the weapons at hand in each case. He lost his temper and struck out with whatever he could."

"March was probably drinking and got into a fight with some stranger," David said.

Sebastian shuffled the reports on his desk. "No, the autopsy report shows a very low level of blood alcohol. He'd had one drink at the most."

"But the killer could have been drinking. To link March's death with Julia's murder a year ago is simply—" David suddenly stood up. "If I'm charged with anything, you'd better read me my rights and let me phone a lawyer. Otherwise, I'm leaving."

The detectives exchanged glances. "You're not charged with anything," Sebastian told him.

"Fine. Goodbye, gentlemen."

He phoned Annie when he got back to the store and told her what had happened. "I tried to reach you this morning," he said.

"I just read about March in the afternoon paper. Do the police really think you're involved?"

"I guess so. I drove around for some time after I left my brother's place and that's not much of an alibi."

"Do you want to say you were with me?"

"No! Besides, it's too late for that. I've already made my statement to the police."

"Would you like to come over for dinner tonight?"

"I want to see you, but let's eat out. I'll pick you up around seven."

The store closed at six that night, and as David locked the door and started across the parking lot he saw a familiar figure emerge from one of the cars. Lieutenant Gerber strode over to intercept him. "I thought maybe we could talk, David. Off the record."

"I have a date in an hour."

"Let me buy you a beer."

"All right," he decided, his curiosity getting the better of him. "But I hope you're not going over the same ground again."

"I'm not," Gerber promised.

There was an Italian restaurant next to the fast-food place and they took a couple of stools at the bar. "I thought we might talk about your wife's death," the detective began. "And about that reporter. Have you thought about why they died, David?"

"I've thought about Julia every day since she was murdered."

"So have I. Despite what you might think, I'm not committed to the idea that you killed your wife. I'll admit it's the most likely theory—that you stabbed her in the kitchen in a fit of anger and then went off to work, leaving her body to be found when you returned in the afternoon. The autopsy placed the time of death as around eight or nine o'clock that morning. I worked on that theory for the first few weeks, talking with everyone who had contact with you that day. They all said you acted normally—you did your job, chatted with the bank's tellers, took care of customers at your desk. Of course, you could be one of those split personalities, or simply a killer without a conscience."

"Do you really think so?"

"I did at first. Then I began considering other possibilities. I wondered about the burglar you insisted upon. I even looked into your family here—your brother and his wife. It's only forty minutes by plane between Central City and Greenbrier. On the day of the killing, your brother was on the road and your sister-in-law was home alone. Either of them could have made the flight and been back in a couple of hours—three hours at the most, counting time from the airport to your house."

"That's crazy. They both loved Julia."

"Were you having an affair with your sister-in-law?"

"Certainly not!" David stood up, ready to leave. "I guess that ends the conversation. When you said you were investigating new leads I didn't know you meant Sam and Francie."

Gerber looked up at him. "I think Carroll March was killed last night because he was getting close to the truth."

"The truth is that Julia opened the door for some passing tramp or would-be burglar and got herself killed. The man's probably a thousand miles away."

"Sit down," Gerber said gently.

David sat.

"I thought about that, too," the detective said. "A burglar who moved to another town and tried the same thing. I even found a case in South Carolina that interested me for a time. A woman, the wife of a branch bank manager like your wife, was held prisoner in her home while a phonecall was made to the banker. He had to take a hundred thousand dollars from the bank and deliver it to a man in the parking lot or his wife would be killed."

"What happened?"

"He did it, but he alerted the police first. The man was arrested and the money recovered. He'd left a partner to guard the woman and that one escaped. Luckily, the woman was unharmed."

"When did this happen?"

"Six months ago. Probably too long after Greenbrier to have any connection with your wife's death, but I went down to South Carolina to question the prisoner. He'd never been in Greenbrier and he blamed everything on his partner. It turned out the arrested man was in a Florida jail the day your wife was killed, so it came to nothing."

"And you're back to thinking the killer is here."

Gerber nodded, reaching for a slim briefcase. "I'd like you to look at the police photos of Carroll March's body. Sebastian was good enough to give me a set." He spread the stark black-and-white enlargements before them on the bar. "Repeated blows to the head, as you can see."

David looked away. "All right, that's enough."

"Funny thing—his jacket and pants were inexpensive, off the rack, but his shirt was a fancy monogrammed one."

At that, against his better judgment, David reached out and picked up one of the photographs.

It was after six-thirty when he used his key to shut off the alarm and enter Monarch's through the rear service door. He walked quickly to the manager's office and went to the fireproof file drawer where he knew McIntire kept the slips from credit-card purchases. He found them at once and turned on the desk lamp so he could study the names and signatures. There was nothing in the first or second folders, but in the third he found the one he wanted. There was the imprinted name and the signature to match it. *Carroll March.*

"I'll take that slip, David," a voice said.

He turned and saw Max Renkler standing in the doorway, holding a small revolver. "What do you want, Max?" he asked quietly. "Who are you?"

Max Renkler smiled without humor. "I thought you knew by now, David. I'm the man who murdered your wife."

David stood very still, the stack of charge slips still in his hand. "Why? And why did you follow me here to Central City?"

The gun in Max's hand never wavered. "I was after the bank's money. I went to your house after you left for work, pretending I had a package to deliver. I forced my way inside, planning to hold your wife captive till you brought me a hundred thousand dollars. But she was a fighter. She grabbed a knife and in the struggle I had to kill her. The rest of the plan went out the window then. I left the house and was far away before you found the body."

David's mouth was dry. His eyes never left the gun. "But you tried it again, in Carolina."

Max Renkler seemed surprised. "You know about that? I teamed up with another ex-con, figuring it had to be a two-man operation. We subdued the wife, but this time my partner bungled the money pickup. The cops got him, and I barely escaped. I was just on the run when I remembered having read in the Greenbrier paper that you'd moved to Central City and you were working in a clothing store here. You didn't know me, and this was as good a hiding place as any."

"Why?" David asked again.

"Call it unfinished business. It was at your house that my luck turned bad. I'd never killed anyone before. I felt you owed me something, and I came to collect. I figured I'd find a way to make some money off you sooner or later. But that reporter came to town for his damned story. He remembered me from when I had a robbery charge dismissed in Greenbrier. He'd seen me in court. He came back last night to make sure, pretending to buy a shirt."

"The new monogrammed one you told me you'd sold. I recognized it in the police photos and figured he'd have charged it, so he could put it on his expense account. I came to find the charge slip that would prove it."

Max nodded. "He admitted recognizing me and I arranged to meet him later. I thought I could bluff him until he started asking about your wife's murder. That's when I hit him with a brick. Just now I happened to see you coming in the back door and I was pretty sure what you were after. I remembered to take his copy of the charge slip out of his pocket, but I forgot the store copy. My sales number is on it, of course."

David nodded. "This is a test market for that particular shirt. It's doubtful he'd have bought it back home. And you told me you'd sold one last night."

"That was dumb, wasn't it?" Max said sadly. Then: "Why did you have to rip his shirt, anyway? Why did he have to come here in the first place?"

"Maybe for the same reason you did," David told him. "Because he thought I owed him something." As he spoke, he pulled the cord of the desk lamp out of the wall with his foot. Max Renkler cursed and fired wildly as David dropped to the floor.

Then Lieutenant Gerber's voice bellowed a command. Max turned and fired out the door and Gerber's revolver answered with two quick shots. When David lifted his head from the floor, Max was down and Gerber was at the door turning on the overhead lights. "You okay, Witan?"

"Just barely. Is he—?"

"He'll live to stand trial. Call an ambulance and then get Sebastian down here."

"You saw him follow me in?"

"Yeah. I figured then that your theory about the shirt was the right one."

After he called the ambulance and the police, David phoned Annie. He'd be late for dinner, he said, but he'd be there.

Antonia Fraser

Your Appointment Is Cancelled

"This is Arcangelo's Salon, Epiphany speaking. I am very sorry to inform you that your appointment is cancelled . . ." In sheer surprise, Jemima Shore looked at the receiver in her hand. But still the charming voice went on. After a brief click, the message had started all over again. "This is Arcangelo's Salon, Epiphany speaking. I am very sorry to inform you that your appointment is cancelled . . ."

In spite of the recording, Jemima imagined Epiphany herself at the other end of the telephone—the elegant black receptionist with her long neck and high cheekbones. Was she perhaps Ethiopian, Somali, or from somewhere else in Africa, which produced such beauties? Wherever she came from, Epiphany looked, and probably was, a princess. She was also, on the evidence of her voice and manner, highly educated; there was some rumor at the salon that Epiphany had been to university.

As the message continued on its level way, Jemima thought urgently: What about my hair? She touched the thick reddish-gold mass whose color and various styles had been made famous by television. Jemima thought it was professional to take as much trouble about her hair as she did about the rest of the details concerning her celebrated program looking into the social issues of the day, *Jemima Shore Investigates.* She had just returned from filming in Morocco (working title: *New Women of the Kasbah*) and her hair was in great need of the attentions of Mr. Leo, the Italian proprietor of Arcangelo's—or, failing that, those of his handsome English son-in-law, Mr. Clark.

But her appointment was cancelled and Jemima wondered what had happened at Arcangelo's.

A few hours later, the *London Evening Post* ran a brief front-page bulletin: a male hair stylist at a certain fashionable salon had been found when the salon opened that morning with his head battered in by some form of blunt instrument. The police, led by Jemima's old friend, Detective Chief Inspector J. H. Portsmouth—more familiarly known as Pompey of the Yard—were investigating.

As Jemima was mulling this over, she received a phone call from Mr. Leo, who told her in a flood of Italianate English that the dead stylist was none other than his son-in-law, and that it was he, Leo, who had discovered the body when he unlocked the salon this morning, Epiphany, who normally did the unlocking, having been delayed on the Underground.

"Miss Shore," he ended brokenly, "they are thinking it is I, Leo, who am doing this dreadful thing, I who am killing Clark. Because of her, *mia cara, mia figlia, Domenica mia.* And, yes, it is true, he was not a good husband, in spite of all I did for him, all she has been doing for him. In spite of the *bambino!*"

He paused and went on as though reluctantly. "A good stylist, yes, it is I who have taught him. Yes, he is good. Not as good as me, no, who would say that? But good. But he was a terrible husband. *Un marito abominabile.* I knew, of course. How could I not know? Everyone, even the juniors knew, working in the salon all day together. *My* salon! The salon *I* have created, I, Leo Vecchetti. They thought they were so clever. Clever! Bah!

"But for that I would not have killed him. She still loved him, my daughter, my only child. For her I built up everything, I did it all. My child, Domenica, and the little one, Leonella, who will come after her. Now he is dead and the police think I did it. Because I'm Italian and he's English. You Sicilians, they say. But I'm not Sicilian. I'm from the North, *sono Veneziano*—" Mr. Leo gave an angry cry and the flood poured on:

"What about *her,* then?" he almost shouted. "Maybe *she* killed him because he would not leave Domenica and marry her!" He now sounded bitter as well as enraged. "No, Clark would not leave my fine business—the business he would one day inherit. Not for one of those *savages,* not he. Maybe *she* kill him—kill him with a *spear* like in the *films!*"

From this, Jemima wondered if Leo was saying that Epiphany had been Mr. Clark's mistress.

"Mr. Leo," she said. "When the salon reopens, I want an immediate appointment."

A few days later, Jemima drew up at Arcangelo's in her white Mercedes sports car. The golden figure of an angel blowing a trumpet over the entrance made the salon impossible to miss. Jemima was put in a benign mood by being able to grab a meter directly outside the salon from under the nose of a rather flashy-looking Jaguar being propelled at a rather more dignified pace by its male driver. She glimpsed purple-faced anger, rewarded it with a ravishing smile, and was rewarded in turn by the driver's startled recognition of the famous television face.

Well, I've certainly lost a fan there, thought Jemima cheerfully. She looked through the huge plate-glass window and saw Epiphany, on the telephone, austerely beautiful in a high-necked black jersey. One of the other stylists—Mr. Roderick, she thought his name was—was bending over her. Epiphany was indeed alluring enough to make a man lose his head.

Pompey of the Yard, being a good friend of Jemima's from several previous cooperations beneficial to both sides, had filled in a few more details of the murder for Jemima. The blunt instrument had turned out to be a heavy metal hair dryer. Mr Clark's body had been found—a macabre touch—sitting under one of the grey-and-gold automatic dryers. The medical examiner estimated the time of death as between ten and eleven the previous evening, more likely later than earlier because of the body temperature. The salon closed officially at about six, but the staff sometimes lingered until six-thirty or thereabouts, tending to each other's hair—cutting, restyling, putting in highlights, unofficial activities they had no time for during the day.

The night of the murder, Mr. Clark had offered to lock up the salon. (Being one of the senior stylists and, of course, Mr. Leo's son-in-law, he possessed his own set of keys.) At five o'clock, he had telephoned Domenica at home and told her he had a last-minute appointment: he had to streak the hair of a very important client and he might be home very late because this client was then going to take him to some film gala in aid of charity, to which she needed an escort—he couldn't offend her by refusing. Domenica, brought up in the hairdressing business and used to such last-minute arrangements, had a late supper with Mr. Clark's sister Janice, who had come to admire the baby, and went to bed alone. When she woke up in the morning and found Mr. Clark still absent, she simply assumed, said Pompey of the Yard with a discreet cough, that the party had gone on until morning.

"Some client!" said Jemima indignantly. "I suppose you've questioned her. The client, I mean."

"I'm doing so now," Pompey had told her, with another discreet cough. "You see, the name of the famous client whose offer Mr. Clark simply could not refuse, according to his wife, was *yours*. It was you who was supposed to have come in at the last minute, needing streaks in a hurry before beginning the new series."

"Needing streaks *and* an escort, to say nothing of what else I was supposed to need," commented Jemima grimly. "Well, of all the cheek—"

"*We* think," Pompey had interposed gently into Jemima's wrath, "he had a date with the black girl there at the salon after everybody had gone. There is a beautician's room which is quite spacious and comfortable, couch and all. And very private after hours."

"All very nice and convenient," Jemima said, still smarting from the late Mr. Clark's impudence. "So that's where they were in the habit of meeting."

"We think so. And we think Mr. Leo knew that—and, being Sicilian and full of vengeance—"

"He's Venetian actually."

"Being *Venetian* and full of vengeance. There's plenty of vengeance in Venice, Jemima. Have you ever been to the place? Mrs. Portsmouth and I went once and when you encounter those gondoliers—" He broke off and resumed a more official tone. "Whatever his genesis, we believe he decided to tackle his son-in-law. That is to say, we think he killed him with several blows with a hair dryer.

"Mr. Leo has no alibi after nine o'clock. After a quick supper at home, he went out—he says—to the local pub, returning after it closed. But nobody saw him in the pub and he is, as you know, a striking-looking man. He had plenty of time to get to the salon, kill his son-in-law, and get back home."

"What about Epiphany? Mr. Leo blames her."

"She admits to having been the deceased's mistress—she could hardly deny it when everybody at the salon knew. She even admits to having an occasional liaison with him at the salon in the evening. But on this particular evening, she says very firmly that she went to the cinema—alone. She's given us the name of the film. *Gandhi*. All very pat. What's more, the commissionaire remembers her in the queue—she is, after all, a very beautiful woman—and so does the girl at the box office. The only thing is, she had plenty of time once the film was over to get back to the salon and kill her lover."

"She has no alibi for her activities after the movie?" put in Jemima.

"Not really. She lives with a girl friend off the Edgeware Road. But the friend's away—a very convenient fact if there was anything sinister going on—so according to Epiphany she just went home after the cinema, had a bit of supper, got into her lonely bed, and slept. Saw no one. Talked to no one. Telephoned no one. As for being late the next morning, that, too, was a piece of luck—stoppage on the Underground. We've checked that, of course, and it's true enough. But she could have come by a slower route, or even just left home later than usual so as to avoid opening up the shop and seeing the grisly consequences of her deed. As it was, we were there before she arrived."

With this information in her head, Jemima now entered the salon. Epiphany gave her usual calm welcome, asking the nearest junior—Jason, who had a remarkable coxcomb of multi-colored hair—to take Miss Shore's coat and lead her to the basin. But Jemima didn't think it was her imagination that made her suppose that Epiphany was frightened under her placid exterior. Of course, she could well be mourning her lover (presuming she had not killed him, and possibly even if she had) but Jemima's instinct told her there was something beyond that—something that was agitating, even terrifying Epiphany.

In the checkroom, Pearl, another junior with a multi-colored mop, took Jemima's fleecy white fur.

"Ooh, Miss Shore, how do you keep it so clean? It's white fox, is it?"

"I dump it in the bath," replied Jemima with perfect truth. "Not white fox—white nylon."

At the basin, Jason washed her hair with his usual scatty energy and later Mr. Leo set it. Mr. Leo was not scatty in any sense of the word. He did the set, as ever, perfectly, handling the thick rollers handed to him by Jason so fast and yet so deftly that Jemima, with much experience in having her hair done all over the world, doubted whether anyone could beat Mr. Leo for speed or expertise.

Nevertheless, she sensed beneath his politeness, as in Epiphany, all the tension of the situation. The natural self-discipline of the professional hairdresser able to make gentle, interested conversation with the client whatever his own personal problems: in this case, a son-in-law brutally murdered, a daughter and grandchild bereft, himself the chief suspect, to say nothing of the need to keep the salon going smoothly if the whole family business was not to collapse.

At which point Mr. Leo suddenly confounded all Jemima's theories about this unassailable professionalism by thrusting a roller abruptly back into Jason's hand.

"You finish this," he commanded. And with a very brief, muttered excuse in Jemima's general direction, he darted off toward the reception desk. In the mirror before her, Jemima was transfixed to see Mr. Leo grab a dark-haired young woman by the shoulder and shake her while Epiphany, like a carved goddess, stared enigmatically down at the appointments book on her desk as though the visitor and Mr. Leo did not exist. But it was interesting to note that the ringing telephone, which she normally answered at once, clamored for at least half a minute before it claimed her attention.

The young woman and Mr. Leo were speaking intensely in rapid Italian. Jemima spoke some Italian but this was far too quick and idiomatic for her to understand even the gist of it.

Then Jemima recognized the distraught woman—Domenica, Mr. Leo's daughter. And at the same moment she remembered that Domenica had worked as receptionist at the salon before Epiphany. Had she met Mr. Clark there? Probably. And probably left the salon to look after the baby, Leonella. It was ironic that it was Epiphany who had turned up to fill the gap. But why had Domenica come to the salon today? To attack Epiphany? Was that why Mr. Leo was hustling her away to the back of the salon with something that looked very much like force?

Jason had put in the last roller and fastened some small clips for the tendrils Jemima sometimes liked to wear at her neck. Now he fastened the special silky Arcangelo's net like a golden filigree over her red hair and led Jemima to the dryers with his usual energetic enthusiasm. Jason was a great chatterer and in the absence of Mr. Leo he really let himself go.

"I love doing your hair, Miss Shore—it's such great hair. Great styles you wear it in on the box, too. I always look for your hair style, no matter what you're talking about. I mean, even if it's abandoned wives or something heavy like that, I can still enjoy your hair style, can't I?"

Jemima flashed him one of her famously sweet smiles and sank back under the hood of the dryer.

A while later, she watched, unable to hear with the noise of the dryer, as Mr. Leo led Domenica back toward the entrance. As they passed the reception desk, Jemima saw Epiphany mouth something, possibly some words of condolence. In dumb show, Jemima saw Domenica break from her father's grip and shout in the direction of Epiphany.

"Putana." In an Italian opera, the word would have been *putana*—prostitute—or something similarly insulting concerning Epiphany's moral character. Whatever the word was, Epiphany did not answer. She dropped her eyes and continued to concentrate on the appointments book in front of her as Mr. Leo led his daughter toward the front door.

"I am very sorry to inform you that your appointment is cancelled . . ." The memory of Epiphany's voice came back to Jemima. Could she really have recorded that message so levelly and impersonally after killing her lover?

Yet why had Mr. Clark lingered in the salon if not to meet Epiphany? He had certainly taken the trouble to give a false alibi to Domenica, who was expecting her sister-in-law for a late supper. Someone had known he would still be there after hours. Someone had killed him between ten and eleven, when Mr. Leo— unnoticed—was still allegedly at the pub and Epiphany was at home—alone.

Jemima closed her eyes. The dryer was getting too hot. Jason, through general enthusiasm no doubt, had a tendency to set the temperature too hot. She fiddled with the dial—and in so doing, it occurred to her to wonder under which dryer Mr. Clark's corpse had been found sitting. She began, in spite of herself, to imagine the scene. Having been struck—several times, the police said—from behind by the massive metal hair dryer, Mr. Clark had fallen onto the long grey-plush seat. The murderer had then propped him up under the plastic hood of one of the dryers to be found when the shop opened in the morning. The killer had left no fingerprints, having—another macabre touch—worn a pair of rubber gloves throughout, no doubt a pair that was missing from the tinting room. The killer had then locked the salon, presumably with Mr. Clark's own keys since these too had now vanished.

"At the bottom of the Thames now, no doubt," Pompey had said dolefully, "and the gloves along with them."

Jemima shifted restlessly, sorting images and thoughts in her head. Epiphany's solitary visit to a particularly long-drawn-out film followed by a lonely supper and bed, Mr. Leo's alibi, Domenica entertaining her sister-in-law in Mr. Clark's absence, Jason's dismissal of abandoned wives—it all began to flow together, to form and reform in a teasing kaleidoscope.

Where was Jason? She really was getting very hot.

Suddenly Jemima sat upright, hitting her head, rollers and all, on the edge of the hood as she did so. To the surprise of the clients watching (for she still attracted a few curious stares even after several years at Arcangelo's), she lifted the hood, pulled herself to her feet, and strode across the salon to where Epiphany was sitting at the reception desk. Both telephones were for once silent.

"It was true," said Jemima. "You *did* go to the cinema and then straight home. Were you angry with him? Had you quarreled? He waited here for you. But you never came."

"I told the police that, Miss Shore." It was anguish, not fear, she had sensed in Epiphany, Jemima realized. "I told them about the film. Not about the rendezvous. What was the point of telling them about that when I didn't keep it?"

"His appointment was cancelled," murmured Jemima.

"If only I *had* cancelled it," Epiphany said. "Instead, he waited. I pretended I was coming. I wanted him to wait. To suffer as I suffered, waiting for him when he was with her—with her and the baby." Epiphany's composure broke. "I could have had any job, but I stayed here like his *slave,* while she held him with her money, the business—"

"I believe you." Jemima spoke gently. "And I'm sure the police will, too."

A short while later, she was explaining it all to Pompey. The policeman, knowing the normally immaculate state of her hair and dress, was somewhat startled to be summoned to a private room at Arcangelo's by a Jemima Shore with her hair still in rollers and her elegant figure draped in a dove-grey Arcangelo's gown.

"I know, I know, Pompey," she said. "And for heaven's sake don't tell Mrs. Portsmouth you've seen me like this. But the heat of the dryer I was under a few minutes ago gave me an idea. The time of Mr. Clark's death was all-important, wasn't it? By heating the body under the dryer and setting the time switch for an hour, the murderer made the police think that he had been killed nearer ten or eleven than the actual seven or eight when he was struck down.

"As it happened, ten or eleven was very awkward for Mr. Leo, ostensibly at the pub, but not noticed in the pub by anyone—I have a feeling that there may be an extramarital relationship there, too. Mr. Leo is still a very good-looking man. That's not our business, however, because Mr. Leo didn't kill Mr. Clark. Between eight and nine, he was in the Underground on the way home, and there we have many people to vouch for him. As for Epiphany, the girl at the box office verifies that she bought a ticket and the commissionaire that she was in the queue. The timing lets her out, lets them both out, but it lets in someone else—someone who kept the appointment she knew Mr. Clark had made. The abandoned wife. Domenica.

"Domenica," Jemima went on sadly, "entertaining her sister-in-law from half past nine onward. Sitting with her, chatting with her. Spending the rest of the long evening with her, pretending to wait for her husband. And all the time he was dead here in the salon. Domenica had worked at the salon—she helped her father build it up. She knew about the rubber gloves and the keys and the hand dryers and the time switches on the stationary ones.

"Pompey," Jemima paraphrased Jason: "it's heavy being an abandoned wife. So in the end, Domenica decided to keep Epiphany's appointment. She even left her baby alone to do so—such was the passion of the woman. The woman scorned. It was she who cancelled all future appointments for Mr. Clark, with a heavy blow of a hand dryer."

William Bankier

Beliveau Pays

Hector Beliveau was wondering what to do. He could walk inside Le Club Big Bang and find out what Tancred wanted from him today. Or he could wander on down Notre Dame Street to Gib Dakin's instrument repair shop and pick up his guitar.

Standing in the entrance to the club, he examined a photograph of Luther Rodriguez, the new saxophone player from Halifax. Rodriguez looked menacing. The tenor horn balanced across his chest brought to mind an armalite rifle. Beliveau could imagine the musician turning on his audience some night and raking the tables with automatic fire.

Beliveau was bored. A year ago, before he won the Quebec lottery and when Lenore was still alive, he was a hard-working detective. Now here he was, the possessor of an investment portfolio providing a good income, alone in the world and with time on his hands to do whatever pleased him. The catch was that few things gave Beliveau pleasure any more.

He made up his mind to go inside. He would find out why Tancred Falardeau had been so evasive on the telephone this morning. Then he would move on to Dakin's, claim the guitar, walk home, and get in an hour's practice before Rocky Peerson came by at seven to conduct his lesson.

Beliveau was in no hurry to see Gib Dakin, anyway. The instrument repairman was not his idea of good company. In the old days, he would have enjoyed putting Dakin away if he could have come up with sufficient evidence. Conducting his unsavory sidelines, Dakin managed to creep along slightly outside the law.

Dallas was behind the bar setting up the pieces on one of the house chessboards. The headband holding his shoulder-length blond hair gave him an appearance of tribal nobility. Beliveau approached out of the sunlit doorway and ordered a beer. "Where's the old gentleman?"

"He may have gone upstairs." Dallas snapped the cap from a bottle. "You want to see him?"

"He wants to see me."

"I'll get him."

The bartender moved between tables to a curtained doorway at the edge of a low stage. Tancred's upright piano was asleep, lid closed, gathering dust from shafts of colored light streaming through a stained-glass window. Thick stone walls retained and released slowly last night's cooler atmosphere.

Beliveau drank his beer and began to feel the cure. He was not alone. He had friends who would stand by him, old buddies who went well back before either the tragedy of losing Lenore or the good fortune of winning a quarter of a million dollars, tax free.

"On his way," Dallas called, returning to his chess game. The time was coming up to five o'clock. Soon the working crowd would be hurrying down Beaver Hall Hill from the glass prisons on Dorchester Boulevard to the freedom of Le Vieux Montréal.

When Tancred appeared, he didn't join Beliveau directly. He went to stand in the doorway like a groundhog at the entrance to his burrow. The club-owner wore a dark-blue beret; his rotund silhouette looked extremely Gallic. Beliveau put on a serious face as his friend advanced out of the sun, working his hands together.

"Am I going to have trouble with you, Beliveau?"

"Depends what you want."

"Quit the police almost a year ago but you can't get suspicion out of your system."

"You sounded on the phone like you were setting up a bank raid."

"Not my style." Tancred went to the end of the room and drew the piano stool into position. He sat down, raised the lid, and looked at the keyboard. "Know what you have to do to guarantee yourself eternal life?" he said. "Lend me a thousand dollars." As he spoke, he played a couple of chords. The notes suggested that life was bare and that there was gloom and misery everywhere.

Beliveau left the bar and crossed the room. He stood with glass in hand looking at the beer rings on the piano. Some of them dated back to those terrible nights in the spring when he had been working hard at forgetting Lenore.

"Why don't you clean your instrument, Falardeau?"

"All I need is a thousand dollars."

"I know people who'll scrub a piano for five. Paint it for ten."

"You're the only person I know who has the money."

"A quart of flat emulsion is what's needed. Two coats on the keyboard." Behind the bar, Dallas laughed without looking up from the chessboard.

Tancred's chords decided to become "Ghost of a Chance," so he began to play the old standard in a soft, shuffling sort of way. "I wouldn't ask if it wasn't important. Life or death, *mon vieux.*"

"You look healthy to me."

"Come across, my friend."

"All I want is to be told why you want the thousand. Even your bank manager asks that much." Beliveau went back to the bar and sat down. It was almost time to go claim the guitar from Dakin and go home. He knew he was being sadistic with Tancred, it would be easy to give him the money. But he resented the way his friend was not leveling with him.

"It isn't for me," Tancred said. "It's for a friend."

"Then let him ask."

"He doesn't know you well enough."

"That hasn't stopped anybody so far." The newspaper stories of his Loto-Québec win had turned Detective-Inspector Beliveau into a celebrity. "I get nine requests every day in the mail." He got up. As he left the bar and moved toward the door, Tancred called after him: "What will I say to my friend?"

The photograph of Luther Rodriguez was in Beliveau's mind as he said: "Tell him I'm stubborn. Luther will understand."

The sun on Notre Dame Street was still penetrating even after five o'clock. Beliveau walked toward Jacques Cartier Square and Gib Dakin's shop a hundred yards away. The guitar had been bought on the advice of Rocky Peerson, the professional who was teaching Beliveau to play. Rocky said it only needed new pegs and some glue. Dakin had promised it would be ready this afternoon.

The repair shop looked like somebody's house, as did many of the commercial establishments in Old Montreal. There was a small girl standing in the doorway. The door behind her was partly open. The girl wore a white T-shirt over a narrow chest. She had an underdeveloped body but something in her face came across as mature. Her hair was dull red, oxblood, reminding Beliveau of a favorite pair of shoes he had once owned. It was tied loosely with black ribbon at either side. Her nose was broad, her teeth slightly protuberant, her eyes a vivid green. She was half ugly, half cute.

When she saw Beliveau intended to enter the shop, the girl reached for something in the back pocket of her jeans. It was a bolo bat—a wooden paddle with a rubber ball attached to it by a length of elastic string. Deftly, she swung the ball in an arc, caught it with a swipe of the paddle, and drove it in his direction. Beliveau had to back off as she pounded it rhythmically, provocatively, bap-bap-bap, within inches of his face.

"You're good," he said after a dozen strokes.

"No I'm not, I'm bad." Her shirt had green letters stenciled on it. HORACE, OF COURSE. Beliveau stared at the words. "You're supposed to ask me who Horace is," she said.

"Who is he?"

"Someday I may tell you."

"What happens if a person wants to go into the shop?"

"Nothing much."

"Do I have to press the magic button?"

"You wouldn't know where to look."

Beliveau felt the child was controlling him, that she was keeping him standing there for reasons of her own. He moved to one side. She shifted her position so that he was still facing the driven ball. She had him skewered on the end of that stiff elastic. "Pretty soon I'm coming past you," he said.

"Touch me and I'll call a cop."

"I *am* a cop."

The batting rhythm stuttered, but she put her chin out. "You don't look like a cop."

Heavy footsteps sounded behind the girl. Somebody was running downstairs. Shoes tripped on risers, recovered, and raced for the door. The girl was brushed aside as Gib Dakin charged past her. He leaped across the concrete steps to the pavement.

"Hey, Gib!" Beliveau caught Dakin's wrist and slowed him down so that the men faced each other, pivoting on the sidewalk.

Dakin did not answer. His face looked elongated, a plasticine face. His nose was running the way kids' noses do on cold days. In a film about cattle, Beliveau once saw a cow clamped in a steel rack after having been driven with electric prods through a sequence of baths following hours packed inside a freight car. Dakin's eyes were like that cow's eyes. He didn't know what the hell was going to happen to him next.

"Hold on, Gib. What's the matter?"

Dakin broke away, ran about twenty yards along the sidewalk, and then, without warning, dashed into the street. A taxi driver blew his horn and hit the brake pedal. Dakin absorbed the impact, then rose in the air and turned over in an extended flip as the car passed beneath him. His passage resembled a slow-motion replay from your world of sports. His shoes went farther than he did, one of them thudding against a parked car, and he came down like a piece of luggage.

Beliveau was the first one to his side. His face looked more relaxed now. He recognized Beliveau and he used his final breath to pronounce one word. "Frogman."

"Say it again?" Beliveau put his face close to the head on the pavement, but there was nothing more. The taxi driver appeared.

"Mon dieu, il est fou! He is crazy! I try to stop but he run right on my car!"

"I saw it," Beliveau said. "Not your fault." The girl in the T-shirt was staring at Dakin's body, her hands winding the elastic string around the handle of the bat. Her eyes met Beliveau's and she frowned as if everything was too complex to be discussed. Then she was gone.

Beliveau noticed a small pocket notebook on the pavement. He picked it up and saw pages of scrawl. The most recent entry was alone on a page, printed awkwardly in green felt pen. The misspelling looked pathetic: "Loother Rodriguez, a thousand dollars, August 20." Today was the nineteenth.

Only minutes ago, Tancred had asked Beliveau to lend him a grand on behalf, possibly, of Luther Rodriguez, saying it was a matter of life and death. He had not specified Gib Dakin's death.

Knowing he should not be doing it, Beliveau tore the page from the notebook and put it in his pocket. He tucked the book under Dakin's body and got to his feet. Then he walked back to the shop with a newly arrived policeman.

There wasn't much to be seen in the apartment above the shop. Dakin was a former golf pro who had made a little money in the game before all those college kids came charging onto the fairways. Repairing musical instruments was the daytime side of his life; after dark, he was a small-time usurer and receiver of stolen goods. As such, he would be a candidate for a robbery or a shakedown. Beliveau could have predicted Dakin's death by gunfire, blade, or fist, but collision with a taxi while in hysterical flight from nothing at all was an esoteric way to go.

"If anybody was chasing him, they've gone," the cop said.

A curtained doorway opened on a corridor leading to a back door. Beliveau checked it out. "Could have gone out through here."

"If Colclough finds you in here, he'll give me a bad time."

"That's my guitar. My name is on the tag."

"I'll have to tell Colclough you took it."

"Tell him. I'll handle any and all complaints from Colclough."

They were sliding Dakin's body through the back doorway of the ambulance as Beliveau headed home. The procedure was impersonal, like a rack of wallpaper samples being rolled into a cupboard. Soon Beliveau would be fingering chords on his reconditioned guitar. Meanwhile, Gib would be applying for a job tuning harps. If he was lucky.

Outside Beliveau's front door on Rue St. Amable, the marigolds were dying in their wooden tubs. Beliveau knew what was needed—regular watering and the dead blooms snapped off. Around the cottage in Cote St. Luc, flowers used to thrive from May till October under Lenore's loving care. Now it was as if he was waiting for her to come back and take care of these withered blooms.

Beliveau unlocked the door and went upstairs to his apartment, moving sluggishly. There was a fragrance in the place, a presence. He opened the bathroom door. Françoise MacDonald was drinking gin and tonic in the tub, her brown and pink shoulders gleaming above the suds, wisps of black hair clinging to her forehead. Her eyes were mischievous, her lips smiling over ragged teeth.

"You can come in," she said, "but only if you remove your clothes." He took the drink from her hand and finished it off. She watched his face. "What's the matter?"

"I just saw Gib Dakin get killed." He described the episode.

"I'm coming out."

"Stay there. I'll get us both a drink."

The radio in the kitchen was tuned to CKGM, which meant the same three girls who recorded everything these days were pretending to be black gospel singers. Beliveau dialed CBM where they were performing Brahms. This was too painful in the other direction, so he switched off the radio and got ahead on the comforting sound of gin over ice in crystal glasses and the twist-hiss of the tonic bottle as the cap came off.

Françoise sat up to accept her glass, eyebrows raised, fragile jaw set. "I should phone first," she said. "I should never just let myself in."

"When I want my key back, Frankie, I'll ask you for it." He sat on the hamper and took a long swallow. "How goes it at the studio?"

"We had a bad day. We tried for hours to get one stupid sequence

in the can. The guy playing Baltazar looks good but he can't remember lines."

"I feel responsible." The *Baltazar* series was based on the character
of Hector Beliveau, inspired by his experience as the youngest officer
ever to achieve the rank of Detective-Inspector. The scripts were
dreamed up by Milton Sangster in his loft on the other side of the
square. Beliveau had attended a few sessions of the early filming.
This was where he met Françoise MacDonald, the director's assistant.

Françoise attended Lenore's funeral, arriving with Sangster in
his motorized wheelchair. She wrote an old-fashioned sympathy letter. Six weeks later, he found himself at a film-editing session where
Françoise was keeping track of shots. Now, here she was in his
bathtub with the water getting cold. She shivered.

"I'd better get out."

He rolled up his sleeve as he turned on the hot water. Then he
reached past her toes and pulled the plug, replacing it when the
level was low enough. He unhooked his belt and slipped out of his
shoes.

"Do you need a bath?"

"I need something."

Afterward they ate salad and slabs of thick ham carved from a
leg left over from the weekend, perched on stools at the kitchen
counter under an orange lampshade slung like a pumpkin on a gold
chain.

"It must have been terrible seeing that man struck by a car. After
what happened to Lenore."

"That's what I don't want to talk about."

"I understand."

"You don't understand anything." It was now be-cruel-to-Frankie
time. Beliveau had never figured out why these sessions had to take
place unless they were needed to maintain a safe distance between
them. Françoise seemed to have a bottomless capacity for soaking
it up. Her face assumed its wounded mask—pointed chin, dark blank
eyes. This is the way she will look when she is old, Beliveau told
himself.

"It might help if you talked about it," she said.

"Talked about what? I wasn't there when Lenore got hit—I didn't
see it. So let's leave it alone. Can you manage that?"

"Yes."

"I'm not asking too much, am I?"

"*Seigneur, fais pas ça . . .*" She cried softly as she ate, like the bad child at the picnic. Beliveau chewed with a steady, grinding rhythm, breathing heavily through his nose.

The telephone rang. It was Rocky Peerson asking if the lesson was on. He had heard on the radio about Dakin's accidental death and he knew Beliveau's instrument had been in the shop. "It's okay, I picked up the guitar."

"Shall I come around, then?"

"Come early. I have to go and talk to Tancred."

In the kitchen, Françoise had put on her linen jacket and was rinsing plates at the sink. "I have to go," she said.

"Don't rush. It's only Rocky."

"I just came by for the bath." Her eyes and mouth gloated over her recent humiliation. He stood in the upstairs doorway as she high-heeled it smartly down to ground level, turning to wave as she opened the door to the street. "Take care of yourself." She blew him a kiss with one finger.

Beliveau went into the kitchen to get things back the way he wanted them. Frankie always left the sponge in a different place or the dishtowel folded the wrong way. He was straightening these things out when he found her key to his front door on the ledge beside the potted African violet. Like the marigolds downstairs, the violet was getting ready to give up the ghost.

The guitar lesson never got off the ground. Peerson kept insisting in his pedantic London accent that Beliveau must place the ball of the thumb just so and arch his hand so that his fingertips would form the chord.

"It hurts."

"You have to train the muscles."

"I don't want to play like Julian Bream, I only want to play simple accompaniments."

"You'll end up playing like Segovia. Arnie Segovia, my building superintendent."

They struggled for half an hour. Finally Peerson said, "You're in a miserable mood. Is it seeing Dakin knocked over?"

"That's part of it."

"What's the other part?"

"Frankie was here. When she went, she left her key."

"You've split with her before."

Beliveau began to pack the instrument away. "Let's go see Tancred. There's something I have to ask him about Luther Rodriguez."

"What's the ugly bastard done now?" Peerson always referred to the saxophone player as the ugly bastard when, in fact, Rodriguez was one of the handsomest black men ever to come up the river from Nova Scotia.

"Maybe nothing. Earlier today, Tancred asked me to lend him a thousand dollars. I think he wanted it for Luther."

"What's the problem?"

Beliveau took a folded slip of paper from his pocket. "I found Dakin's notebook on the pavement. This is a page from it."

Peerson read the message. "Rodriguez owed Dakin a thousand. Due August twentieth—tomorrow."

"And Dakin was terrified when he ran out of the place."

"You think Luther may have been inside?"

"It's possible." Beliveau was assuming the girl blocking the door could have been Luther's friend. He took back the paper. "I'm going to show this to Tancred and Luther and give them a chance to explain."

"You'll be tipping him off. Give it to the police."

"There's no reason."

"You're concealing evidence. Are you that anxious to start up with Colclough?"

"There's no need for Colclough to come into this."

"Let *him* question Luther. He'll do a more thorough job than you will."

"He would indeed. Broken teeth, fat lip, no saxophone playing for a long time. Then you could be Tancred's number-one soloist."

"Why not? When was the last time I played a gig at the Bang? It was the weekend before Rodriguez showed up. I'm as good on the guitar as he is on tenor—but he has me at a disadvantage. I won't sleep with Tancred."

As they crossed Notre Dame Street to enter the club, Beliveau and Peerson encountered Milton Sangster purring along in his wheelchair in the direction of the square. Sangster had his yachting cap jammed down hard on his close-cut prematurely grey hair. One hand was on the chair's control box, the other moved the steering bar. Tinted glasses and a cigar completed the characterization of captain in charge of nothing smaller than a supertanker.

Sangster saw his friends and stopped. "Evening, lads. How goes?"

"Come and have a beer with us," Beliveau said. "Catch Luther's first set."

Peerson kept on walking to the phone booth on the corner. He went inside and closed the door. Beliveau watched as he inserted money and dialed.

Sangster said: "Luther is good—he's the best thing since Lester Young." The writer was hyperenthusiastic about everything. Beliveau believed it was Sangster's way of coping with the existence forced upon him after he was shot in both knees by persons unknown.

When it happened, they said Sangster brought it on himself. He was unwise to name names in a newspaper story he wrote about collections being made in Montreal to fund the Irish Republican Army. A number of important people were embarrassed. Three months after the article ran, Sangster came home to find a man and a girl in his flat. The girl had an automatic in her hand. The man punched Sangster and knocked him down but not out. He heard the shots and felt the shock in both legs. The pain at the time was minor compared with what he felt these nights when he tried to turn over in bed.

"Come on in," Beliveau said. "First set starts at nine."

"I've got to get back to the loft. The girl won't be able to get in." Sangster winked. "Come over later. I've got a story line for a Baltazar episode. We can talk about it." He pressed a button and hummed down the street. There was something sinister about that blocky torso moving ahead like a dummy in a house of horrors.

Beliveau and Peerson went inside the Bang. There was a good house. Dallas was busy behind the bar, pausing to make moves on two chess games in progress. The drinkers grouped around each board reacted to the bartender's moves like peasants pitted against a grandmaster.

"Same as this afternoon," Beliveau specified. "And for my friend."

The public-address system coughed and Falardeau's voice echoed through the room. "Showtime, *mesdames et messieurs*. Here he is, the man they let get away from Halifax, the man we will hold onto as long as we can, the incredible, the sensational, the very sexy—Luther Rodriguez!"

The crowd applauded. A tall black man appeared through the curtain beside the stage and approached the piano where Tancred had just taken his place. He had a lanyard slung around his neck and he was carrying a tenor saxophone in one hand. The black-lacquered instrument gleamed like an extension of that sinewy arm.

The battered upright was a cartoon piano, but it was filled with quality strings. Tancred sat like a gnome on a mushroom, elbows tucked in and fingers hanging down, barely touching the keys. What came out was Tatumesque. Luther stood behind his saxophone and hardly moved at all. They played a slow version of Ellington's "Sophisticated Lady" that lasted for twenty-five minutes. The same musical idea never came by twice, and when the performance ended Beliveau said to Rocky over the applause: "What do you think of that?"

"He's good. He'll help any prison orchestra in the country."

"When you hate a guy, you don't give up."

"Did you notice he's wearing a pair of Tancred's boots?"

The musicians departed and the crowd raised their glasses and their voices. Through the buzz, Beliveau said: "Let's go talk to Tancred."

Peerson glanced at his watch. "I may run over to the loft."

"Okay. Tell Sangster I'll be along."

Beliveau went through the curtained doorway, down a narrow hall, and into a tiny room that held a desk, a filing cabinet, one chair, and a section of a church pew. Tancred was standing beside the desk. Luther was lying on the pew, his head propped on a fist. Rodriguez always made Beliveau feel uneasy. He had eyes that were almost oriental, high cheekbones, a beautifully shaped mouth with the flat lower lip of the reed player. His hair was a modified afro.

Beliveau sensed he had walked into a situation. "Sorry."

"No, come on in," Tancred told him. "Sit here." He spun the swivel chair.

"About that thousand dollars," Beliveau began.

"I was telling him, Hector. If he wants a loan, he has to ask for it himself."

Luther brought his hands together below his chin. "Please, Mister Rich Man, can I have a thousand dollars?"

"You can have it in quarters if you promise to stuff them up your nose one at a time."

"They told me you gave up the police, but you didn't. Once a cop, always a cop."

"You show a lot of hostility for somebody who needs a loan."

"You think money makes you special? The cops in Halifax *steal* more than you'll ever have."

Beliveau got to the point. "What happened to Gib Dakin?"

Tancred looked alarmed. "He must have been drunk."

"Let Luther talk."

"I don't know anything about Dakin."

"Money lenders charge heavy interest. And they get rough when it isn't paid."

"Tell him the truth, Luther." Tancred moved behind the pew and massaged the young man's shoulders. "It isn't anything to be ashamed of. Your sister gambles. She owes a man in Halifax."

"I'm sorry I told you."

"You want to send her money. Tell Beliveau and he'll lend it to you."

Rodriguez closed the subject. "There's other ways to handle the situation down there."

"What about this?" Beliveau showed the notebook page. "Dakin had you down for a thousand."

"Two o's in Luther—that isn't even how I spell my name."

"So Dakin couldn't spell. But he kept careful records."

"I was here all afternoon."

"I didn't see you. I was drinking beer and Tancred was playing the piano."

"I was upstairs sleeping."

"That's the truth, Hector. After you left, I went upstairs. He was in bed."

Beliveau put the slip of paper away. "I believe you owed Dakin a thousand dollars—otherwise he wouldn't have marked it down. But I accept that you weren't in his shop when it happened."

A light flickered on the internal telephone. Tancred picked it up. "*Oui,* Dallas. At the bar? I'll come out." He threw the receiver at the cradle. "It's Vince Colclough."

Tancred led the way down the hall with Beliveau at his heels. They entered the main room and found Detective-Sergeant Colclough at the bar. His narrow-brimmed fedora was tipped sharply forward, his tweed jacket unbuttoned and hanging from shoulders that might still have been wearing the pads he wore as a defensive halfback with the pro football Alouettes. He tried to frown when he saw Beliveau but his face wasn't good at expressions. "I come in to open an investigation," he said, "and I find the television cop is already on it."

"What investigation, Coleslaw?" Beliveau used the nickname that had followed the man to Montreal from his days as a college player in New Mexico. Not big enough for the NFL, Colclough was one of the many American players who had plenty of talent for the less-demanding Canadian league.

"I'm talking about the Gib Dakin assault case," Colclough said.

"I was there. I saw no assault."

"Dakin was a shylock. He had about as many enemies as there are users in this place tonight. One of them could have been Luther Rodriguez."

"That's crazy. Luther is my saxophone player."

"He owed Dakin a thousand dollars, due tomorrow. This afternoon, somebody scared Dakin so badly he ran into traffic. Your saxophone player had the motive. I'm here to see if he had the opportunity."

Beliveau said: "We'd better go back and see Luther." Tancred led the way. As they walked, Beliveau asked Colclough: "Who told you about Rodriguez owing money?"

"My old friend, anonymous phone call."

Luther wasn't in the back office. They trudged up the stairs to Falardeau's apartment and he wasn't there, either. The detective said: "If he comes in, tell him to call me."

They left Falardeau in his office. Beliveau followed Colclough and stood with him in the club entrance as he appropriated Luther's photograph. "Do you believe he made Dakin run?"

"You're retired from the force," Colclough said. "Stay off the case."

They went outside to where a uniformed officer was waiting at the wheel of a cruiser. Colclough got in and they drove away. Beliveau watched them go. Then he started out in the direction of Milton Sangster's loft. Rocky Peerson would be there, drinking the free booze and chatting up whatever talent the writer had persuaded to fraternize. It could have been Rocky who telephoned and blew the whistle on Luther. That would be why he took himself into the phone booth when Beliveau was talking to Sangster. It was typical of the guitarist's ambition. If Luther was hassled and put away, Rocky could become the club's top musician once again.

Beliveau couldn't avoid some sort of response. As he came to the alleyway beside the Hotel de Gaspé on the far side of the square, he slowed his pace. If he made allowances for Peerson's behavior tonight, it wouldn't be for the first time. He remembered that afternoon at the house in Cote St. Luc three summers ago when he returned unexpectedly—Lenore and Rocky in the kitchen, two damp towels in the bathroom, the heavy presence of Lenore's cologne. Whose feelings had he spared with his quiet dignity? His wife's? His friend's? No, he realized as he headed for Sangster's loft. He had been trying to go easy on himself.

He walked down the alleyway into darkness. He came to an iron door painted blue. There was a button on the frame and he pressed it. A buzzer released the lock, allowing him to push the door open and walk inside. He was standing on a rough board floor, facing an elevator shaft that contained the workings of a freight elevator.

He opened the door and stepped inside. The cage was spacious and he could see through it to the brick walls of the shaft. After a slow climb to the top floor, he walked down a corridor toward a panel of light that was the entrance to Sangster's studio.

Inside, he found Rocky Peerson submerged in a leather beanbag holding a glass of red wine. Sangster had driven his wheelchair onto the converted golf cart he used as his mobile command center at home. Seated behind his desk, his file cabinet on one side and a small refrigerator on the other, he was very much the commodore on the bridge of his flagship. "Come on in," he said. "Want a drink?"

"Not yet. How are you, Rocky?"

"Getting by," Peerson said.

"Why is it the bastards always get by?"

"I thought you guys were lovers," Sangster remarked.

"This one shafted me an hour ago, Milt. He sneaked away and made a telephone call."

"For your own good," Peerson said. "Let Colclough investigate Rodriguez."

"I don't believe Luther was in the shop this afternoon."

"Then he has nothing to fear."

"From Colclough? You're joking. He'll tell Vince to take a hike and Vince will put him in the Royal Vic with a ruptured spleen."

"I'm getting the message," Sangster said cheerfully. He popped the seal on a can of beer and cruised with it in Beliveau's direction. "This is about good guys and bad guys."

Beliveau sidestepped the cart as he accepted the beer. It was like being in a room with an aircraft carrier. "We discussed this," he confronted Peerson. "You *knew* I wanted Colclough left out of it."

"You should never have been a policeman." Peerson's face rose from the glass arrogantly, his lips wet with wine. "You should have been in charge of discipline at a nursery school."

Beliveau bent down and took hold of Peerson's jacket, hauling him onto his feet. "How would you like to go downstairs without waiting for the elevator?"

Peerson turned his head away. "I'm not about to damage my hands," he said.

"I've owed you for quite a while."

"Maybe you have. Let go, I have to be able to play."

"You blew the whistle on Luther so you could take his place at the Bang."

"If you make me fight you, I'll take something and kill you with it. I swear I will."

Sangster moved the cart closer. "There's a girl in the other room."

Beliveau released Peerson. "I'm all done."

"Find a psychiatrist," the guitarist said, "and invest in some therapy. Lenore died and that was terrible, but you've had good luck, too."

Beliveau said quietly: "I don't want you mentioning Lenore."

The loft was silent. The men heard a movement behind a door at the end of the room. Peerson headed for the corridor. "Thanks for the wine, Milt. Apologize for me to the little lady."

When the elevator sounds faded away, Sangster said: "Don't you go weepy on me. I don't tolerate melancholy."

"Sorry, Milt. I'm all right." Beliveau stood by the window and looked down into the square. It was almost midnight but the tables on both sides of the cobbled road were full. Rocky Peerson walked out of the laneway and headed up the street. The window was a large pane of glass reaching from ceiling to floor. By changing the angle of his head, Beliveau could see his own reflection. He turned away. "Did you want to talk about a script idea?"

"I did but I don't." Sangster was looking thoughtful. "Didn't Peerson live with you and Lenore for a while?"

"A short while."

"He seems like a reasonable type. Most of the time."

"So am I, most of the time." Beliveau drank some beer. "He's helped me with my music."

"How's the music going?"

"Tougher than being a policeman."

"I liked the song I heard at your place the other night."

" 'Lazy Love'? That's my entry in the CBC Songwriting Competition. Rocky made me enter it. He says it could win something."

"When does it happen?"

"Middle of October. If I'm still alive."

"Hang in. Follow the example of Milton Q. Sangster. When I was in hospital after the shooting, I thought I was finished. Not many paraplegic reporters chasing stories these days. So there I was, choosing from a range of quality tin cups for my new career as sidewalk pencil vendor when the idea came to me. A cop named Beliveau was investigating my case. He had an American wife. He liked baseball, she taught school, they both liked jazz. We got on well together."

"That we did, Milt."

"The idea for a television series called *Baltazar* just popped into my mind. I woke up one morning and it was all there. I only had to write it down."

Beliveau said: "There was a girl at the scene this afternoon, I think she may have been involved." He described the child, her skill with the bolo bat, her unusual T-shirt, and his suspicion that she was keeping him outside while something took place.

"How do you think the girl is involved?"

"I don't know."

"I suppose you want to find her."

"Yes, but I'm not sure why." Beliveau set his empty beer can on the floor beside the window. "I'm bored, I don't have anything to do."

"That's how a lot of continents got discovered. Never get tired of boredom."

Beliveau headed for the corridor. The golf cart maneuvered after him like *Ark Royal* entering Portsmouth harbor. He stopped by a sash window and raised it high. "I can't face that elevator again." He stepped out onto the fire escape.

"Please yourself."

Beliveau began to climb down. "Good night, Milt. Let your woman out of the cage."

Sangster ran the cart back into the studio. He switched on his wheelchair and rolled down the ramp onto the floor. He changed direction and moved close to the door at the end of the room. "You can come out."

The door opened and she walked in on bare feet, dressed only in the T-shirt with the legend, HORACE, OF COURSE. "I was going crazy in there. Your books are terrible."

"You weren't reading, you were listening."

"Who the hell is George Orwell?"

"Beliveau was talking about you, Tina."

"Is he really a cop?"

"He used to be. What were you doing in Dakin's doorway?"

"I want a ride. Take me once around the room."

"No rides. You can sit on my lap, but no rides till you tell me what happened this afternoon."

She eased herself onto his lap. She took off his cap and put it on her head. "Nothing happened. I was just hanging around."

"Beliveau thinks you were keeping him out of the shop."

"He's crazy."

"He's an experienced observer."

"Who do you believe, me or him?"

"I've known Hector Beliveau a long time."

"You're not going to know *me* much longer." She slid off the chair and padded toward the bedroom. "I made a mistake coming here."

"Why did you, then?" He motored to the doorway and watched her as she put on her jeans.

"Are you going to tell Beliveau?"

"If you were just hanging around the shop, you tell him."

When he was seeing her into the elevator, she said: "Promise me you won't do anything tonight. You won't tell Beliveau I was here."

"He'll have to know sooner or later."

"But not tonight."

"If it makes my little girl happy."

Beliveau was in no hurry to go home. He sat at a table across the square from Sangster's loft and ordered a cold quart. After a while, he went inside to the men's room. When he was away from his table, a girl in a white T-shirt emerged from the alleyway beside the hotel, crossed the square, and disappeared down St. Paul Street.

Beliveau returned and poured himself another glass. The population was thinning out. Spaces of half a minute separated passing cars. He couldn't see the river beyond the dark warehouses, but he could smell it. All around him, the night was buzzing softly.

Something was floating around in his mind. Dakin, just before he died, had said one word: Frogman. It could be something or nothing. Concussed as he was, he might have been talking from his subconscious. Except that Dakin didn't seem to be out of touch when he said it.

The waiters were stacking chairs when Beliveau left the café. He was still in no hurry to go home. He walked along Notre Dame Street instead. As he passed the Bang, he saw the lights were out. The front door opened and closed and the lock snapped. Beliveau squinted to see who was there. He made out shoulder-length hair and a headband. "Dallas!"

"Lots of bad characters this time of night." The bartender crossed the road. Green letters on his T-shirt made the statement, HORACE, OF COURSE.

"Where did you get the shirt?"

"I sweat so much these nights my own shirt gets saturated. I put this on to walk home."

"Where does it come from?"

"Northway Beverages. Their rep came in a few weeks ago promoting a new mixer. It's pale-green and minty and it's meant to go with vodka. Great if you like drinking mouthwash. They've invented a cocktail they call a Horace Collar."

"Who's this rep?"

"Guy called Davey Blackburn."

"Could I find him?"

"Call the plant. They're on Decarie Boulevard."

"Have you seen a lot of these shirts around?"

"Besides this one, I've seen two. Blackburn was wearing one when he came in. His daughter had on the other."

"Daughter?"

"I think her name is Tina. She's been with him once or twice on his rounds. Funny kid. Looks eleven and behaves like thirty."

They were at the corner of Beaver Hall Hill. "Come on up to Ben's," Beliveau said. "I'll treat you."

"I never refuse a free meal."

As they approached Dorchester, Dallas said: "Tancred is going out of his mind. After you and Colclough left, Luther showed up. He'd been hiding in a closet. He came down the back stairs with a suitcase in one hand and his tenor in the other. By the time Tancred spotted him, he was loading his stuff into the Landrover. Then he took the keys out of Tancred's pocket—practically mugged him—and he drove away."

"That's bizarre."

"Tancred ran halfway down the alley after him. Then he came in and called the cops."

Beliveau shook his head. Why was Luther so anxious to escape? Colclough had been tipped off about the money he owed Dakin, but there was nothing incriminating about that. Or was there?

After the late meal with Dallas, Beliveau went home and walked from one room to another, staring out of windows, looking at tiny framed photographs. What did lonely people do? He had tried drinking; he was semi-drunk now. The answer was to establish himself with another companion. But that would mean exposing his emotions again with somebody who might disappear at any moment.

The telephone rang. "Hector, it's Milt. Can you listen?"

"Go ahead." Sangster sounded as if he was suppressing nervous laughter.

"That script we were talking about. The one about the old lady alone in her apartment—"

"What old lady?"

"That's the one. She's upstairs alone and she can't get out. And the window is open and she thinks she heard something."

"Somebody's in the apartment, Milt?"

"You've got it. And she wants to cool it so they don't get excited. I've been playing around with ideas—"

"I'm on my way," Beliveau said. "I'll hang up, you keep talking."

Out on the street, his heels echoed as he covered a hundred yards at a run. In the square, he looked up at Sangster's window. He could see a seated figure and a much larger shape looming behind the chair. The chair was dragged abruptly away from the window.

Beliveau ran harder, but before he reached the alleyway he heard breaking glass. He looked up in time to see Sangster in his wheelchair drifting several feet in front of the building. The electric motor was humming, the wheels turning. But the chair's power alone couldn't have carried it so far. It had been slung like a projectile from a catapult.

Sangster was breathing when Beliveau reached him, but there had to be internal injuries. Now came a difficult choice. He could call an ambulance or he could go down the alley and try to intercept Milt's assailant. If there was a struggle or a chase, precious minutes would be lost. Beliveau stared into the black gap beside the hotel. Then he ran in the other direction to the telephone booth at the bottom of the square.

As it turned out, he might as well have gone on the chase. In the short time Beliveau was away from his side, Milton Sangster took it upon himself to die.

Beliveau passed a restless night after the police ambulance took Milt away. In the morning, he plugged in the kettle, went downstairs, picked up the *Gazette* inside the front door, and brought it back to the kitchen. He made toast and ate it while he drank his coffee. There was nothing in the paper yet about Sangster, but there was a small item on Gib Dakin. His death was treated as a fatal case of jaywalking, Montreal's favorite all-weather outdoor sport.

He went to the telephone and dialed Françoise MacDonald's number. A male voice answered, sounding cheerful and loved. He went away calling Frankie's name down the scented corridors of the semi-basement apartment off Cote des Neiges. Beliveau waited, feeling himself growing thin, afraid to look in the mirror across the room.

"Allo?"

"It's me. Did you hear what happened to Sangster?"

"Yes." She waited. "You don't sound very good."

"Last night, very late, Milt telephoned me. Somebody was in the loft. I ran across the square but it was too late. I saw him come through the window."

"*Mon Dieu.* That must have been terrible for you."

"Milt didn't like it very much, either."

"I'm trying to sympathize with you. I can't do anything for Milt."

"How about the stud who answered the phone? Are you doing anything for him?"

"Did you call me to argue?"

"I wanted to hear your voice." Beliveau counted the drops of sweat falling from his chest to the bedroom carpet. At drop three, he said: "I've got an idea. What if I put that key in an envelope and mail it to you."

"I've got a better idea. What if I only come over when you invite me?"

Half an hour later, having taken part in a frustrating telephone conversation with somebody named Claire Hitchen at Northway Beverages, Beliveau was dressed and on the street, looking for a taxi. He hailed one and gave the Decarie Boulevard address. After a hectic drive, he paid the fare and got out. On the sidewalk in the sunshine, he felt exceptionally alive, like a man who has run safely in front of the Pamplona bulls. Northway Beverages, Inc., was housed in a converted residential building. Beliveau went inside, wondering what Claire Hitchen was going to look like. Closing the door behind him, he felt he was in somebody's living room. There were upholstered chairs, flowered wallpaper, numerous photographs of ancient people. These dead Hitchens watched Beliveau for any false moves.

A woman entered the room. She was probably in her forties, smartly dressed in a wine skirt and off-white blouse with pearl buttons and drawstrings tied at the collar. She was bone slender, small pink fists compressed as she faced Beliveau, chiseled chin tilted upward, sharp cheekbones under a cloud of taffy hair in a poodle cut that was stylish twenty years ago.

"Inspector Beliveau?"

"Formerly. Just Hector Beliveau now."

"And you want to talk to Davey Blackburn."

"If you'll be so kind as to give me his number, Miss Hitchen."

"I'll trade you Claire for Hector," she said. "How about coffee while we talk?"

Standing close to her, he could feel her electric energy, could smell her perfume. "I'd like a coffee."

She served him where he sat in one of the puffy chairs, then brought her cup and sat facing him, skirt riding up over slender, tapered legs. "Why do you want to talk to Davey?"

She struck him as a woman who would respond to the truth. "I want to find his daughter, a girl named Tina. Do you know her?"

"I know *of* her. Tina Blackburn is what they call a problem child. Davey has his hands full trying to look after her without a mother." She read Beliveau's expression. "Didn't you see it in the papers? Three years ago, I think it was. They lived in a highrise apartment. Mrs. Blackburn tried to throw Tina over the balcony railing. But the girl was too strong for her so she gave up trying to kill her daughter and settled for committing suicide."

Beliveau remembered the episode. "The papers said they were from someplace in Ontario."

"Baytown. That's where Davey comes from anyway. The late Mrs. Blackburn was a Montrealer. He married her after he came here to find work. Tina was born almost immediately after the wedding." Claire looked at her watch. "If you're going to see him, I'll come with you. He's never let me see the inside of his apartment."

They drove in Claire Hitchen's car to an address on Bleury Street. There were two taverns on the block as well as a souvenir shop and a second-hand clothing store. "Are you sure this is it?"

"He's never asked me here," Claire said. "Now I know why."

They rang the bell and waited. The green door opened, its latch controlled by a length of string the other end of which was held by a man standing at the top of a lengthy flight of stairs. "Claire, me darlin'," he called, affecting a broad Irish accent. "What's up?"

"This man wants to talk to you." She was on her way up, so Beliveau fell in behind her. "Hector Beliveau—he used to be a detective. He wants to find Tina."

Beliveau moved into the apartment. It was painted bottle green like shutters on a summer house. Part of one wall was grey where the paint had run out. The only ornament was a calendar from a Chinese grocery store. The girl in the photograph was wearing a bathing suit, circa 1936.

"When are you going to have your phone reconnected?" Claire said.

"I had a disagreement about money with the phone company," Blackburn told Beliveau. He led them down a hallway into a kitchen, a small room with a two-ring gas cooker, a refrigerator, and a square yard of counter space. A large upholstered chair occupied most of the far end of the room.

Blackburn had been cutting up a slab of raw meat. He took up a knife and began trimming fat, slicing the lean portions into cubes. He scooped these up several at a time and threw them into a pot standing on the nearest burner. Claire said: "You've been holding out on me."

"I'd never hold out on you, me darlin'. Stay for supper if you want."

"How about it, Hector? Shall we take him up on it?"

"Thanks, but I can't. I have a man I want to see." Beliveau thought he might drop in on Colclough and ask about Rodriguez and the stolen Landrover.

"I think I'll stay." Claire stood behind Blackburn, a wrist balanced on his shoulder, her hip cocked. "Look at all the stuff in that pot. Who else is coming?"

Blackburn emptied his face of intelligence. "It's me perpetual stew, love. Specialty of the maison." His hair was black and parted in the middle. His ears were batlike, cupped to the front, and, together with the alert expression in his eyes, they created an impression of an animal deciding which way to run.

"I'd like to talk to your daughter," Beliveau said. Blackburn had his back to the room and his knife was going cluck-cluck-cluck on the wooden surface. "Does she live here with you?"

"Nobody lives here but me. Tina used to live here for a while after I moved in. She has her friends, now. Places to go. I don't know who or where. I don't even have her phone number."

"Then you can't help me locate her."

"Not really." The cheery voice altered in tone as he began peeling a potato. "Could you tell me why you want to talk to my daughter? Unless it's none of my business."

There was something threatening in the air, beyond Blackburn's emerging hostility. Beliveau had picked it up minutes ago. It was like being near a calm sea and knowing there is a deadly undertow just below the surface.

"Tina may not be involved," Hector said. "There was an accident in the Old Town yesterday. A man named Dakin ran in front of a taxi and got killed."

"I haven't even been out for a paper."

"I was about to enter the shop but Tina stood in the doorway and prevented me."

"Are you sure it was my little girl?"

"She's been identified to my satisfaction."

"Why would she do a thing like that?"

"That's what I'd like to ask her."

"There's no school in August. A child should be able to bat a rubber ball without the police making a federal case out of it."

Beliveau wondered if Blackburn's remark had registered with Claire. Her expression told him nothing. He stood up. "Since you don't know where Tina is, I'll just have to keep my eyes open. Thanks for the lift, Claire. I'll let myself out."

As he was working the latch on the door at the top of the stairway, he heard a movement behind him. He looked over his shoulder and saw another flight of stairs leading upward into darkness. He held his breath. The movement was not repeated. Could it be Tina? Was Blackburn lying about her absence? His reference to her batting a rubber ball could only mean that he himself had been at Dakin's yesterday. Or else his daughter had been talking to him since.

Beliveau went outside and took a couple of air-conditioned short-cuts through the department stores on his way to the police station on Maisonneuve Boulevard. He made his usual splash walking into the department. His big money win was still recent enough to pro-voke comment.

"Here comes the landlord."

"Hey, Beliveau, I hear you took out a mortgage on city hall."

"Put me down for a Christmas basket, Beliveau."

Colclough was on the telephone in his office. The photo of Luther taken from the club lay on his desk. Behind him, a gallery of framed photographs showed Colclough in action on the gridiron. A dusty football on a shelf was covered with fading autographs. He put down the phone.

"I'm curious to know how it's going with this guy." Beliveau picked up the Rodriguez photo. "Did you pick him up?"

Colclough put his feet on the desk. He was wearing a straw hat with a pink polka-dot band. His eyes were just visible under the snap brim. "Not yet."

"Why not? He was driving a Landrover. It shouldn't be hard to spot a Landrover in a world of Fords and Chevies."

"We've got the car but not your friend. It was driven off Highway 11 not far from Rouse's Point. Walking distance from the border."

"He's sneaked into the States?"

"So we could be looking for one more black saxophone player in New York City."

"Why bother? You've got the car back."

"I think he's trying to get to Halifax. He could take a bus through Maine and one of the ferryboats over to Nova Scotia. I telephoned Halifax this morning. They're keeping an eye open."

"What makes you think he's going there?"

"I spoke to your friend Falardeau. He says Rodriguez has a sister who gambles. The money he got from Dakin was to bail her out with some bad people."

"I don't think he got any money from Dakin. He was trying to borrow a thousand from me."

"The kid has terrible judgment."

Beliveau's apartment was less lonely now than it had been when he woke up. He took a beer from the refrigerator, poured it into a crystal glass, and carried it to the piano in the back room. He sat and began playing the few chords he knew. A word came into his mind. Frogman. He could not forget the clarity of tone with which Gib Dakin had made his dying statement. Gib believed he was passing the word to somebody who would know what to do with it. Beliveau softened his touch on the keyboard and began to sing:

> "Laaaazy love,
> Everything hanging fire.
> Me and my slow desire,
> Needing a shove,
> Self-satisfied governor of
> This lazy, laaaazy love . . ."

As he sang, he tried to imagine strings and brass accompanying the winning entry on the CBC telecast in October. Rocky Peerson insisted it was a good song, but Rocky might not want to say anything to alienate his rich friend. Before his lottery win, Lenore was the only one who knew he cared about music. She had said if you feel it, go ahead and do it. Which was not the same thing as saying she thought the songs were worth anything.

Unexpectedly, Beliveau's mind produced a view of the dark stairway in Davey Blackburn's apartment. He stopped playing, stopped singing. He sensed again the movement overhead, felt the cold ripple of fear. Suddenly he knew what he was going to do. He would enter Blackburn's apartment and he would climb those stairs. The plan forming in his mind would require assistance. Beliveau went to the kitchen, where he dialed Rocky Peerson's number. The guitarist answered and said: "Oh, it's you."

"I need your help."

"Why call on me?"

"Why not?"

"I'm the guy you had by the throat last night. You tore my shirt, you sonofabitch."

"I'll buy you a new shirt for Christmas."

"Do that, and then eat it. Preferably while it's still in the box." After a pause, Peerson asked: "What happened with Sangster? There was a mention on the news."

"He wouldn't give me another beer so I threw him out the window."

"They said you found him in the street."

"That's my specialty these days."

"Who would want to kill Milt?"

"It could be a spinoff from what he wrote about the IRA."

"What sort of person throws a crippled man through a window?"

"The sort of person who puts a bomb where people shop. Anyway, never mind that now. I need your help with something else."

"All is forgiven when you need the old minstrel."

"I yelled at you because I had a reason. Do you want to drag it out again?"

"I don't appreciate being humiliated in front of Sangster."

"Sangster will never mention it again. Okay?"

After a pause, Peerson said: "What do you want?"

"I want to enter a place and have five minutes there alone. I want you to keep somebody occupied."

"Here we go again," Peerson said, "bending the law with Hector Beliveau. Switch on the fan and cue the custard."

It was seven o'clock when Beliveau approached the door on Bleury Street for the second time that day. He pressed the bell hoping that Claire Hitchen would not be upstairs. Her presence would complicate things. His cover story was simple. In his investigation, he had discovered new information that let Tina off the hook. He thought her father would want to know.

The latch snapped and the door creaked open. He stepped inside. "Mr. Blackburn?" He could barely make out the figure on the shadowy landing.

"What can I do for you?"

"Is Claire with you?"

"Claire left. She got one of her headaches. Between the two of us, we get lots of headaches."

"I'd like to talk to you. Can you come out and have a beer?"

"I'm having my supper."

"It's about Tina." With his hands behind his back, Beliveau was wedging a broken matchstick into the tongue of the lock. "Just one beer. We'll go across the road to the Alouette."

The little man made up his mind. "I'll get my jacket."

The door at the top of the stairs swung shut. Beliveau had time to examine his handiwork—the lock was effectively blocked. Blackburn reappeared and skipped down the stairs. On the pavement, Beliveau closed the door gently. "Is the Alouette okay for you?"

"They sell the same beer there as anywhere else."

Beliveau found a table at the far end of the L-shaped room, around the corner and out of sight of the front door. They sat down and he ordered four glasses of draft beer, which were delivered in seconds. Beliveau paid, raised a glass, said "Santé!", and drank.

"You said it's about Tina." Blackburn glanced at his watch.

"Since I spoke to you, I heard something. Apparently there's a musician who was into Dakin for a lot of money. This guy has stolen a car and taken off. It's in the hands of the police."

"So that's it, then."

"I owe you an apology about your daughter."

Rocky Peerson came drifting by, reading a tabloid newspaper. "Hey, Rocky," Beliveau said.

"The people you run into when you don't have a gun."

"Sit down, have a beer. Davey Blackburn . . . Mark Peerson."

Blackburn tried to push one of his beers on Peerson but Beliveau was signaling a fresh order.

"I saw Françoise when I went by your place," Peerson said. "She wants you to call her."

"You can't escape." The beer arrived and Beliveau paid again. "You used to be married, Davey. You must know what I mean."

"Good times and bad," Blackburn said.

"Hector," Peerson said patiently, "don't be a bastard all your life. Go to the phone and ring up Françoise."

Beliveau sighed. He took some change from his pocket as he stood up. "All right, I'll phone my girl friend." He headed for the telephones, a route that took him around the corner of the L, out of sight of the table. He picked up speed as he went through the doorway and was on the trot when he crossed Bleury Street. Blackburn's front door swung open from the pressure of his hand. He stepped inside, pinched the matchstick loose, let the tongue of the lock spring free, and closed the door firmly behind him.

On the top landing, he eased the door open and was greeted by light from the kitchen. He stood listening. Silence. He waited for the sensation he had experienced earlier, the pressure of danger from above. He could not feel it.

Beliveau closed the door and moved down the hall into the kitchen. The stew pot stood on the stove. He peered inside and found it empty. This surprised him. Claire Hitchen had said the stew looked enough for a crowd. Blackburn had explained it was to last for days. Now here it was gone in one meal. A faint vibration in his gut told Beliveau it was time to be afraid.

He had to make a move. Rocky couldn't hold Blackburn in the tavern forever. He moved out of the kitchen, down the hall, and into the shadowy doorway. He could count six steps, after which there was darkness. He wished now he had brought a weapon. He had convinced himself he would find Tina up those stairs. Now he was not so sure.

He climbed five steps and waited. Ahead lay a vertical band of grey. That would be the door, slightly ajar. "Tina?" He saw no harm in speaking. His movements in the hall and the kitchen would have been audible to anyone up here. He held his breath, listened, heard nothing except muffled traffic noises from the street.

Beliveau took the last step and faced the partially closed door. He put his head into the opening to see and hear whatever he could.

The door was slammed so suddenly he couldn't draw back. The sharp edges caught him on either side of the head and he saw white light.

As he went to one knee, he was gripped by the hair and hauled into the room, skidding helplessly across cold linoleum, trying to get a grip on something. At the same time, he smelled an overpowering odor, a cage smell, the stink that fills the rhino house at the zoo. "Jesus, Jesus," he heard himself whimpering and then he was lifted into the air, his clothes tearing, his flesh bleeding, and the wind was driven from him as he was thrown against a wall.

He was conscious though hardly able to breathe. Up he rose again and he was flying, released and turning in space. A door frame smashed against him and it must have hurt but he felt no pain. Shock had obliterated his sensation. He saw himself caught in a machine. He would be dead in seconds and there was nothing he could do about it. And he would never know who was doing this to him, or why.

The hands took hold of him once more. He was vertical now and he could see a face, but not a human face. Globular eyes with heavy lids observed him sleepily. An upside-down crescent mouth protruded, half opened and emitting a chemical breath. Beliveau tried to swing a fist at it, but he was weak and everything was happening too fast. He was being thrust upward, slammed against the ceiling again and again, smashing a light fixture, breaking the plaster, over and over like a toy being destroyed by an hysterical child.

Just before Beliveau blacked out, he remembered Gib Dakin's meaningless word, Frogman. And he saw Milton Sangster silhouetted against the sky, driven through a plate-glass window with savage force. He was beginning to understand. It was too late, but he was beginning to understand.

Beliveau opened his eyes and saw gold. It was white gold, so bright that he couldn't look at it. He tried to turn his head but it didn't want to move. He closed his eyes. His eyelashes were wet and he realized he was crying. It took him a while to understand that he was crying because he was alive.

"Thank God." A warm hand touched his cheek. "I was afraid you were never going to wake up." Françoise was standing beside the bed, a china rose pinned to the collar of her white blouse. She was smiling and trying not to cry.

"Which day is it?"

"Thursday. You've been out for three days."

A nurse looked in. She went away at a run and came back with a doctor. He observed Beliveau, listened to him, took a blood-pressure reading, and looked into his eyes with a light.

"When can I go home?"

"Don't think about going home yet." The doctor flashed his patient the satisfied grin of one rich man to another. "You aren't worried about the bill, are you?"

When the door closed and he was alone again with Françoise, she said: "Why did you go up there by yourself?"

"I'm trying to find a girl. She knows what's behind Gib Dakin's death. If I sort that one out, I may know what happened to Milt Sangster."

Françoise looked out the window. Her face was sad, as if she were on the stern of a ship departing from a friendly country. "When they let you go home, I can come and stay with you."

"It might lead to a relapse." There was a fuzzy plan in his mind that had something to do with leaving town. "Let's talk about it later."

She gave him a wry smile as she prepared to leave. "Take care, my love." She pulled on a lacy white glove.

All Beliveau wanted to do was close his eyes and let sleep rise like the tide and carry him off. He floated for a while and then opened his eyes. He was on a raft. It belonged to Lenore's father, Louis Angelo, who was at the outboard motor now, guiding the raft across Long Island Sound. It was not much more than a board surface riding high above the water on oil-drum floats. Beliveau was sitting in a canvas chair. He did not get on well with Lenore's father, but he loved the man's raft.

"If you get the time, you might bring Lenore down here to see me," Angelo said.

"I can't."

"Why not? Do you need money? I understand you won a pot full of money."

"She's dead, Mr. Angelo."

The news did not seem to trouble the older man. "You were supposed to take care of her. You promised to cherish her in sickness and in health."

"Till death parted us. And I still do."

"How did it happen, anyway?"

"She was waiting for a bus and this car came along."

"What bus? Lenore had her own car."

"She left it at home. She was at a Christmas party with a bunch of teachers from her school. Somebody offered her a lift but she refused because the man had been drinking. She went down to Dorchester Boulevard and waited for a 66 bus."

"Must have been cold waiting for a bus."

"A car came along going about sixty miles an hour. It went into a skid on black ice. He wiped out the whole line. Two dead, four badly hurt."

Somebody was standing over Beliveau, staring down from behind glasses with heavy frames. "They told me you came out of your coma. Welcome back."

"Rocky, it's you. I'm going to need you."

"What for?"

"There's something we have to do. We have to go someplace."

"You're going nowhere, my friend."

Beliveau began to remember the scene in the tavern before he crossed Bleury Street. "How come I'm not dead?" he asked.

"The girl saved you. Tina? She must have come along as it was happening."

"Tell me what happened."

"I sat with Blackburn. I detained him as long as I could, but he finally left and I went after him."

"Where did you find me?"

"In the kitchen. You were unconscious. The girl was there and she seemed mad as hell. She said something to Blackburn about Uncle Conrad."

"What about Uncle Conrad?"

"She said she'd given him his medication. She said if she wasn't around, nobody took care of him."

"What did Blackburn say?"

"He was scared. He dragged out a suitcase and started packing. She asked him if he was dumping Uncle Conrad on her. He said: 'Conrad belongs with your grandmother. Take him home. I'm going with Claire.'"

"So Blackburn is gone with Claire Hitchen. And Tina's gone home with Uncle Conrad. Home to Baytown."

"Where the hell is Baytown?"

"I remember what I want us to do. We have to go to Baytown."

"Prior commitments, old friend. I'm touring Tasmania with Jazz at the Philharmonic."

Beliveau closed his eyes. "Why did Sangster go out his window the same day Gib Dakin ran in front of a taxi?"

"Must have been a double-header."

Beliveau was becoming more lucid. "Uncle Conrad could have sent Sangster through the window. The only other thing would be the mechanism that fires jets off an aircraft carrier."

Peerson stood up. "You'd better rest."

"But if it was Conrad in Dakin's shop, and Conrad again in Sangster's loft, what's the connection? Why was Tina in Gib's doorway keeping people from going in?"

"I'm going now, Sherlock."

Beliveau stared up at his friend with dangerous eyes. "I'll be out of here soon and then we'll make plans."

Beliveau was waiting for Peerson at the top end of Jacques Cartier Square. "I thought you weren't coming."

"You thought wrong, didn't you."

They walked toward the alley, Beliveau limping on the crutch issued him by the hospital appliance department.

"I must be crazy," Peerson said. "I'm the one who's going to climb the fire escape."

"It's perfectly safe. I came down it a couple of weeks ago."

They moved down the alley, past Sangster's door, on into the back yard. Tired of arguing, Peerson took hold of the bottom rung of the vertical ladder, swung himself up, clambered onto the iron stairway, and began to ascend toward the window thirty feet above.

Beliveau dragged himself back to the door. The hospital crutch had been used by others before him and was soiled. He couldn't bear to think how many arms it had been under. It was worth any risk to be rid of it.

He leaned against the door. His head had been shaved and revealed now a new growth of hair with scars visible through it. It was the haircut of a marine recruit who has failed the assault course. Slender at the best of times, Beliveau looked delicate now in slacks and short-sleeved shirt. Behind the door he could hear the elevator on its way down. It stopped, the door opened, and Peerson let him in.

"It's spooky up there. The window Milt went through is boarded up."

In the studio, the golf cart was on its side, a sight that tightened the muscles in Beliveau's stomach. He looked at the panel of plywood nailed over the broken window. He peered around the edge of it into the street below. They were drinking beer at the sidewalk cafés.

"I don't see any crutches," Peerson said.

"Hunt for them."

In the bedroom, there was a built-in wardrobe. Peerson swung open both doors and got down on his knees and rummaged under garments. "You're in luck," he said, drawing out a pair of aluminum crutches. "A matched set of all-weather, radial Gimpmaster Specials with polystyrene hand grips."

It was a pleasure to balance on the light shaft with its brand-new pad. Beliveau checked himself in the mirror. "I'm all set."

The telephone rang as they were about to leave the bedroom. They stood looking at each other. "What we do is let it ring," Peerson said.

Beliveau picked it up. "Hello?"

"I have a collect call for anyone there from Baytown, Ontario. Will you accept the charges?"

"Yes."

"Mr. Sangster, you don't know me but you know my granddaughter. I've heard her speak of you." It was the voice of an old woman. She sounded more than a little drunk. "I see your programs all the time. You're a wonderful writer. I never thought much of Tina, but if Milton Sangster is her friend there must be more to the girl than I thought."

"Tina's a good girl. A little wild sometimes . . ."

"Her father spoiled her. Davey is the one at fault." She began to cough, the line echoing with the croupy noise. "I can't talk long. Tina is over in the summer house putting Conrad to bed. I found your number in her purse."

"Why did you call me?"

"I'd like you to take them back and give them a place to stay. Not in your house—nobody would want Conrad all the time and Tina is just a child. But if you could take them off my hands . . ."

"It's a difficult problem."

"I know. But I'm an old woman." The voice became a hoarse whisper. "She's coming back. Do it if you can. You'd oblige me."

Beliveau set down the telephone. "We have to go to Baytown. They're both there."

"Doesn't she know Sangster's dead?"

"Obviously not."

"I don't see why you need me. Hire a driver."

"I'm about to do that. I'm going to tell Tancred I want Rocky
Peerson booked for a two-week solo gig starting the end of September. If he refuses, I'll call in the loan I gave him to fix his roof."

Peerson followed Beliveau into the elevator. "Two weeks?"

"We'll go there now and confirm it."

Out in the alley, moving slowly toward the square, Peerson said:
"I hear Baytown is lovely this time of year."

Beliveau and Peerson emerged at the top of the stairs in Tancred's
sitting room, a polished area of black glass and white vinyl. The
only light came through a row of windows above half sized louvered
shutters painted midnight blue. A tape was playing somewhere out
of sight—Miles Davis giving his muted rendition of "Bye Bye, Black-
bird." Beliveau smelled a trace of incense.

Tancred's voice came from another room. "In here!"

Beliveau moved into the doorway of the bathroom. Tancred was
immersed in the tub, his barrel chest gleaming over a crust of bub-
bles. There was only one chair, a cane job beside the tub. It was
occupied now by the telephone and a folded towel. Beliveau said:
"I've got an idea for your September booking."

"I was thinking of screening old movies."

"That's a terrible idea. You need a fortnight of Rocky Peerson
playing in different styles. A guitar retrospective. He could do Mot-
tola, Django, Oscar Moore—all the way up to the rock players of
today."

"Let me think about it," Tancred said. "Go in the other room, I'll
be right there."

Rocky sat in a white wicker chair padded with a black-velvet
cushion. Beliveau took the petitpoint chair without arms, placed his
crutch on the carpet, and found a comfortable angle for his plaster
leg. Tancred came into the room and sat down facing them on a
black-velvet hassock, a wine-satin robe cinched at the waist, his
chunky calves tapering to slab feet planted on the polished parquet.
"It's a good idea," he said. "Let me think about it."

"Rocky and I are going away for a while, but when we get back,
he's available."

Nobody spoke for half a minute. Then Beliveau said: "That phone
in the bathroom, is it on a long cord?"

"Yes, it usually sits in here. Want to make a call?"

"Not at the moment. What do you hear from Luther Rodriguez?"

"He must be miles away in the States."

"Colclough thinks he may be on his way to Halifax."

"Did Colclough say that?"

"He said you told him about Luther's sister who gambles."

"Shall we go downstairs and have a drink?"

Beliveau said: "I'd rather stay here and talk to Luther."

"What do you mean?"

"I mean I'd like Luther to appear from wherever he's hiding."

Tancred gave a short laugh. "You're incredible."

"Come out, come out, wherever you are!" Beliveau's voice echoed through the apartment.

"How did you guess?"

"When Dallas announced us from downstairs, it took a long time for you to answer. But the telephone was on the chair beside you. Somebody must have carried it into the bathroom and let you answer it. My guess is the somebody is Luther."

Rodriguez walked out of the bedroom. He was unshaven and his suit was wrinkled. "They needed a place to rest up," Tancred said.

"They?"

"Come on out, May," Luther called. "This is my big sister, May." A tall, slender woman came out of the bedroom, carrying a tin of beer. She moved from the hips down, holding the top of her torso rigid, which gave her a statuesque appearance. Her skin was café-au-lait, lighter than Luther's. She was not as good-looking as her brother, her features too sharp, her head too small. She wore her hair cut almost as short as Beliveau's. "This is the Beliveau I told you about. And Rocky Peerson. Plays good guitar."

"Hello, boys." She raised her free hand in a faint salute as she lifted the tin and took a sip. She must have been in her forties. She wore a floral-print housedress of a style Beliveau hadn't seen for years.

He moved his crutch, allowing Luther to get to a chair. "So you did go to Halifax."

"You wouldn't lend me the money, so I had to sneak back and bring her out."

"Somebody should have leveled with me," Beliveau said. "Told me what the money was for."

"He has a point," Tancred sympathized. "Everybody thinks Beliveau is the money tree. Beliveau pays. It isn't fair."

"Let us rest a couple of days," Luther said. "Then we'll move on."

"Let's try Vancouver," May said.

"I've still got a problem," Beliveau said. "The page from Dakin's

notebook." He took out his wallet and extracted the dogeared slip
of paper. "It says you owe him a thousand dollars. Would he list you
if you didn't owe him?"

"You never mentioned this." May came and took the paper from
Beliveau's hand.

"It's phony. Somebody's framing me."

"He can't even spell your name," she said. "There's no o's in Luther."

Beliveau tried again. "Do you know a girl named Tina Blackburn?"

Rodriguez hesitated. "I know *of* her. She's a kid."

"She was blocking the doorway of Dakin's shop. If you were inside
terrorizing the man, and if Tina is your friend, it might make sense.
She would have been covering for you."

"Except I wasn't there." Luther took the slip of paper from his
sister. He lit a match and touched the flame to a corner of the page.
In seconds, it was consumed and he dropped the flickering corner
of it into an ashtray. "Now can we shut up about the goddamn
thousand dollars?"

"You're impulsive, Luther," Beliveau said. "But I don't mind. I've
never believed you did anything to Dakin. I think Tina Blackburn
is more involved than you are. That's why Rocky and I are driving
down to Baytown to talk to her."

"Baytown?" Rodriguez looked interested.

"A little place in Ontario." Beliveau struggled up. "Come on, Peerson. Let's go hire a car—one big enough to take this plaster leg of
mine."

The grey Daimler rolled quietly down Baytown's main street. It
stopped at the tattered canopy of a hotel called the Coronet. The
driver emerged first, slamming the door and hitching up his slacks.
The passenger climbed out awkwardly because his left leg was in
a cast. As he drew himself erect, the driver reached inside and found
an aluminum crutch which he handed to his companion.

"Is this where we're supposed to stay?" Beliveau said.

"This is the place the car-rental girl recommended." Peerson had
the trunk open and was hefting out two suitcases. "Walk on in."

The desk clerk was a compact man with hair so fair it was almost
invisible. He slammed a bell and called in a theatrical voice: "Front!"
A youth in a white mess jacket, unbuttoned, wandered through a
doorway at the end of the lobby. His hair was long and glistened

with vaseline. His trouser legs were ankle high, his shoes brown
and warped. He looked as if he had climbed from a river and taken
a long time to dry. "Sam, these gentlemen are for room 109."

"Yes sir, yes sir." The youth spoke with a cigarette in his mouth
and it flickered up and down, sprinkling the grubby jacket with ash.

"Can we get a drink somewhere?" Peerson asked.

"The beverage room is through there, Mr. Peerson," the clerk said,
reading the name from the card as if he was announcing a candidate
for an Academy Award.

It was three-thirty in the afternoon. The beverage room was
sparsely populated. A waiter came and stood with his head tilted
forward, his eyes half closed, as if he was in a funeral parlor in the
presence of the bereaved. He had the mottled face of a fighter who
has taken a pasting for eight rounds but plans to go to fifteen.
Peerson ordered four beers and the man went off.

"There's a police station down the road," Peerson said. "Let's go
tell them we have reason to believe the Blackburns have been up
to naughty tricks in Montreal. Let them send a constable."

"The local cops would never understand. Stop fretting, we're going
to proceed with caution."

"Yeah, sure."

"Only at the last minute will we start screaming and running
through plate-glass windows."

"And what about the Landrover I saw behind us on the highway?"

"You were dreaming."

"I saw it. Definitely once and maybe another time."

The beers came and for a few minutes they drank in silence. At
last Peerson said: "I'm a glass ahead of you, Beliveau. Drinking
alone here."

"Time was when I would have blinded you with the action of my
elbow. That was before I met Lenore."

Beliveau remembered a chilly February afternoon years ago in
Le Vieux Carré in New Orleans. He was at the bar in Lafitte's with
the gas fire blowing beside him, a Ramos gin fizz in hand and Carly
Simon singing "You're So Vain" in the background. Using up some
accumulated vacation time, he had decided to put the Canadian
winter behind him. He drove to New Orleans in three
stages—Hagerstown, Maryland; Chattanooga, Tennessee; then the
arrival on a Monday afternoon in pale, sweet sunlight. For a few
weeks, he rolled around Bourbon Street, Royal Street, drunk every

afternoon, over to Jackson Square to sleep on the grass. As his money
ran low, he reduced himself to cheap grades of wine.

Then he struck it rich in a poker game with some musicians from
Crazy Annie's and that brought him to Lafitte's and his gin fizz on
that February afternoon. He was half asleep by the fire, drowning
in homesickness as Carly sang about Nova Scotia and a total eclipse
of the sun. Then he raised his eyes and there, looking directly at
him with a thoughtful expression on her face, was Lenore Angelo.

She had a companion, but the boy only lasted a few minutes.
Angelo and Beliveau came together in the simple relationship people
depend on to banish loneliness. But first of all, the drinking had to
stop. It was easy.

These recollections slipped through Beliveau's mind in less time
than it took him to tell Rocky: "I learned a long time ago there are
better things to do than drink."

"You are an intolerably wealthy man," Peerson said. "It's a good
thing you've got money."

Time was slipping by. Beliveau said: "In a town this size, the
Blackburn family must be known." They went back to the lobby.

"Mrs. Blackburn works here," the desk clerk said. "She comes in
three mornings a week as a chambermaid."

"I'm interested in locating Dave Blackburn. I owe him money."

"If he's here," Sam the bellboy said, "he'll be out at the house on
Station Road. Where Moira lives."

"Moira is Mrs. Blackburn," the clerk explained.

"When do you get off, Sam?"

"Five."

"Five-thirty," the clerk said.

"We'll go and unpack," Beliveau said. "At five-thirty we'll come
down and you can take us to Mrs. Blackburn's."

Room 109 was rectangular with two sagging beds. There was a
dresser with a mirror, a solid chest of drawers, an upholstered armchair, and a wooden chair with cane seat and harp back. Beliveau
lay down on one of the beds and rolled to the middle of the mattress.
"I'm having a nap."

Peerson busied himself with his suitcase, popping hasps, sighing
as he took out garments and slid them away in various drawers.
"If Françoise could see us now," he said.

"Shut up," Beliveau murmured. He was drifting off.

"One of these days that nice French-Canadian bird is going to rebel. She hated us coming here and I don't blame her. *I* hate us coming here. But you bought me with your influence over Tancred. Beliveau pays, everybody dances."

Beliveau listened to his friend's voice with the top of his mind. Then up came pictures from deeper down. He saw Lenore Angelo approach the balance beam, holding herself on tiptoe, her buttocks attractively rounded under the stretchy leotard. She rose gracefully and mounted the beam in a sideways vault. The television caption gave her name and her score in white computer letters.

The crowd applauded everything she did. Her skill on this difficult piece of apparatus was outstanding, the nearest the USA had come in a long time to having somebody capable of competing with the East European women. Then the back injury occurred, not enough to cripple her but enough to take the edge off her performance. Beliveau considered himself lucky to have seen her at her peak. He was luckier still to have run into her in New Orleans.

The gas fire was hot against his back. Beliveau looked around Lafitte's bar for another place to sit. He got up and went outside. It was cold on the street, an icy wind blowing down from the mountain, funneling between the buildings on Dorchester Boulevard.

The car approached from the east, running the light at Metcalfe Street. The light changed and the driver hit the brake—the car swerved on black ice and came at the waiting people broadside on. Beliveau watched Lenore bending and turning in the air as the car went through beneath her. She was beautiful, her legs tucked, blonde hair flying. Beliveau ran to take her hand and help her to her feet. But as he drew her up, it was Gib Dakin and blood ran from his mouth.

A hand touched Beliveau on the shoulder and he shot bolt upright. "We're all right!"

Rocky Peerson pulled back as if he had been stung. "Jesus, when you take a nap you don't kid around."

"Sorry. What time is it?"

"Five-thirty. If you still want to get murdered, let's go and have it seen to."

The bellboy was waiting in the lobby. He led the way outside. Peerson put a hand on Beliveau's arm. "What did I tell you?" He pointed ahead.

"You were right." Beliveau walked past the Daimler and stopped beside Tancred's Landrover. He looked in through the open window. "Hello, May. Hi there, Luther."

"I want to see Tina," Luther said.

"We're going there now."

"I'll follow along."

"I'm not sure that's a good idea."

"If Tina Blackburn is going to say anything about me and Dakin, I want to be there."

"Could she say anything about you and Dakin?"

"I told you, I never knew the man."

"Then you're in the clear."

May Rodriguez turned to her brother. "Maybe we should drive on. Let these gentlemen get on with whatever they're doing."

Beliveau made up his mind. "All right," he said, "we'll take both cars. But there's an old woman there as well as the girl. And I'm pretty sure her uncle, and he could be dangerous. So keep cool, Luther."

"Man, I'll be like a choir boy."

The road was not much more than a country lane. It had been paved, but not in this quarter of the century. Two lines of railway track snaked along between coarse weeds. On the other side, there was shrubbery, then thick grass, then stands of birch and maple. It was after six and the September evening was serving notice that it would soon close down. There was a mild, moist smell in the air.

"Does the old lady live alone?" Beliveau asked.

"Most of the time," Sam said. "Conrad is in and out of the hospital. And her old man disappeared years ago. The cops tried to make something out of that."

"Cops?"

"Yeah. Sean Blackburn, Moira's husband, was a vicious bastard. Drunk most of the day. I never saw him—it was before my time."

"What happened?"

"When he disappeared? Moira told the police he ran off and left her. Nobody believed it. A nasty character like Blackburn would never be that obliging."

"Somebody killed him?"

"And not a moment too soon."

After a quiet spell, Beliveau said: "I never met Davey's brother Conrad."

"Spends a lot of his time in the asylum. They're the only people who can handle him. They shoot him full of drugs." Sam fired his cigarette through the window. "They call him Frogman."

"He sounds like a hazard."

"When the hospital gets him in shape, they send him home. Then Moira can take care of him. When he starts acting funny again, they bring down a platoon with torches and a net." Sam lit another cigarette, crouching under the dashboard to shield the match. "I heard Conrad Blackburn was okay when he was a kid."

"What happened to change him?"

"I don't know. Moira told me he wasn't always like this. I never heard what happened." Sam pointed. "That's the place, the house with the flowers out front."

Moira Blackburn's place was a tarpaper shanty. Its slanting roof was shedding its shingles. There was an unscreened porch and a picture window containing a red café curtain with a lamp burning behind it. The house looked homemade.

The Daimler rolled onto grass and stopped and the occupants climbed out. They waited for Luther, who came alone, leaving May in the Landrover. The group approached the house along an overgrown gravel footpath.

Two bathtubs were partially buried in the ground on either side of the front door, filled with earth and planted with petunias, marigolds, and pansies. The flowers were thriving, the dark earth between the plants showing signs of weeding and watering.

Sam mounted the porch and rapped on the door. The others waited on the path. As Beliveau stood there, he sensed something in the air. It reminded him of the hint of danger he had felt in Blackburn's apartment, only this time the feeling was not as intense. He turned and looked behind him. There was a pathway through shrubbery and, beyond it, a couple of chestnut trees. Their branches formed a canopy over a circular roof shingled in cedar.

"Hello, Moira," Sam said. "These people are from Montreal. They want to talk to you."

Mrs. Blackburn stepped onto the porch. She was a tiny woman, frail yet giving the impression of being a worker. Her skin was wrinkled and dark, her cheekbones high, her hair silver-grey and pinned on top of her small skull. Beliveau decided there was Indian blood in her veins—he had seen this face in sepia photographs taken by early settlers. She was wearing faded jeans and a short-sleeved white blouse drawn by a string at the neck.

She looked at the parked limousine. Her eyes met Beliveau's. "Is that your car?" Her grin showed teeth like kernels of golden bantam corn.

"It belongs to a company in Montreal. I hired it."

"What do you want to talk about?"

"I'm trying to find your granddaughter, Tina."

"Are you the police?"

"I used to be. My money's invested now and I live on the income. I don't have to work."

The old woman grinned again. "Come in and tell me what it's like."

They trooped inside. The house seemed to be all kitchen. There was a wooden table and four chairs and an old-fashioned iron stove that burned coal. Mrs. Blackburn opened the door of an ancient icebox. "All I've got is beer."

"We'd love a beer," Beliveau said. They sat down around the table as Mrs. Blackburn snapped bottle caps using an opener screwed to the doorframe, letting the caps roll away out of sight on the linoleum floor.

"Why do you want to find Tina?" She passed the bottles around and sat with her knees apart, a bony fist jammed into one thigh, a beer in her other hand.

"A friend of mine had an accident. I want to find out what happened and I believe Tina was a witness."

Luther spoke up. "The cops are giving me a hard time. Tina can say I wasn't there when it happened."

"Are you Tina's boy friend?"

"I'm too old for her. She's just a kid."

"She might say otherwise."

"Can we speak with Tina, Mrs. Blackburn?"

"She isn't here."

"I understood she might be," Beliveau said.

"I haven't seen her or her father since two Christmases ago."

"What about Conrad?"

"My older son has trouble with his nerves. He spends a lot of time in the hospital."

"I see." Beliveau pushed back his chair and made a business of getting onto the crutch. "Then there's no need to bother you any longer. Thanks for the beer." He took a business card from his pocket. "This is my number in Montreal. I'll be back there tomorrow. If you hear from Tina, would you ask her to give me a call?"

Outside, Rodriguez said: "We drove a long way for nothing. I want this thing cleared up."

"Trust me, Luther. When and if I confront Tina, I'll see you get a fair shake."

"What about Colclough? If he gets hold of Tina she can say what she likes about me and he'll buy it."

"He isn't even looking for her."

It was almost dark. Peerson got into the Daimler and turned on the lights. The twin beams illuminated twinkling columns of insects. "Why don't you drive on out to the west coast?" Beliveau said. "Write me when you get there." He handed over another business card. "I'll write back and tell you what's happening."

"I must be crazy," Luther said. "Corresponding with a cop."

"A former cop."

In the limousine, moving in the right direction, Peerson said: "I understand now."

"I thought you would eventually."

"You wanted rid of Luther. So you let him believe *you* believed the old lady's story."

Sam looked at his watch. "You guys want to come to a ballgame? Paragon Café versus Canada Cement."

"Sounds incredibly dull," Beliveau said. They let the bellboy out near a playing field where inadequate lights shone on a dirt field occupied by men in street pants and colorful jerseys and drove on.

"Did you see that building among the trees?" Beliveau said.

"At Mrs. Blackburn's? No."

"When she telephoned and thought she was talking to Sangster, she said something about the summer house. They aren't supposed to be using it."

"If that evil bastard is in there—"

"Calm down. We can drive out there and do a little recce."

"When?"

"Tonight. As soon as we stop at the hotel and borrow a flashlight."

Rocky Peerson could not see. He wanted to stay where he was, but Beliveau was making progress and he was terrified of being left alone in this jungle.

"We're there." Beliveau aimed Peerson's chin toward a dark shape. "That's the summer house. Conrad may be inside or he may be up at the house with Tina and the old woman."

A globe of light was approaching from the direction of the road. It advanced slowly, raising and lowering its distance from the ground.

"Which way do we run?"

"We stay put."

The light turned out to be a kerosene lantern. The holder was only partly visible, a blurred silhouette in a vignette of yellow light screened by leaves. "Mr. Beliveau?"

"Tina?" Beliveau stood up. He and the girl stepped forward and met in a cleared area. "My friend tells me you saved my life, coming along when your uncle was beating me up."

"Conrad isn't responsible. It was my father's fault. It was all his idea."

"Where's Conrad now?"

"In the house behind you. You've nothing to worry about. He's on his pills now."

They left the shrubbery, walked to the house, and entered the kitchen. Moira Blackburn sat at the end of the table, a cribbage board beside her. She held a hand of cards. Tina's cards lay face down on the table. "You're trespassing on my property," she said.

"I knew Tina was here," Beliveau said. "And Conrad. I was the man who took the call when you telephoned Montreal."

Tina was extinguishing the lantern. She looked up. "I never knew you telephoned, Gran."

"I can't keep Conrad here. Or you, either, for that matter. Are we finishing this game or not?"

Tina snatched the pegs out of the board and dropped them on the table. Mrs. Blackburn began gathering the cards.

"Can we talk about Milton Sangster?" Beliveau said. "It seems you knew him, Tina."

"I met him around the sidewalk cafés. We used to say hello."

"But you had his name and phone number in your purse."

"When I heard he was famous I asked for his autograph. I put down the phone number because I thought he might help me someday."

"Somebody threw him from his upstairs window. Could it have been Conrad?"

"I didn't keep track of Uncle Conrad every minute."

"What about Gib Dakin? He ran like he was scared to death."

"I knew something was going on," Mrs. Blackburn said.

"How about it, Tina? You were keeping me out of Dakin's shop."

"All right, I'll tell." She made an exasperated face. "They were threatening Mr. Dakin to get money out of him. It was my father's idea."

"And did Dakin pay?"

"Not at first. We came back a second time with Uncle Conrad. I don't know if he gave my father any money. All I know is he came running past me, and you know what happened then."

"So it was a shakedown racket."

"Yes."

"And the same thing with Sangster?"

"There won't be any more trouble," Tina said. "We can forget the whole thing."

"Two men are dead," Beliveau said. "We can't forget that."

Mrs. Blackburn stared through the open doorway into the night. "None of you understand what it was like. Conrad was my best child. He was born beautiful because he was a cesarean—he was so big I couldn't have him the regular way."

"Then he changed."

"His father changed him. Sean would come home drunk and the baby would start crying. He'd slap him and Conrad would cry louder. I found him once holding the baby's face down on the covers. I told him to stop and he punched the back of his head. I thought he was dead that time."

"You never told me this," Tina said.

"He damaged him. That's why Conrad goes crazy now."

"Gran, why didn't you do something?"

"You keep hoping he'll quit. And when it happens again, you hope that's the last time."

"How long did it go on, Mrs. Blackburn?"

"Till Sean got arrested for breaking and entering. A householder caught him and he beat the man up so they put him away in Kingston Penetentiary. Conrad was three years old. A year later, Davey was born."

"While your husband was in prison."

"Davey's father was a deckhand off the lakeboats. When Sean was released, Davey was six and Conrad was ten. Too big for beating like babies."

"What happened to Sean?"

"Who cares? One day he was here, next day he wasn't around. I don't question luck as good as that."

It was time to go. Beliveau asked Tina to walk them to the car. In the darkness, the insect chorus filled the night. "Tina," he said at the side of the road, "you can tell me the truth about Dakin now."

"What truth?"

"Is there ever more than one?"

"I'm not with you."

"When people extort money, they usually have something on the victim."

She was silent.

"Dakin had a reputation. What had your father found out about him?"

"All right," she said at last. She was cheerful; it was as if she had wanted to tell all along. "I was Dakin's playmate. He liked teenage girls. The story was my Uncle Conrad would kill anybody who laid a hand on me. For all I know, it's true."

Beliveau felt weary. He leaned against the car. "What about Sangster? Were you involved with him, too?"

"A man like him? No, I just had his autograph." She clawed at her leg. "Can I go inside? I'm getting bitten to death."

"Go ahead."

Tina walked toward the house. She wasn't worried that Beliveau had managed to get this close. She was sure she could handle him. Men had always done their best to please her. Women were not the same thing. Her grandmother was a soft touch, but even Gran could get up in arms sometimes and start acting toward Tina as if she was some kind of savage.

Her mother had always been the hardest one to figure out. She seemed to change from hour to hour. One minute, she would be screaming, shaking with anger and causing drops of spit to land on Tina's face. Nothing had happened except she had got some grape jelly on her overalls. Finally the screaming would stop and then, minutes later, her mother would be trying to pick her up, which was stupid because Tina was so tall her shoes scraped the floor while her mother squeezed her, pressing her wet cheek against Tina's face, smelling of whatever she had been drinking.

The first time Uncle Conrad came to stay with them in the apartment was bad. Her mother didn't want him, but her father said he needed his brother with him. Tina's memory of the visit was vague. The episode that stood out in her mind was when her father went to work and her mother began yelling at Conrad in the kitchen. She said she couldn't stand the way he smelled. Tina ran into the kitchen and faced her mother. "You shut up. Don't say that to him."

"Get to your room."

"You stink of gin."

"I'll swat your face. Get out of this room."

The argument subsided and Conrad went to wait for his brother outside the apartment building. He always did that. Tina's father was never home before six and sometimes Conrad would wait out there all afternoon.

Tina went looking for her mother and found her standing on the balcony. She had her arms folded, a cigarette in one hand. Tina watched from the doorway. As her mother was grinding the cigarette under her shoe, she noticed Tina. "Come out here. Don't sneak away, I want to talk to you."

"I'm not sneaking."

"Don't use that tone of voice with me."

They were arguing without any reason. Tina told her mother all the things her father had said about her on their walks. These disclosures brought surprise and pain to her mother's eyes, so Tina went on to exaggerate her father's statements. That was when her mother caught her wrist and they began to struggle. They had not fought physically in quite a while. Tina was pleased at how easily she could handle her mother.

The fight ended and Tina ran inside. She forced her way behind the sofa and stayed there, trembling with fear and excitement, until they came and got her.

The Daimler engine rumbled as Beliveau's car moved away. Humming confidently, the girl went into the shanty to face whatever hassles her grandmother might have in mind.

Inside the car, they were arguing. "You'll have to call the cops," Peerson raved. "That maniac caused Dakin's death. Maybe he caused Sangster's."

Beliveau remained calm. "Davey Blackburn is the one I'd like to get. But he's in the States with the Hitchen woman."

"Conrad is the killer, man. The danger is here, in that summer house."

They drove slowly past homes hidden behind acres of lawn on into the commercial district, down the main street to the Coronet. As he locked the car farther down on the market square, Peerson spoke again. "The police station is right here, Hector. Let's tell them what we know."

"Leave it," Beliveau said. "Leave it till I say when."

There was a telephone message waiting for Beliveau at the hotel desk. He recognized his home number. How had Françoise discovered where he was staying? Wearily, they climbed the stairs.

"You want me out of the room while you talk?" Peerson asked.

"In the bathroom brushing your teeth will be sufficient."

Beliveau dialed the Montreal area code and his home number. The telephone was lifted after two rings and he heard Françoise, her voice close to the mouthpiece, sounding urgent.

"Hector?"

"How did you find out where I'm staying?"

"I called Murray Hill car rental. The girl told me she'd recommended the Coronet."

"What's up? How are the plants?"

"Skeptical. They don't understand regular watering. You had visitors today—a man and a woman. They didn't give their names."

"What did they look like?"

"She's thin, pretty years ago. Thinks she still is and probably gets away with it. He sounded Irish. Big ears."

"Claire Hitchen and Davey Blackburn."

"The man whose apartment you broke into?"

"Tell me what happened."

"Nothing happened. They showed up around five. They seemed disappointed you were out of town."

"Did they say they'd be back?"

"No, they just went away. Can I call Colclough?"

"Don't. He'll have to know I'm here and what I'm doing."

"What *are* you doing?"

"Sorting things out. I've traced Tina Blackburn." Beliveau stared through the window at the town-hall clock across the street. "I'm going to coast for a day or two until I decide my next move."

"What is there to decide? You have to call the police."

"The police means Colclough. And that means violence, which I'm trying to avoid." The clock announced the half hour with one devastating bong. "Frankie, do me a favor. Call my friend Kiniski—his office number is in my book by the kitchen phone. He's a stockbroker. Ask him for a quick rundown on Northway Beverages. I'd like to know if the company is healthy. Can you do that by ten in the morning and ring me back here?"

"Of course." She was scribbling a note. "I wish you'd come home tomorrow."

"A few more days. This affair is almost finished."

Peerson came out of the bathroom as the call ended. "We ought to go home like she wants."

"You know we can't do that."

"Call the police and turn Conrad in."

"My mind is made up."

"The city of Montreal don't know their luck." Peerson crawled into his bed. "They lost one pain-in-the-ass cop when you won that lottery."

Françoise telephoned at 10:30. Kiniski's information was that Northway Beverages was in trouble. There were cash-flow problems and word was that old man Hitchen was ripe for a takeover. "It confirms my theory," Beliveau said. "Davey Blackburn thought Claire could support him but he's learned that she can't. Or won't. So he came back to squeeze some money out of me."

"This crazy scheme has to end." Françoise sounded angry.

"It will in a few days."

Beliveau and Peerson went to an afternoon movie at the theater across the street next to the town hall. When they came out into the early evening light, they could see Sam the bellboy sitting on the steps in front of the hotel. As they crossed the road, he stood to greet them. "You missed all the excitement."

"What excitement?"

"A convoy of cops took off for Moira's house. Two cars full of guys from here and another with Provincial Police in it. The Montreal cop was with the Provincials."

"You're sure he was from Montreal?"

"The guy who used to play football. Vince Colclough."

Beliveau moved as fast as he could to where the Daimler was parked on the market square. As he fished out the keys, Peerson said: "Françoise didn't waste any time blowing the whistle on you."

"Never mind Françoise," Beliveau said. "If I know Colclough, he's brought guns. And if I know Conrad Blackburn, he'll give them something to shoot at."

It was after eight o'clock. The last of the light was fading from a cloudless sky. Most of the cops were staked out in the grounds around the summer house. Beliveau stood near the open doorway of the shanty. Vince Colclough had drawn a chair onto the porch and was sitting there, staring at the door of the summer house just visible through the trees.

"Are the lights ready?" Colclough sounded bored.

"All set now."

"Let's have them. I can't see a damn thing."

A generator motor coughed and started, and several lights on standards illuminated the gazebo like a stage set. A derisory cheer rose from the men crouched in the woods.

"Go back inside, Beliveau. Keep out of the way."

"You can't start anything with Tina in there."

"That was my mistake, letting you persuade me to allow her inside."

Beliveau went into the kitchen. Rocky Peerson was sitting on the floor at the far side of the room. His forehead rested on his arms; he might have been asleep. Mrs. Blackburn was working a late shift at the distillery. They wouldn't see her much before midnight.

"Figure they're really going to shoot him?" A photographer from the *Baytown Banner* had seen the police cars and followed them.

"I hope they don't."

There was movement at the summer-house door. It opened and closed. A small figure was coming sideways down the stairs, now moving quickly across the grass. It was Tina Blackburn, looking like a kid playing hookey. The police were all standing, their guns at the ready. Tina confronted Colclough on the trampled grass below the porch. Her eyes were white patches in a dirty face. "He's afraid. He's seen all the people out here. When the lights came on, it made him worse."

"Kill the lights," somebody said.

"Hold it!" Colclough shouted. "Leave the lights! Christ, he wants the lights out so he can make a run for it!"

"That isn't true," Tina wailed. "He's afraid."

"So am I. I'm afraid he's going to come out here and have another go at my friend Beliveau."

"Let me go in, Vince," Beliveau said.

"You're out of your skull."

"With Tina. We'll go in together, she can keep him calm. Maybe I can get him to give you his rifle." Beliveau watched Colclough's face, the flinty eyes clocking up calculations like the dials of a slot machine.

"All right, go in," the detective said. "Maybe you can get him to part with the gun. But I give you ten minutes. After that, the pair of you better hit the floor."

Beliveau followed Tina across the lawn and down the path through the shrubbery. As they approached the summer house, she said: "There is no rifle. I only told them that so they wouldn't come in after him. He'd fight and they'd have to hurt him."

"We may get out of this without any trouble."

With Tina's help, Beliveau made it up the steps and through the screen door. She tapped on the inner door. There was a sudden movement inside. "It's me, Uncle Conrad."

The door opened inward. There was a light coming from a kerosene lantern hanging from a nail in the wall. Tina went inside and Beliveau stumped after her, closing the door behind them.

Conrad Blackburn had gone back to the floor in a corner. He sat on one hip, his legs bent at the knees and tucked to one side, his weight resting on a straight arm, the flat of his hand on the plank floor. The posture reminded Beliveau of a child allowed to stay up late and watch television on Christmas Eve.

"This is Mr. Beliveau." Tina moved across the room and crouched beside her uncle. "He's the man you hurt in Dave's place. That's why he has the crutch. But he isn't mad at you."

The giant turned his face from the girl to Beliveau. His mouth hung slack and when it caught the light, Beliveau saw a quantity of saliva cupped in the lower lip like dew in a curved leaf. "You can tell I'm not mad." Beliveau bent to lay the crutch on the floor and managed to sit with his leg extended. "You were just defending yourself."

Conrad looked at Tina. She nodded. Something moved behind his head. What Beliveau had thought was thick black hair turned out to be a cat resting on the massive shoulders. It stood now on stiff legs, arching its back. The giant scooped the cat up in one hand. Gently, he placed it on his knee.

"Mr. Beliveau came to tell you there's nothing to be afraid of."

"Saw guns out there."

"If you come out with me and Tina, nothing will happen."

Conrad ran a finger through the cat's fur. He shook his head and Beliveau thought of a seven-year-old who has made up his mind. "Why won't you come?"

"I killed that man. Now they'll kill me."

"That isn't the way it works." Beliveau was feeling more secure. "Tell them it was your brother's idea. Tell them Davey made you do it."

"Davey said kill the old bastard." Conrad was staring into space. "Davey said he beat you when you was a baby."

Tina took her uncle's head on her shoulder. The cat scooted away. "What's he talking about?"

"I think I know." Beliveau touched Conrad's arm. "Did Davey tell you to kill your father?"

"Yeah."

"When?"

"Long time ago."

"Your mother thinks he went away."

"Naw. He's here."

"Where is he, Conrad?"

Tina frowned at Beliveau. "What are you doing?"

"Where is your father? Can you show us?"

"Yeah."

Beliveau struggled to his feet. "Come on, let's go outside. You can show us where your father is." He limped to the door. "Don't worry. When you pay for what you did to that man, you'll be paying for your father, too."

They appeared on the screened porch in a glare of artificial light. Beliveau called: "Hold everything, Vince! We're coming down."

Colclough's voice rang out. "Throw the rifle down where I can see it."

"There is no rifle. He was unarmed."

"Keep coming straight and at a steady pace."

When they reached the grass, Beliveau moved ahead, screening the other two. He glanced back and saw Tina was holding Conrad's hand. He limped on.

What happened next was so unexpected he could only stand and watch. A small shape darted down the steps and ran between Conrad's legs, tearing up grass. Conrad made a lunge for the cat. It escaped and ran for one of the chestnut trees, leaping and hitting the trunk a yard above the ground, scrambling upward. Conrad ran after it, arms extended. Tina screamed as she saw the policeman nearest the tree raise his shotgun. Blasts rang out simultaneously from various directions. Beliveau hit the ground.

When the shooting ended and there was a few seconds' silence, he struggled to his feet. As he worked his way through the crowd of policemen, he was almost blinded by the photographer's flash. He reached the inner circle, where Colclough was bending over Conrad. "Take the girl away," the detective said.

Beliveau got down quickly to hear what Conrad was trying to say. "Can show you," the dying man said.

"Show me what?"

"Where my father is."

"Don't show. Tell."

"In the tub. Under the flowers."

Beliveau could see the bathtubs at the front door of the shanty filled with marigolds and petunias. "Which tub, Conrad?"

"Both."

Conrad's hand took hold of Beliveau's arm and drew him close. "Afraid." It was barely a whisper.

"I know."

"Don't want to be alone."

"You won't be. You're only doing what everybody does."

"Getting dark."

"It'll be light soon."

Conrad squeezed Beliveau's arm so hard it was agony. Then the grip was released and the hand let go.

A woman screamed near the house. "Who the hell is that?" Colclough said.

"Moira Blackburn—the mother. She's home from work."

"That's all I need. And what about the father? Didn't he say something about his father?"

"Come on," Beliveau said wearily. "I'll take you to the father."

The hardest part was making arrangements to keep Tina Blackburn out of the hands of the authorities. There were homes for difficult teenaged girls, but he knew this would be the wrong environment for Tina. Françoise needed some persuasion. "You'll like her, Frankie. She's a decent kid."

"I'm not sure I want her in my apartment. I've never considered myself a foster mother."

"You'd be friends. She's mature for her age."

"That's putting it mildly."

Beliveau held her by the shoulders, their faces eye to eye. "She's been led along a nasty path. But it may not be too late if we take charge and convince her she's a worthwhile person."

Françoise decided at about half past midnight that she would give fostering a try. "But you won't be able to sleep here any more," she said with malicious pleasure.

"All I want is to sleep here tonight but you keep talking."

Tina moved in with Françoise and settled down and the weeks

went by. In mid-October, the terrifying evening of the CBC Song-writing Contest arrived. Beliveau laid on a television party. Françoise was helping with the food. "You must be nervous about your song," she said.

"It'll all be over in a few hours," he said, sounding like the con-demned man.

The television set went quiet in the other room and Tina wandered into the kitchen. "When do we eat?"

"Eight o'clock. That's when the show starts."

"I don't think I'm watching the program."

"We were counting on you," Beliveau said.

"I know, but that music isn't my scene." She snatched a ring of green pepper and bit into it. "May I have my allowance, please?" She put the palms of her hands together below her chin. "I know I had it two days ago, but I bought a couple of books."

"We like you to read," Beliveau said. He found a five-dollar bill and gave it to her.

"Could it be more, please? I'm meeting a friend and she never has any money. She doesn't have somebody as generous as you."

"Ever get the feeling you're being manipulated?" He gave her another five.

When Tina was gone, Françoise said: "Don't give her so much money if you think she's taking advantage."

"I'm not complaining."

"You've been too generous. A thousand dollars to the old woman . . . "

"Are you suggesting I telephone Baytown and ask Mrs. Blackburn if she got the money?"

"Do you think Tina kept it?"

"She said her grandmother was too shy to come to me." Beliveau massaged his face. "I'm having a bad day. I think it's that letter from May Rodriguez."

"The letter said everything was okay."

"Okay with her. She's got a job in Vancouver. She's got a boy friend, she has a flat. But not one word about Luther. Why write to me?"

"Why not?"

"I think she's trying to tell me something."

"Tell you what?"

"I don't know."

The front door-buzzer sounded. Rocky Peerson arrived, carrying his guitar case. "The music is on television," Beliveau said. "You don't have to play."

"This is for later. I'm doing the ten o'clock spot over on Stanley Street."

"Can't be bad."

"You sound depleted, Hector."

"I'm not over the Baytown thing yet."

"But those bones under the flowers. That was the end for me."

"I *hope* it was the end."

Beliveau would never forget the pungent smell of marigolds as he knelt in the dark by the rusted bathtub with a garden trowel in one hand, lifting out the plants with their clots of root and damp earth, trying not to damage the golden blooms. Colclough was taking less care at the other tub. He got to his half of the skeleton first. His tub contained the skull, the rib cage, several long bones. Beliveau unearthed the pelvis, then a ball-in-socket knee joint. This was where Sean Blackburn had disappeared to all those years ago. The fact that his sons had cut the corpse in half did not bear thinking about.

Colclough advised the Baytown police to arrest Moira Blackburn as an accessory after the fact of murder. She was taken in and interviewed, held for a couple of days, then allowed to go home. There would be a hearing later. The feeling in Baytown was that the old woman would not spend much time in jail. Conrad was dead. Davey Blackburn was the man they wanted to find.

Tancred arrived wearing a blue-denim visored Russian student's cap which he kept on when he sat down. Françoise brought him a glass of white wine. "What do you hear from Luther?" Beliveau said.

"I hear nothing. I hope he's enjoying the use of my Landrover. So much for gratitude."

"I thought he might have drifted back and got in touch."

"After the experience they gave him here, I doubt it."

There was no luck with "Lazy Love." The top fifteen songs were performed one after the other. The screen was filled with tuxedos and ruffled shirtfronts, fashionable gowns and pricey hairstyles, and there were lots of views of soloists seen through the strings of the harp.

"Let's hear it for our director," Peerson said at one point, "Arty Longshot."

Each song sounded better to Beliveau than the one before. Where had he acquired the idea that he could succeed in this business? He drank more during the hour than he had done in the past month, his disappointment evolving into hostility. "It isn't the end of the world," he said when the show was over. "It's only the end of my career as a songwriter, so called."

Peerson switched off the set. "At least four of those songs are not as good as yours."

"You never did have an ear."

"Stop feeling sorry for yourself," Françoise said.

"I'm disappointed. Is it okay if I feel disappointed for a few minutes?"

"If this is what it means to be in the music business," she said, "I wish you'd go back to being a policeman. Not that you ever stopped."

In a cleared space at one end of the Stanley Street jazz club, Rocky Peerson sat alone. The customers were packed around small tables. Beliveau was lurking at the bar, half out of things. Times past, when he was still on the force, he spent many a relaxing hour in these surroundings, insisting on paying for his drinks. It was understood in bars and restaurants all over Montreal—Beliveau pays.

Peerson was concluding a spectacular rendition of "Limehouse Blues." After the applause, he said: "This next song was written by somebody most of you have heard of. I'm lucky enough to be his friend—Hector Beliveau. He wrote a good one here . . . 'Lazy Love.' "

As Rocky began singing, Beliveau listened to the song objectively. He was hearing it for the first time under professional conditions. By the time it ended a few minutes later, he had learned something. It was not a great song, certainly not a prize-winner, but neither was it rubbish. It was a pretty good song.

Beliveau departed soon after. He strolled east with his hands in his pockets, past the Peel intersection and the Dominion Square Building. The cinemas had emptied after the final shows and the crowds has dispersed. He was sharing the street with drifters and lovers and the occasional cop.

He stayed on Ste. Catherine as far as Bleury, then turned and began to descend toward Dorchester. He was passing the Alouette when he remembered the evening he raced out the door and headed for Davey Blackburn's place. He looked across the road at the green door and saw something sticking to it. It looked like a message.

He crossed the road. He was between streetlights but the printing on the scrap of paper was large and dark, done in green felt pen. The note was fastened to the door with cellulose tape.

"Loother—back soon. Bringing Dad. Tina."

A car drove past slowly from the left and another gunned by from the right. Beliveau began to feel the warning tingle in the back of his neck. He turned and looked across the street. The parking lot beside the Alouette was closed for the night. Somebody moved near the operator's hut. Beliveau took his hands out of his pockets and crossed the street again. There wasn't much limp left in his mended leg. He stopped a few feet inside the paved area.

"Luther?" Nothing moved. "You want to come out now?"

Rodriguez stepped forward and stood with his arms folded high on his chest. He was looking good. His face was a little fatter. He was wearing a black-velvet pullover styled on a pro football training jersey with horizontal pockets at the waist. Under it he had on a blue checkered shirt open at the neck.

"How's your big sister?"

"She's fine. She said she was going to write you."

"She did. When she didn't mention you, I figured you might be on your way."

"You figured right."

"How much of the thousand did you spend on plane fare?"

Luther grinned. "It was Tina's idea to ask you for the money and say it was for her old lady. She's a stubborn kid. She was determined I was going to get a grand out of this thing."

"If not from Dakin, then from me."

"You figured that out, too?"

"Only just now. It came together when I saw the way Tina spells your name. Loother with two o's. She must have written that item in Dakin's notebook. I thought it was Dakin keeping track of you. But it was Tina reminding him he had to pay you a thousand."

"Or she'd go to the cops and say he was making it with a child."

"But her father and uncle were already shaking him down for the same thing."

"That was the main scheme. The thousand for me was Tina's own little ripoff. Her old man never knew about it."

Two people were at the door across the road—Tina and Davey Blackburn. Tina used a key to open the door, then she worked at removing the taped-on message while her father went inside. With the scrap of paper in her hand, she followed him in and closed the door.

"Why is she doing this?"

"Doing what?"

"Bringing her father here at the same time as you?"

"I don't understand half of what the kid does."

They crossed the street. Beliveau pressed the button on the door-frame. Within seconds, the latch snapped and the door sprang open. He pushed Luther ahead and followed him inside.

"Come on up, love," Tina said. Then she saw Beliveau. "Oh, hello."

Rodriguez took the steps two at a time while Beliveau limped upward at a slower pace. When he reached the landing, Luther had finished talking to her. "You know it all, then," she said, facing Beliveau.

"Not quite. I've been told the extortion game was as much your idea as anybody's. And I know the note in Dakin's book was written by you. And the thousand for your grandmother was really for Luther."

"I thought you'd like that."

"What I don't know is why we are gathered here this evening."

"Isn't it obvious?"

"Not to me."

"We're getting married. I want my father to meet my fiancé." She took Luther's hand and led him into the kitchen. Beliveau followed. Davey Blackburn was sitting at the table holding a bottle of beer. He looked the worse for wear. "Mr. Beliveau. I wasn't expecting you."

"I hear you and Claire came around to see me while I was away."

"A business proposition. I can't pursue it now."

"Daddy, we've got something to tell you."

"Tina, hold on a minute," Rodriguez said.

"Shut up, Luther. Daddy, you don't have to worry about me any longer. I'm going to be Mrs. Rodriguez." She was pressing herself close to the musician, her arm around his waist.

"What are you talking about?"

"I wanted to marry Mr. Sangster but it didn't work out. He found out what happened to Mr. Dakin, so I had to get Conrad to shut him up. He was too old, anyway. And he was crippled. Don't you think Luther is lovely?"

"I don't know what the hell she's talking about," Rodriguez said.

Beliveau spoke up. "Luther, I can't think of any reason to hold you. I suggest you get out of here."

"Don't you leave." Tina took his hand.

"You're free to go. Go back to your sister in Vancouver."

Beliveau kept an eye on Tina as Rodriguez went down the hall, closing the apartment door behind him. He was afraid the girl might try to disappear but she seemed in no hurry to go. "Davey," Beliveau said, "I'm going to have to arrest you."

"I expected that."

"Will he go to jail?" Tina asked.

"Depends on how good a lawyer he has."

"Can I be a witness? I could tell them everything."

"Yes. In fact, the police are going to want to keep you now. You won't be staying with Françoise."

"Tina, don't talk to any cops," Blackburn said.

"I want to."

"If you shut up, we'll both be all right."

"I liked Uncle Conrad, but he's dead now. Why should I care about you?"

"The child is sick," Blackburn confided to Beliveau.

"No wonder, growing up around you," Tina said. "Where's that skinny bitch you ran away with? Did Miss Hitchen desert you, too?"

"We'd better go," Beliveau said.

"Just a minute." Tina's voice was authoritative. "There are two things I want my father to know. I've been saving them. First of all, I'm pregnant. Luther is the father. Okay?"

The blood left Blackburn's face. "Holy Mother of God."

"And the other is from a few years ago. Remember when you came home from work and Mum had tried to throw me off the balcony, and when she couldn't she jumped herself?"

"Tina, don't." Blackburn closed his eyes.

"It wasn't like that. We were having an argument. I pushed her over the railing. I did it on purpose to get rid of her."

"She's making it up. She wants to hurt me."

"The suicide note—I wrote it myself after I went inside. I'd been faking Mum's handwriting on notes whenever I skipped school."

"You could never do such a thing."

"You wanted me to kill her. You told me to."

"No such thing. Never."

"I take after Gran. She knows how to survive and have fun." Tina put her hand through Beliveau's arm. "We can go now."

Beliveau telephoned the CBC at four o'clock in the afternoon. The December light was so far gone, he was sitting in near-darkness.

From the kitchen radio he could hear the sound of a dead singer dreaming of a white Christmas. The girl at information confirmed that they were rehearsing an episode of *Baltazar*. She gave him the studio number and wished him Joyeux Noel.

He got into his overcoat and pulled the scarlet toque down low on his forehead. His hair had grown almost all the way back. He picked up his fur-lined gloves, walked heavily to ground level, and let himself out.

The report had said it would go to eleven below zero tonight. Beliveau breathed in and felt the hairs in his nostrils congeal. He blew a cloud of vapor and set out on a fast walk up the hill toward the Radio-Canada Building.

The *Baltazar* cast were taking a break, sitting around the studio drinking machine coffee. The floor was taped to represent the set in which they would be shooting in a few days. Many of the performers knew Beliveau. They greeted him and exchanged superficial conversation.

Françoise came down the iron stairs, ran to his side, took his arm, and led him out of the studio into a corridor. "Where have you been?"

"Home," he said.

"I called you there. I kept leaving my name on the tape."

"I didn't feel like talking."

"And now you do. You leave things rather late."

"It's my style."

"It isn't mine. I have to know where I am."

"Is he a nice guy?"

"I've known him for years. He has a good job."

Beliveau leaned his back against the tile wall. She stood before him, very feminine despite the severe haircut, the plain blue sweater and the stopwatch on a leather cord around her neck. "It was the announcement in the marriage column that shook me."

"That was his mother." She clicked the watch repeatedly, playing with time, sending it back and starting over. "How is Tina?"

"She's in a detention home. I haven't checked with her."

Beliveau left the CBC Building and punished himself by walking all the way down into the Old Town. Inside the steamy atmosphere of Le Big Bang, the clients were being served two drinks for the price of one. Dallas handed Beliveau a free beer. "Merry Christmas."

Tancred was sitting at his table in the corner. He was not alone. Beliveau recognized the back of Rocky Peerson's head. He carried his beer to the table and sat down. "Ask Falardeau about his music policy in the new year," Peerson said. "Never mind, I'll tell you. I'm to be the house guitarist, permanently."

"Nice going."

"I didn't say permanently," Tancred said. "Six months."

"In my life, that's permanent."

The conversation came to a halt. They drank while listening to a piped-in Christmas carol. Beliveau finished his beer and pushed the empty glass away. It fell over and he picked it up on the third attempt.

"What's happening with him?" Tancred asked Peerson.

"It's the Christmas blues."

"He's been bad since he came back from Baytown. He never recovered from that beating."

Beliveau sat looking at his hands, listening to his companions discussing him as if he weren't there. "Where are you going?" Tancred asked, catching his glass as Beliveau got up, nearly upsetting the table.

He couldn't speak, nor did he look back. He went to the bar and bought a bottle of bourbon from Dallas. Outside, the night was so black it threatened the streetlights. Packed snow crunched under his boots as he moved down the alleyway beside the club. He opened the bottle and swallowed a long drink. Then, with the bourbon in his overcoat pocket, Beliveau began walking.

He followed an uphill route through the business district, where there were plenty of alleys in which he could hide while he drank more bourbon. A thought occurred to him. If he finished the bottle and lay down in some isolated place, all his problems would be solved. He would not be faced with the unwelcome duty of waking up tomorrow.

Beliveau wished he could believe in a Sunday-school hereafter. If he did, getting out of this world would be easy. He could look forward to seeing Lenore, telling her it didn't matter that she had gone to bed with Rocky. He could compare notes with Conrad on the routine experience of dying. He could assure Gib Dakin the guitar he fixed plays like a dream. He could tell Milt Sangster that without him, the TV series was falling apart.

"You were the soul of your creation, Milt," Beliveau said out loud at the corner of St. James Street. People made space around the colorful drunk.

He managed to arrive on Ste. Catherine Street and was standing in a group of parents and children on the pavement in front of a corner window at Eaton's. Behind plate glass, a collection of stuffed animals bowed and pivoted roughly in time to a recorded carol.

Beliveau felt a hand on his arm. "Is it you?"

He turned and looked down on a fur hat with a fringe of crisp, poodle-cut hair. He saw high cheekbones, alert eyes, full red lips. It was Claire Hitchen—he could smell the perfume she wore. "Hello," he slurred.

She took the bottle from his hand and tucked it into the satchel she was carrying. "I never knew you were a loner. Look at you, bombed out of your mind." Their faces were inches apart. She kissed him on the lips. "Merry Christmas, Beliveau."

"I'm sinking, Claire. Won't see Christmas."

"You look to me like you need some sleep." She took his arm. "Come on. Did you know we sold the beverage business? I was never so happy about anything in my life. I'm working downtown now, managing a boutique in Place Ville Marie. It's paradise. My apartment is up here on Sherbrooke."

He allowed himself to be led, could not prevent it. "I thought I had a life. But everything comes apart."

"I know, it's terrible." She put her arm through his and forced him to move ahead in a fairly straight line. "Come home and you can tell me all about it."

He slept until four o'clock the next afternoon. He ate something and slept again until eleven. It was only then that he could sit up in bed with her head on his shoulder and her thin, strong arms locked around his waist and begin talking to her, surprisingly, as if he had known her all his life.